RILEY
AND THE
ROARING
TWENTIES

RILEY
AND THE
ROARING
TWENTIES

JAMES ANDERSON O'NEAL

Three Ocean Press

Vancouver, British Columbia

Copyright © 2018 by James Anderson O'Neal

Riley and the Roaring Twenties is a work of fiction. Names, characters, places, and incidents are either the product of the author's imagination or used fictitiously. Beyond historical characters and events used for purposes of fiction, any resemblance to actual persons, living or dead, or to actual events or specific locales is entirely coincidental.

Library and Archives Canada Cataloguing in Publication

O'Neal, James Anderson, 1953-, author
    Riley and the roaring twenties / James Anderson O'Neal.

(Tales of the American century ; book 2)
Issued in print and electronic formats.
ISBN 978-1-988915-04-3 (softcover).--ISBN 978-1-988915-06-7 (ebook)

    I. Title. II. Title: Riley and the roaring 20s.

PS3615.N42R57 2018   813'.6   C2018-905561-8
                                            C2018-905562-6

Copy Editor: Kyle Hawke
Proofreader: Carol Hamshaw
Cover Designer: Maddy Haigh
Book Designer: Patti Frazee
Cover Image: *Roaring Twenties* © 2018 Wade Edwards
Author Photo: Kristina Perkins

Three Ocean Press
8168 Riel Place
Vancouver, BC, V5S 4B3
778.321.0636
info@threeoceanpress.com
www.threeoceanpress.com

First publication, October 2018

Contents

Prologue: Three Mysteries...1

Homecomings

1. Riley Redux...5
2. Back to Independence 9
3. Cobb, Rothstein, and Runyon..............................19
4. No Spooning on Blue Road.....................................33

Cornelius on Broadway

5. The Black Hand 43
6. Creatures of the Night...49
7. Round Tables and Jungle Animals 61
8. Literary Ladies 75
9. Lords of the Cosmos 83
10. Massacre in Gowanus 93
11. Cornelius Plays Shamus...99
12. A Close Call 109
13. The Pope's Usurer 121
14. The Man Who Could Sink Anybody.................131
15. A Rat Reappears 135
16. An Honest Cop 145
17. Mr. Rothstein Reveals His Nature 151

The Death of Arnold Rothstein

18. A Break from Reading...161
19. Death Comes to Independence 163
20. Cornelius Goes Home...169
21. Bad Times 175
22. Deep Waters..179
23. The Big Bankroll Meets a Bigger Bankroll 183

24. The Pointing Nun 189

25. The End of Frankie Yale 195

26. Marta's Lament..201

27. A Rich Man Takes a Dive 203

28. Rothstein Feels the Pinch 217

29. Marta Gets Fed Up...223

30. Recruiting Titanic 225

31. Riley's Breakfast 231

32. The Lady of the Hacienda 233

33. Coney Island 237

34. "I Like to Drink and Smoke" 245

35. The Game 247

36. Marta Makes a Plan...259

37. Rothstein the Welshman 261

38. The Key to Every Man 265

39. A Secret Compartment.......................................269

40. Big Night on Broadway 277

41. In the Beach Cottage 283

42. Bullets on the Boardwalk...................................287

43. Charlie's Suit...291

44. The Bandit's Cave..293

45. Two Knives..295

46. Polly Adler's Peace Conference...........................299

47. Marta's Prayers..307

48. So Who Did It?..309

49. The Son of My Sorrow 311

50. An Old Testament Kind of Way 313

51. Wrapping Up 315

Author's Note 321

For Sally

Prologue

Three Mysteries

My grandfathers must have been the two biggest liars of the twentieth century.

The following story of theirs is a prime example. It takes place in the New York of the nineteen-twenties and purports to give the solutions to not just one, but three notorious murder mysteries.

The victims:

Frankie Yale

Gangster boss of Coney Island, Yale was gunned down in the streets of Brooklyn on July 1, 1928 by killers known to work for Yale's friend Al Capone. Why was he killed?

Alfred Loewenstein

On July 4, 1928, a European financier said to be the second-richest man in the world went to the bathroom in his private plane over the English Channel and somehow fell out the plane's exit door to his death, without any of the other passengers noticing. He became known as "the Man Who Fell from the Sky." Subsequent investigation established that a lone man could not have opened the door in flight and that, even if he did, the plane would have lurched so violently the other passengers would certainly have felt it. How could this have happened?

Arnold Rothstein

The brain behind the creation of modern organized crime in America and a famous gambler who was said to have fixed the 1919 World Series, Rothstein was shot dead in a New York hotel room on November 4, 1928. The man accused of the murder, George "Hump" McManus, was acquitted. Who did it?

While putting the second autobiographical notebook by my grandfather James Cornelius O'Neal together with my other grandfather Walter Riley's oral recollections and my grandmother Marta's diary excerpts, I did some checking. I found that these three deaths happened when and generally how Cornelius and Riley describe them. In all the many writings that discuss these deaths, I found no confirmation of my grandfathers' solutions to the mysteries associated with them, nor any mention of my grandfathers, nor any suggestion that these three deaths were related other than the odd fact that financier Alfred Loewenstein actually did meet with gangster Arnold Rothstein in New York shortly before Loewenstein's dramatic fall from the sky, for reasons no one seems to know. It is also true that Rothstein followed Lowenstein to Montreal after their meeting.

Is there any truth at all to my grandfathers' tales? I don't know and, after all these years, I don't much care. I'm just assembling the memoirs and then I'll have done my duty for those old men.

I do miss Riley and Cornelius, though. And Marta.

JAMES ANDERSON O'NEAL

Part One

Homecomings

1

Riley Redux

Jim

The study in Riley's hacienda looked just as I remembered from
the last time I had seen it, eight months earlier. That was during
the trip for Grandpa Jimmy's funeral in early 1991, when Riley and I
talked through the first of the autobiographical notebooks written by
Grandpa Jimmy, whom Riley called Cornelius. Cornelius wrote the
notebooks throughout the 1980s, when he was an old man.

I was sitting on the same sofa, Riley in the same chair. There
was the same wistful portrait of my grandmother Marta watching over
us. We were drinking the same brand of bourbon, Riley was smoking
the same brand of cigarette. The pack on the desk might have been the
same pack, except Riley would have smoked about a thousand packs
since we last met. Only his mustache was different, in that it now had
more white hairs than gray. Holding the second Cornelius notebook in
my lap, I stared at my taciturn grandfather and waited to hear what the
next wild tale would involve.

"How much have you read?" he asked through the blue smoke
from his cigarette.

"Nothing."

"Jesus. You could at least have read a little on the plane down here."

Riley grimaced, showing that his disposition hadn't improved greatly since I last saw him. He took another sip of bourbon and another drag on his smoke.

"Well, maybe it's just as well. This time, it's a little different. There's something else to read."

He walked over to his desk, removed some sort of journal with a featureless rose-colored cover from a drawer, and tossed it in my lap. It looked and smelled old.

"What's this?"

Riley sat back down.

"Off and on over the years, your grandmother kept a diary. She was a good writer, not just her poems but everything she wrote. It all had her voice, her kind of quiet elegance. I thought so, anyway."

I weighed the book in my hand and flipped some pages. The leaves were inflexible, cracked with age. Most of the pages were filled with a woman's handwriting in purple ink. It must have come from a fountain pen as there were blots here and there.

"Did she let you read any of this?" I asked Riley.

"Not while she was alive," he said. "She was real private about it. I knew she was keeping a diary, but she hardly ever wrote in it when I was around and she sure didn't let me see it."

"You didn't ever sneak a look?" I asked him. I would have.

He snorted and shook his head.

"Not until she died. Then I read them. Some of it was hard for me. Not like I was a real good husband to her."

He was gazing solemnly into his cigarette smoke.

"You said 'them.' Are there more than this one?"

"Some. She'd keep one for a while, then quit, just as the mood struck, I guess. This is the longest one. I figured you should read it, too. Maybe you can put some of her writing in with Cornelius and me. I'd like her voice to be in there, somehow."

I nodded, not knowing what to say. I asked myself why I was committing to this task, which now looked to require even more time and work than the first one. I would have to read Marta's entire diary to select the excerpts relevant to the story and place them where they seemed to belong. Why should I devote all that time and effort? Simply because my grandfather asked me to?

Riley may have sensed my thought, for he went right to business. He stubbed out his cigarette and leaned forward in his chair.

"Cornelius starts his book on the twenties by talking about how he got a job as a reporter in New York, but there's things to tell about before that. Things Cornelius left out of the story. You remember where the first notebook ended? We were on the troopship, just coming back from Europe and the Great War, due to be discharged in New York. Spring of 1919."

Once again, he drew me into his story.

2

Back to Independence

Riley

Lindbergh turned out to be a cold son of a bitch when I met him, but you have to admit he made his mark. Nobody did more to make aviation available to everybody, which cracked open the whole world like nothing else ever did. I mention that because I can't see why anyone would want to travel the world if everybody had to cross an ocean on one of those old ships they sent the boys home in after the war. Flying beats that hands down, just because it doesn't take so damn long.

It was *boring* was the thing. Even though the war had been over for months, there were still a lot of men to bring home. We were soldiers officially, but we were going to be mustered out as soon as we landed, so nobody bothered to make us drill or scrub the decks or anything like that. I'd just sit and listen to Cornelius prose or I'd pace the decks and think about Marta, wonder about being a father to a baby girl I'd never seen except in pictures. Cornelius had gotten a woman pregnant just before we left home to join up, so we had that in common. He hadn't married his woman though and she'd run off and left their baby son with Jack and Rose, Cornelius' parents, in Independence.

The most useful thing I did on that ship was improve my poker. There was always a game going and I got to where I sat in more often

9

than not and did pretty well. Cornelius said it was because I always had a poker face whether I was playing cards or not. He was terrible at the game because he didn't have the patience. I took to learning when to fold, when to raise, and how to read the weaknesses of the other men. I was never a pro at it, not like people we'd meet later in New York, but I did all right.

Anyway, the closer we got to home, the quieter Cornelius got. Quiet isn't a natural state for Cornelius, not like for me. Cornelius was always a talker and a laugher and kind of a show-off and I was the opposite. Maybe it's why we took to each other. He was round-faced and funny and smart as all-get-out, while I was just me. We complemented each other, like people say.

As the ship got closer to New York, Cornelius stopped talking and walked around looking, I don't know, thoughtful. At first, I thought maybe it was because he was worried whether we'd be put in the brig back in the States. After all, we'd both gone AWOL back in Europe. We thought we'd be in trouble when we finally reported in, but instead nobody said anything and we were just put on a ship for home. Maybe Cornelius figured that was too good to be true.

That wasn't it. I should have guessed.

Word got around the ship that we'd see the Statue of Liberty tomorrow, take a few days on Governors Island to get processed, and then be mustered out. Men were pretty excited, laughing and even singing some. I walked up and down the bunks trying to get a poker game going, but nobody was interested. Not even this guy named Billy, or Willie maybe, a kid from Philadelphia who was always willing to lose his money.

"You got to be kidding, Riley," Billy or Willie said to me. "You took almost all my dough already this trip. I ain't going to lose what little I got left on the last night out."

That seemed to be the general feeling, so Cornelius and I climbed up on deck to take a stroll. I was walking along the railing, looking out at the waves all around, smoking, not thinking much of anything. Cornelius walked beside me and it was only when he finally started talking that I realized how unusual it was that he'd walked for almost five minutes in silence.

"Riley, tell me about Marta."

His blurting out such a damn fool request stopped me right where I stood.

"What do you mean, tell you about Marta? What do you want to know?"

"I guess what I mean is, tell me about being married. What's it like? You lived with Marta, man and wife. Did it ever weigh on you? On your soul?"

If I were a good man, I felt, I wouldn't know what he meant. I'd just tell him marriage is wonderful. But I knew what he meant.

"Cornelius, I don't see that this is a profitable subject for us to be talking about. You're not married and not likely to be any time soon, since your girl run off."

"She wasn't my girl. She was just *a* girl."

"She gave you a baby."

"Well, don't talk like it was a present. The baby's part of what I'm thinking about."

We reached the foredeck and Cornelius gestured over to a bench, or whatever they call it on a ship.

"Let's sit down a minute," he said.

I threw my cigarette butt over the side, sat, and lit another. Cornelius dropped down beside me on the bench, a man much preoccupied.

"Riley, I don't think I can go back to Independence. I can't live there and I can't even live in Kansas City. They're just not places enough for me."

"What do you mean, they're not 'places enough'? Either something's a place or it's not."

Cornelius gave me his old impatient look, like how could I be so dumb.

"I was speaking figuratively," he said. "Think of the big cities we've seen. Think of the action there, the culture, the chances they give to smart young fellows looking to move up in the world. You know what I'm talking about. We've been there, Riley. We've been to Paris, Berlin, New York…"

"Well, we were in Paris and Berlin when they were under siege or in a revolution and it's a wonder we didn't get our heads shot off. As for New York, all we saw of that was a glimpse of some tall buildings from across the river at the camp at Governors Island."

"Doesn't matter. Just looking at that city, I could see it. Hell, I could almost feel it, feel the life and the sights and the sounds…"

"You don't feel sounds."

"Oh, stuff it, Riley. I'm being poetic and you're just throwing water on me. Maybe you should go back to Independence and be a farmer like you claim you're going to."

"I don't claim anything, that's just what I'm going to do. Just like I did before we joined up. And I don't see that this has anything to do with you asking me about Marta and being married and the like. You're being strange tonight, Cornelius."

Cornelius let out a big sigh.

"I should have known," he finally said. "You're right when you say you don't claim anything, you always do just what you say you're going to do. I've never known a man with less imagination."

That seemed unkind, but I let it pass. We sat for a minute in silence.

"Riley, I thought I could talk you into coming with me. I know damn well you got bored before the war, just working the farm and staying home. That's why we joined the army in 1917, why we ran off to chase Pancho Villa back in 1916. You think you want to stay home and be a good man, but you get bored and run off. It's happened before and it will always happen. But I know you better than you know yourself, so you'll go home and you're going to have to find it out again on your own. That's why you're not coming with me."

"Coming with you? Where are you going?"

"Well, not to Missouri, that's for damn sure. Riley, when we get mustered out, I'm heading over to the island of Manhattan and I'm going to make something of myself there. I can't be nobody, I can't live in a place that's not the center of the world. I'm staying in New York and I'm going to be somebody."

So that was it.

"You can't do that."

"I have to do it."

"You have a baby now."

"So did the boy's mother. That didn't stop her."

"She was wrong, but that doesn't mean you should do wrong. Is Hal going to be deserted by both his parents? What does that do to a boy?"

That stopped him, but only for a moment. He put his hand on my arm, which meant he was serious since, where we came from, men don't touch each other.

"Riley, I've been thinking about this the whole trip. My folks can care for the boy, better than I ever could. I can't have him in New York, I don't have a job, no money, and I'll have to spend all my time getting ahead. Hal will be fine. And you and Marta and Ma will all be around for him, too."

For the second time in that conversation, I closed my mouth to keep from saying something hard. Cornelius was my best friend in this life. He was smart and fast-talking and brave and he saved my skin many times. I always found him a good man in a tight spot. But when his personal life got to weighing on him, on his soul like he said, Cornelius didn't hesitate to put the weight over on the people close to him, especially the women. Maybe it's why he was to have four wives over the course of his long life and none of them would take. I had my own issues, of course, but Marta stayed with me and I with her. I always ran off for adventure, but I always came back. I never cheated on her, not once.

I didn't talk much to Cornelius for the next few days. When we mustered out on Governors Island and were free men, I watched him board the Manhattan ferry with his head high, walking toward New York like he was walking into a party set up just for him. We barely said goodbye to each other. He was excited and I was mad. I kept wondering how I'd explain this when I got back to Missouri.

There was no fuss about my discharge papers. Years later, I would see my file and it said I'd been honorably discharged in November 1918, which was news to me. Cornelius and I never figured out who fixed it for us, whether it was Pershing or Patton or whoever. Maybe even Churchill.

Lord, I'll never forget pulling into the train station in my home of Independence. I was still in uniform, to make an impression and because I didn't have any decent clothes. I had two sprigs of flowers, one for Marta and one for Ma, that I bought when I'd changed trains in Kansas City. In my duffel I had some toys for my baby daughter Fern and for Cornelius' baby son Hal, whom neither of us had ever seen. My heart was beating fast and I was happy on one level, but on another level, I dreaded having to deal with the obvious fact that Cornelius wasn't there, had *chosen* not to be there.

I leaned out the window as the train pulled in. Old Mr. Murray was still the stationmaster and he turned up his nose at me on account of how I punched him in the face back when Cornelius, Kip Miller, and I snuck out of town to go chase Pancho Villa with General Pershing. The man never did forgive me. That didn't matter though, for in the next second, I saw my family gathered on the station platform, smiling and waving. I don't think my heart ever melted so fast and so completely as it did at that moment, except maybe the first time I saw Marta back in Mexico.

Ma was there, of course, looking stout and solid as ever but wiping back the tears for all of that. Ann, Hazel, and Fayette, three of my sisters, were gathered around her, waving and bouncing like schoolgirls. My other two sisters were gone: Bessie had become the first woman admitted to Harvard Divinity School, God help them, and for some reason Gussie had run off to Florida. Fayette was hanging onto the arm of a good-looking fellow that I later found out was her boyfriend, George. Jack and Rose O'Neal were there too, grinning and waving. Their smiles must have been a little forced, as they knew from his telegram that Cornelius wouldn't be with me.

My eyes were taken up by the center of the picture. There stood Marta, my beautiful wife, holding in each arm a baby born in August 1918, making them about seven months old when I finally met them. I thought Marta was showing off a little, holding both of these little ones when she was surrounded by women who would have happily shared the burden, but I expect Marta wanted it to be this way when I first saw her. My eyes clouded with tears at the sight of them. Lickety-split, I was off the train and in Marta's arms. I guess she shucked one of the babies over to Ma as I ran over. All I know is that we joined in an embrace that I hoped would never end. Ma was hugging the two of us with the other baby in her arm, while Jack O'Neal was pounding my back and telling me how proud he was. Old man Murray managed to give me a sneer over Marta's shoulder as he slouched by, but what was that to me? I was home.

After I held the hug as long as I could, I looked into Marta's eyes

14

and kissed her. Finally, I turned my attention to the babies. Frankly, I couldn't tell them apart for sure, but I figured the one Marta was still holding was our daughter Fern. She was well out of the newborn phase and turning into a real person. She had a round red face and was sucking on her fingers, but she looked pleasant and placid and just a fine baby all around, far as I could tell. I grinned at her and at Marta, not able to speak just then. I kissed little Fern, who was clammier than I expected and who drooled just when I leaned over to her.

"*Te amo*, Walter," Marta said to me. "Do you like your daughter?"

"*Te amo*, Marta," I said. "She's the most beautiful thing I've ever seen, next to you. I'll never leave you again."

"And meet the other new member of the family," said Ma, holding up Walter Hal.

He looked scared to death and began to squall lustily. I didn't know what to do and felt put out that he reacted to me that way, which was stupid but I hadn't been around babies much.

"I think he's teething," Jack O'Neal said, drawing an elbow in the ribs from his wife Rose.

"What do you know about it, Jack O'Neal?" she asked him.

"Hush, Rose," Ma said, "Jack does just fine with the babies. Better than any other man I know would, sure better than my John ever did with our babies."

I came to learn that was true. Jack would bathe and feed and generally fuss over both babies almost like a woman, probably singing communist songs to them while he did it. Jack was a faithful Marxist, remember.

There was no sense putting it off, so I didn't.

"Cornelius will come home," I said, looking at Rose and Jack. "He just wanted to see the big world a little more, I think. He'll be home."

I wasn't so sure myself, but they nodded and said nothing.

We walked out of the railroad station and I glanced around. Independence was still a small town then. It was a pleasure to look again at my hometown, which had never seemed so American to me before. The courthouse square, Doc Clinton's drugstore, the old jail —all still there, all as they should be. There was no band, no parade, no throng of townspeople to cheer me. Folks were fed up with that by

15

March of 1919, I guess, and wanted to go back to life without thoughts of some European war they didn't really understand anyway.

Jack poked me in the ribs.

"Got a surprise for you," he chuckled.

Everyone was smiling and looking like the cat with the cream, so I knew something was about to be sprung on me. I saw the old wagon that I'd ridden a thousand times to the east acreage and into Kansas City to box at Skelly's gym. There was a new mare I hadn't seen before hitched to it, so I guessed that was the surprise and got a big laugh.

"Next to the wagon, Walter," Jack said. "The automobile!"

There was a new-looking Ford Model T parked next to where the mare was tied up to a post. I stared at it. Could it be?

"It's ours, you slow-wit!" Fayette finally burst out, unable to contain herself. "Ma bought it with the O'Neals! It would be the greatest thing except Ma won't let us girls drive it."

"Driving ain't for womenfolk," Ma said definitively.

Ann nodded, Hazel looked down, and Fayette tossed her head impatiently.

I went over to the car and ran my hand over the engine. The world was sure changing on me.

"How could you afford something like this?"

Jack seemed embarrassed.

"Well, your Ma paid for most of it," he said.

"Oh, the farm's been doing all right, Walter," Ma said. "And we'll do even better now that we have you home."

Home. I thought back on how urgently I longed for it over in France and Germany, how I dreamed of Marta and Fern, how I swore if I ever made it back, I would never leave again. I'm ashamed to admit that right then, just minutes after I dropped my bag on the station platform and took Marta in my arms, I started feeling uneasy. Restless, I guess. I remembered farming, which I hated, to be honest about it. I remembered long nights in the Riley house, listening to Bessie preach and the other girls jabber, until Ma would hush them and they'd be silent for a minute or two. I remembered how flat everything looked to me and how I wanted to see the world and have some adventure in my life. Now I'd be back, with a wife and baby—maybe two babies, if Cornelius never came home—and responsibilities that stretched on forever into an endless flat future. I wondered what was the matter with me, why I could never be happy with what I had, instead always thinking there was something else out there, something I was missing. You'll think I'm fibbing, but right that minute I realized that this was how I was and how my life was going to be. I was a wanderer.

And now I'm ninety-three years old, and that's how it's been. Still is. I'm a wanderer. Only now I just wander in my mind.

3

Cobb, Rothstein, and Runyon

Cornelius

I didn't arrive in New York and walk down that gangplank quite as unprepared as Riley probably thought. I had a plan and I had the name of someone to find. At twenty, you think that is all you need and sometimes it is.

The plan was to become a newspaper reporter. When in high school back in Independence, I started our first school paper with the help of a sympathetic English teacher. I did pretty much all of the writing. Probably did pretty much all of the reading of the paper too, but I thought I was the next Mencken. The name I carried in my head was Irv Cobb, one of the best-known journalists in New York. Like many other writers from the New York scene—including Alex Woollcott, whom I'd later meet—Cobb had covered the Great War as a war correspondent.

I'd seen him at the great mustering site in southern France in early 1918, soon after Riley and I had arrived in Europe. Cobb had been writing a story on training camps and he'd interviewed Riley and me. Well, he'd interviewed me while Riley sat there looking at us without saying anything. With that much of a connection, I was bold enough to think Cobb would help out a war veteran by giving him a leg up into the newspaper business. I had no Plan B.

Trouble was, I didn't know which newspaper employed Cobb. This was more of a problem in 1919 than it would be today, with the number of daily newspapers shrinking so much. Newspapers were important then and there were lots of them, especially in New York. The city was the heart of the American newspaper business, as of so much else. There was no counting the number of papers that existed, morning editions and evening editions in probably a dozen languages. The papers in New York of the twenties employed real writers whom people still read today, not just columnists but also street-level reporters: people like Ring Lardner, O. Henry, Heywood Broun, Damon Runyon, and Franklin Pierce Adams, known as FPA. With so many papers, there was an insatiable demand for content. Words, words, words were needed to fill all that white space with black, smeary newsprint. The best words were smart, cynical, slangy, and jazzy, fitting the times and the city and the new American cockiness in the air.

I used the cooking skills I'd been taught by old Mrs. Rodriguez back at Riley's farm to talk myself into a job frying eggs and bacon at a Greenwich Village diner. Next, I needed a place to stay. As it happened, I had some family members in New York, the Toolans. They were my cousins, sons of my mother's brother, all policemen. I hardly knew them though and didn't want to have to account for my whereabouts and plans to nosy relatives. Besides, they lived in Brooklyn, which seemed like the back of beyond to a boy craving to satisfy his obsession with Manhattan. Accordingly, I avoided the Toolans and took a bed in a flophouse near the diner, using the small amount of service pay I had set aside.

So accommodated, I set myself to reading all the newspapers I could find, looking for the name Irvin S. Cobb. I enjoyed the task, braced by the crisp writing and the abundance of attitude displayed by the writers. Here was a fraternity to which I could belong.

It didn't take me long to find Cobb's byline, for he was a well-known columnist for the *New York World*. I found its offices one day after the lunch shift at the diner. The *World*, owned by the Pulitzer family, was high in the pecking order of New York newspapers at the time, right behind the *Times* and William Randolph Hearst's sister newspapers, the *Journal* and the *American*. The *World* came out in the morning, which reporters liked because they could sleep until noon, carouse on their beats in the afternoon and evening, and meet their deadlines at midnight or so. Of course, the boys who wrote for the afternoon papers seemed to populate the bars just as much as those on the morning editions, so it may not have mattered much.

The receptionist at the *World* was what we called a looker, with bobbed hair and red lipstick on a wide mouth, legs crossed to show off two very passable gams. She found it amusing when I appeared and asked for Mr. Cobb, still wearing my greasy kitchen whites. She paused in the noisy mastication of her chewing gum, which she seemed quite partial to, and let out a hoot of a laugh.

"Kid, you don't know much about reporters if you think you'll find a fellow who writes for the mornings in the office at this time of day. Cobb's deadline is midnight. You'll find him here then."

She turned back to pecking at her Underwood.

It tells you how intently I was focused on getting into the newspaper business that I didn't try to chat this girl up. I just went back to the flophouse, changed out of my kitchen uniform, and threw myself down on my bed to try for a quick nap. Sleep didn't come as I was rehearsing in my head what I would say to Cobb. All I needed was a job, any job that would get me in proximity to the newspaper business. Once in, I knew I could talk my way up the ladder to a reporter's desk, but getting in the door was crucial and Cobb was my only hope.

I wanted to catch him just when he had finished his column and would be able to give me his attention, so I cadged a free plate of beans at the diner and possessed my soul in patience. At about 11:30 that night, I climbed the stairs to the *World* newsroom again. No receptionist this time and no security—busy people were passing in and out of the newsroom, so I just walked right in.

The *World's* newsroom was much like every other such room that I've seen since, but this was my first and I was enchanted. The air was filled with smoke from a hundred cigarettes and cigars. The room was extremely large, cavernous and crammed with desks covered with papers and typewriters. Along the back wall were glassed-in offices for the more important editors, who wore vests and smoked cigars. The reporters were easy to distinguish as they were all seated behind Underwoods, tapping out their stories with an air of intense concentration, cigarettes hanging from their lips, fedoras pushed back on their heads. I don't recall seeing any women in the room. Boys were running from desk to desk, fetching copy as reporters ripped their stories from the typewriters and barked for a copyboy. The boys would run the copy to the desks of older men, the night editors, leaving the reporters to glare at the editors as though daring them to change a sacred word of their stories.

I took it all in, more determined than ever to sit at one of those desks. Then I looked around for Cobb, without success. A snide-looking reporter at my elbow finished his story, gave it to a copyboy and sat back with his hands clasped behind his head. I must have caught his eye.

"What the hell do you want?" he asked me.

"Looking for Irvin S. Cobb," I said.

The reporter smiled and got a twinkle in his eye.

"Are you? Then I suggest you talk to that man over there," he said, pointing. "He's looking for Mr. Cobb, too."

The man he pointed at was one of the editors, just stepping out of his glass office. Squat and beetle-browed with a big balding head, the editor had a mean and scowling look about him. He glanced at his pocket watch, then folded his meaty arms across his chest and watched the door, tapping his foot. I didn't like the idea of bracing him in such a mood, but I was left with no alternative so I threaded through desks and stepped up to him.

"Sir?" I ventured. "My name's Jimmy O'Neal. I was told you might help me find Irvin Cobb."

The little area of the room within the sound of my voice became motionless and silent. The editor's eyes narrowed as he glared at me.

"You bein' a wise guy, kid?"

"Not me, sir. It's just I was in the army with Mr. Cobb"—close enough to accurate, I figured—"and I wanted to look him up."

The editor closed his hairy hand on my shirt front and I thought he was going to strike me.

"So you want to look him up, do you?" he asked as he pulled me into him, nose to nose. "Well, you just do that, kid, and when you do, you ask Mr. Cobb why in the fuck he's not in the newsroom writing the copy that's due in ten goddam minutes from now!"

A passing copyboy saved my neck, or at least my shirt.

"Boss," he said, pointing, "there he is."

The editor's eyes and my own followed the boy's finger to the entrance to the newsroom, where stood the man I remembered from training camp in France. Irv Cobb was a big, beefy, dark man, generally wreathed in cigar smoke, confident and humorous in demeanor. He burst into the room grandly and strode down the aisles of desks waving at his pals, a cigar in his teeth and a folded newspaper under his arm. The editor glowered grimly at Cobb as he approached, but Cobb was unperturbed.

"Hiya, boss," he said gaily, his accent betraying just a slight trace of his native Kentucky. "You're looking especially lovely tonight."

"Goddam it, Irv…" began a long and inventive string of profanity that the editor unleashed on Cobb, but the writer ignored him completely. Cobb sat himself at a typewriter, rolled in a blank sheet, and began to write with great facility and hardly an instant's pause for thought. The editor continued cursing directly into Cobb's ear, with no effect whatsoever on the effortless flow of words. From the grins around the room, I gathered that this was not a cause for concern, but rather a comedy enacted nightly. Fascinated, I watched the clock in the newsroom as Cobb typed away. At midnight exactly, Cobb pulled a third page of copy from the machine and handed it to the troll cursing over him.

"There it is, every word a gem. And don't let the night goons fuck it up this time."

Cobb blew his boss a kiss and headed for the door. The editor thrust Cobb's story at the copyboy and marched back to his office. I ran after Cobb eagerly, calling his name and almost bowling him over when he stopped suddenly.

He looked down his nose at me curiously, but without hostility.

"Who might you be?"

"My name's Jimmy O'Neal," I said, a little breathless. "We met in France. You interviewed me for the *Saturday Evening Post*."

"Did I now? Why did I do that? Were you a hero?"

I decided not to stretch it that far.

"No, sir. I was at training camp and you came down to do a story on the camp. Do you remember?"

Cobb thought a moment, looked at me hard and shook his head.

"Nope. Good to see you, kid."

He made to leave and, in my eagerness, I clutched his arm and held him fast.

"I'd like to talk to you, sir. I'd like to get into the newspaper business."

"Jesus H. Christ, why would you want to do something like that?" He smiled when he said it, his eyes then lighting up as though an idea had occurred to him. "You're a job-seeker, huh? Well, boy, if you seek, you must first deliver. It is the witching hour and at the witching hour I develop a thirst that must be slaked. You, my boy, if you crave a moment of my time, will pay for it by buying a few rounds of scotch. Release my arm, son, and let us hie to a watering hole. You interest me strangely."

You may be wondering how we could legally buy scotch given that it was 1919, the year the Volstead Act was passed and Prohibition became the law of the land. Actually, the act wasn't passed until months after my meeting with Cobb, though everyone knew it was likely to be coming. Even after it was passed, it didn't go into effect until January of 1920, which gave everyone plenty of time to make plans for violating it. No one ever had trouble getting a drink in New York, or most anywhere else, regardless of Prohibition. The effect of the Volstead Act was only to worsen the quality of liquor for the working man (the rich could always get good liquor) and to create a magnificent opportunity for enterprising mobsters.

Cobb and I were able to saunter over to the bar at the Park Central Hotel, just off Times Square, with perfect legality. Well, not quite perfect as I was still a few months underage, but no one in New York seemed to care about that. We planted ourselves at the bar and Cobb loudly and theatrically hailed the innkeeper. He seemed to think he was Falstaff and he was starting to irritate me, but I was in no position to complain.

I paid for our scotches out of my precious and dwindling resources.

"Scottie," Cobb said to the barkeep, "what's the plan if Prohibition passes? Tell me this bar isn't closing down."

Scottie smiled.

"Not to worry, Mr. Cobb. You won't go dry. Just head up to room 416 and you'll find me working the bar like always. The plan is to knock out a wall so two suites will be put together into the nicest little joint you ever saw."

Cobb smacked the bar with the palm of his hand.

"I knew I could depend on you, Scottie."

Cobb downed his drink and ordered another. I figured I'd better make my pitch before I went completely broke.

"So, Mr. Cobb, I want to be a newspaperman more than anything. I started the high school newspaper back in Independence, Missouri, all on my own. I can do it, I tell you. I just need a chance…"

Cobb held up his hand in mock surrender.

"Okay, kid, okay, I hear you. You're the bee's knees, Lincoln Steffen and H. L. Mencken rolled into one. Here you go."

He pulled the cocktail napkin on the bar over to him, took out a pen, and started to write.

"You just keep this safe and don't get it wet, and take it over to Damon Runyon of the *Journal*. We don't have any openings at the *World* right now, but the *Journal* is always hiring. Runyon is a particular buddy of mine and he'll fix you right up."

He finished scrawling and handed me the napkin. Through the water stains, I could just make out what he'd written:

Dear Runyon:

I am doing you the favor of introducing to you the bearer of this note, the most promising young talent in American journalism.

Cobb

This was beyond my wildest hopes, as Damon Runyon was the leading reporter in New York City. In fact, he was New York City personified. Runyon knew everybody and everybody knew him. Even I knew that, not a week in New York. I folded that wet napkin like it was holy writ and bought Cobb another scotch. I was on my way!

"Now listen to me, kid," Cobb said.

I listened raptly.

"Don't even try to get to Runyon at the *Journal*. They're a bunch of prigs over there and won't let you in. Sunday is wash day. You can find Runyon at Lindy's on wash day, clearing his accounts. That's where you want to beard him."

"Wash day?"

"Oh, yes, wash day." Cobb smiled. "Every Sunday, all the gamblers on Times Square show up at Lindy's to clear accounts with their bookies, to wash everything out so everybody's even. Runyon always loses and he's always there. You'll meet some interesting characters too, you can write about them. Show up about seven, eight o'clock."

"At night?"

"This is Broadway, kid. There ain't no mornings." Cobb wiggled his empty glass. "Running dry here."

I slapped whatever money I had left onto the bar and got to my feet.

"Mr. Cobb, I'm in your debt," I said. "I won't forget this."

"Not a problem," said Cobb. "Just keep your eyes open around Runyon. He's quiet, but he don't miss a trick. He's a piece of work, that guy."

So he proved to be.

Come wash day, I showed up at Lindy's as directed. If there was ever a place undeserving of its prominence in history, Lindy's Delicatessen was that place. The food was mediocre and the service was actively poor. There were dozens, maybe hundreds of Jewish delis in New York that were better than Lindy's. It became famous in part because of its location on Seventh Avenue at Times Square, which made it easy for theatre types to nosh there, but mostly it became famous for two men. One was Damon Runyon, who immortalized it as Mindy's in his stories of Broadway's guys and dolls. The other was Arnold Rothstein.

I'd never heard of Arnold Rothstein that rainy Sunday evening when I pushed open Lindy's doors. I brushed rain from my face and looked around. Directly in front of me was the cashier. Off to my right were rows of tables and a deli counter, like a thousand other joints including the one I slung hash in every day. Nothing to see here.

The place was crowded, though. I thought of Cobb's comments about "wash day." At every table, I saw wise guys with fedoras and broad lapels and loud ties, slurping coffee and downing cheesecake. Sitting by himself at the table next to the cashier was a trim little man, neatly dressed, with nothing on the table in front of him but a glass of milk and a notebook, the size that fits into a man's inside suit pocket. Something about this fellow took my eye. His brown hair was slicked down and parted in the middle. He had a prominent nose and his teeth stuck out a little over his lower lip, like he had dentures that didn't quite fit. He was showing signs of going bald in a few more years. His suit and his polka-dotted bow tie were a touch on the flashy side, but obviously expensive so that would be forgiven even in the best of clubs. The notebook was open in front of him. His eyes were flying up and down the page, reviewing columns of figures, sucking in the numbers like a hummingbird sucking nectar.

As I watched from just inside the door, letting the night's rain drip off me, I saw a wise guy sidle up to the little man's table with the attitude of a supplicant, hat in hand. He sat and leaned over the table, speaking softly to the little man sipping milk. Suddenly the little man reached out and seized the hand of the wise guy, pulling him close and whispering intensely to him. Then he took an enormous wad of dough, big as your fist, from his side pocket and counted out some moolah, which was quickly pocketed by the wise guy. The little man pulled out a fountain pen and made careful notations in his ledger. The transaction over, the wise guy made himself scarce, only to have his place taken by another supplicant, bent on the same routine.

I asked the counter guy for Damon Runyon and he pointed to a corner table by the window. I thought he had the wrong dope, for the individual seated at that table was far too well-dressed to be any reporter I had seen so far. He wore a well-tailored suit, pearl gray, with wide lapels and a snap-brim hat perched just so on his head. His conservative tie was perfectly knotted. An impeccably folded handkerchief peeped from his breast pocket. All in all, he was quite the dude, as Runyon might have said of himself in his own writing. He would have used the present tense, of course, as he always did in his short stories, but this was before the short stories, when Runyon was only the top reporter in New York.

He drew on his cigarette and read the evening paper that lay on the table in front of him. His eyes were looking down at the paper through rimless glasses on wire frames. The newspaper lay over the remains of some sort of meal, something with gravy. The ashtray on the table was full of evidence of Runyon's tobacco habit, which would kill him one day. Runyon's mouth was compressed into a tight line, suggesting he was less than happy. Given what Cobb had told me about wash day and Runyon's infatuation with slow-running horses, I was not surprised. Anyway, I decided that this was indeed the great Damon Runyon of the *Journal*. I walked over to him.

Runyon sensed me staring.

"So," he said in his dry, high-pitched voice, without looking up, "did you get a good gander at the Big Bankroll, kid?"

It took a second, but I realized he was talking about the little man near the cash register with the big wad of cash.

"Yes, sir, I guess I did," I replied. "It surprises me he'd show that much cash. Doesn't have a bodyguard even. That I can see."

This brought Runyon's cool eyes up to face me as he took a sip from the glass in front of him. He was drinking water, which was something of a relief after I had to buy Cobb all those scotches. I later learned that Runyon didn't drink liquor.

"I surmise you're new to town. If you'd been in New York a week, you'd know who that fellow is. And if you knew that, you'd know why he doesn't need a bodyguard."

I didn't follow this at all, but decided to let it pass.

"Excuse me, are you Damon Runyon?"

Runyon looked back down at the newspaper.

"That's what everyone calls me, so I suppose I am."

Like a fool, I sat down on the chair across from Runyon, which he didn't like at all but was too polite to say.

"Mr. Runyon, my name is James Cornelius O'Neal. I mean to get in the newspaper business. I really admire your work and I'm honored to meet you."

Runyon just stared at me over his cigarette.

"I have this letter of introduction from Irvin S. Cobb."

I pulled out Cobb's note and held it out to him over the table. Runyon didn't move, just stared at me like I was offering him a dead fish.

"Mr. Cobb and I worked together in France during the war," I added. Each time I told the story, I made my relationship with Cobb a little closer. Soon I'd be saving his life over there.

Runyon still didn't move, so I dropped the note on the table in front of him. My aim was bad, as the wet napkin that Cobb had written on dropped right on the wet napkin Runyon had used to wipe dinner off his lips, no doubt doing it no good. Left little alternative short of rudeness, which he shunned, Runyon picked up my napkin and read Cobb's note. Then he sighed.

"Kid, you know Cobb hates me?"

Uh oh.

"I see that you don't," Runyon continued. "It's just that Irv wants my job, like most reporters in this town. Happens that I have circulation, or my boss Mr. Hearst does, and circulation is a reporter's lifeblood. Why would you want to get into a crummy business like that?"

"It's all I got, Mr. Runyon," I said. This was my one shot, so I laid it out for him. "You see, I'm from Missouri. I came back from the war, got off the boat, and walked into New York because this is where it is, where everything is. I can write. I'm a good writer. Mr. Cobb was right about that. I need the newspaper business and I'll be good at it. Can't you help me?"

"Kid, there's a million yokels who come to New York, wanting to be writers or actors or God knows what. I know, I was one of them. It takes more than wanting."

Runyon turned back to his newspaper like he was done, but I wasn't finished.

"What does it take?" I asked him.

He looked up, confused.

"What?"

"What does it take? You said you were a yokel once. How'd you make it?"

Runyon stabbed out his cigarette on his plate.

"Kid, if I made it, I wouldn't be here on wash day getting another marker put into Arnold Rothstein's ledger." He reached in his pocket for another smoke and his irritation increased when he realized the pack was empty. "I didn't just come into New York as a punk kid with no experience. I'd worked for papers in Colorado. I fought in the Philippines. Then I worked my way up for Hearst, writing baseball, covering Pershing in Mexico. I've been around, kid."

I couldn't believe my luck.

"You were with Pershing? Going after Pancho Villa? So was I!"

Runyon looked at me skeptically.

"You were just a kid then. I mean, even more of a kid."

"Me and a friend ran off to find Pershing and we met Pershing and Patton both."

Instinct told me to hold back mentioning that I also knew Pancho Villa. Generally speaking, a listener can only handle so much truth at one time.

"A less charitable observer might suspect you were feeding me a helping of horse patoot, kid," said Runyon. "You are really asking me to believe that you were with Pershing in Mexico?"

"It's the ever-loving truth, Mr. Runyon."

I'd read enough of his articles, I figured I could show off a little of his patois. Then he grilled me, fast.

"How is Patton related to Pershing?"

"Brothers-in-law."

"Name three of Villa's commanders."

"Lopez, Cervantes, Fernandez."

"What sparked the expedition?"

"Villa's raid on Columbus, New Mexico."

"Describe Pershing. Quick now."

"Rod up his ass. Cautious."

"Patton?"

"Brave. Show-off. Kind of crazy."

Runyon pursed his lips and considered.

"Okay, kid," he said finally. "I'll ask around at the paper tomorrow and see if there's something for you. Be here at Lindy's tomorrow at one and I'll let you know if I find something. Now get scarce."

And get scarce I did.

The next day, I showed up at Lindy's as instructed and almost ran to Runyon's table. A sense of panic hit me when I saw that the table was empty and Runyon was nowhere to be seen. Was he avoiding me? Had he only said he'd find me a job in order to get rid of me?

A soft voice called me from behind.

"Young man?" It was almost a hiss.

I turned. My sense of panic did not subside when I saw that I was being called by the neat man with the little notebook and the big bankroll, Arnold Rothstein.

That morning at the diner, I had asked around about Rothstein. His story was well-known in the city and it didn't take long to pick up some of the details. He was born in midtown Manhattan in 1882, the son of devout Jewish parents named Abraham and Esther. Abe was a wealthy dealer in cotton goods and what they call a pillar of the Jewish community. He was famously nicknamed "Abe the Just" and was much in demand for his wisdom and fairness. One of Arnold's brothers became a rabbi. A.R., as he was called, took a different path. So different that his father disowned him, proclaiming Arnold dead to him, a powerful proclamation for anyone, but especially for Orthodox Jews like the Rothsteins. A.R. still visited his mother every month, they told me.

The quiet man who sat looking at me from his regular table at Lindy's was the leading gambler in a gambling town, the leading fixer in a corrupt town. A believer in making an impression, he would flash a bankroll in the tens of thousands, even the hundreds of thousands. He kept detailed records of his transactions in the famous notebooks that he always carried with him. He was said to have his fingers in everything shady in New York and to have an unrivaled nose for making money. Still, he was mostly a loner. He sat in Lindy's for anyone to see, no henchmen in sight, just A.R. drinking milk and figuring the odds.

Physically he was short, about Riley's height of 5′7″. He was trim and pale, quick and jerky in his movements. He had thinning brown hair and a tendency to squint and there was something clammy about him. He was the sort of fellow you instinctively didn't want to touch. If he appeared suddenly, like he did with me that day at Lindy's, you shuddered a little. I expect he had that effect on people his whole life. Some people are just that way. Cold.

He was finishing his modest lunch, which he did not invite me to join. The ever-present notebook was on the table in front of him.

"How do you know Damon Runyon?" he asked me.

"I'm sorry?"

I pretended not to hear, so I could think of an answer.

"I saw you sitting with Damon yesterday and here you are, today. I'm a curious man. I like to know what my friends are about and Mr. Runyon is a friend of mine."

A voice at my elbow interrupted, thank God.

"A.R., to be your friend, I'd have to be colored green and have a picture of a dead president on my belly."

It was Runyon, who had just entered the restaurant. He turned to me.

"Sorry, kid, I got hung up. You'll work in the print shop for the *Journal*. You'll be what they call a printer's devil—which is aptly named, so don't thank me. The shop's at Second Avenue and 34th Street. Show up Monday, a week from today, at eight in the p.m. You'll work nights. Best I could do, but it's a newspaper job."

It wasn't reporting, but I figured it was a start. I was about to launch into profuse thanks, but Runyon moved away and hurried to his table while a supplicant moved in on Rothstein, seeking a loan or a favor.

It was enough. I had a toe in the newspaper business and I knew my whole body would follow. I was on my way. I loved New York.

4

No Spooning on Blue Road

Marta

March 21, 1919:

At last I begin. I have thought so long of writing a journal, but I could never start. If I'd spent the same time writing that I've spent thinking about doing it, I would have a box full of journals by now! I am so excited that my Walter is coming home, I have to express my feelings somewhere, so I bought this notebook and I will record them in these pages. It will be good practice for me to write in English.

It was really Mr. O'Neal's encouragement that led me to take up my pen and start a journal. He was always so encouraging about my poetry, even though it must look so immature and foolish to him. What a kind man he is! If I may say so here secretly, I wish his son Cornelius took after him more. It is hard for me to believe Mr. O'Neal is really an atheist like he says he is. How can someone so kind not believe there is a God from whom all kindness comes? He asks me to call him Jack, but I do not think that would be appropriate for a girl of my age. Do you, dear diary? I suppose I must call you that, now, like the girls in the story books. But "diary" sounds so childish.

Walter is due back in two days! Back from the war, back to stay. He has been gone so long, he has never even seen the babies, and they have never seen their father! Look at that, I wrote as if Walter was father to Hal as well as to baby Fern. I admit, sometimes I feel that way, and I feel like I am mother to both of them. It is so bad of Cornelius not to come home with Walter. Baby Hal is so wonderful, the sort of strong, handsome son any father should want. Sometimes I not only feel like I am mother to both of them, I wish I were!

I will have to watch myself. I am barely on the second page and already I have written things I would not want others to see. If I keep on at this rate, I will reveal all my secrets…

I'm sorry, I am back now, my journal. I am so foolish. When I wrote the word "secrets," suddenly the bad thoughts came back to me, the memories of what happened before, to me and to Papa and poor Miguel. When the bad thoughts come, I have to stop.

March 25, 1919:

Now I can truly start this journal. Now my wonderful Walter is home and we have our beautiful Fern and I hope she has sisters and brothers to come! For now, at least, we also have poor Hal, only seven months old and already deserted by both his parents. Such a sad thing for this little one, though of course he knows no better and is such a good, quiet baby, taking in the world so seriously. Not like our Fern, who is beautiful but I have to admit, fusses rather more than it seems a baby should. I worry it is because my breasts were unable to make her enough milk and she has had to be bottle-fed like Hal. Ma Riley tells me it is normal, and in fact she said that after she had so many babies, she's convinced anything in the world would be normal! Ma can be very funny, but she is also a formidable woman, a challenge to have as one's mother-in-law, for sure.

I know that a person is supposed to use a journal to tell of events that happen day by day, so I should be talking about Walter's arrival home. He looked so handsome when we met him at the train station, I started to cry. I made sure that I was holding both babies when he first saw me. It is silly, but I didn't want baby Hal to feel left out. I hope the O'Neals were not offended. Hal is their grandson and not blood kin to me, but I feel as though he is.

Everyone made such a fuss over Walter that I think it embarrassed him. We came home in the automobile (I am still frightened by that machine!) and Walter carried Fern in his arms so carefully and gingerly as he walked into the living room and eased onto the sofa.

"Don't be afraid, my love," I teased him. "She won't break."

"'Course, I wouldn't advise you to drop her," Ma laughed.

She followed us in and plopped Hal down into his playpen, a brand new one that Jack and Rose bought at the general store in Kansas City. Rose and Fayette followed Ma toward the kitchen to put out the spread we had prepared for our returning warrior. I tried to join them to help, but Ma wouldn't have it.

"You've been waiting for this boy for near two years, Marta, go talk to him!" she said.

I was glad to obey. I put Fern in the playpen with Hal and I sat next to Walter and snuggled into his side.

"*Te amo*," I said to him, and we kissed.

I laughed that he sneaked a look toward the kitchen, as though hoping Ma didn't see us kissing.

Jack O'Neal sat on a small chair opposite us, next to the playpen. He's a dear man and very good with the babies. He leaned over the pen and patted them both, bringing a smile from Fern and a typically serious look from Hal. Mr. O'Neal does not really look like a bookseller. He is a broad-chested man of middle height, with close-cropped and curly brown hair going to gray. He has a strong chin, a large nose, and deep brown eyes that seem to take everything in without judging any of it. He is quick to laugh, and so smart that he can be very hard to follow, but he is never a show-off about it. I told Rose once how lucky she is to have a man like him. She just laughed.

"Yes," she said, "my Jackie's a good man. He just never learned the knack for making money. I guess that means he's a good communist, too."

Communist or not, I knew that Mr. O'Neal was one of the world's gentle souls, just by how he rubbed Fern's back and made her smile. His brown eyes were serious when he turned back to Walter.

"What was happening over there, Walter? We heard Cornelius was dead and you were in a hospital, then we heard you ran off, then we heard you were both alive and coming home, then just you come home. We don't understand."

Walter grimaced. He nodded slightly.

"You've got a right to know. It's a long story. Let's have supper, then I'll tell all of you. There's no dishonor in any of it and Cornelius is fine. He's trying his fortune in New York, like he told you. I'm sure he'll be back for Hal."

Mr. O'Neal didn't look so sure, but he let it pass.

Oh, journal, I don't have the strength to tell you all that Walter told us over the supper table after the babies were sleeping. It was such a long story. Cornelius disappearing after a big battle, Walter wounded, Walter leaving the hospital to go help Cornelius in Germany, involvement with some rebellion in Germany that got Mr. O'Neal very excited. It sounded like Cornelius wanted to fight for the communists over there, which made Mr. O'Neal happy, at least. He was especially astonished that they met some woman named Rosa who apparently was one of his heroes. It all seems so unreal and so irrelevant to our simple life here working on the farm and caring for Fern and Hal. I am proud that Walter is so brave, but I hope he has been brave enough for one lifetime by now and he can stay with his family for the rest of our lives.

We had our special reunion together, my journal, but that is too sacred to share even with you. I do wish I could be more womanly with him. Much as I want to please him, I cannot pretend the memories of the cave in Mexico do not come back, even in our private times together. Especially then. Will I ever escape them?

April 2, 1919:

My Walter has been home so short a time, yet already he seems restless. Today especially, as Ma talked to him about the farm. They sat at the kitchen table this afternoon while the babies napped. I was sewing a baby dress for Fern in the parlor, but the Riley house is not a large one and I could hear them clearly.

"Here's the books for the last three years, Walter," Ma said as she spread the farm's account books across the table. "It's been a good time for farmers. Corn's been up to a dollar-twenty-five, a dollar-thirty a bushel on account of the war. Farmers in Europe are all blown up, so the world's been getting all its corn from the US of A. Back when your father was alive, some years John was lucky to get sixty cents a bushel. You remember?"

"Not really. I was just a boy." Walter sounded bored, or lost.

"Boys farm, too, Walter. Anyway, I figure Europe's got to take a while to get back up and running, so the good times should keep going for now. With you back, I know we'll do better than ever. It'll be nice to have a man around again."

Walter said nothing.

"Anyway, I had to go ahead and buy the seed for this season without waiting for you. I went with all corn this time, since corn prices have been so good. If the weather holds, we need to start planting in a week or two. I was thinking, though, maybe we should mix it up for next year, in case the corn prices go down. Maybe sorghum? What do you think?"

Again, Walter said nothing.

"John pretty much stuck to corn, but I've been trying other things. Two years ago, we grew sorghum and did all right. But this will be your call now, Walter." Ma chuckled. "Listen to me, you just been home a week and I'm asking you to make decisions for 1920. It can wait."

I heard Walter's chair scrape back on the floor as he pushed away from the table.

"Is that it?"

There was a long pause, but Ma must have nodded since Walter then came into the parlor. It hurt me to see the frown on his face.

"Come, husband," I said. "It's a beautiful spring day. Let's go for a walk."

We always enjoyed our walks together on Blue Road in the time before Walter left for war. Today, we turned west, toward town. It is pretty country where we live, very green and with gentle hills, so different from the Mexican desert where I grew up. There are neighbors, but not many since we are three miles from town. Their houses are pleasantly spread along the road, with much room in between. We liked to wave at those neighbors who were outside and maybe chat with them. Well, I did. Walter is a very quiet man.

Today, I felt I knew why he looked especially solemn. I put my arm through his.

"You must not worry, Walter. The farm does well. It will only do better with you here, but Ma will help you."

"Sure, I know," he said. "It's just… I'm not sure I'm cut out to be

37

a farmer. I never much cared for the work. Pa was always disappointed in me that way."

"Nonsense, Walter. You were only a boy when he died. Why would you say that?"

"Boys work on farms, Marta. Just ask Ma."

"Well, if you want to do something else, what would it be? Go back to school?"

Walter laughed at that.

"I was never much for school, Marta. Ran away from it when I was seventeen, don't expect to go back. Besides, Ma needs me at the farm. It's ours."

I'm not so sure Ma needs him. She has the Mexicans and she has a very good head for farming herself. But I didn't say that. Instead I worked up my courage to raise something I've been thinking about for a long time.

"I might want to work at something. Something besides the babies, I mean."

I thought he might laugh at me or even get angry. He always did when I would imagine having this conversation, which I did many times, but I was unjust to my Walter.

"What would you want to do?" he asked.

"Oh, that's the problem," I admitted. "What could I do? I am only a woman. I know I am not strong, I am not smart."

Walter turned to me and took both of my arms in his hands.

"What are you talking about, Marta? You're one of the smartest people I know. Everybody says so. You read more books than anybody in town. As for being a woman, Ma's a woman and she's as tough a bird as I ever saw."

"But I am not tough, Walter. You know it. You know I cannot forget what happened in Mexico."

He pulled me close, clasped me in his arms.

"Oh, Marta. Of course you can't forget it. No one can forget a horror like that. Lots of people couldn't live through it, but you did. And now we have each other and the babies. If you want to work at something, that's just what you'll do. You like books, maybe you can work at the bookstore for the O'Neals."

"Walter, they hardly have enough customers to keep themselves busy, how could they take on an employee? No, I want to find a real job, some way I could make a difference somehow. Ma is such a whirlwind, she runs the house and the farm and cares for the babies all by herself. I think if I could only feel I was doing something worthwhile and helpful, I could be a better mother to Fern and a better wife to you and I could let the past stay in the past."

"Then you'll find something, Marta. I'll help you."

"And I will help you, my husband. I know you better than you think. You need excitement and adventure and you don't find it at the farm. You can have your excitement, Walter, even if it means you must go back to your boxing. Just never leave me or our baby again."

"*Te amo*, Marta."

"*Te amo*, Walter."

We kissed. We were interrupted by the noisy rattles of the Rileys' Model T, driving from town. It was Jack O'Neal, who stopped the car and leaned over to talk with us.

"No spooning on Blue Road," he laughed.

"Where are you off to?" Walter asked.

"Your place, of course. Got an urge to see my grandson and your sweet little baby. Come on, get in. I brought a new book of short stories by Theodore Dreiser for you, Marta. Hard to keep up with you, much as you read."

So Mr. O'Neal gave us a ride back to the house. I asked him what he thought of women working and, my goodness, he went into a long speech about how women are oppressed and in a communist future, they will be equal to men in the workplace and everywhere else. I love Mr. O'Neal. I know communism is evil, but he makes it sound so nice.

When we got home, the babies were awake and anxious for their bottles. All in all, it was a good day. I pray for good days to come.

Part Two

Cornelius
on
Broadway

5

The Black Hand

Cornelius

Cobb thought he was milking the rube, of course, making me buy him scotch and then referring me to his rival. He figured Runyon would laugh me off and I'd be riding the rails back to nowhere in no time. He was wrong. For unknown reasons of his own, Runyon took a shine to me and became my best friend in New York. In the twenties, if Runyon was your friend, all doors opened.

Nobody thinks much about Damon Runyon nowadays, except when there's a revival of *Guys and Dolls* or you turn the television to an old movie that was made from one of his stories. Runyon's main strength was as a reporter, the best sports reporter of his day, and for the most part nobody reads even a reporter's best stuff two days after he writes it.

I give you the straight and honest dope when I tell you that New York City in the twenties would not have been what it was without Damon Runyon. He invented it, he chronicled it, and he devised for it a language that I don't recall hearing anyone actually speak: wise guy slang mixed with painfully high-brow locutions, all in the present tense. In the thirties, he made a lot of money writing funny, sentimental stories about Broadway crooks, none of which were remotely accurate.

In the twenties, when Runyon was a reporter, his style brought him access, unparalleled access. Runyon knew everybody there was to know in Manhattan, everybody knew him, and everybody knew that Runyon was okay. This meant that you could let Runyon hang around and he wouldn't bother anybody. If he happened to see something he probably shouldn't have seen, like a drug deal or a beating administered to some guy, he would have the good taste and discretion not to mention it. In all his years in New York, he never embarrassed anybody and he never mentioned anybody who mattered in any way that could be a source of unhappiness. He covered murder trials as well as sports, but only murder trials involving personal matters and citizen killers. If the killing was business and the killer was connected, Runyon didn't write it. Of course, there were usually no arrests and no trials in such cases anyway, so it wasn't a problem.

It was a grand time to cover sports. Runyon wrote of Red Grange, Babe Ruth, Jack Dempsey, and a little jockey whose principal distinction was that his name rhymed with "handy," allowing Runyon to write catchy poems about "a handy guy named Sande." Runyon slept until noon, went to ballgames, bet on losing horses at Aqueduct, and tagged along with the nightlife of New York, even the most criminal of nightlife like that offered by his close acquaintance and bookie Arnold Rothstein. I couldn't imagine any life better than Runyon's life, which he lived until the cigarettes caught up with him and his ashes were scattered over Broadway from a plane flown by Eddie Rickenbacker. Not a bad way to go out.

I was privileged to see New York in the twenties from a front row seat, for I became Runyon's protégé. For a time, I was Watson to his Holmes, Toklas to his Stein. I stayed silently at his elbow, just as he was mostly silent, and I thereby came to put my hand right on the steamy, beating heart of the city. Runyon got me a job, first as a printer's devil at the *Journal*. In six months, I worked my way up to copyboy and soon came to be Runyon's personal copyboy, sounding board, and slave. Runyon talked me up, first to the editorial staff, then to the boss himself, Mr. Hearst. I started writing obituaries. Then, in 1924, I was given a beat and made an actual reporter. My first paycheck went for a snap-brim fedora, of course. I accompanied Runyon nightly on his rounds. He smoked and didn't drink, I drank and didn't smoke: we were a perfect match.

My initial beat was considered dangerous, low-class, and a

professional dead end. I loved it. I was made the crime reporter for Brooklyn and the Lower East Side, areas teeming with recently arrived Italians and Jews fighting for turf with the Irish gangs who had been there for decades. Prohibition was in full effect by this time and stakes were high in the illegal liquor business. Runyon, of course, set the table for me.

"Kid, I don't know that I did you any favors getting you this job," he told me over pastrami omelets at Lindy's. "I suggest you work there a year or so and, if you write well and don't get yourself killed, you can move to a better desk."

I forked pastrami into my mouth.

"What do you mean 'get killed'?" I asked through the pastrami. "I'm just a reporter."

"You'll be fine," said Runyon, "but these places aren't like Times Square. You need to watch your step a little. See, the Irish used to run the show in the Bowery, but now the eyeties are everywhere down there and they brought a history of maybe a thousand years of crime. You know about the Black Hand? Downtown, that's for real, mainly run by this tough Sicilian name of Joe Masseria. Word is Masseria has the roughest bunch working for him this town has ever seen, young animals who'd do anything and kill anybody for a buck. And then the place is full of Jews and there's some young guys who run together and are called the Bugs and Meyer gang. That's Meyer Lansky and Ben Siegel, who they call Bugsy—but don't call him that so he hears it, he don't like it. And all of them have to deal with the Irish gang, the White Hand, led by a guy out in Brooklyn. Not that I recommend you write about any of this, of course, but you'll want to understand it."

This sounded to me like interesting material to write about, but I wasn't going to argue with Runyon.

"What about the cops?" I asked him. "Is corruption as bad as everybody says?"

Runyon smiled.

"Depends what you mean by 'bad.' Corruption as a system has some things to recommend it. Me, I like a man who's on the take. You know where he stands."

I nodded over at Rothstein.

"They say our friend there is the main fixer in town. Should I ask him if the police are all on the take?"

"You could try, but I don't think you'd get much of an answer. Why don't you ask your cousins? Aren't they cops?"

"I did ask them," I told Runyon. "I didn't get much of an answer."

"Well, there you go, then. Better not write about that, either."

I pushed away my plate.

"If I can't write about gangsters and I can't write about crooked cops, what am I supposed to write about? I'm the crime reporter."

Runyon smiled through his cigarette smoke.

"There's plenty of crime, kid. You just need to know what crime is okay to cover. Domestic stuff, home burglaries, pickpockets, and con men, those are for you. If you have any questions whether something should be written about, just ask me. Or him."

He pointed at Rothstein, who was sitting by the cash register counting his big bankroll. In fact, Rothstein's nickname was the "Big Bankroll." When he wrote his stories, Runyon would call him "The Brain."

Since it was my first day on the beat, Runyon agreed to take me downtown and show me around. We went to the Tombs, the prison in Lower Manhattan where wise guys who were a step slow spent unwanted vacations. We sat in on night arraignment court, which was the same undisciplined zoo that it is to this day and that it is in big cities all over the world. We walked the streets and I felt transported to the slums of Naples with pushcarts and social clubs and gaudy Catholic icons, to the ghettos of *Mitteleuropa* with Hassidim and Stars of David and kosher markets, and even to Hong Kong with fish markets and sweatshops and opium dens. All within a few blocks, too.

The night's highlight occurred on Mulberry Street, in the heart of Little Italy. Runyon suddenly stopped at the unmarked door of a social club, such as were located all over the Lower East Side. When their doors were open, you could look inside these clubs and see older men with bellies taking their leisure and their drinks in easy chairs while they chatted over the events of the day. Usually, but not always, the denizens were Italian. Always, not just usually, the clubs were rigidly segregated by ethnicity. Often, young men lounged outside the doors to the clubs, acting as security. I had seen such places many times in my perambulations around the city and I never even considered trying to enter one of them. It wasn't done.

But all doors were open to Runyon. He stood politely at the door while the young tough on the street looked him over, Runyon and I standing out from the surroundings in our suits and fedoras. I barely drew a glance. The kid jerked his head to allow us admittance without a word. Runyon nodded amiably and stepped in, me on his heels. The room inside was dark, dark as tar, dark as Dante's vision of Hell. The only light, once the door was closed behind us, came feebly from small candles placed on each of the round tables that filled the room. Here and there, I could make out the sight of old Italian men drinking espresso or wine. Not many, maybe six men scattered about. Only one had a companion and only one, the same one, was eating. A burly, jowly middle-aged man with a dark complexion and a protruding belly, he sat eating a plate of noodles and red sauce, swilling wine each time he filled his mouth with food. His short tie, white shirt, and linen suit were all liberally stained with sauce. Next to him sat a young Italian man, about my age, wearing a dark suit and looking bored. He wasn't eating and I didn't see him touch the glass of wine in front of him.

Runyon motioned for me to stay rooted and he took a few steps toward that table.

"Mr. Masseria, I appreciate the chance to see you again," he said. I was startled to realize that I was in the presence of the boss of the Black Hand. "You know that Tom Kelly has retired?"

Masseria nodded curtly.

"I thought you'd like to meet the young man who will replace him. He came to show his respect."

Runyon waved me forward to center stage.

I stood there feeling like a fool while Masseria and his stooge looked me over. Finally, Masseria said something in Italian to his companion and they both laughed. Then Masseria deigned to speak to me, in very heavily accented English.

"This man before you, this Kelly." He took a forkful of pasta and chewed it loudly, ruminating on my predecessor. "He was Irish, but he did all right. Never had any trouble with him, you know? Will you make me trouble, boy?"

I wanted to tell him to go fuck himself, but I didn't. I said I always listened to Mr. Runyon.

Masseria nodded.

"Okay," he said, "but I got my eye on you. *Basta!*"

Lacking Italian, I thought he had impugned my parenthood.

47

Runyon hustled me out and informed me that he simply meant the interview was over.

"What was all that about?" I asked, a little heatedly.

"I know. The guy's a prick, but he runs the show down here and you're going to be walking these streets a lot. It won't hurt if he remembers you paid your respects."

That was my introduction to Joe "the Boss" Masseria. More importantly, that was my introduction to the silent young man seated next to him, Charles Lucano. People called him Lucky. The newspapers later got his name wrong: they called him Lucky Luciano.

6

Creatures of the Night

Cornelius

Looking back from the vantage point of a comfortable old age, I see that my career in the New York of the twenties was based on a series of introductions that led me, unknowingly, deeper and deeper into the heart of the times. Cobb to Runyon. Runyon to Rothstein. Rothstein to Polly Adler. Polly Adler to Benchley, Benchley to Parker, Parker to Anne Morrow, Anne to J.P. Morgan. I just kept dancing the Grand Right and Left, hand extended, smile on my face, looking for the main chance with all the other hustlers of the decade. If I had known how it would end, with Riley, Marta, and me facing some of the worst bad men of the century on the Coney Island boardwalk, I might have gone back to being a daddy and working on the Riley farm. Probably not, though.

I worked my crime beat. One day, I wrote a story about the handling of an arson case by the famous New York trial lawyer Bill Fallon. I called it "Fallon and the Firebug" and it was quite popular, which it should have been because it was funny. I copied Runyon's style, but who didn't? It was at lunchtime a couple of days later that I strolled into Lindy's, hoping to talk Runyon into celebrating with me by going to the Polo Grounds to watch the Giants. Runyon was not at his usual table, but Rothstein was at his. I heard his soft, sibilant voice from behind me, calling me over to talk to him. It was like being summoned by the rattle of a snake from under a rock. Nevertheless, I trotted over, hat in hand.

Across from Rothstein at the little table near the cashier sat a dark-haired dame, maybe forty, wearing a fur coat and one of those dainty little hats with a veil. She looked like she should be lunching at the Waldorf with white-gloved ladies, not at Lindy's with Arnold Rothstein. On a second glance, though, her eyes were bright with intelligence and humor, so maybe she was a wiser doll than she first appeared.

"Mr. O'Neal, let me introduce you. This is Miss Polly Adler. Miss Adler, this is Mr. O'Neal."

The lady's smile grew broader, either at my name or at the look on my face when I realized I was being introduced to the madam of the most famous and exclusive whorehouse in all of New York. A Russian Jew who emigrated at a very young age, she spoke with a slight accent.

"I know who you are, Mr. O'Neal. That story you wrote on Fallon was funny as hell. All my girls know about it."

I bowed, trying to be debonair.

"Miss Adler, all New York knows about you. I am honored to meet you."

Rothstein's frown was as severe as Adler's grin was infectious.

"Mr. O'Neal, I must ask you. Are you an anti-Semite?"

My smile fled from my face instantly, as did Adler's. Rothstein's tone was deadly, with no hint of humor.

"What are you talking about, A.R.?" Adler responded. "Why would you ask him something like that?"

Rothstein calmly held my eyes.

"You used an offensive term in your story, Mr. O'Neal. Perhaps you did not realize it, but such terms can only perpetuate the unfortunate stereotypes that contribute to the prejudices against people of my background, which are so rife in this city."

Adler snorted.

"You seem to be doing okay, A.R. Besides, who are you and me to get on a high horse about being Jews? Not like they'd welcome the likes of us at temple. What about it, Jimmy O'Neal?" she asked, turning her attention to me. "Are you a Jew-hater?"

Screw Rothstein.

"Miss Adler, I am in no way a Jew-hater," I said. "If I were, one look at your smile would turn me around and make me think seriously of enrolling in Hebrew school."

Adler cackled with delight.

"A.R., you are definitely full of shit on this one," said the lively Miss Adler. "This boy is welcome at my establishment any time."

With a girlish simper, she reached into her purse and pulled out a business card with only a phone number on it, which she placed into my waiting hand.

"What did the article even say, anyway, A.R.?" she asked. "I don't remember anything that offended me. Of course," she said, smiling flirtatiously at me, "I may not offend as easily as some."

"In his story, Mr. O'Neal referred to an arson for insurance purposes as 'Jewish bankruptcy.' It is an old joke and an offensive one."

"Oh, fudge, A.R., I call it that myself. Don't be so serious. It was just a funny story."

Rothstein's glare cooled the steam off his soup.

"I am a serious man," he said.

I muttered something about being more careful with my words and Rothstein and Adler went back to whatever they were talking about. I wondered briefly what Adler needed from Rothstein, protection or financing. Likely both. Meanwhile, a certain business card was already starting to burn a hole in my pocket.

Polly Adler was known to all levels of society in the city and the fact that she could still run her highly illegal establishment was a testament to her sagacity and connections, as well as to the flexible views of properly-oiled law enforcement officers. She moved frequently, renting suites of apartments with multiple bedrooms and large living rooms. You located her by obtaining one of her precious business cards. You would call and inform Polly of your desires, whether it be a raucous party or a private tête-à-tête. Polly would decide if she wished to accommodate you and, if so, call out her stable of girls as needed.

While Polly certainly attracted more than her share of mobsters and rough trade, she also enticed the highest circles of Wall Street and Park Avenue society. At Polly's, the living room was almost as much an attraction as the bedrooms, for Polly was hostess for a social club that a man could enjoy without ever taking off his pants. When Polly agreed to accept your business, she would do everything possible to ensure that you were surrounded only by customers you would find agreeable and who suited your social background. If you were a Wall Street tycoon, you would find the living room populated with similar businessmen, with whom you could share Arnold Rothstein's whiskey and make deals in a relaxed atmosphere, surrounded by adoring women who were more than willing to celebrate the transaction with a visit to the boudoir. The drinks and cigars were always the best to be found in Prohibition New York. Bob Benchley took to using Polly's as his office, writing some of his best stuff there and sometimes not bothering to bed any of the girls. Sometimes—but not often, though.

Polly was famous for treating her girls well and there was always a long line of applicants for positions in her stable. Still, it was prostitution. Girls were beaten, girls took drugs, girls were degraded. That's how prostitution is and there is no getting away from it. I never knew Polly well enough to decide how much she kidded herself about the effect this line of work had on her girls. I suspect not much. She came to America all by herself as a child from a tiny village in Russia, without a cent to her name and without speaking any English. She clawed her way up a very slippery ladder to fame and wealth in one of the most dangerous of professions. Despite her line of gab and her charming smile, I doubt that she harbored any illusions about her girls' prospects in life or about much of anything else.

I was definitely torn at the thought of calling Polly. I had never used a prostitute in my life and the thought was unpleasant to me. I was reasonably successful with women and was generally able to find bedmates without paying them. I even married a girl from the print room back in 1921, though the marriage didn't last a year. Looking back, I don't think I even wrote my parents or Riley about the marriage. I figured all along it wasn't going to last and didn't see the point, I suppose.

As you probably expect, I did eventually dial the number on Polly Adler's card. I told myself it was professional curiosity, as so many of the city's top mobsters were regular Polly customers, as were most of the politicians and judges in town, but I knew it was more than that leading me to dial the number. The notion of a gentleman's club, with good liquor and good conversation, and with pretty girls who would never turn you down or make you feel slighted, was overpowering to any heterosexual American male, as Polly well knew. Perhaps at this special place, the girls wouldn't be drug addicts, wouldn't be beaten and abused, would really mean it if they said they liked you. At minimum, perhaps they'd do a wonderful job of pretending all of that. I wanted to find out.

Polly's warm voice answered with a simple hello.

"Miss Adler?" I said, taking a deep breath, though I knew very well who it was. "This is Jimmy O'Neal. The reporter?"

From her welcoming tone, I might have been Santa Claus.

"Why, Mr. O'Neal, at last. I thought you'd forgotten me. I'm so delighted you called."

I stammered like a schoolboy.

"I remembered your kind invitation, Miss Adler, and, well, I've been thinking about it and, well..."

"Now, you must stop by, Mr. O'Neal, you really must. And call me Polly, for pity's sake. I can tell right now, we're going to be good, good friends."

"And you call me Jimmy, then, Miss—I mean, Polly. Or Cornelius, if you like. That's what my best friends call me."

Polly gave a delighted little squeal.

"Cornelius! Oh, the girls will just love you. You must come over! When can it be?"

Right now, I thought.

"Whenever suits your convenience, Polly. And the girls' convenience, of course."

"Well, aren't you a sweetheart, Cornelius. Let's see..." It seemed as though she was checking a datebook, but she may have been seeking to give that impression. "Tonight would simply not be appropriate. We have a sizable party coming in and while they didn't insist on exclusivity, I'm afraid this is rather an uncouth crowd that you wouldn't want to associate with. No, I think Wednesday is the best night for you. So far, all we have reserved for Wednesday is a gentleman who is a long-time customer and just a dear—you will like him very much—plus a theatrical person who is coming with him. I'm sure you all will get along and I will make very sure to have my prettiest girls available to entertain you. How does that sound, Cornelius?"

It sounded good to me. My feet might be cold, but other body parts were very warm indeed.

"I'll be there with bells on," I said cleverly. "What time?"

53

"Let's say ten o'clock, Cornelius. My girls are late sleepers and creatures of the night. Come to apartment 8D, 766 West Fifty-Fourth Street. You got it?"

"I got it, Polly. See you then."

I hung up, the phrase "creatures of the night" reverberating in my head.

I killed an afternoon in Brooklyn trying to get acquainted with Frankie Yale, the boss of the Red Hook docks. I took the subway to the joint he owned on Coney Island, which was called the Harvard Inn. Frankie was originally named Ioele, but he Americanized it and he thought it was funny that he owned the Harvard Inn. I didn't get an interview though, for as soon as Frankie learned I was a reporter, he had me tossed out by his chief enforcer, a sleazy creep named Willie Altieri.

Wednesday finally came. The time between seven and ten that evening was the worst, for I just had to wait patiently for the hour when I was to knock on Polly's door. The minutes dragged with excruciating slowness as I sat in my apartment, watching the clock. I wanted a drink, but thought I shouldn't drink. I'll be frank: I considered masturbation so I would not spend myself too quickly later that night, but I decided it would be even worse to be unable to arouse an erection at all. I was like a teenage boy, obsessed with his own performance and how he might be perceived by whatever lady of the evening should be assigned his case. I was pathetic.

At ten o'clock on the nose, pathetic me knocked on Polly Adler's door. A colored maid opened the door instantly, as though she were waiting.

"You must be Mr. O'Neal," she said. "I'm Lion. Now you just give me your hat and come on in, sugar. This place is your home."

In a funny way, that's how it felt. I gave over my precious snap-brim to Lion and walked on in. All my worries and insecurities melted away. I stepped into a large room that looked comfortable as could be, not like any whorehouse I had ever imagined. A portly young man with a mustache sat in an easy chair, smoking a pipe and chatting away with three nice-looking girls who might easily have stepped out of the pages of a Sunday magazine. A tough-looking fellow with a prominent nose sat at an upright piano, plunking the ivories while two more girls sat on the bench on each side of him, snapping their fingers and keeping time. He was playing "California, Here I Come" if I remember right, a big hit that year for Al Jolson.

Polly came in from what I assume was the kitchen, holding a tray of drinks.

"Cornelius!" she exclaimed. "Welcome to the party! What are you drinking?"

The fellow at the piano belted out the finishing lines of the song and his fingers shot the keys in the closing arpeggio. I asked for a Gin Rickey, a cocktail that was the rage of Broadway at the time. The chubby fellow with the mustache leaned forward and offered his hand.

"Cornelius, I'm Bob," he said. "Very pleased to make your acquaintance. Welcome to the finest house in New York."

I fell gratefully into the seat next to Bob. A girl in a short flapper dress sat on my lap.

"Happy to see you, Cornelius," she said. "Polly told us all about you and I knew you and I were going to be friends."

Was I in Heaven? Bob smiled, as if he were reading my thoughts.

"Not a bad welcoming committee, is it? Come over here, Blanche."

One of the girls, apparently Blanche, sat on Bob's lap just as my new friend had perched on mine.

"This is the life, I must say," said Bob contentedly.

The tough-looking piano player took one of the girls by the hand and drifted down the hall, into a bedroom.

Polly brought me my drink.

"You come here a lot, Bob?" I asked.

"All the time, Cornelius. Polly knows what soothes the troubled soul." Bob was rubbing his hand on Blanche's bottom, a blissful look on his face. "I must confess, Cornelius, I am about to violate the rules of the house. I know who you are and don't see a reason to pretend that I don't."

I took a quick peek under my girl's bodice, drawing a slap on my hand and a giggle.

"So who am I, Bob?"

"You," said Bob, "are Jimmy O'Neal, crack crime reporter for the *New York Journal*. Do you know who I am?"

Of course I did.

"You are Robert Benchley, funniest writer in New York."

"Well, I'm glad to see you're as perceptive as you are talented, Cornelius," he said. "I think we'll get along."

There was a knock on the door. Polly came again from the kitchen, a concerned look on her face. She put on a smile when Bob and I looked at her.

"Don't worry, gents. I'll get rid of whoever it is. This night is all yours."

She looked through the peephole and seemed to recognize whomever she saw, for she unlocked the door and began to open it. It slammed into her as though kicked and a big lug barged into the room, followed by a handful of cronies. Polly almost fell down, backing away as they marched in like they owned the place. It took me a second to realize that I knew the lug in the lead. It was Hump McManus.

"You're a lucky lady, tonight, Polly," said the Hump with a mean grin on his face.

He looked several sheets to the wind, as did his hangers-on, who were already ambling into the room and eyeing the girls.

"My friends and me," he continued, "we've been up and down Broadway looking for a place to party and we decided on yours. This all the girls you got on hand? Better call a few more, I'm feeling peckish."

Hump licked his big Irish gob with his big purple tongue.

Everyone on Broadway knew Hump McManus. He hailed from a law enforcement family not unlike my cousins, the Toolans. His father was one of a famous band of Manhattan cops nicknamed the Immortals and Hump had two brothers who were well-known crooked coppers. Hump, though, never joined the force. He was a gambler and a small-time political fixer, generally known as a big dumb ox who was a good time if you weren't craving intellectual stimulation. He wore loud suits and ties, set up floating dice and card games, and could fix a small problem that a wise guy might have with the political or legal establishments. Big problems, though, were beyond the Hump and went to Arnold Rothstein.

I saw Hump here and about, as did everyone on Broadway, but I never gave him much thought. He seemed an amiable lummox capable of providing occasional amusement and that was about all there was to him. I had never seen him as he appeared that night at Polly's, liquored up and sporting an obvious hard-on, both literally and figuratively.

His buddies weren't any better, low-rent hustlers and crooks looking to let off steam. I pushed my girl off my lap and rose to my feet quietly, wondering where this was headed.

Polly, being experienced in such matters, remained cool.

"Hump, you need to call me," she said. "My parties are by appointment, you know that. These gentlemen have the house for tonight. I'm sure I could find a place for you and your pals to be accommodated."

Hump swaggered to Benchley's chair, where Bob still sat with Blanche on his lap. One of his companions wandered into the hall where the bedrooms were located.

"These gentlemen?" said Hump, contemptuously. "These gentlemen?"

He grabbed the girl by the arm and threw her across the room, then placed his mammoth foot on Benchley's crotch.

"I don't think these gentlemen will give us any trouble, do you, Polly?"

"Boys!" Hump's companion suddenly called out from the hall. "Look at this!"

Hump kept his foot on Benchley's crotch, but the rest of us hurried into the hall. Hump's friend stood at an open door to what was apparently the chamber where the piano player had taken his chosen lady, for he suddenly stormed out of the door and knocked the wise guy to the floor, savaging him. I said he was tough-looking and his looks did not belie him: this piano player knew how to use his fists and the wise guy was quickly beaten like an egg. The wise guy's buddies did not stand apart, they began to kick and stomp and pound the piano player with great abandon. I should mention that the piano player was stark naked, which is not ideal in such a situation.

Things looked bad for the pure in heart and no one seemed to be rising to the occasion. Benchley simply sat and looked with displeasure at the foot in his crotch. Polly stammered and waved her hands, but did nothing to influence the course of events. I decided it was up to me.

"Hump!" I shouted in my deepest voice. "Think what you're doing here."

Hump looked at me quizzically, apparently not having previously noticed that I was in the room.

"Who the fuck are you?" he asked, befuddled.

"I the fuck am a friend of A.R.'s," I replied. "Look at me close, Hump. Don't you remember me?"

Hump removed his foot from Robert Benchley's nether regions and lumbered over to me. I had spoken loudly enough that the boys paused in beating on the piano player. Hump gazed drunkenly into my face.

"You're that reporter. I seen you at Lindy's."

"Yes, Hump, you seen me at Lindy's. You seen me with Damon Runyon and I believe you know Damon Runyon. I believe you also know that Mr. Runyon and I have a relationship with a gentleman named Arnold Rothstein. Would you really want me to discuss your behavior here tonight with Mr. Rothstein?"

Hump drew himself up to his full, quite massive height.

"You think I'm scared of Arnold Rothstein?"

I placed my hand on his shoulder.

"Hump, in fact I think you are fucking stupid, but I do not think you are so fucking stupid as not to be scared of Arnold Rothstein."

I smiled and patted him. He seemed to appreciate my confidence in his intelligence.

"What the fuck, Hump?" asked a fellow who was kneeling on the piano player's chest.

You could trace the progress of thoughts clomping slowly through the Humpster's dim mind. He had serious doubts that I was truly as connected with A.R. as I let on. On the other hand, he had seen me both with A.R. and with the great Runyon. If he was going to be wrong, the downside of thumping a friend of A.R.'s greatly outweighed the downside of foregoing a violent evening at Polly's. You could imagine his hard-on receding as he thought.

"Come on, boys," he finally said. "Nothing happening here. Let's find a joint with some action."

Slowly, they took themselves away.

The party was pretty much ruined. Benchley, the piano player, and I said our goodbyes and went for a late-night breakfast at Lindy's. Benchley explained that the piano player, whose name was Leonard, was appearing with his brothers in some sort of comedy revue on Broadway. This surprised me: Leonard seemed far more of a wise guy than he did a theatrical type. It takes all kinds.

As we parted, Benchley again complimented my writing.

"I want you to have lunch with me at the Algonquin. You might fit right in."

I said I would.

The next day, I explained to Runyon what had happened. He was horrified and said I must never use A.R.'s name again unless I had specific authorization. He said he would fix it for me this time, but not to do it again. As it happened, Polly Adler was a favorite of Rothstein's and A.R. thought Hump McManus was an oaf, so Runyon's intervention was unnecessary. Rothstein did make a point to personally tell me not to use his name again. I never sought the services of Polly Adler's workers either. I decided being a john just wasn't for me.

Two days later, I met Benchley for lunch at the Algonquin.

7

Round Tables and Jungle Animals

Cornelius

The Algonquin is a rather small hotel on 44th Street between Fifth and Sixth Avenues, closer to Sixth. It is on the edge of the theatre district and the lobby of the Algonquin has always been an excellent place to stop for drinks and dessert before or after a show. Even today in the nineteen-eighties, the lobby feels like the New York of my youth. Richly upholstered, dark and cozy, the lobby is crowded with little tea tables at which people sip cocktails and discuss the subjects of the day. Most people still dress reasonably well at the Algonquin. While tourists do sometimes intrude, wearing their shorts and sandals, such occurrences are rare and the tourists generally leave quickly. It is still the Algonquin that I visit when I want New York City straight, no chaser.

I believe the day I met Benchley for lunch was my first visit, for the Algonquin was not yet as famous as it later became as the host of the Round Table. The lobby was less dark then, the upholstery less worn, but otherwise it was much the same that day as when I last stopped there. Frank Case, the hotel's owner and a gentleman of the first order, stood behind the front desk. I flicked my hat brim at him and smiled as I walked by, trying to look at home, and indeed I had started to feel that way already. I threaded the tea tables and walked to the door of the hotel's restaurant, the Rose Room.

Today, when you stand at the door of the Rose Room, you see on the wall facing you a very large portrait of the now-famous Algonquin Round Table. In the painting is an image of the restaurant and at a very large table in the center sit caricatures of all the principal Round Table folk: Kaufman, Benchley, Parker, and so on. I am not depicted, which I suppose is fair as I didn't spend nearly as much time with that crowd as the others did. Still, I was part of that gang for a while and it would have been nice to have a little bit of recognition in the painting, even if my back was turned.

When I entered the Rose Room on this first occasion, Benchley was seated at a table to the right of the door. The table was indeed large and round. Benchley sat back to the wall and face to the door, waving at me. On his left was a tall, stooping fellow with a horse face and a long mustache: I recognized him as Robert Sherwood, a movie critic who would later become a successful playwright. On Benchley's right was a very tiny woman, like a doll, with dark bangs and bright eyes that devoured the room despite her demure expression. Across the table, turning to look at where Benchley was waving, were a burly, well-fed bruiser and a thin, tall, Jewish-looking fellow with wire-rimmed glasses perched on the end of a long nose. I can't say they were looking at me with kindly expressions. It was more like a pride of lions sizing up a new addition to the pack, wondering if they could dominate him or would have to kill him.

"This is the fellow I was telling you about," Benchley said, waving me to a seat next to the bruiser. "James Cornelius O'Neal, pride of the *New York Journal*. You can call him Jimmy or you can call him Cornelius, just don't call him late to dinner."

Humor at the Algonquin Round Table was not always what it was reputed to be.

Benchley quickly reeled off the names of Sherwood and the others at the table. The bruiser was Heywood Broun, a reporter and left-wing activist. The Jew was George Kaufman, the playwright, who proved to wield the deadliest wit I have ever run across, with the possible exception of the lady sitting across the table from him: Dorothy Parker, of course.

This whole Round Table thing started because Parker, Benchley, and Sherwood were friends and fellow writers at *Vanity Fair*, located just around the corner. They had taken to lunching at the Algonquin. When Parker was fired by the editors in a fit of poor judgment, Benchley and Sherwood immediately resigned as well, a show of solidarity that left Parker eternally grateful to them. Perhaps in token of her appreciation, she never (as far as I know) slept with either of them. Since the same is not true of myself, I can say that the boys thereby avoided some very stressful evenings.

Benchley, Parker, and Sherwood all progressed in their careers after the *Vanity Fair* debacle, as all were very talented. Word spread in the literary and theatrical sets that the Algonquin was the place to lunch. A particular boost was given when Franklin Pierce Adams, the famous FPA, joined the set. Adams wrote an extremely popular column called the Conning Tower and he was considered one of the great wits of New York. If the Round Table was good enough for FPA, it was good enough for anyone in town who aspired to his crown. Over the years, with greater or lesser regularity, the table hosted Kaufman, Broun, Edna Ferber, the artist Neysa McMein, Marc Connelly, the Lunts, and many others. Most notable, perhaps, was the great eunuch Alexander Woollcott, who dominated most conversations, organized insufferable parlor games, and generally made everyone feel part of a special and exclusive club. These friends, if such they were, not only lunched together but also went on weekends, played poker, and went out on the town together. One of their number, of course, was Harold Ross, founder of *The New Yorker*, the magazine that published pretty much all of them. When I first appeared in the Rose Room in the summer of 1924, however, *The New Yorker* was still in the future.

"Risky of you, asking a beat reporter for the *Journal* to join us, Bob," said Broun. "Comes from hanging around whorehouses."

Obviously Bob, though married, had freely shared our experience at Polly Adler's with the table.

Parker immediately spoke up for her friend.

"Mr. Benchley does not hang around whorehouses," she sniffed. "If he was at Polly Adler's, I expect it was for the purpose of improving the ladies' minds."

"Exactly, Mrs. Parker," Benchley said as he clinked glasses with her.

"Now, Dorothy," said Kaufman, "you know you can lead a horticulture, but you can't make her think."

There was polite laughter, plainly feigned. This was my first exposure to the Algonquin practice of thinking of spontaneous witticisms in advance, repeating them at every opportunity, and honing them until you got them right. Benchley, for example, famously said "Let's slip out of these wet clothes and into a dry martini." In fact, he must have said it at least a hundred times, fifty of them in my presence. And sometimes Algonquin wits would borrow and improve upon the lines of another, often in his or her presence. Come to think of it, I believe it was Parker who originated the "horticulture" joke now fed back to her by Kaufman. Not an easy job, being a wit.

Runyon despised the Algonquin crowd and warned me to stay away from them. He pointed out that most of them were not only writers, but critics, and they used their positions to write good reviews of each other's work and talk each other up generally. While Damon Runyon didn't need such backscratching, I was still a hungry young reporter, eager for any advantage I could get. If talking myself into a seat at the Round Table could get me some good press, it was jake with me.

I came out swinging.

"I've heard about this joint. Runyon tells me you've got a good thing going."

Kaufman wrinkled his brow at me.

"I have no idea what that means."

Broun knew Runyon and was to some extent his rival.

"Damon Runyon thinks we give each other good reviews because we're friends and because we expect return favors," Broun said. "That old story."

"It's not true," Mrs. Parker murmured. "I was a drama critic and I thought George's plays were terrible." She mimed a kiss at George, who returned it. "Of course, I'm not a drama critic anymore. Now I have no favors to give. Well, none I'd give to this crowd, anyway."

A presence loomed in the entrance to the restaurant. I knew immediately that it was Alexander Woollcott, because Woollcott looked like no one else in the world. Not tall, he was broad and fat, with the face of a peculiarly unpleasant and unattractive baby. He affected the clothes of an old-fashioned dandy. On this occasion, he wore a large broad-brimmed hat and a three-piece suit with very wide lapels, and he carried in his hand an expensive-looking walking stick. He did not wear an opera cape, but only because it was lunchtime: I saw him many times in the evening with a scarlet-lined cloak flung dramatically over his shoulders, typical wear when he attended the theatre in his capacity as a critic. Woollcott, more than anyone, inspired the backscratching charges we had been talking about, for he praised the work of his friends and pets in embarrassingly florid prose while savaging others mercilessly.

Woollcott was gazing profoundly at our table from under his bushy and unkempt eyebrows. He raised his arms like Moses, an effect heightened by the cane he was holding.

"I give you: Pan!" he intoned in his high-pitched voice.

This was a poser. I didn't know whether to look for a cooking utensil or a flying boy in a green suit. It appeared he meant neither, however, for he gestured dramatically to a nondescript man standing just behind him whom I hadn't even noticed until Woollcott pointed him out.

I was startled, for at first I thought it was Leonard, the fighting piano player from Polly Adler's. He had the same big nose, the same eyes, the same tough look about him. Then I realized his face was a little fuller, his head a little balder, his eyes a little brighter than Leonard's. Benchley cinched it.

"You mean Harpo?" he called out.

Woollcott walked the few steps to our table. All eyes in the restaurant were on him, which was his intent. The man named Harpo looked mortified and kept his eyes on the carpet.

"You call him Harpo. Soon the world will call him Harpo. But I say he embodies the spirit of Pan, with all Pan's fierce comedic fire. Pan plays his pipes, Harpo plucks his harp, together they represent the inner animal in man, the primitive id unchecked by societal restraint. This is the man—nay, the genius—whom I bring to lunch today."

Woollcott turned to Harpo, looking for some appreciation of his prose. Instead, Harpo issued the longest, biggest yawn I have seen a human perform. It was as though his face were rubber and shifted shapes at will, perhaps at random. Seeing that Woollcott was staring at him, Harpo then made a grotesque grimace in which his eyes crossed, his tongue protruded, and his cheeks blew up like a frog's. I later learned that this particular face, called "the Gookie," was a standard part of his stage routine. Harpo then loped about the restaurant, eating off people's plates, sitting on the laps of attractive women, and sliding silverware into his pockets. Finally, with everyone except the stuffed shirts convulsed with laughter, Harpo sidled into a chair next to Kaufman and put his leg across George's lap.

"I usually charge good money to let people do that," Kaufman told him.

Harpo handed him one of the forks from his sleeve.

Woollcott chortled as he took his seat.

"Gentlemen and Mrs. Parker, I believe our little gatherings will now be considerably enlivened."

Suddenly Woollcott noticed my presence. He did not like it when newcomers joined the group, unless they were invited by him.

"And who is this individual?"

Benchley spoke up for me.

"This is Jimmy O'Neal, whom you can call Cornelius. He's a top crime reporter and a good fellow who got me out of a jam the other night, so you be a good boy, Alex."

Harpo, who still hadn't said a word, picked up on Benchley's tone and shook his finger at Woollcott as though to scold him. Woollcott was besotted with Harpo and laughed, though he wouldn't have taken such treatment from anyone else.

Kaufman gently lifted Harpo's leg off his lap.

"Would you take this back? I fear if I don't return it soon, I'll have to pay a late fee."

"Forgive my ignorance, Harpo," I said. "I take it you're on the stage?"

Woollcott spoke for him.

"Ignorance should not be forgiven, sir. Don't you read? My review of *I'll Say She Is* is on the streets today and it's one of my finest efforts."

"Pay no attention to Alex," said Benchley, "he's just being bitchy. This is Harpo Marx. He and his three brothers opened on Broadway last night in a revue called *I'll Say She Is*. You met his brother Leonard the other night. Onstage, they call him Chico. Darn funny show. Have you seen it, George?"

Kaufman shook his head.

"Well, you should," Benchley continued. "You'll want to write for these boys. They're the real thing. Never laughed so hard at the theatre in my life. No offense, George."

"Well, this is a pleasant lunch," George complained. "This fellow mauls me with his leg, you say he's funnier than my plays, and Dorothy says my plays stink. Why do I come here?"

"Because the watercress salad is very nice," said Parker, with a smile to the waiter who had finally arrived at the table.

The staff in the Rose Room were used to the Round Table crowd and knew not to interrupt the witticisms with actual food very often. A person could get very hungry at the Algonquin Round Table.

After we ordered, Broun asked Harpo if he actually talked.

"I do," said Harpo in a disappointingly normal voice, "but I'm not as funny at talking as my brothers. We figured out that the act works better when I don't say anything."

Over the next few years, I became friends with Harpo. He was one of the sweetest men I ever knew, but I've always been a little sorry that I heard him speak. Silent, he made a magic that I've never seen any other performer achieve, maybe barring Chaplin. Knowing what his voice sounded like spoiled the trick a little.

The lunch wore on and eventually ended, leaving me torn. On the one hand, I couldn't stand Woollcott, Kaufman and Broun annoyed me, and the constant effort to be witty and sophisticated grew thin quickly. Balanced against this, Benchley was a great companion, Harpo was hilarious, and the whole experience felt good for my career.

I decided to come back as long and as often as they'd let me. I met others of the group: FPA, Harold Ross, Edna Ferber. Ross was a sweaty hustler who looked like a Missouri farmer, but he was working day and night to create a magazine that would be the epitome of New York sophistication. I sat in on the frequent poker games hosted by FPA in a suite upstairs, which he referred to as the Thanatopsis Literary and Inside Straight Club. I rarely bet large sums since my funds and my skills were both limited. I drank with Benchley, went to Kaufman's shows, and stayed as far away from Woollcott as I could. I did not, in my first few months of hanging on with the Algonquin crowd, get much of a bead on Dorothy Parker. She spoke rarely, though when she did, she was the funniest and most acerbic of the group. I learned from Benchley, her closest friend, that there was indeed a Mister Parker.

"Dottie married him when she was quite young," he said one night over drinks at a speakeasy. "She claims she did it to lose her Jewish name, but that's just Dottie cracking wise. He's got his own life and she's got hers. I guess they make it work."

I watched Bob take another drink.

"You always seem a little sad when you talk about Mrs. Parker," I said. "Do you have history with her?" "We have friendship, Cornelius. That's better than history. She's very talented and good-hearted, and this world is hard on her. I don't like to see her hurt, but I'm afraid she's hurt all the time. Hell, what am I talking about?" Benchley raised his hand for the bartender and pointed to both our glasses. "Broken hearts are boring, Cornelius, because they're too common. It takes genius to make broken hearts interesting. Since genius is a rare commodity around this town, whatever Woollcott likes to say, we need to focus on fun, laughs and triviality."

So we drank to that. But Bob wasn't quite finished with the subject of his friend, Mrs. Parker.

"You don't know this, but she's asked about you, Cornelius. I see her look at you, like she looked before at Charlie MacArthur and who knows who else. You're a big boy and she's a big girl, but remember. She's easily broken, like glass. If the occasion arises, just be careful of her."

I wondered if he meant to take care of her or to take care of myself. I didn't ask.

I went to see Frankie Yale again late in 1924, because of a rumor that was swirling around the streets. It was said that Frankie had just murdered Al Capone's Irish rival Dean O'Banion in Chicago. Yale gave me the bum's rush the first time I visited the Harvard Inn, but I was paid to try.

I'd heard about Frankie Yale for years from Runyon, from my cousins the Brooklyn coppers, and from wise guys on the street. Frankie was a big, expansive, friendly guy who took care of the poor, stayed loyal to his friends, and made sure his enemies spent little time breathing. His headquarters at the Harvard Inn was tucked right underneath the Wonder Wheel, a big Ferris wheel on the boardwalk at Coney Island. You can still ride that attraction today, if you are so inclined. Ferris wheels, invented by an engineer named George Ferris, achieved massive popularity after they were introduced at the 1893 Chicago World's Fair. The Wonder Wheel, built in 1920, was 150 feet tall and was the biggest attraction at Coney Island, at least until the Cyclone roller coaster opened next to it in 1927. You can still ride the Cyclone, too.

The subways still had a new feel to them when I went to see Frankie Yale. You never quite believed that for five cents, you could ride almost anywhere in the boroughs and get there quickly and in one piece. Of course, a lot of workers died to construct such a marvel and riders still not infrequently faced delays or accidents along the way, but the subway was definitely a wonder of the modern world.

I got out at the Coney Island station and walked a few blocks to the Harvard Inn. Nathan's was off to my right, selling Coney dogs to the eager masses. I turned to my left and strode down Surf Avenue toward the Wonder Wheel, which loomed over its surroundings with all its immensity and engineering mastery. It was simply a very large mechanical wheel that rolled round and round without going anywhere, providing thrills and views to parties of four to six per car, depending on hip width and willingness to fraternize. All the rides were closed for the season, of course, as it was late November and a cold wind was blowing in from the Atlantic. I wondered why Frankie Yale chose Coney Island of all places as the location for his headquarters, from which he waged an implacable war with the Irish for control of the Red Hook docks, directly across the borough.

I knew the background of the O'Banion hit. Dean O'Banion, mistakenly called Dion by the newspapers, led the Irish mob in Chicago, which was becoming a very hot town indeed. The leading Italian gangster was Johnny Torrio, who moved to Chicago from Brooklyn and was looking to take over the city. His chief lieutenant was another Brooklyn boy, one Alphonse Capone, who had worked for Frankie Yale as a waiter at the Harvard Inn as a young man. Indeed, it was at the Harvard that young Capone got in the fight that gave him one of his nicknames, Scarface.

Word was that Yale and Capone remained close, with Capone frequently returning to Brooklyn to visit his old haunts. He must have been proud to show off to the home folks, for Al was making quite a name for himself in Chicago. While his boss Torrio liked to remain in the background, Capone was flamboyant, loud, and intensely violent. It was clear that the Italians were going to dominate the whole city, politics and all, leaving O'Banion the scraps, at best. Border clashes between the mobs became more frequent and more violent. Then, one evening, three men walked into O'Banion's flower shop and shot him dead as he was clipping violets. Yes, Dean was clipped while clipping. Word I got was that the killers were led by Frankie Yale, doing a favor for his old friend Al.

Frankie was indeed in Chicago when the shooting occurred, supposedly to attend the funeral of one of Al's men. I paused at the door to the inn and took a quick drink from my flask to give me a little courage. Frankie had been none too welcoming the first time. I did not expect his hospitality to improve when I asked him if he had just murdered Dean O'Banion.

I walked into the tavern, which had only a few customers on this unpleasant night. It didn't make me feel any better to see that one of them was the skinny, blond, ice-eyed little bastard Willie Altieri, whom I had met the first time I came to the Harvard Inn. Wise guys talked about Frankie Yale all the time, but I heard very little about Willie Altieri other than that he was Yale's chief enforcer and he was bad news. People seemed to clam up at the mention of Willie's name, as though it were bad luck to talk about him. I suspected Willie had been bad luck for a lot of people.

Yale was not present. Rather than ask for him, I took a seat at a little round table in the corner and ordered an apple juice, meaning a shot of whiskey. I purposely selected a seat where Altieri would have his back to me, though I doubted he would remember me. He was sharing his table with a big, broad, thick-necked, muscular-looking fellow dressed like a longshoreman. I was to learn that he had indeed been a longshoreman, he was a union official, and despite his young age he was also a murderer, extortionist, smuggler, and ex-convict. His name, I later learned, was Albert Anastasia.

When the waitress brought my "apple juice," which must have been from Arnold Rothstein's crew as it was quite good, I asked her if Frankie was around. She said she didn't know any Frankie, but then she walked through the door behind the bar to the office in back. She caught Anastasia's eye as she did so. He nodded and Altieri turned to look at me. He recognized me, for he squinted in an unfriendly way and walked over to my table. He sat next to me, uncomfortably close. An especially strong gust of wind rattled the bar.

Altieri peered intently at me and pursed his lips, looking like some sort of malignant fish.

"You're the reporter."

I tried to be casual.

"I'm a reporter, Willie. New York is full of reporters. I expect they've been pestering your boss lately, too."

"I don't know what you're talking about, Mr. Reporter," Willie hissed. "You're talking foolish. That's a dangerous habit in Brooklyn."

"Who's that fellow you're sitting with? He looks like a longshoreman. Frankie says he's just a saloonkeeper with no ties to the docks, so why are you sitting in Frankie's place talking to a longshoreman with a face like a Halloween mask?"

The gangster smiled thinly, showing no teeth.

"That's Albert. I could introduce you. But be careful what you wish for, Mr. Reporter."

Frankie Yale stepped out from the office, the waitress following behind him. When he walked into the main room, he flashed a grin, donning his charisma like an overcoat. He was elegantly dressed, as if he were going somewhere with swells. My eye was taken by a broad black belt he wore, straining against his ample middle. It was studded with diamonds, reflective of Frankie's wealth and status. He nodded warmly to acquaintances in the room, including Albert, as he made his way to our table.

"Mr. O'Neal, right?" he said to me. "I think I owe you an apology."

This was unexpected.

"Why's that?" I asked.

Frankie pumped my hand and landed his substantial weight on the chair across from me.

"I recall when you came here before and I think I was rude to you. Must have been in a bad mood." Yale turned to his enforcer. "You should read this guy. Really, he's good. I like when you write about what goes on at the criminal courts. People are crazy, huh? You like your whiskey?"

I must say, if Frankie wanted to take me aback with his charm, it was working.

"Sure. It's good stuff."

Frankie waved to the waitress to fill my glass.

"So, can I call you Jimmy? You call me Frankie."

I nodded.

"Let me tell you, Jimmy, I'm glad you came in tonight. All this time I felt bad, enjoying your stories in the paper and remembering that I was a bastard to you when you just came to pay your respects. Jimmy, you're welcome any time at the Harvard Inn."

The girl brought a glass for Yale and poured drinks for all three of us, and Yale drank my health. Willie wasn't looking happy about all the *bonhomie*.

"This guy says he wants to meet Albert," he told Yale.

Frankie's grin turned into a frown.

"You don't want to meet Albert, Jimmy. Nobody really wants to meet Albert." Frankie leaned toward me and whispered. "Truth is, Albert is not a very pleasant guy. Works hard on the docks over at Red Hook. Makes him grouchy, I guess."

Against my will, I glanced over at Albert. He was staring darkly into his whiskey glass, paying us no attention. His huge, hairy hands were folded around the glass as though to strangle it. I could believe that he was not a pleasant guy.

"Never mind about him," I said. "Actually, Frankie, I came here to ask you about your trip to Chicago."

Yale nodded affably, without a hint of defensiveness.

"It's the damnedest town, Jimmy, just crazy. It's sad how violent it is there. I went for the funeral of an old friend and then while I'm there, that O'Banion killing happens. It's all so unnecessary, you know? It's very sad. O'Banion had a great funeral, though, I'll say that for him. It was in all the papers. Parades and everything. Those Irish know how to go out. You Irish, Jimmy?"

I took a deep breath.

"You know, Frankie, I gotta say, not everybody thinks it's coincidence that you were in Chicago when O'Banion got rubbed out. There's word on the street that you did it as a favor for Al Capone."

Altieri's pale face reddened, the scarlet flush popping out on his cheeks like clown make-up.

"You come into this place and you talk like that?"

He made to rise, but Yale waved him back peacefully.

"It's all right, Willie, it's okay. Jimmy's a reporter. He hears things, he wants to check them out, I understand. Listen to me, Jimmy. Al used to work here when he was a kid. Far as I remember him, he was a good guy. I liked him. I still like him. I don't know his business and I sure don't like him well enough to do favors like you're talking about. I was in Chicago, I saw Al, sure. We're friends. He gave some parties, we went out, we had a good time, and we went to an old friend's funeral. That was it. This other business, this O'Banion, this killing that goes on over there—that, I had nothing to do with. I'm a saloonkeeper. Violence frightens me."

I looked at Altieri for a smile, but there was none. Frankie leaned toward me over the table.

"Now, Jimmy, like I said, you are welcome here any time. I was rude to you before and I've apologized. You asked me something that some people might consider rude and I answered you. I'd say we're even now. I would appreciate it if you would not ask me questions like that again."

I said nothing, drained my glass, and rose to go.

"This garbage you heard on the street," Yale said. "You going to write about it?"

"Nope," I said. "It was just rumor. Tomorrow I've got a story on a dame who poisoned her ever-loving's mashed potatoes for the insurance money. Check it out."

"I will."

I took one last look around the room as I left. Frankie was waving me a regal goodbye, Anastasia was still gazing brutishly at his whiskey, and Altieri was looking at me as though measuring me for a coffin. They were like jungle animals. Frankie the king of the lions, Albert the killer gorilla, and Willie the viper. The hell with Runyon. One of these days, I was going to get something big on these guys and write about it.

8

Literary Ladies

Cornelius

Don't think me boastful, but I believe that both Dorothy Parker and I felt it was inevitable that at some point we would become lovers. It's not that I particularly craved Dorothy or did anything intentional to bring about our relationship. Dorothy was known for taking lovers with whom she would invariably break up quickly, with a maximum amount of pain and unhappiness on both sides. It just seemed natural that one of those lovers should be me. As it happened, the event that finally brought this about involved me with not just one, but two of the best-known literary ladies of the century.

There was a fellow back then named Herbert Bayard Swope. Hardly anybody today would recognize his name, but he was well-known in the twenties. Born rich, indeed very rich, he nevertheless chose to work for a living and, being talented as well as rich, he succeeded at the things to which he turned his hand. These included reporting, writing for magazines, publishing, and later in life, government service. Being talented, amiable, and wealthy, Swope came to know virtually everyone worth knowing on the eastern seaboard and he mixed in highly various circles. One of these was the Algonquin Round Table, which Swope occasionally visited, but never made into a habit.

I think it was the summer of 1925. I know it was summer, for the ever-dapper Swope was wearing a straw boater and well-tailored seersucker suit. He made me think of the boulevards of Paris, although when I had made my only visit to that point, it was under invasion by the Germans and straw boaters were not in evidence. I was at the table with Parker, Benchley, Woollcott, Harpo, Edna Ferber, and probably one or two others of the regulars. On Swope's arm was a lovely young girl whom I pegged at about nineteen, which turned out to be quite a good guess as Swope introduced her as Anne Morrow and said she had just finished her freshman year at Smith College.

"Anne's parents are Dwight and Betty, of course. Anne came all the way into the city from Jersey to meet you, Dorothy."

Parker said nothing, she merely looked depressed and took a generous slug of her lunchtime martini which, given Prohibition, was disguised in a ceramic bottle. Anne was not to be daunted.

"I'm sorry. I'm sure I sound foolish, but I so admire your work, Mrs. Parker. Oh," she added hastily to the table in general, "and the work of all the rest of you, too."

"Come over and sit next to your heroine, Anne," said Swope, a touch too heartily.

He plumped a chair next to Dorothy and Anne sat down on it, tentatively, very aware that her idol was ignoring her. Swope sat next to Woollcott, who was frowning at Parker. Rude as Alex could be, he was generally courteous to the young, especially to attractive young ladies whom he might convince to admire him.

"How are you enjoying Smith, Miss Morrow?" Edna Ferber asked gamely.

Parker gave a little snort.

"Now, Edna, isn't it more relevant to ask how the Yale boys are enjoying Smith? That's what you girls up there at Smith are for, isn't it, dear? Providing appropriate mates for all those Bulldogs? Bow wow wow and all that?"

Benchley ostentatiously slid the martini bottle away from Dorothy, but she just slid it back.

"Well, Mrs. Parker, I think some of the girls do believe something like that," Anne said diplomatically. "But there are also serious young women who want to make their own marks in the world. Many of us who feel that way take inspiration from your career, your writing. I especially like—"

"Oh, Christ, don't. I may vomit."

"Dottie," said Woollcott.

"What's the matter, Alex?" Parker said innocently. "I'm just making conversation. Tell me, Miss Morrow, did you go to the Yale Prom?"

Anne was working hard to keep her composure. Swope looked sick.

"No, Mrs. Parker. Freshmen aren't allowed."

"Too bad," said Dorothy, sucking at her martini bottle. "I was once in New Haven the night of the Yale Prom and I saw all the Smith girls with their dates. I remember thinking, 'If all of these sweet young things were laid end to end, I wouldn't be at all surprised.'" Dorothy laughed and added to Woollcott, "That was a good one, Alex. Write it down."

"I wrote it down the first two times I heard you say it, Dottie," Woollcott snarled. "Honestly, I don't know what's gotten in to you, besides about a quart of bathtub gin."

"Why, Alex, you know that about half the men in the theatre district have gotten into me at one time or another," Parker cooed.

She was totally out of hand and the party was within a heartbeat of breaking up in disgust, so I decided to seize the moment.

"That does it," I said.

I stood and marched around to stand behind Parker's chair. I signaled to Harpo, who instantly caught my drift and came to my side. I wrapped my arms around Parker's tiny frame and hauled her bodily out of her chair. Harpo grabbed her legs. Dorothy squalled like an angry sailor, but we carried on.

"I'm sure she will apologize when she's feeling herself," I said to Anne.

Harpo and I marched out of the restaurant with Dorothy held aloft, shouting bitter obscenities at us. Frank Case waved discreetly as we passed the front desk. "Room 518," he said, without prompting, and he tossed me a key. Dorothy continued cursing, but she wasn't fighting very hard and seemed to be going along with the prank. The Algonquin was as woefully under-elevatored in 1925 as today, so we waited a considerable time for one of the two slow, tiny cars to arrive. A distinguished-looking elderly couple came to wait for the elevator with us.

Parker stopped cursing long enough to turn to the woman.

"Excuse me, these gentlemen are white slavers," she said. "If you let them take me, they will come for you next."

The woman looked at Harpo with some alarm, whereupon Harpo flashed her a Gookie. The elevator arrived and the five of us crowded in, Mrs. Parker still up in the air and cursing creatively. If memory serves, Harpo removed her shoes and was playing with her feet as we reached the fifth floor. We deposited Parker on the bed in room 518. I told her to stay there until she could be civil and Harpo and I returned downstairs.

On the way back to the Rose Room, I was struck by a call of nature. Then, as now, the restrooms in the public area of the Algonquin were located downstairs, below the lobby. I let Harpo head back to the table, his job well done, and I started down the narrow staircase to the bathrooms. Suddenly, coming upward and blocking my path was Anne Morrow.

She'd plainly been crying and was trying to put herself back together. I couldn't blame the girl. Simply for accepting the invitation of a family friend to meet her idol, she'd been insulted and humiliated, then was in the center of a public spectacle of a sort which her whole sheltered upbringing would teach her was simply not done. I felt sorry for her. Also, truth be told, she looked darned cute holding back her tears.

"Miss Morrow," I said, drawing to a sudden stop. "This whole crowd owes you an apology."

"No, no. I'm sure it was my fault."

"That's nonsense, Miss Morrow. When you're young, somehow it seems like everything is your fault, but it's not true. Dorothy was drinking and she acted like a bitch. None of that was your doing at all."

She flinched a little when I said "bitch," which was my intent. I wanted her to understand that I was a man of the world.

"We haven't even been introduced," I said. "I'm Jimmy O'Neal. I write for the *Journal*."

We shook hands, very seriously.

"I don't customarily carry women bodily out of restaurants. Only when the occasion demands."

Anne smiled delightfully. She leaned forward.

"I was glad you did," she said in a conspiratorial whisper. "She really was being horrid, wasn't she?"

"Miss Morrow, you said a mouthful."

We smiled at each other for a moment.

"Listen," I offered, "you need to have a better trip into the city than this. How about I take you to dinner? Maybe walk you around and show you some of my old beat, some of the seamier sides of the city. What do you say?"

She seemed to think for a moment, then she pulled a piece of paper from her purse and scribbled a number on it.

"I'm afraid I live with my parents. In Englewood, New Jersey. Hopelessly provincial, I know. But I'd love to have dinner with you. Thank you, Mr. O'Neal."

She was past me and up the stairs before I could tell her to call me Jimmy. I went down to the bathroom and took care of business, quite pleased with myself.

The day wasn't over. I returned to the table. In deference to Miss Morrow, there was no discussion of Mrs. Parker's exit, but Benchley and Woollcott both nodded their silent thanks to me. At the end of lunch, I went back upstairs, still jingling the key to room 518 in my coat pocket. I knocked, then opened the door.

Parker flew off the bed in a rage and tried to claw my eyes. I held her off, pulling her hands away from my face while also working hard to get the door closed behind me. I pushed her back on the bed.

"What's the matter with you?" I demanded. "You deserved everything you got. You humiliated that poor girl for no reason when all she wanted was to tell you how much she admired you. I don't know who the hell you think you are, but you can't behave like that."

Parker put her hands over her ears and screamed. Screamed loud and long, like a madwoman. A screw down deep was definitely loose. Then, suddenly cool as could be, she looked me in the eye.

"I suppose you're going to fuck me now," she said.

"What?"

"You heard me. This is when men always fuck me. So come here and fuck me, Jimmy O'Neal."

She stood up. She pushed her dress down over her shoulders and dropped it to the floor. Her slip followed. She kicked off her shoes, rolled off her stockings, slipped off her bra, and pushed down her panties. There before me stood the Complete Works of Dorothy Parker.

We went to bed and made love. If you want to call it that.

My affair with Dorothy was an on-and-off thing that lasted several months. I'm told that was a little above par for her. I'm being hard on Dorothy, I know, because she was so often troubled and mean. There was another side, as there always is with people.

That first day, when we finished the lovemaking, Dorothy clung to me and sobbed.

"I was just a shit to that girl," she moaned, over and over.

I could hardly disagree, but I tried to comfort her.

"You were drinking, probably rotgut stuff. Where do you get your liquor, anyway?"

She wiped her eyes.

"Where anyone gets it. Here and there."

"No good. Only liquor worth drinking in this town is Arnold Rothstein's. I know him. I'll fix you up."

"How do you know Rothstein?"

"I'm a crime reporter, Dorothy. I know some criminals. Part of the job."

She smirked.

"Well, you're one of the first men to go to bed with me and then offer me something useful, I'll say that."

"Why do you act so hard, Dorothy? Why all the time with the wisecracks?"

"Oh, God, if we're going to have that conversation, I need another drink." She looked around, but her ceramic bottle hadn't followed her to the room. "Damn. I'll get us something."

She started pulling on her clothes. I lay back and watched her, glad of the respite and the comfortable bed. It occurred to me to wonder who was going to pay for the room. Money was tight for me then.

When she was dressed, Dorothy looked me up and down.

"On second thought," she said, "I'm scramming. I'm going to go write something and if you're lucky, I won't put you in it."

She then leaned over and kissed me, passionately, on the mouth.

"I wisecrack to get through the day, Jimmy. It's a man's world in New York and it's especially hard on a smart dame. I decided a long time ago: they can fire me, they can fuck me, they can hurt me. But nobody's going to push me around."

She gave me one more kiss and walked to the door.

"Thanks for the action, Jimmy. If it's okay with you, we'll do it again. I'd warn you not to fall for me, but I don't think you need it."

And she walked out.

I wondered if she was right, if I needed that warning or not. I decided I didn't need the warning, as I wasn't going to fall for her. Dorothy was one of those people who had set herself on the road to hell and wasn't going to do herself any favors by turning around. She paid for the hotel room, I'll say that for her.

The months that I saw Dorothy Parker were by turns exciting, warm, stimulating, and intensely irritating. Probably the dominant feeling was exhaustion. I worked my usual beat and produced content for the paper while being witty at Algonquin lunches, making love to Parker, and escorting her to dinners, shows, and speakeasies. There were weekends at Woollcott's or at the country place of one of the wealthier members of the crowd. And there was drinking, lots and lots of it. As we've already seen, Dorothy's moods were variable to say the least, but she was always a challenging companion. Between trying to keep up with her wisecracks and regularly nursing her through drunken stupors and hangovers, I completely understood why Mr. Parker was nowhere in evidence.

Somehow, in the midst of all of that, I found time for Anne Morrow. One day, I called the number she had scribbled for me and a young woman's voice answered, sounding exactly like Anne. When I called her by that name, she immediately let out a sort of girlish whinny and informed me that I was not speaking to Anne, but to her much more attractive sister. When Anne came on the line, I introduced myself and apologized for the mistake.

"Oh, that happens all the time," Anne said. "Serves her right for always being the one to pick up the telephone. She practically takes her meals by the instrument hoping it will ring for her."

"That's a lie," a female voice exclaimed, followed by loud shushing from Anne. "Now then, Mr. O'Neal, better state your business quickly before my sister grows any more obnoxious."

"I hope you recall our discussion on the Algonquin stairway, Miss Morrow. I promised you a dinner in the city to make up for that unfortunate lunch."

Anne seemed far more confident back on her home ground.

"I do recall that discussion, Mr. O'Neal, but I would describe it as more of an offer than a promise. I didn't exactly accept."

"You gave me your number. I don't think you expected me to call to ask your father for stock tips."

Her father, Dwight Morrow, was a partner in the House of Morgan and thus a genuine Wall Street bigwig. He was also an old college pal of the president, Calvin Coolidge, leading to frequent speculation that Morrow would be put up for a major political job.

"Well, perhaps you should ask my father for stock tips. He'd give you good ones." Her voice grew more serious. "It's very tiresome, I know, but my parents will want to meet you before I go out to the city with you. If that makes you withdraw the offer, I fully understand."

This took me aback, for a second. I was twenty-six and it had been a long time since a girl's parents had figured into my dating equations in any way. On the other hand, Dwight Morrow sounded like a good fellow to know.

"I completely understand, Miss Morrow," I said, musing on the contrast with my relationship with Dorothy, whom I had left naked and soused an hour before. "Um, how do we go about this?"

"Oh, that's easy," she said, now fully in control. "My parents are having a few people to dinner tomorrow night here in Englewood. It's just very close friends: Uncle Jack, Uncle Tom, Aunt Florence, and I think that's all. We can tell the cook there will be one more and it will be all set. If you're free, of course."

"I'm free," I said hastily. "What time?"

We agreed that I would arrive at 7:30 the next evening. She gave me instructions for the train and said their driver would pick me up at the station.

I should think so. If I were to meet Uncle Jack, also known as J.P. Morgan, I'd better arrive in some style.

9

Lords of the Cosmos

Cornelius

How do you dress for dinner with the Lords of the Cosmos?

The House of Morgan was a shadowy presence for those outside the business world, but its discretion only heightened its legend in the minds of ordinary folks like me. The late J. Pierpont Morgan had been the master, in some respects the creator, of Wall Street and all it stood for. He was the very model of a banking tycoon, striding gruffly down the streets of the financial district with a top hat on his head, a cane in his hand to knock down impertinent reporters, an imperious scowl on his face, and an immense nose protruding from his head like the figurehead of a frigate. Morgan had provided the money that fueled the age of the robber barons. In return, he'd demanded a seat on their boards and a say in their futures. Indeed, since corporations ran on the money Morgan provided, Morgan in many cases had *determined* their futures. He'd decided where railroads would run, what canals would be built, what banks would fail. In 1907, when the stock market plunged and looked to crash beyond repair, it had been Morgan who pulled together the nation's financiers and made the deal that saved the economy. Since he despised all journalists and strove his whole life to avoid publicity, he'd become exceptionally famous, the universally known symbol of Wall Street finance.

All that said, Pierpont died in 1913 and so missed the bankruptcy of Europe that resulted from the Great War. In the great Morgan's lifetime, American bankers were not in the same league as the financial houses of the old world. Immense as Morgan's influence was in the burgeoning arena of American commerce, and familiar as he was with Europe, the nations of the world still looked to the Bank of England, the Rothschilds, and similar venerable houses to finance their wars and back their currencies. Then four years of very expensive stalemate on the plains of France bled not only Europe's young men, but the treasure in its banks. When Armistice came, one nation was perfectly positioned to dominate the world, with its mostly unspent military might, its vibrant and expanding corporations, and the money of Wall Street. That's why it became the American Century.

There was still a J.P. Morgan at the helm of the great house in the twenties, but it was J.P. Junior, known as Jack to his intimates, of whom he had hardly any. Fairly or not, he suffered from the inevitable comparisons with his father. Regardless, the House of Morgan now played on the world stage, thanks to the effects of what we then still called the Great War. It was led not only by Morgan himself but by a band of strong partners who were international figures: Tom Lamont, Dwight Morrow, and others. No longer content with funding the Rockefellers and Fords, these bankers traveled the world and met with heads of state, floated their bonds, paid for their programs. These were the titans with whom I would be sharing dinner table conversation. I hoped they would like the Fallon and the Firebug gags, but it didn't seem likely.

Dressed in my best suit, which felt uncomfortably cheap and flashy for my destination, I took a train to Jersey and was met by a chauffeur who walked me to a shiny limousine for transport to the Morrow estate. It was a grand place. There was a great stone wall with massive gates that opened onto spacious grounds, like those of an especially well-tended English country house. The Morgan partners, in fact, had a fondness for all things English, especially the country houses. We pulled to the front door and I was met by Anne herself, flanked by two other young women whom I took to be her sisters. They were a bouncy, giggling threesome who put me in mind of the "Three Little Maids from School" in *The Mikado*. All were wholesome and pretty, but for my money, Anne would have been given the lead part of Yum-Yum hands down. Yum-Yum would have been a good name for her.

"Hello, Mr. O'Neal," said Anne as I stepped out of the car.

I had brought her flowers and handed them over to her. She simpered prettily at them, though I sensed her sisters thought them scruffy.

"These are my sisters," she added. "You can ignore them."

"Ignore that, Mr. O'Neal," said the youngest, offering her hand to me. "I'm Constance. I'm the pretty one."

Anne gave her a push.

"I'm Elizabeth. I'm the smart one," said the third, shaking my hand. "Of course, there's precious little competition for the slot."

The others stuck out their tongues at her. It put me in mind of a moneyed version of Riley's sisters, minus Bessie.

"Ladies, I stand helpless," I said, raising my hands in feigned surrender. "Were I Shakespeare, I could write a sonnet, but I am left bereft in the face of such loveliness."

It fell flat. There was an awkward pause and Anne led me into the house. I thought it was a good line, actually.

I call it a house, but its size and magnificence made it unlike any house in my limited experience to that point. The massive foyer which we entered was teeming with well-dressed and demure folks who, it turned out, were servants. Anne later told me she didn't know just how many servants there were in the Morrow household, but the number was somewhere in the twenties. Even so, the Englewood estate was basically a weekend place for Anne's parents, who spent the workweek at a luxurious apartment in the city.

The Morrow sisters led me through the lines of servants, who bowed their heads at us in a friendly way. A fellow who looked like a butler opened two large doors.

"Mr. O'Neal," he intoned, the way they do in English plays.

I was a long way from Lindy's. Inside the elegant library we now entered, a middle-aged woman who looked a lot like Anne was trying gamely to fix the cravat of a short, owlish-looking fellow in formal evening dress. I assumed these were the mistress and master of the house, which proved to be the case.

"Now, Dwight, stand still," the lady admonished.

Dwight was reading a sheaf of papers in his hand and obviously lacked interest in the state of his neckwear.

"I swear," his wife said, "you'd come to dinner in your pajamas if I didn't watch you like a hawk."

She gave her husband's cravat a final pat and turned to me with a charming smile of welcome.

"Mr. O'Neal," she said, extending her hand. "We're so delighted you were able to come."

Betty Morrow was a muckety-muck at Smith College, her alma mater and the school of choice for all her daughters, and she simply dripped social skills. Understand, I do not say that disparagingly: quite the opposite. She immediately made me feel welcome and appreciated in very foreign surroundings and no doubt would do so no matter who walked into her library. There really is such a thing as breeding and, while it doesn't make people smart or talented or honest in and of itself, it does give them an ease in social situations that people like Riley and me couldn't learn, copy, or buy.

Mr. Morrow was still distracted.

"Hello," he said without looking at me.

He strode out of the room with his eyes glued to his papers.

"Don't mind Papa," said Anne. "He's like that with everyone."

"Usually worse," said Constance.

"Our father is famous as Wall Street's absent-minded professor," said Elizabeth. "At work, they assign a man to stand in the restroom and make sure he adjusts his trousers properly."

"He's forgotten to remove his clothes before getting in the bath," Constance rejoined.

"You girls need to stop," said Mrs. Morrow firmly. "Mr. O'Neal is getting a terrible impression."

"Not in the least, ma'am," I responded. "I am very aware of Mr. Morrow's reputation in the financial district. If he is absent-minded, I'm sure he's thinking of far more important things than I can even imagine."

Betty Morrow shook a finger at me.

"You are a smooth talker, Mr. O'Neal. We will have to keep an eye on you."

Then drinks were distributed and the conversation kept flowing until the butler fellow, who I guess actually was the butler, announced

"Mr. and Mrs. Lamont." In walked the most handsome, connected, and smooth couple of the nineteen-twenties. I was indeed mixing in the highest of society.

Tom Lamont was the dominant partner at J.P. Morgan and the leading banker on Earth, despite his feudal obligations to Jack Morgan. He had been Woodrow Wilson's principal economic advisor during the negotiation of the Treaty of Versailles. He had the power to say yea or nay to the financial needs of the great rulers of the world. He thrived in the diplomatic age of banking, when Wall Street held the purse strings that supported every treaty, every bond issue, every war that took place anywhere on the globe. He was lean, handsome, immaculately dressed, and walked with such confidence that you suspected he invented walking. If Morrow was an absent-minded professor, Lamont was the Prince of Wall Street. He grinned and wrapped Betty Morrow in an embrace, while his wife Florence smiled warmly.

"Betty Morrow, you look lovelier every time I see you," Lamont said.

"What on earth are you wearing on your feet?" Betty responded.

"There, you see, Tom?" said his wife. "I told you."

Tom looked down at the offending footwear.

"Spats!" he said. "All the rage, latest thing. The Emperor of Japan loved them."

"The Emperor of Japan wanted you to loan him money," Mrs. Lamont chided. "No one here wants your money and no one will compliment those wretched things."

"I'd love your money, Mr. Lamont," I volunteered, "and I love your spats."

Actually, they looked a great deal like a pair I had seen on Hump McManus. Spats were big on Broadway that year.

A question appeared in Lamont's eyes for a moment as I spoke, but Betty introduced me and he reverted to charm. He shook my hand, greeted the Morrow sisters, and inquired after his host. Betty responded that she was sure he was in his office, as he was buried in a project for the United States Aviation Board, which he chaired. Nothing would do but that Lamont raced from the room and pulled Morrow by the arm back into the library, to join the party.

As it turned out, Dwight Morrow was also quite a charming man once you had his attention. He and Lamont accepted cocktails from a waiter and began telling stories of their trips around the world, which their wives could supplement as they often accompanied the men. We heard lively tales of the Versailles conference, Latin American dictators, and Asian potentates. Not wishing to be left out, I mentioned that I had met Pancho Villa. I quickly regretted it, as Morrow immediately subjected me to close questioning which gave me a difficult time. It turns out that Morrow was quite an enthusiast about Mexico, being responsible for the Mexican loans floated by his firm, but I wasn't anxious to have the details of my Villa experience become the subject of cocktail party conversation. Somehow the fact that I shared a cave with Villa and a sadistic German maniac did not seem calculated to amuse the dinner party.

To change the subject, I asked if Mr. Morgan himself were coming and said I was very honored to have the chance to meet him. The faces in the room fell.

"Is Mr. Morgan coming?" Dwight asked his wife.

"Yes, dear," she responded.

"Poor Jack," said Lamont. "He's still at sixes and sevens since Jessie died. It's very sad."

Jessie was Morgan's wife, who had recently passed away. Lamont didn't really look sad. He looked more like he was an actor, playing sad. He was good at it, though. Mrs. Lamont also frowned for poor Mr. Morgan.

"It truly is so very sad," she said, accepting a glass of champagne.

As if on cue, the butler stepped in and announced, "Mr. Morgan."

I stepped back and tried to melt into the wallpaper as the Morgan partners and their wives hurried to greet their master. I knew what Morgan looked like, of course, as he was one of the most famous men in New York. I knew him to be tall, stout, handsome in an arrogant and self-assured way. Hardly surprising in a man who since birth had been one of the wealthiest and most important human beings on the planet, a man surrounded by servants and sycophants, a man who never left his protective cocoon of privileged luxury.

I was shocked, then, by the man who entered. His elegant suit hung loosely on his frame, as though he had lost his late wife's weight from his own body. The balding brow that in photographs looked Roman and noble was beaded with sweat. His mustache and receding hair were changing from gray to white. He raised the corners of his lips in an attempt at a smile when he entered the room, but the effect was ghastly. J.P. Morgan, Jr. was a beaten man. He obviously was taking the loss of his wife very hard, which I later learned was not surprising. His wife was said to be a lively, down-to-earth woman who was Morgan's one real tie to normal human beings. Without her, he faced a lonely life indeed.

Morgan handed Betty Morrow a bottle of a very expensive-looking Bordeaux.

"I brought wine," he mumbled, somewhat unnecessarily.

"Oh, Mr. Morgan, how thoughtful of you," Betty gushed. "Come in. Come in and let's get you a cocktail. You remember the girls."

I am not joking, each of the Morrow sisters actually curtsied for the grieving banker, bringing to his face a smile that looked much more genuine than his first attempt. Then they ran to him and each gave him a demure hug, which would have done me a world of good, I assure you.

"And this is Mr. O'Neal," said Mrs. Morrow, gesturing to me. "He is a journalist."

Morgan blanched and froze in place, causing Betty to wince as she realized her *faux pas*. Lamont and Morrow each grabbed one of Morgan's arms to keep him from either fainting or bolting from the specter before him. Morrow calmed him down, with more presence of mind than I would have expected from Wall Street's famously absent-minded genius.

"Don't worry, Mr. Morgan, don't worry," he whispered, patting Morgan's arm. "He's not *that* kind of journalist. He's a friend of Anne's. He won't write about anything tonight. I wouldn't have allowed that sort of thing."

I stepped forward a bit, causing Morgan to quiver like a dog that's been beaten.

"That's true, Mr. Morgan," I said. "I'm just a crime reporter and that can certainly have nothing to do with you. I will not write about anything tonight. I give you my solemn word."

Morgan looked sour, but he nodded and it seemed to suffice. Betty Morrow redeemed herself by launching into an amusing story about a recent trip to Egypt and the moment passed. Morgan, like his pugnacious father before him, plainly harbored a virulent hatred and fear of reporters. Perhaps this was understandable, since the House of

Morgan is an irresistible target for muckrakers, being richer and WASP-ier than anyone else in America. Both Jack Morgan and his father Pierpont were repeatedly castigated in the popular press. Whether they deserved it or not is a matter of opinion and not an easy question.

The dinner passed, as dinners do. I spoke less than is my custom, both because of the lofty nature of the company and because I was focused on eating. The food was wonderful, each dish a complex and sumptuous experience. It occurred to me to wonder what it would be to live like the people around the table, for I was sure that their each and every meal was like this. I wondered if Anne Morrow was a girl I could truly know. I was interested to try.

I don't know how many courses we went through. It seemed like a lot. At the end, after a dessert of Peach Melba (which I recalled discussing in Paris with Winston Churchill), Betty Morrow suddenly stood.

"Ladies, shall we?" she said.

All the women at the table—Betty, Mrs. Lamont, and the three Morrow sisters—rose, nodded their heads to us, and walked out. We, of course, leapt to our feet to acknowledge their departure. Being only a rube, aspiring to be at most a wise guy, I was unaccustomed to the tradition of ladies leaving gentlemen to their brandy and cigars. I found it a very strange custom.

Morrow led the gentlemen to the library and there we were, the three titans at the top of the House of Morgan and me. We accepted cigars and snifters of some brown liquid that I expect was cognac. I had trouble snipping off the end of my cigar and wound up with tobacco all over my lap, but that was as nothing compared to Dwight Morrow, who attempted to light his cigar at the wrong end until the butler discreetly corrected him.

Once the cigars were lit and the servants had disappeared, Mr. Morgan started the conversation.

"Dwight, what is happening with your Aviation Board?" he asked. "I hear that is taking a great deal of your time."

"Don't bother Dwight about that, Jack," Lamont interjected, looking down at his spats pensively. "Dwight's aviation work is good for the firm. It shows his close ties to the president and it positions us for close relations with aviation companies when they start exploding, which they will. I'm far more concerned about Dwight's infatuation with Mexico than I am about the Aviation Board. The only thing that interests me about Mexico right now is that bond issue we floated for them. If the government doesn't maintain at least some pretense of stability, our bondholders will be holding the bag. You need to talk to them."

"I talk to them every day, Tom," responded Morrow with some heat. "Do you think this is easy, like talking to the board of some steel company? These are unsophisticated, passionate people. They live and they die with commitment, passionate commitment toward matters far different than bond issues."

"Bollocks!" exclaimed Jack Morgan, pounding his fist on the end table and spilling his brandy. "My father took me to endless meetings of steel company boards and they were passionate and they killed people too. In the end, it is the interests of our clients that matter. And in the Mexico affair, our clients are the bondholders."

There was a moment of silence as we absorbed this wisdom. I remembered Mexico: the ambush in the desert, hiding in a closet with a knife at my throat, Marta's rape and torture in the desert cave. It all seemed very remote from this Wall Street discussion of bondholders, yet I knew that it was not. These men, and lesser men like them, provided the money for nations around the world, meaning they held sway over elections and wars and government policies just as surely as did the first J. Pierpont Morgan over the American companies he financed. By now, even I realized that this would be the American Century, although Henry Luce had not yet coined that phrase. While that would be true in part because of our military and our motion pictures and our consumer goods, it would also be because of the purse strings of the three older gentlemen with whom I was sharing an after-dinner drink.

Dwight Morrow seemed to have had enough discussion of Mexico.

"Shall we join the ladies?" he asked.

The next day at Lindy's, I described the entire evening to Runyon and Rothstein. I couldn't tell if A.R. was interested or not. He remained silent until I was done, then he asked an odd question.

"Did they discuss Jews?" he asked, not looking at me.

"No," I said. "Why would they discuss Jews?"

"A.R. doesn't care for the House of Morgan," Runyon said. "Thinks they're anti-Semitic."

"All Wall Street is anti-Semitic, Damon. This is simply a fact."

Runyon lit another cigarette.

"There are lots of Jews on Wall Street. How about Kuhn Loeb? Otto Kahn is Jewish, last I knew."

"The fact that there are Jewish houses like Kuhn Loeb proves my point, Damon." Rothstein's voice was soft, like always, but he spoke with an intensity that clearly meant he felt the issue deeply. "They have to exist because the Protestant bankers won't take on Jewish partners and won't get too close to Jewish clients. And Morgan is the worst of all. Even Catholics aren't good enough for him."

I tried to lighten the atmosphere.

"Well, you're in the money-lending business, right, A.R.? If Morgan won't lend to Jews or Catholics, leaves more for you."

"I don't find anti-Semitism amusing," Rothstein said coldly.

The next time I asked Anne Morrow for a date, she turned me down. I wasn't to see her again until after she married Charles Lindbergh. Guess we weren't meant to be.

10

Massacre in Gowanus

Cornelius

You hear lots of conflicting accounts about the massacre at the Adonis Social Club, but no reporter knows more about it than I do. I wasn't there, though. At the time it happened, I was in bed with Dorothy at the Algonquin. It was our last night together, Christmas night, 1925. Dorothy's drinking and depression, both heavy, were weighing on me, as were her occasional bursts of frenzied anger at me for reasons that didn't seem much related to me but far more to her childhood or her treatment by her absent husband or her general contempt for men and for herself. Anyway, I'd had enough. In fact, I planned to break up with her over dinner that Christmas, but what with the holidays and all, I put it off. It occurred to me that I didn't have another woman lined up and had no way of knowing when I might be able to have sex again, so I thought I should take advantage of the opportunity and hoard the memory. Like a squirrel storing for the long winter, in a way.

So Dorothy and I were tucked away at the Algonquin when Al Capone and Frankie Yale's crew butchered three prominent Irish gangsters in the middle of a Christmas celebration at a social club dedicated to good fellowship and brotherhood between the Irish and the Italians. It was the event I worked hardest to investigate and report on as a journalist, up until the Lindbergh kidnapping a few years later.

Here is what you would have seen, if you had been celebrating the holiday at the Adonis Social Club on Christmas night, 1925:

The club was located in the Gowanus neighborhood of Brooklyn, near the Gowanus Canal and not far from the Red Hook docks. It was a tough neighborhood, with hatred and pitched battles among the Irish, Italian, and Jewish ethnic groups who fought for control of the borough. I wrote once that the Gowanus Canal was so full of bodies that if you stared at it long enough, someone you knew was bound to come bobbing up.

In the nineteenth century, crime in Brooklyn and indeed throughout New York City was dominated by the Irish, who enjoyed the favors of the Irish political machine in a fashion generally similar to what I knew about the Pendergast operation back in Kansas City. The overwhelming influx of Jews and Italians at the beginning of the twentieth century changed the calculus and set off insanely violent turf wars that largely tipped in the Italians' favor by late 1925. The Brooklyn Irish mob in particular, which some called the White Hand, was in notable decline. Their most recent leader, a violent drunk named Wild Bill Lovett, had been murdered in his sleep by persons unknown. The current head of the Irish mob was Lovett's lieutenant, Peg Leg Lonergan, another mean drunk distinguishable from his predecessors by his wooden leg and not much else. For believers in the Great Man Theory of History, nothing about these Irish leaders inspired much confidence.

There are still social clubs throughout Brooklyn and they still play a prominent role, though perhaps not as much as in the twenties. Then, they played two important roles that are less urgent now. First, they were a place where working men could gather with people of their own ethnicity, who spoke the same language, shared the same customs, and would not look down on them as did so many of the Americans they met in their daily life. Second, they were a place where a working man could freely drink, regardless of the ridiculous social experiment called Prohibition. Never were social clubs so necessary as in the New York of the nineteen-twenties.

Of the social clubs, the Adonis was unique. It was formed by a young Italian man from the neighborhood, who had served in the First World War and returned misty-eyed over how soldiers in his unit from all ethnic groups had worked together in a common cause in stark contrast to the ethnic hostilities and segregation back in the Gowanus neighborhood. In forming his new social club on his return, he violated all custom by opening the club to all ethnic groups (well, not blacks, of course) and making it clear that, within the confines of the club, the Irish and the Italians were expected to get along.

How did it work out? Truth be told, most of the patrons of the club were Italians, like the owner, but undoubtedly there were some Irish and possibly even some Jews who would show up at the club to drink and dance and fraternize after a hard day on the docks or in the shops or on the factory lines. Generally speaking, the atmosphere was friendly and happy, though perhaps not as entirely relaxed and comfortable as in single-ethnicity clubs such as the one where Runyon introduced me to Joe Masseria. Girls crossing ethnic lines could still raise hackles and blows were sometimes exchanged when people had too much to drink. On the whole, though, the Adonis Social Club proved to be a worthwhile venture.

Diners who went to the Adonis on Christmas night, 1925, would have seen the usual squat, nondescript brick edifice adorned with red and green bunting for the holiday. A friendly but not demonstrative Italian doorman would have nodded his head curtly and waved them inside. The guests would enter and see the dining room looking much as usual, with a scattering of tables and a small bar at which stood a middle-aged woman who looked rather the worse for wear and smoked incessantly. A knot of working men at the bar would be ordering beer or wine, unhampered by Prohibition. The clientele around the tables would vary depending upon what time the guests arrived: families with children up until eight o'clock, increasingly inebriated party-goers thereafter. A trio of elderly Italians played, respectively, an accordion, guitar, and piano, bouncing their heads to "Che la Luna" and a variety of peppy Italian songs that sounded much like "Che la Luna." An occasional Christmas carol was mixed in.

The liveliest and biggest table was off in the back corner. Diners around the room shot glances at them, but said nothing. One couple, Poles named Kinsky, didn't know who the men at the table were and

Mr. Kinsky frowned over at them when they grew especially noisy or obscene. Fortunately, the men didn't notice. Sal and Connie Matteo, who sat near the loud table, both knew who the men were. They were careful not to look.

Seated at the loud table were seven men and six women, all well-oiled with bootleg wine and in a party mood. The men were plainly Italians, from their slicked-down black hair and their accents and their occasional ventures into the mother tongue. Anyone from Brooklyn would recognize their leader, Frankie Yale, who sported a tuxedo as he sat at the head of the table and presided over the festivities. Most of the men were known to be Yale gang members.

The women at the table did not look like wives. They were young, chubby, wore flapper outfits, and seemed drunker and happier than the men, as well as louder. They frequently whooped with laughter and spilled their drinks while clapping to the music. Sometimes they sang. They tolerated with varying degrees of receptiveness the groping and grabbing of their escorts. The waiters kept the wine coming, knowing better than to give Frankie Yale bad service at his Christmas party.

To our eyes today, the most interesting man at the table would have been a smiling young fellow sitting just to Yale's left, with his back against the wall. He was overweight and balding, his chubby cheeks glistening with sweat. What would really strike the modern observer would be his youth. He was only twenty-six, yet he was a very powerful man in Chicago and about to become the best-known gangster in history, if you don't count politicians. He'd been born and grown up in Brooklyn, not far from the Red Hook docks. Now, Al Capone was back home on a visit, after taking his ailing son east for an ear operation. It had been nice of Frankie to invite him to the Christmas party.

Other men, by themselves, stood here and there about the club. They drank, but sparingly, and a few diners wondered about them. Again, no one said anything. In Brooklyn, it is better not to ask.

Yale turned to his principal guest.

"So, Al," he said softly, "you think they're coming? Getting late."

Al considered his cigar.

"Wouldn't worry about it, Frankie. They'll come or not. Just have a good time."

That was normally what Yale did best, but this night he seemed preoccupied. The band struck up another song, "Alexander's Ragtime

Band," with a wheezing vocal from a heavy woman with impressive cleavage.

It was about three in the morning when the White Handers arrived.

They were led by Peg Leg Lonergan, newly anointed leader of the Irish gang that traditionally ruled the Red Hook docks and that still stood in Frankie Yale's way there. He was just a skinny mean guy who rose through the mob because he had an aptitude for hasty violence. Usually, he would have been smarter than to go into a predominantly Italian social club on Christmas night. This night, though, he'd gotten heroically drunk and had been needled into it by little Paddy Maloney, who for some reason had it set in his head that they should end the evening in Italian territory to show they weren't afraid.

Lonergan threw open the door and barged in.

"Hello, dagoes," he boomed in a loud voice.

A waiter hurried up to intercept him, but Lonergan ignored him and walked to the bar, followed by four of his gang. Casting his eyes around the room, Lonergan saw Yale at the far table, but did not acknowledge him.

"Whiskies all around," he demanded of the bartender. "And Rothstein stuff, none of that wop swill you people drink."

Lonergan looked belligerently around the room. Inevitably, his gaze lighted on Yale's table. An Irish girl he knew from the neighborhood was sitting with one of the mobsters.

"Jesus Christ, Katie," Lonergan said. "Go out with white men for a change."

A man at Yale's table told him to keep it down. Lonergan simply gave him the finger while downing the whiskey he'd been handed.

Maybe to lighten the mood, maybe just because he was drunk, one of Lonergan's men stepped up to the bandstand. Joe Howard was nicknamed "Ragtime" because he'd spent his youth cadging for nickels thrown by crowds who would watch him sing and dance on the sidewalks and in the bars in Red Hook and Coney Island. He really wasn't a bad singer, better than the fat Italian woman. He told the band to "do 'Jingle Bells' in C," but they ignored him, glancing furtively at Yale's table and putting down their instruments. That led Ragtime to sense something was up.

"Dickie!" he shouted.

Dickie was Lonergan's real first name, but it was too late. Dickie's time was up.

The lights went out. On that cue, the men at Yale's table, led by Capone, pulled guns from under the table and let loose, showering the Irish with lead before they could even reach for their pockets. Some of the men scattered about the room did the same. Paddy Maloney, who had headed for the bathroom a moment before, escaped out the back of the club. Ragtime Howard hid among the band members and wasn't hurt. Lonergan and one of his men lay dead on the floor. The last White Hander, badly shot, stumbled out the front door and died on the sidewalk.

Yale sat motionless throughout. Capone pocketed his gun and slapped his old boss on the shoulder.

"Hell of a party, Frankie," he said. "Merry Christmas."

And that was what came to be called the Adonis Club Massacre.

11

Cornelius Plays Shamus

Cornelius

I got back to my apartment around dawn, following my last night with Dorothy. Our farewell was uneventful, pretty much an afterthought. I was dressed and about to head out the door. She still lay naked in bed, covered by a sheet, looking hung over. I put my hand on the doorknob and turned back to her.

"Dorothy, it's been fun, but I'm not sure we should do this again."

She didn't open her eyes.

"Okay by me," she said.

I put on my hat, went into the hall, down the elevator, through the lobby, past the hotel Christmas decorations and into the New York street. I felt relieved. Dorothy was funny as hell, but everything she touched turned dark and bitter. Years later, when Charles Addams started doing his gloomy, morbid cartoons for *The New Yorker*, I wondered if he had been Dorothy's lover too.

I took a cab home, splurging for the holiday. A telegram was waiting for me at my apartment, slipped under the door. It was from my editor: "Shootings at Adonis Club. Lonergan dead. Get there." Before I finished reading, I was back out the door, chasing down my departing taxi, piling in, and telling the driver to head to Gowanus. This felt big. With Lonergan dead, Yale would be the undisputed ruler of Brooklyn and ruling Brooklyn meant ruling the Red Hook docks, maybe the biggest prize in town. I was a crime reporter so I'd have covered the Adonis Club killings as a matter of course, but my instinct told me this was no ordinary story, that maybe this was the way to show Frankie Yale and his friends that James Cornelius O'Neal wasn't to be trifled with.

We pulled in front of the plain little building that held the social club. I'd been there once or twice before, as it was a regular watering hole for various Brooklyn tough guys. It didn't look like the owner's desire to make the Adonis Social Club a safe haven for all ethnicities had worked out so well this Christmas. A corpse lay face-down on the sidewalk, well-ventilated with bullet holes. There were coppers all over, stamping their big feet in the cold, likely obliterating any traces of evidence that might have been in the area. Lucky for me, one of the first cops I saw was Mikey Toolan, my cousin. I visited Mikey and his brothers once in a while and sometimes they gave me tips on what was happening among the wise guys or who on the force was on the take. The list of who wasn't on the take was shorter.

"Mikey!" I called him over.

Mikey was broad-shouldered and good-natured. Tall for a Toolan, he wore his uniform proudly and didn't take more graft than was polite. I always liked him. He grinned when he saw me and twirled his billy club like a copper on the stage.

"Cousin Jimmy," he said. "You're a little late. Place has been crawling with newspaper men already."

Damn, I thought, but it figured.

"Any of them get inside yet?"

"Can't say about initially," Mikey said, pointing his stick toward a knot of my competitors who were being held in check in a little circle on the sidewalk by yet more police. "I think a couple of them snuck in and maybe got some pictures before the coppers took control, but we got them all out of there. Bloody mess, Jimmy. Not a very nice Christmas, you know?"

I saw Feinberg, one of the Hearst photographers, in the crowd and waved him over, then I put my arm around Mikey's shoulder.

"Get us in there, Mikey. Come on, you can do it. Mr. Hearst will be very grateful."

Family was an important thing to an Irish cop in those days, but so was money.

"Just how grateful is your boss prepared to be, Jimmy? This is a big story, not a time to be parsimonious, is it? And I made sure all those poor boys over there were kept out, just so we'd be having this conversation."

Naturally. But I could have kissed the greedy pig.

"So how much, you fucking Irish thief?" I said.

He had it all figured.

"Hundred for me, hundred for the officer in charge inside, fifty for each of my boys who are over there babysitting your competitors. It's a bargain at the price, Jimmy."

I wasn't going to argue. It was Hearst's money, he had lots of it, and a few bloody photos that the competition didn't have would make him forget any quibbling over price. I agreed and Mikey knew I was good for it, so in two shakes Feinberg and I were through the line and into the building. To construct the club, the owners had pulled down all the walls on the ground floor except the bearing wall that divided the social area from the kitchen, so we stepped right into a large room set up with café tables, a bandstand, and two dead Irishmen. Cops stepped over and around them, not paying much mind. The official photographers had wrapped up and somebody from the medical examiner's office was looking over the bodies, not making much of a show of it. Feinberg knew his job and immediately started taking flash photos of the gore, which was plentiful. The dead gangsters had more holes in them than Mayor Walker's account books and blood was everywhere.

I looked for the man in charge and settled on Rory McGunnigle, a plainclothes detective from Mikey's precinct. Not all New York cops were Irish in those days, but it seemed like it. McGunnigle was standing over Lonergan's body, looking pensive, perhaps watching to see that no one heisted the corpse's peg leg as it would have been a fun souvenir. He didn't wince when I walked up to him, since he knew he'd get his cut.

"I grew up with these boys," he said to me. "Could've been me on this floor, easy."

"Cheer up, McGunnigle, you may get shot yet. What can you tell me so you get your name in the papers?"

McGunnigle snapped out of his reverie.

"Write that the Brooklyn PD is all over the investigation and asks the community to come forward with any information. Like that will happen."

"So was this a dagoes against the Irish thing?"

"Well, you got a Christmas party with about a hundred eyeties and three micks and we got three dead micks. What would you call it?"

"I want to know what you call it. Was it just a spur of the moment blow-up between assholes or was it Frankie Yale making a move? Looks like the Italians were carrying a lot of firepower to a Christmas party."

"Ah, these dagoes are packing when they go to bed," McGunnigle said dismissively. "That don't mean nothing."

"Witnesses?"

"What do you think? Owner and staff all got amnesia. They don't remember anybody who was here, don't remember how it started, don't remember shit. Think they're all in shock, maybe? Got to hand it to these Black Hand boys, they've sure taught the neighbors to dummy up."

"Your boys walking the pavement looking for patrons?"

"Sure. This'll be in all the papers, so we got to go through the motions, you know that. Gonna be a big outbreak of amnesia in Gowanus today."

"You get any names, you'll call me?"

"Fuck me," McGunnigle said. "You sure want a lot for your money. We get any, it'll be a hundred a name, but you can tell your boss to save his money. Wasn't anybody here who's gonna talk to cops, nor reporters neither."

"Yeah, but you need the dough more than Hearst. Call me."

He nodded and I wandered the room, looking for God knows what. I'm not Sherlock Holmes. I did notice one thing, though. Most of the tables in the room were café tables, littered with the usual remnants of a dinner since nobody had cleaned up after the massacre. But off in the corner, several tables were pushed together in a line, tables more laden than any of the others, with lots of evidence of lasagna and other Italian dishes scattered all over. Judging by the number of red sauce stains that surrounded the plates, I guessed that the diners were free with the booze. I counted thirteen chairs around that table, several of them tipped over and lying on the floor. Two glasses were broken, their shards on the tables and the floor. A cake so big it looked like a wedding cake sat untouched on a little table in the corner. There were a lot of cigarette butts, some lipsticked.

I looked at the wall behind the table, near it. It looked fine. Then I walked across the room and looked at the opposite wall. I saw bullet holes all over it. I made sure Feinberg got photos of everything, but I needn't have bothered. Feinberg knew his business. The picture he got of Lonergan's dead face was classic and came to be plastered all over our front page.

Somebody had a Christmas party and three Irish hoods walked in on it and got dead. One of the hoods was Lonergan, Frankie Yale's only rival for control of the Red Hook docks. I was getting hard just thinking about this. I strolled back over to the long table and took another look. This time, I noticed something shiny near the head of the table, half-covered by a napkin. I looked around to be sure no one was watching, then I picked it up.

It was a distinctive-looking diamond stud and I recognized it. When I saw it before, it was fastened to Frankie Yale's belt, straining to hold in his belly. The big dinner must have popped it off. Now I knew something the cops and the other reporters didn't: Frankie Yale was at the Adonis the night of the massacre. I slipped the stud into my pocket, figuring I could always give it to the cops after writing about it in the *Journal*. I got out of there as soon as I could and headed out to find Frankie Yale.

I didn't go to the Harvard Inn, for it had burned down earlier that year in one of Coney Island's many fires. To replace it, Yale had bought a beach cottage on the boardwalk that he now used as his headquarters and that was where I headed. In the cold December wind, I felt the old churning feeling in my stomach that I remembered from my prior visits with Yale. If I was right, the big man had made a major move and would be on alert, watching for reactions from the cops or the White Hand. I needed to play this carefully.

I walked up the stoop of the beach cottage, looked in the window and froze. There were five men sitting around a table in the cottage's parlor. What men they were. Frankie Yale sat at the head of the table, wearing a vest opened to reveal his expansive belly. His cold little killer Willie Altieri sat next to him. Charlie Lucano and Albert Anastasia sat across from Altieri. Next to Willie was a round-faced fellow I had never met, but recognized as Al Capone from newspaper pictures. Quite a gathering, when you think about it. I was especially surprised to see Lucano, who worked for Masseria and not Yale, as far as I knew.

The men were smiling and drinking red wine, though it was still morning. The smiles on their faces disappeared for a moment when I knocked on the door, but Yale recognized me and gestured me in. Frankie quickly recovered his pleasant equanimity.

"Hey, it's the Firebug man," he said happily, using the nickname he'd had for me since the Fallon story. "Nice of you to stop by. To what do we owe the pleasure?"

I decided, what the hell.

"I heard your Christmas party got a little too exciting, Mr. Yale. Wanted to be sure you weren't hurt."

Everyone at the table stared daggers at me, but it was hard to keep Yale unhappy for long. He actually threw back his head and laughed. He even slapped the table in his mirth.

"You hear this guy? That's what I love about reporters, they care, you know? Hear that, Al? He wants to be sure we're okay."

Al wasn't amused. He shifted moodily in his seat and I got the sense he was wishing he was back in Chicago. Yale noticed his discomfort and turned back to me.

"We're all okay, Firebug," he said. "Maybe you should go now."

"Let me just ask you—" I started, but Yale's suggestion was the only authorization that Willie Altieri needed.

The skinny creep oozed from his chair and slithered over to me, planting his reptilian little kisser right up against my face so we were nose to nose.

"You're not welcome here," he whispered, breathing garlic into my face

I felt two pokes in my middle and looked down to see he was holding a stiletto in each hand and was pointing them into my abdomen.

"Jesus, fucking Two Knives Altieri," Yale said, making it a joke. "That's what we call him, Two Knives, you know that? It's a thing he has." Yale shrugged, like it was just a matter of taste, like a fondness for anchovies. "Seriously, though, you should go. Now."

Altieri kept the points of his two knives pricking my belly and, from the look on his face, if he was going to move them, it was going to be in my direction. Lucano looked bored, Anastasia, as always, looked psychopathic. I was about to back discreetly away when Rory McGunnigle walked in behind me, backed by Mikey and two other patrolmen.

"Hello, Frankie," McGunnigle said. Then he looked at me. "The fuck you doing here?"

"Leaving," I said.

I walked out with as much of a swagger as I could muster and ran around to the back, hoping to sneak in the kitchen and listen to the conversation. No luck, as a shabby old man was coming out of the back door as I approached it. Deciding I'd brace Mikey later about what happened inside, I scooted. As I left the alley next to the cottage, I opened the lid and took a glance into the garbage bin. I saw garbage.

I spent a substantial part of the next three months working the Adonis Club story. Capone was arrested, along with some other Yale cronies, but no witnesses were talking and the cases were dismissed for lack of evidence before Capone's cappuccino got cold. He was apparently arrested just for visiting Brooklyn at the wrong time. Yale lived in Brooklyn and never got arrested.

I walked the streets of Gowanus, working hard, ringing doorbells, and I got bupkis. Cold stares, slammed doors, smiles that turned into frowns when they saw where I was going. The eyeties could sure keep their mouths shut, but I got nothing from the Jews or the Irish, either.

Speaking of the Irish, I braced Lonergan's remaining gang mates, naturally. They were pretty much always drunk when I talked to them, not so much because of grief as because it reflected their general state of being. The handwritten notes from my interview of Ragtime Howard give the basic idea:

Fuck. Takes drink.

That was a bad fucking night. Fucking dagoes.

We'll get those fuckers. Fucking dagoes.

Takes drink.

Who are you again?

That's about all I got from Ragtime. The only other Irish survivor, Paddy Maloney, just dummied up completely and I didn't have a fulcrum to move him with. Not at first, I didn't.

The weeks wore on, then the months. I wrote other stories about that night. Editors and reporters gave me grief about my Adonis Club obsession. One day, the phone at the *Journal* rang for me and it was Rory McGunnigle.

"The hundred still goes?"

I knew exactly what he was talking about.

"Absolutely," I said.

"Kid named Sal Matteo. Gowanus." He gave me the phone number and an address that went with it. "That gets me the hundred, right? Ain't saying he'll talk to you, he gave us nothing. But he was there."

"You're covered, Rory. Thanks."

"Much good it'll do you. Watch yourself, Jimmy."

He rang off. I dialed the number he gave me and a woman answered.

"Um, could I speak to Sal Matteo please?"

There was a moment of silence.

"Who is this?" the woman asked.

I realized that I was an idiot for calling, since there was no way this person would talk to a reporter over the telephone. I couldn't think of how to extract myself with any grace, so I hung up. Smooth.

I hit the street, hopped a subway, and rode to Brooklyn. The address was quite a distance from the station so I had to hoof it for several blocks, not exactly sure where I was going, but I found it. It was a tenement apartment building, maybe five flights, with no buzzer or doorman so you could just walk right in. A good thing, given my stupidity on the telephone. I hiked up the stairs to Matteo's apartment on the third floor, passing little kids playing in the hall and an old lady lazing on the stairs. On the ride across town, I'd considered my knock: gentle for reassurance? Or stern and authoritative to scare the lady inside into opening up? I couldn't decide, so I just knocked.

A female voice, the same voice from the phone, spoke from within and asked who it was.

"Mrs. Matteo," I said, "my name is James Cornelius O'Neal. I'm the man who spoke to you on the telephone a little while ago and I rudely hung up. I didn't mean to be impolite, I just got nervous because

I knew you didn't know me and might not want to talk to a stranger on the telephone. I apologize."

Silence.

"Mrs. Matteo, is your husband at home?"

"Yes, he's home," she said after a moment. "He's here and he says you should beat it. He don't want to talk to you. He's a real big guy so you better scram."

Right.

"I see," I said. "I'll tell you what, Mrs. Matteo, please ask your husband to come out here. I'd like to talk to him."

"Shit," I heard her murmur, barely. Then she said in a louder voice, "No, you don't want that. He'll beat your ass, he's real big."

"Well, I probably deserve it, dumb as I was on the telephone. I'll tell you what, Mrs. Matteo, I'll just wait right here. You go on about your business and let me know when you or your husband have a few minutes to chat with me."

I put my back against the wall opposite their door and sank down so I was sitting on the floor, legs sticking out into the hallway. I really wanted to find out what happened at the Adonis Club and didn't have any other leads.

Hours passed with me sitting on that dirty hallway floor. If I smoked, I'd have smoked. I wished I had a rubber ball I could bounce against the wall. But I was devoid of amusements, so I just sat and waited, like a hunter in a deer stand. Right about the time I started needing to pee, when I was sensing that it was getting dark outside even though no windows were handy, I heard footsteps coming up the stairs. Heavy steps but quick. Soon a young guy appeared, dressed in a longshoreman's canvas pants, sweatshirt, and jacket. There was something likable about Sal Matteo right from first sight. He was a good-looking young guy: curly black hair, Roman nose, face that smiled as its default expression. I smiled back at him, not to shuck him but because it was a natural response.

"Mr. Matteo?"

There were other apartments on the third floor, but I knew it was him. His eyes narrowed and his expression turned quizzical, but still good-natured.

"Yeah? Who are you?"

I jumped to my feet, looked him earnestly in the eye and started talking. He frowned when I said I was a reporter, frowned more when I mentioned the Adonis Club, but he kept listening. His wife burst into the hall and tried to shoo me away, but Sal kept listening. I cursed myself silently for not bringing a bottle of something to offer them. Fortunately Sal was the hospitable sort and before you knew it, we were seated around their tiny table in their tiny kitchen, drinking some of the bathtub wine that no Italian could do without. I smiled, I joked, I apologized, I entreated. I promised never to use their names. I said whatever they had to say wouldn't matter anyway because we knew everything, but some details might help give some human interest to the story, all without involving the Matteos at all. I kept filling their glasses, especially Connie's. Eventually she got drunk enough and he got friendly enough that the story came spilling out.

Sal and Connie had been splurging, having a big Christmas dinner at the club because they knew the owner from around the neighborhood. They'd seen the whole thing as it happened: Frankie Yale's party, the Irish hoodlums arriving, Ragtime Howard singing, the insults, the gunshots. They'd never forget it.

The one thing that stuck out to me was when they told me one of the Irish guys had gone to the bathroom just before the shooting started. The only Irish guys who had survived the massacre were Ragtime Howard up on the bandstand and Paddy Maloney. Paddy's life was apparently saved by a timely bladder attack. Made me want to talk to him again.

12

A Close Call

Cornelius

Paddy Maloney was gone. Just gone. I walked his streets, combed the bars all around Red Hook and Gowanus, asked every Irish plug-ugly I could find where he was, and got nothing. The Toolans knew a lot about the Irish mob in Brooklyn, but they had no idea what happened to the unpleasant drunk with a very convenient bladder. I figured he was dead and I had a shrewd guess why. If he did sell out his own people to the Italians, leading Peg Leg and his boys into a trap at the Adonis Club, his life wouldn't be safe from either side. Betrayal of your own people was an unforgivable sin in Brooklyn, unless you got away with it.

Without Maloney or any other angle, my Adonis Club stories petered out and then stopped entirely. I'd broken the news that Frankie Yale's Christmas party was at the club that night, but I had no witness who'd vouch for the fact that his men did the shooting. Sal and Connie Matteo were frightened to their souls at the thought of how much they had told me and I couldn't get another word from them after my story appeared, even though I never mentioned their names. As always, other murders took the place of the Adonis Club in the public consciousness. By spring of 1926, nobody even remembered what happened.

Except the Irish mob. The massacre pretty much broke up any

chance the White Hand might have had to retain any real power in Brooklyn. The boys who worked for Frankie Yale in Brooklyn and for Joe Masseria in Manhattan were just too tough, especially when Charlie Lucano made an alliance on behalf of Masseria with the Bugs and Meyer crew from the Lower East Side. I didn't dream then how much of a role Arnold Rothstein played in all this. I found out later.

Being young, I was impatient. I was tired of seeing these arrogant hoods all around me and not having anything meaningful to write about them. Runyon thought I was obeying his advice to stick to crimes that are safe to write about, but the truth was I didn't yet have anything I could publish about men like Masseria and Yale and Lucano because no witnesses would talk about them and I had no other proof. I burned to build a national reputation by sending these mobsters to prison, but I needed real facts that would put them away. Without them, anything I wrote would do nobody any good and would get me tossed in the Gowanus Canal.

I decided to get me some facts. I got serious about heisting the notebooks of Arnold Rothstein.

It came about because of a lunch I had with Runyon at Lindy's, one of maybe hundreds that we shared there over the years. Runyon liked to listen to me yapping about the newspaper business and the doings of the mob and the miscellaneous criminal strangeness that I covered, while I never stopped learning from Runyon about being a reporter. We always ate at Lindy's because that's where Runyon always ate and sat, endlessly soaking in the Broadway scene.

"Anything new with your friend over there?" I asked, nodding at Rothstein's table.

As always, he sat alone, scribbling in his notebook, granting audiences to supplicants and flashing his big bankroll.

"A.R.?" Runyon shrugged. "Same as always. Got his fingers in everything, but it's hard to say how. Did you hear he bought an art house?"

"What's an art house?"

"Well, a lot of things, but this one is legit. Place called Vantine's, been around a long time. They import art from Europe and Asia, all over the place, and sell it to the swells uptown. The owners came on hard times and A.R. bought the business. Doesn't seem like his usual play, but you never know with A.R. He's figured more ways to make money than Ruth has hit home runs. Speaking of which, you think the Giants will ever win a series with the Yankees what they are?"

We talked baseball and finished our lunch. As we walked out, Runyon stopped at Rothstein's table to congratulate him on his purchase of Vantine's.

"Thank you, Damon. I'm very pleased. As you know, Vantine's has an excellent reputation and only imports the finest."

"Well, that's not really my line, A.R.," Runyon said. "Most beautiful piece of art I know is a winning ticket at Aqueduct. You coming to the races with me?"

Rothstein closed the notebook in front of him, which I saw was at its end and filled with notations.

"I will certainly do that," he said. "Just let me stop at the office to pick up a new notebook. I've got a beautiful piece there I acquired as part of the Vantine's purchase, a painting from the Italian Renaissance. I thought if I own the business, I might as well enjoy some of the art in my office before I sell it. Care to see it?"

"I'd like to," I piped in. "I love the Italian Renaissance."

Both Runyon and Rothstein looked skeptically at me, which was justified because I didn't know the Italian Renaissance from an Italian ice. But I had an idea.

Rothstein nodded and we headed over to the Park Central Hotel nearby, where A.R. rented a suite on the sixth floor that he used as an office. This was the hotel where I bought drinks for Irvin Cobb seven years earlier. It was just off Times Square and served as a second home for numerous Broadway citizens. As I would later see, it would become the setting for two notorious mob murders, but that was still in the future when Rothstein led Runyon and me to his office there.

Rothstein unlocked a nondescript hotel suite door and showed us in. The office of New York's leading gambler, fixer, and all-around shady individual was disappointingly normal. I saw a large desk, a conference table, and a few chairs in the living room. The one notable feature of the room was the painting from Vantine's, which hung on the wall directly opposite Rothstein's desk. It seemed a very fine painting. It showed purple storm clouds lowering over a cruel-looking lancer on a horse that was rearing in a threatening way over three large-breasted ladies who seemed quite upset about it. Rothstein told us the name of the artist, but I've forgotten it. It was Italian and sounded vaguely familiar and had lots of o's in it.

While Runyon and I were nodding at the painting the way people do, wondering how long before they can decently move along, Rothstein walked behind his desk. I watched from the corner of my eye, as this was what I had come for. I saw Rothstein take his notebook from his breast pocket, open the middle right-hand desk drawer, and place the notebook inside. I could just barely see that a number of similar notebooks were also in that drawer. Then he took a fresh notebook from the left-hand drawer. I hurriedly turned my gaze back to the painting as Rothstein straightened up.

Runyon and I gushed compliments about the artwork, as it seemed like they would be expected.

"Yes, it's beautiful, isn't it?" Rothstein said.

I noticed Rothstein never really looked at the art himself.

"Time for the races, Damon?"

Rothstein and Runyon went to Aqueduct and I headed for the *Journal*. Hot damn! I knew exactly where Rothstein kept his old notebooks and he didn't even lock the drawer! Another few days and James Cornelius O'Neal would be the top reporter in New York.

I went at the problem logically. I wanted Rothstein's notebooks because they would give me a roadmap to all the dirty deals in New York for the last twenty years, enough mud to launch my career to the stratosphere. To get them, I had to get into the right-hand drawer of Rothstein's desk in his office in the Park Central Hotel. I could not take the notebooks with Rothstein there, so I had to do it when he was out and could be depended upon not to return. That part wasn't so difficult. Lindy's was too close to the hotel for comfort, but it wouldn't be hard to find a time when Rothstein was at Aqueduct or locked in an all-night poker game.

How to get into the office? That was harder. Either I needed a key or to pick the lock. But I have no lock-picking skills and no professional cracker would break into Arnold Rothstein's room, nor could I trust him to keep quiet if he did. I needed a key. Rothstein had a key to the room, of course, and so did the hotel desk, but it was another key that interested me.

Back in the twenties, hotels typically had not just room-specific keys, but one, two, or three copies of a skeleton key that would open all the rooms. These master keys were closely guarded for obvious reasons, but two members of the hotel staff always had them: the general manager and the hotel detective. It so happened that the detective for the Park Central Hotel was a friend of mine as well as being, to my knowledge, unique in the ranks of New York City hotel detectives in one respect. She was a woman.

That's right. In 1926 the Park Central, one of the liveliest and most action-filled hotels in the city, employed a female detective named Christy Cole. The wise guys called her the dickless dick. She had started as a secretary for the police department in Manhattan, then talked and fought her way into a job as a patrolwoman. When a Women's Police Precinct had been formed in 1921, with all of the city's twenty patrolwomen on the staff, Christy became the assistant director. The patrolwomen had been harassed, patronized, and not trusted with any real action, so Christy quit and hung out her shingle as a private shamus. She earned the wise guys' respect against all odds and, after a couple of years of the usual divorce peeping and investigating cases for lawyers, she impressed the Park Central management with her discreet handling of an actress overdose in the presidential suite and she got the hotel detective job.

I liked Christy. She was smart, tough, and funny, kind of like Dorothy Parker with less booze and bile. She was only a little more than five feet tall, with bobbed hair like a flapper and a skinny little body I thought about doing detective work on myself. No one would figure her for a shamus, which was how she liked it. You thought she was a sweet, giddy little thing right up to when she stuck her revolver up your nose. She had a partner, a big lug of an assistant hotel dick who provided the muscle if necessary, but with Christy, it usually wasn't necessary.

Christy and I flirted on a regular basis when I'd visit the speak at the Park Central, which was in the renovated room 416 as the bartender had promised Irwin Cobb. I worked out my approach to her. Christy would never even think about letting me have the key if she thought I was going to break in on Arnold Rothstein, so I had to have another reason. I took that day's *Journal*, in which I had a boring piece on a department store heist, and planted myself in the lobby of the Park

Central across from the front desk. I read that rag cover to cover, then read it again so I'd have something in front of my face while I sat there. I was about to start a third time through when my mark arrived.

He was a tall, stooping, insignificant-looking fellow in a well-worn suit, carrying a suitcase in one hand and what looked like a sample case in the other. The sample case marked him for a traveling salesman, everything else about him screamed out-of-towner, probable Midwesterner. I sidled toward the front desk to hear the conversation.

"Howdy, friend," he said to the young desk clerk. "Name's Hartigan. Got a reservation."

The clerk checked his book.

"Yessir," he said. "Bill Hartigan, three nights?"

"That's right. Maybe more, if the people around here need typewriting machines. Think they do?"

The clerk offered a phony smile.

"Folks in New York got everything and need everything at the same time," he replied.

He was quick at his job, that clerk, I'll say that for him. Hartigan was checked in and on his way in a snap, despite the obligatory salesman's joke that he offered and that the desk man brushed off by making his smile even phonier.

Once Hartigan disappeared into the elevator, I sauntered up to the clerk.

"Where's that fellow from? He looked kind of familiar."

"That why you've been sitting in the lobby for two hours with your hat over your eyes, hoping you'd see somebody familiar?"

New York's full of wiseacres.

I shrugged and headed to the door, figuring I had all I needed, but the clerk relented and shouted after me.

"Omaha!"

Perfect.

"Hartigan. Bill Hartigan," I said to Christy Cole over drinks in the room 416 speakeasy. "Not his real name, natch. Real name's Soapy Malone, biggest con man in Omaha."

Christy squinted her eyes skeptically and smiled at me.

"Do they have a lot of big con men in Omaha?"

"Don't get snooty about the Midwest, Christy. I'm from there, so's Runyon, so's F. Scott Fitzgerald, for Christ's sake. Sure, there's con men in Omaha. And Soapy's slick as they come, that's how he got the name."

Christy finished her Old Fashioned, the second I'd bought her. I gestured to the barkeep for another round. While Christy was taking in my tale of Soapy Malone, I was taking in Christy. She was truly an attractive lady, pert and good-humored and funny. She was also street smart in the extreme and she was plainly weighing the likelihood of Jimmy O'Neal giving her the straight dope.

"Tell me again," she said. "This Hartigan or Soapy or whoever is staying here under a phony name, looking to run con jobs on our guests. And you got onto him how?"

"I told you. You know I'm a crime reporter and I got cousins on the force, so I have connections. I'm also from Kansas City, where Soapy would run cons when he wasn't home in Omaha. He's a very wanted guy, all over the Midwest, maybe that's why he's branching out to New York. Anyway, I'm in your lobby today thinking maybe I should get a haircut, when I see this gent checking in who says his name is Bill Hartigan. I swear to God, it's Soapy. I know him from pictures I saw back in Kansas City. If Soapy Malone's in your hotel, it's bad news, believe me. So I figure, I'll do my good friend Christy Cole a favor and tip her off."

Christy swirled her finger around in her drink.

"Tell me, Jimmy. If you're the one doing me a favor, why aren't I paying for the drinks?"

"Christy, I would never allow a lady to pick up my tab."

She snorted with laughter, as I intended.

"Besides, it's not like I have evidence or anything. I only got a quick look at the guy. I need to be sure before I put it in the paper and blow the whistle in Kansas City or Omaha. If he's really Soapy Malone, there'll be something in his room that says so. I just need to get in there, so I need your master key."

I waited. Christy took a deep breath and seemed to make up her mind.

"You wouldn't shit a shitter, Jimmy O'Neal?"

I crossed my heart and kissed my pinky. She sighed, reached down the front of her dress and pulled out a key, which she handed to me.

"Jeepers, dames really keep stuff in their bras?"

"You need to get around more, Jimmy."

I looked at the key. It was funny-looking, long and with not many doodads along the spine.

"You sure this'll work? It looks pretty simple."

"That's why it works, you dope." Christy placed her hand over mine on the bar. "Now listen to me, O'Neal. You go in the room, look around, and get out, then that key comes right back to me. Any funny stuff and I'll break your legs myself."

"Sounds like an interesting proposition to me," I said, "but you'll get the key back. And you'll thank me."

Well, that didn't end up working out.

Even in 1926, I hadn't yet realized how serious a man was Arnold Rothstein. I don't know that I'd have dared to burglarize the offices of Frankie Yale or Joe Masseria, but Rothstein didn't seem in their league. Arnold Rothstein sat in Lindy's and drank milk, for God's sake. He was well-connected in society: maybe a debauched society, but society. He was a well-known gambler and bootlegger and political fixer, but those were venial sins in the New York of the twenties if they were sins at all. I didn't associate Rothstein with violence. Gradually, I was to learn the extent of my ignorance.

Despite my misunderstanding of Rothstein's real nature, my heart pounded a little that midnight as I slipped up the two flights of stairs from the speakeasy to Rothstein's office. I figured I was less likely to be seen entering the sixth floor if I took the stairs rather than the elevator. When I reached the sixth, I eased open the door a crack, to be sure no innocent bystanders were lurking. I didn't want to explain to Christy Cole or anybody else what I was doing on that floor at that time of night.

The hallway was empty. I scurried to Rothstein's door, skeleton key clutched in my right hand. I knew that Rothstein was supposed to be in an all-night poker game with Hump McManus and some heavy players from Jersey. Still, I took a deep breath and held it as I quietly turned the key in Rothstein's lock and slipped into the dark suite.

Everything was going smoothly. Nobody home. I moved across to the desk, which faced the door, without even barking my shin. The last obstacle I had imagined faded away when I found that the middle right-hand drawer of the desk was indeed unlocked and still loaded with the precious notebooks. There was just enough light coming in from the window for me to see the darling little things which would make me the most famous and feared reporter on Broadway. I didn't bother turning on any light, I just pulled from my pocket the big pillowcase I'd remembered to bring and I started stuffing it with Arnold Rothstein's records.

Shit! Right when I got the first handful into the case, there was a loud click at the door. Somebody was unlocking it and coming in! There was no time for any other action but to duck under the desk and hide myself in its capacious knee-well. Rothstein was a small man, but fortunately he favored a big and old-fashioned desk with a panel that covered its entire front, blocking me from the view of whoever entered the room. As long, of course, as he stayed on the other side of the desk, an unlikely prospect since I'd left the goddam pillowcase and a couple of notebooks scattered on the desktop.

That realization came to me just as the room became flooded with light. I heard maybe two footsteps, then my visitor stopped short, drawn up by the sight of the objects on the desk. I tried not to breathe. I heard the unmistakable sound of a handgun emerging from a holster. I heard heavy breathing, but no speech. Oh, Jesus, what if he just started banging away at the front of the desk?

Footsteps approached. I considered the options I would have when Rothstein, or whoever it was, saw me. I could spring at him, but unfortunately I was on my hands and knees facing the front of the desk, so that the first sight of Cornelius that the intruder would get was of my butt. Hard to spring from that position. Oh, how I wished for Riley at that moment.

I was lucky. The footsteps moved in the direction of the bedroom, where my nemesis would no doubt check out the bathroom and closets for any sign of the burglar who'd disturbed Rothstein's notebooks. Quick as I could while making minimal noise, I was out from under the desk and across to the door, which saved me fractions of a second by being open. They were important fractions, for a gunshot cracked and a bullet tore into the door jamb just as I streaked down the hall, a bullet that would have lodged in my back if that door had been closed. A voice, which I recognized as belonging to Rothstein hard guy Legs

Diamond, told me to stop and called me a cocksucker as another shot echoed down the hall. I was on the stairs then, practically jumping from flight to flight. Diamond followed, occasionally getting off a shot from which the stairway shielded me. I was out the basement door, across a laundry area, and in the alley before Diamond could make up any ground. I was one fast reporter that night. I hoped to God that Diamond didn't recognize me.

Christy Cole plainly got an earful from Rothstein about the break-in, for the next day she practically spat in my eye when I gave her back her key. She really should have been more careful with it.

Christy was angry, but I was mortified. Paddy Maloney had disappeared, the Adonis Club story was dead, and now I had blown my best chance to get my hands on Rothstein's notebooks. Whether Legs recognized me, I couldn't decide. He didn't treat me any differently when we next met on the street, but Rothstein acted funny with me two days after the failed burglary when I passed his table like usual at Lindy's.

"Mr. O'Neal, it's good to see you," he said, grabbing my forearm to slow me down.

He had his notebook out and a milk in front of him and all seemed right with the world.

"Since you are a crime reporter, you might be amused to hear that I was the victim of a crime myself this week."

My spine stiffened and my throat closed.

"Oh, it was nothing. A trivial burglary at my office. Fortunately, I had sent Mr. Diamond there to get some more cash for me for the poker game I was attending, so he foiled the plot. The man got away, though."

He sipped his milk and smiled blandly at me.

"Would you like to write about that in your paper?"

He knew. Was he toying with me, so I'd quiver in fear until he took revenge? I still thought of Rothstein as just a gambler, but Legs and his brother were tough monkeys and A.R. was obviously closer to them than I realized.

Still, I put on a bold front.

"Doesn't sound like a piece for the *Journal*, A.R.," I said as breezily as I could. "Maybe if the crook had gotten something, that would've been worth writing about."

"Yes, it may have been. Strangely, the man seemed more interested in my little notebooks than in anything else in the office. Don't worry, I've learned my lesson. My notebooks are now under lock and key and they will be kept in a location where no burglar would ever think of looking. I mention it so you won't worry on my account. I'll see you around town, Mr. O'Neal."

I winked and tipped my hat to him as I moved on. Well, the notebooks were out of reach and Rothstein seemed to be out of my reach as well. I didn't know that Arnold Rothstein would later make a very strange request of me, one that would have momentous consequences for me, for Riley, and for Marta.

13

The Pope's Usurer

Cornelius

L ots happened in New York in 1927.

Lindbergh was the man of the year for his solo flight across the Atlantic. He depressed Runyon deeply, because Runyon did not believe in heroes and as far as anyone could tell, Lindbergh was the genuine article. Also, Babe Ruth hit sixty home runs and two obscure Italian radicals named Sacco and Vanzetti were executed up in Boston on what all my communist and almost-communist friends in New York were convinced was a bum rap.

It was truly a notable year, 1927. It was also the year that Arnold Rothstein brought me into contact once again with J.P. Morgan.

The first time I'd slept with Dorothy Parker, as I've described, she'd been impressed that I knew Rothstein. I finally got the chance to introduce them. I still saw her as a friend even though our love affair was long over. Dorothy had taken a job writing and sometimes reviewing books and plays for the new magazine started by Harold Ross. That was, of course, *The New Yorker* and many of the bright lights of the Round Table wrote for it. I wanted to myself, but Ross never seemed to think much of the stuff I submitted to him. Benchley, Parker, and Woollcott were all regular contributors.

New plays opened on Broadway far more often then and Dorothy was at a theater almost every night during the season. I accompanied her occasionally, though as little as I could manage as many of the shows were junk and Dorothy and I were wearing on each other even as friends. Her sharp tongue was making her seem to me less of a witty sophisticate and more of a shrewish fishwife. Perhaps the difference is simply a matter of acquaintance.

Anyway, one evening, Dorothy and I had a quick drink of bootleg gin in FPA's suite at the Algonquin and headed to a dreadful little domestic comedy that was universally reputed to be a stinker before it ever left New Haven. Dorothy kept her eyes closed and sighed audibly throughout the first act, drawing dirty looks from a dowager in front of us. Finally, the woman lost patience and snapped at Dorothy.

"Madam, can't you keep silent?"

Dorothy did not bother to open her eyes.

"I could, but then I might have to listen to the play."

Intermission blessedly arrived and we agreed to leave. Dorothy felt no compunction about limiting her exposure to an author's cherished work to one act and then writing a blistering review in the morning. One act can be a long time, after all.

We hurried down the stairs, crossed the lobby and stepped into the street, no doubt passing an anxious producer or two who recognized the look in Dorothy's eye. On the sidewalk in front of the door, perched as though waiting for us, was Arnold Rothstein. He blocked our path and leaned in to us, looking for all the world like a salesman offering us a miracle product. His hands were shoved in his coat pockets and his fedora pulled down over his ears. I could not imagine what he wanted.

"Mr. O'Neal," he hissed, "if I could have a word?"

Dorothy had no idea who he was.

"You know this man, Jimmy?" she asked me.

I took a moment to think, but didn't see the harm.

"Dorothy, permit me to introduce you to Arnold Rothstein. Mr. Rothstein, this is Dorothy Parker."

Not every day you get to make an introduction like that.

"Mr. Rothstein," said Dorothy, smiling as she offered her hand, "I find you morally reprehensible and a disgrace to our tribe, but I truly appreciate your liquor. Damned good stuff."

Rothstein had no humor. He looked at Dorothy blankly, then turned to me.

"I'd like to speak to you, Mr. O'Neal. Privately."

"Not really a good time, Mr. Rothstein. I need to escort Mrs. Parker home."

"Like hell you do," Dorothy chimed in. "Let's get a drink and hear what Mr. Rothstein has to say."

Rothstein looked back to her.

"I don't drink, Mrs. Parker. I know who you are. As for being a disgrace to our tribe, as you put it, I don't see that you're in a position to speak. You married outside the faith and you drink and whore around."

"Hey!" I interjected. Though he did have a point.

"We are both fallen Jews, Mrs. Parker. But if a rabbi were here, who would he say has fallen further?"

I was amazed. Dorothy, the ballsy and indefatigable Mrs. Parker, looked down at her feet and said not a word. I was just enough in awe of Rothstein's mystique that I simply took her elbow and pulled her away down the sidewalk. I heard Rothstein's voice behind me.

"My office at the Park Central tomorrow. Ten."

And we were gone.

Dorothy slammed the door of her apartment in my face. The next morning, Rothstein made me his proposition.

"I want to sell J.P. Morgan a valuable piece of art that Vantine's recently acquired," Rothstein said to me in his office, sitting at the same desk I had so pathetically tried to pilfer. "I'd like you to broker the transaction."

This, of course, was all kinds of crazy. I met J.P. Morgan a total of once, at that surreal dinner at the Morrows'. He didn't like me at the time and he wouldn't remember me now. I was supposed to set up a transaction between the most respectable, reclusive, and anti-Semitic millionaire in New York and a Jewish gambler who represented everything he hated? Ridiculous.

"I'll tell you how you will do this," Rothstein continued. "With everything you know about me, everything you have heard, do you think I haven't thought this through? I will tell you what you will do and how you will do it. If you make this sale for me, I will pay you ten thousand dollars."

My eyes widened.

"Ten thousand? That's more than I make in a year."

"I know, Mr. O'Neal," he said, smiling coldly. "I considered the number carefully."

Alarm bells were clanging in my head. I'd seen Rothstein many times since the failed burglary and all had been normal, so that this might be some sort of revenge plot didn't even enter my mind, but taking ten thousand from this icy little villain felt like a deal with the devil. Besides, the whole idea made no sense. J.P. Morgan would almost certainly not remember me and I was hardly someone the reclusive millionaire would blindly follow into making a deal with a shady gambler, loan shark, and who knew what else? Still, ten thousand dollars…

Rothstein read my thoughts.

"You will not tell Mr. Morgan that I am involved in the transaction. Given his deplorable attitude toward Jews, that would be inadvisable. He will do business with you, for you will be offering him something he wants and wants desperately, though he doesn't yet know it." Rothstein placed his fingertips together like a tent, in front of his nose. "Have you heard of the Pope's Usurers?"

This was too much.

"Is the Pope involved in this deal too?"

Rothstein winced.

"No, Mr. O'Neal. Or at least, only historically. As a crime reporter, you should broaden your field of interest. The Pope's Usurers are currently the subject of the most hotly discussed crime in Europe."

"If it gets much further east than Flatbush, it's out of my beat."

"Let me enlighten you, then."

Rothstein rose and began pacing the room as he filled in the gaps in my knowledge.

"About three weeks ago, a wealthy Italian art collector named Arturo Gaetano reported that a unique and highly valuable piece of furniture in his collection had been stolen. It was a desk, an ornate, exquisitely-carved desk made for a Tuscan banker named Giovanni Medici in the late fourteenth century. Now, this desk is not only a beautiful work of art, it has historical significance, especially for bankers like Mr. Morgan. Here is where the Pope comes in."

Rothstein sat back down and looked at me with more than his usual intensity.

"You see, in medieval times, Jewish merchants had a great

advantage because the Catholic Church forbade Christians from loaning money at interest. Kings were forced to go to the Jews to finance their wars, landowners went to the Jews for loans against the grain crop, and it was the Jews who financed the Crusades, which I believe is what some men call an irony."

Rothstein paused, perhaps musing over why anyone wastes their time thinking of such things as ironies.

"Of course, Christians could not continue allowing Jews such a commercial advantage. First, the Church came to recognize doctrinal fictions, such as pretending that instead of charging interest on loans, Christian merchants were merely selling insurance against the loan's repayment. Eventually, the Pope licensed certain Christian bankers to loan money at interest despite the religious prohibition. These men came to be called the Pope's Usurers and one of the most prominent was Giovanni Medici of the famous Medici family in Florence, who commissioned for his bank the beautiful desk that was allegedly stolen from Arturo Gaetano. Are you following me?"

"I think so," I said. "All except that word 'allegedly' you just used."

He smiled, or rather he made the simpering expression that passed for a smile on Arnold Rothstein's face.

"Mr. Gaetano alleges that he was robbed, but he was not. He was paid for the piece by my art house Vantine's. It currently resides, secretly, in one of my warehouses in Queens. You see, Mr. Gaetano found himself in extreme financial distress owing to an unfortunate opium habit that seems to grow worse each day. Yet, he is a prominent merchant and social figure in Lombardy and he does not want either his financial straits or his personal addiction to become common knowledge. He came to Vantine's looking to sell some of his collection secretly, which means that unknowingly, he came to me."

The picture was beginning to come into focus for me.

"You bought it, but promised him to keep the deal a secret and let him pretend the desk was stolen."

Rothstein nodded.

"Correct. I extracted a price reduction for the secrecy, of course, but I knew I could sell the piece even with that restriction. Here is the bill of sale."

He reached into his desk and pulled out a piece of paper with Vantine's letterhead.

"Wow," I said, looking at the handwritten notations on the paper. "That's millions of something."

"Lira," Rothstein said. "In dollars, we only paid two hundred thousand. I expect to get three, maybe four times that from Mr. Morgan. Or rather, I expect you to get that. I fear that, even with the bill of sale, Mr. Morgan would not believe this to be an honest transaction if he knew I were involved."

Well, that made sense.

"Mr. O'Neal, you are to approach Mr. Morgan and tell him you represent Vantine's. Let him know you have the desk of the Pope's Usurer, show him the bill of sale, and explain matters. You will ask nine hundred thousand dollars for it, he will offer you less, you will agree to an amount no less than six hundred thousand, more if possible. For that, you will be paid ten thousand dollars, by me. Are we agreed?"

He stuck out his hand.

God knows I should have known better. There are certain people you do not do business with and Arnold Rothstein was one of them. But then, half of Broadway did business of one sort or another with A.R., on pretty much a daily basis. And ten thousand dollars…

I shook the man's hand. There were no lightning bolts or hordes of demons flying about. There should have been.

I couldn't decide which was the bigger challenge: getting in Morgan's presence long enough to pitch the deal or convincing him to agree. Regardless, the former clearly involved the most physical danger. Morgan emulated his famously reclusive father by surrounding himself with bodyguards wherever he went. He did not take meetings with anyone he didn't know and anyone who dared approach him on the street would likely find himself beaten senseless by Morgan's attendants, if not smashed over the head by the banker's umbrella. Rothstein explained to me that I needed to get within earshot of the great man himself and that I would have at most three seconds to attract his attention.

Rothstein also told me where I could get close to him. Morgan lived on an island in the East River which featured a number of great estates including those of Tom Lamont and the House of Morgan's chief lawyer, John W. Davis. It was called "the Island of Millionaires," for obvious reasons. Every weekday morning, Morgan and Lamont would take a ferry over to the piers on the south side of Manhattan, where cars would be waiting to take them to the office. Lamont was often away on business, but Morgan dependably arrived at the pier each morning around 9:30. As Rothstein instructed, I was waiting for him, dressed in a denim shirt and workpants so I could pass for a dockworker, but neatly groomed and wearing a tie so I would look respectable. Overall, I looked like I was playing a part in a bad play.

I leaned against a wall across from the pier. Dockworkers lazed about, smoking, waiting for the brief moments of activity when ferries would arrive and unload their passengers. Men, all in business suits, many accompanied by servants, hurried off the boats and headed by foot or taxi or private car to their Wall Street offices. No women in sight, as I recall. It was a side of New York I hadn't seen, not much like Broadway. I didn't think I'd like it.

I gave a boy a buck to tip me off when the Morgan boat was coming. It was wasted money, since anyone in the city could have spotted the right boat as soon as it got close enough. The man himself, the great J.P. Morgan, Junior was standing in the prow of the boat, arms folded, cigar jutting from his mouth, looking over the magnificent New York harbor like he owned it, which maybe he did for all I knew. He had recovered his girth since I last saw him and his portly build, his elegant cane, the Homburg perched on his head, and the fur collar on his coat, all combined to give Mr. Morgan the exact appearance you would expect of the country's greatest banker. Morgan and his late papa may not have liked publicity, but they couldn't seem to change the behavior that made it inevitable.

Three seconds, Rothstein said, was all I had to get and hold his attention. He made me practice my lines over and over so I wouldn't waste the precious moments. Unlike the ferries that carried the normal Wall Street crowd across the East River, Morgan's boat was a pleasure yacht, a trim little steamer with plenty of deck space for cocktail parties and sightseeing. The captain eased the boat gently against the pier. Morgan took off his heavy overcoat, worn to deflect the ocean breezes, and stepped to the gangplank. He was preceded by two flunkies who plainly served to keep interlopers like me away from the great man.

I stuffed my hands in my pockets, put my head down, and walked quickly toward the dock. Timing was everything.

I arrived at the end of the dock just as the flunkies did. They held up their hands to stop me, but Morgan was only ten feet behind them. He was in earshot, that was the important thing, and I had my three seconds.

"Mr. Morgan, you know me. I'm a friend of Anne Morrow's. We had dinner in Englewood. I have an art transaction to propose, an entirely legitimate one. It involves the Pope's Usurer."

Morgan stopped in his tracks and stared at me. Rothstein said an avid collector like Morgan would know all about the Pope's Usurer and the desk theft. The tall millionaire looked troubled and dubious, but he also looked intrigued.

He waved the flunkies aside and gestured me over. He peered in my face closely, then nodded.

"I remember you. You're a journalist."

"Not today, Mr. Morgan," I said quickly. "Today I'm just an intermediary acting on behalf of the Vantine's art house. The desk of the Pope's Usurer was not stolen, Mr. Morgan. That was a ruse made up by Arturo Gaetano to cover up his financial problems. He sold the desk to Vantine's, secretly. Here is the bill of sale."

I flashed it in Morgan's face quickly, as Rothstein instructed, so as not to give him time to read the price.

"This is an opportunity for you to have the world-famous desk of the Pope's Usurer, sir. You can't show it to others, but you can have it for yourself and at a price that is ridiculously low for the value of the piece."

I'd made my pitch. Now, it was up to my quarry.

Morgan thought for several moments. Cupidity warred with caution and, as usual, cupidity won.

"Where can you be reached?"

Lindy's didn't seem appropriate. I told him to send a wire to Vantine's.

"My confidential assistant will be in touch."

Morgan looked me up and down one more time, then strode away with his minions in tow.

It wasn't long before the wire arrived, inviting me to a meeting with Morgan's "confidential assistant," who proved to be a public relations man named Ivy Lee. He didn't try to bargain with me, but agreed to the nine hundred thousand on the spot. More money for the Big Bankroll. He filled in the amount on a blank check that had been signed by Mr. Morgan himself, which I cashed at one of A.R.'s friendly banks as per his instructions. Then I passed the money along to him, keeping my ten grand as commission. All in all, a nice piece of work for me. As far as I could tell, J.P. Morgan and Arnold Rothstein deserved each other.

14

The Man Who Could Sink Anybody

Cornelius

It was early in 1928 when I was introduced to the incomparable Titanic Thomas. The introduction came from Runyon, naturally. I was sitting at Lindy's when Runyon came up behind me and tapped the top of my fedora.

"Kid, there's a guy outside you'll want to meet."

"Who?"

Runyon smirked, like he was about to amaze and delight me.

"Right outside that door, standing in Times Square, is Titanic Thomas." Runyon leaned down to me and spoke softly. "He's come to New York to bust Arnold Rothstein."

I don't think my reaction was enthusiastic enough for Runyon. He'd told me about the great Titanic Thomas, rather like gold miners might share stories of the Lost Dutchman over a campfire. Alvin Thomas had blown out of Arkansas and quickly became the greatest road gambler and proposition man the country ever knew. He bet on everything, always with an angle that put the odds in his favor. He was a master of poker, dice, pool, golf, and anything else that gambling men bet on. He had an endless array of tricks, like throwing five hundred cards in a row across a room and into a hat. People would bet him he couldn't do one of his propositions, just to see how he did it. Some said he was called Titanic because he'd survived the sinking as a boy, but it wasn't true. In those days, when a gambler busted a man, he sunk him. Alvin Thomas was called Titanic because he could sink anybody.

Titanic had spent the last twenty years or so on the move, driving his roadster into a town, busting all the local gamblers and suckers, then moving on before he became too well known and somebody shot him. He always carried a pistol in his pocket and sometimes carried one of his series of wives in his car. Runyon said he was known to have killed four men who tried to rob him of winnings. He'd partnered with Nick the Greek in Chicago and they turned the Gold Coast into Poverty Row. Now, for the first time, he'd come to New York, looking to bust the greatest gambler in the biggest city. I'm not much for gambling, as I've said, but Runyon was born for this sort of story.

He pointed to a rube who was standing on the corner outside Lindy's, gazing up at the tall buildings.

"That's him."

I couldn't believe this was the legendary Titanic Thomas. He was tall and whippet-thin. His face was round and handsome, with high cheekbones and sharp eyes, but he wore the cheap checked suit, battered hat, and scuffed shoes of an Arkansas hick. I was later to learn that Titanic could be a classy dresser when he wanted to be, but these were his working clothes. He was hunting for prey and wanted to look an easy mark.

"Ti!" Runyon called as we walked over to him. "This is the fellow I mentioned, the reporter. Jimmy O'Neal, meet Titanic Thomas."

Titanic's narrow eyes looked me up and down as we shook hands. I had the sense that with that one scan he could discern how much of a gambler I was and how much money I had in my wallet.

"Shore pleased to meet you," he said in a backwoods drawl that was also part of his act. "Shore are some tall buildings in this city, yessir. You got any gamble in you, Mr. O'Neal?"

"Excuse me?"

"Well, it's plumb foolish of me, but these buildings being so tall, they make me all rambunctious. Tell you what. I'll bet you one thousand American dollars I can take this here shoe I got on my foot and I can throw it all the way to the top floor of the Park Central Hotel, one toss. Can't say fairer than that, be the easiest money you ever made.

Come on, Mr. O'Neal, take advantage of this Arkansas rube, it's all right. Let's gamble."

This was crazy.

"You're saying you can make one throw and get your shoe all the way to the top floor of the Park Central?"

Titanic smiled an innocent smile.

"That's the bet, Mr. New York man. You know you want to see me try."

I glanced at Runyon, who was studiously watching the passing traffic.

"Mr. Thomas," I finally said, "my father is a very wise man who owns a bookstore in Independence, Missouri. He once said to me, 'Son, gambling is a foolish pastime and you should not gamble, but if you do gamble, do not gamble either with people who are more intelligent than you or with people who try too hard to seem less intelligent than you.' I've always taken his advice."

Titanic's face clouded.

"Well, doggone it, Runyon, if folks in New York don't have more gamble than this fellow, I came to the wrong town."

"You came to sink Arnold Rothstein, Ti, not some impoverished reporter. Come on, let's nosh a little and you can tell some stories."

Titanic looked at Lindy's dubiously.

"They have boiled squirrel in there? Been ages since I had some good boiled squirrel."

Even Runyon was nonplussed.

"I don't think so," he said. "Like to see you ask them, though."

"Rothstein in there?"

Runyon shook his head.

"Not now, but he always shows up eventually."

"Then I'll come back eventually," Titanic said. He turned to me and added, "Nice to meet you."

He shoved his hands in his coat pockets and ambled away, looking up at the tall buildings, radiating Arkansas country boy. Some folks were going to lose their money that day.

Runyon later told me he'd seen Ti pull the shoe trick on Irv Cobb just two days earlier. Cobb made the bet and Titanic tossed his shoe to a confederate in the Park Central elevator who took it to the top floor. Cobb groused, but you don't welsh on a man who carries a gun with four notches on it.

Titanic was known for placing huge bets when the time was right. Asked if a game had a limit, his automatic response was "Sky's the limit." So, when Runyon put a Titanic character in the story that became *Guys and Dolls*, he named him Sky Masterson. I always preferred his real nickname, Titanic: the man who could sink anybody.

15

A Rat Reappears

Cornelius

One afternoon, a few weeks after I met Titanic, I got a call at my apartment. I was not especially pleased when I picked up the phone to hear Dorothy Parker's voice.

"You're there, good. Don't you work anymore?"

"You called me, Dorothy. Don't knock me for answering."

"Listen, I need a favor."

I considered this. I hadn't had a woman in a long time and maybe Dorothy was interested in a return engagement.

"What favor?"

"You're a communist, right?"

"Not anymore. Not so's you'd notice, anyway. I kind of grew out of that."

"Oh, for Christ's sake, of course you're a communist. You went on and on about how you and Rosa Luxemburg were such great lovers, you must be a communist. Don't lie to me."

Coming from a drunk and a Park Avenue leftist, this was a little much.

"Just tell me what you want, Dorothy."

"You remember Sacco and Vanzetti, right? Even you must know about Sacco and Vanzetti."

She was referring, of course, to the Italian anarchists who'd been executed in Boston the previous year because they may or may not have blown up some people. The New York progressive crowd had been all hot about it at the time, thinking they were framed. Dorothy had been especially wrought up and devoted a lot of time to protesting their execution. It was one of those stories that hadn't interested me and I didn't pay much attention to it. I didn't have an opinion on the case, except the opinion that most of their supporters whom I met were rich and among the first people Rosa Luxemburg would have humbled if our crazy communist revolution in Germany had succeeded.

"I remember Sacco and Vanzetti," I said.

"Well, Heywood Brown thinks there may be new evidence that will show those boys didn't commit the murders!"

"Little late, isn't it? What's this supposed new evidence?"

"You dope! If we had the new evidence, would I be wasting my time talking to you? Here's the thing. I just came from a meeting of progressives at the Waldorf—"

"The Waldorf?"

I was torn between amusement and indignation, but she went on, oblivious. She was the queen of irony, but she wasn't always much for turning her perceptive gaze back on herself.

"Broun says he's heard there are witnesses in Manhattan somewhere who could show the whole case was a frame-up if they told what they knew. We were given assignments to comb the city to look for those witnesses. I'm supposed to talk to the members of a group down on the Lower East Side that's involved in the cause."

"What cause?"

"*The* cause, you twit! Communism!"

"Are you a communist, Dorothy?"

"You know me better than that. Last thing I joined was the human race and I've regretted it ever since. For Christ's sweet sake, O'Neal, these Massachusetts boys were hanged just because they were communist and Italian. We can't let the government get away with that."

"Does this group on the Lower East Side have a name?"

"Jimmy, they're not a singing group, they're a secret communist organization. I don't know of any name for them. They probably don't have a mascot, either."

"What do you want from me?"

"They meet every Tuesday night at eight in a little Italian joint on Mott Street," Dorothy said. "I need you to walk me in there and walk me out again. I don't know much about these fellows. I figure it won't hurt to have a male escort and you almost qualify."

I thought about it. Dorothy was poison for long periods, but she could be fun in small doses and watching her play at secret agent could be amusing.

"Dorothy, I don't know why I'm saying this, but I'll go. If nothing else, I want to see you crack wise with one of those seedy Italian bomb-thrower types."

She snickered.

"It is pretty funny, I have to admit. You should see Benchley. He was assigned to canvas a tough neighborhood in Brooklyn and he dressed up in overalls, a black turtleneck sweatshirt, and a soft cap. He looked like Wimpy trying to pass for a Bowery Boy."

"Pick me up at seven-thirty tonight, Dorothy," I said. "You pay for the cab."

The meeting was a frost, as I figured it would be. We knocked on a dingy door in Little Italy. It opened to reveal a hulking brute who obviously had no intention of letting us in. Behind him, swarthy middle-aged men with droopy mustaches shouted passionately at each other in Italian. We looked ridiculous standing on the sidewalk trying to talk our way inside, Dorothy in a simple but chic black dress, a little hat with a veil, and the only silk stockings visible on Mott Street that night. As instructed, I dropped Rosa's name as quickly and loudly as I could, only to meet with a black stare. Dorothy's name drew no reaction at all. Apparently the brute didn't read *The New Yorker*. Finally, I took Dorothy firmly by the elbow and led her away as the door slammed shut behind us.

"What's the matter with them?" Dorothy fumed. "We're trying to help the cause and they won't even talk to us?"

"You aren't really dressed to relate to those fellows," I replied. "They probably thought you were with the Salvation Army."

"Salvation Army, my ass! I paid a hundred bucks for this dress!"

I steered her around the corner and over to Mulberry Street. I figured I'd buy her a cannoli at Ferrara's and a cab ride home, then see what the action was at Texas Guinan's. I was remembering why my tolerance for Dorothy's company had waned.

Suddenly, though, I realized it was a lovely night, unseasonably warm for early spring. Mulberry is one of my favorite New York streets, far better in those days before tourists took it over: the smells of garlic and peppers and red sauce, pushcarts lazily rolling along with their wares of Italian ice and sausage rolls, dark-haired boys playing stickball, fat old men in the chairs on the sidewalk taking in the evening, fat old women sitting on their stoops laughing and gossiping. Music wafted from the buildings, lively tarantellas and heartbreaking ballads, even opera. I had not yet seen Italy, but Mulberry Street seemed like a perfect re-creation, a slice of the old country lovingly reconstructed in the midst of the Manhattan slums. Since the neighborhood was under the protection of Joe "the Boss" Masseria, there was no safer place in the city.

Even Dorothy Parker settled down under the influence of the warm breeze and the sleepy Mediterranean street. We crowded into Ferrara's and found a small table where we could eat our cannoli and drink our espresso. Dorothy told me stories of *The New Yorker*, the theatre, the Algonquin. I talked of Lindy's, the criminal courts, the gamblers, the press. Realizing that all these worlds and many more were here, in this town at this one time, made me ache with love for New York. I knew I could never live anywhere else and I never have. Misanthropic and ridden with personal devils as she was, Dorothy felt just the same. It made for a bond of sorts, I suppose.

As we strolled out of Ferrara's and down the sidewalk again, I contemplated asking Dorothy to join me at Texas Guinan's. I knew the downsides, but suddenly I was again enjoying her company and I hadn't been with a woman in weeks. I was about to make the suggestion when I saw something that drove that and everything else out of my head.

We were approaching the door of the social club where Runyon had brought me on our first night together, when he'd introduced me to Joe Masseria. The same young tough was loitering near the door, screening the entrants. What stopped me cold were the two men who stood at the entrance to the club. One was handsomely dressed in a dark, well-fitting pinstriped suit with a white fedora. He had his hands on the lapels of the other, pulling him forward, lecturing him in a quiet voice. The other man was much shabbier, a typical street rat common to Brooklyn and the Lower East Side. I knew immediately that the well-dressed man was Charlie Lucano. I gazed intently at the other, for he looked familiar. Dorothy pulled at my arm and asked why I'd stopped, but I shook her off. I then remembered who the man was, even though I had only seen him once. He was Paddy Maloney, one of only two Irish survivors of the Adonis Club Massacre.

My instinct was to hide, but the two men seemed so involved with each other that it was clear they wouldn't notice us. Lucano apparently finished lecturing the man, for he shoved him backward into the chest of the tough young doorman. Maloney puffed up for a moment, thought better of it, and walked off down the street in the opposite direction from where we were standing. Lucano shook his head and went into the club, likely to meet his boss. I knew this was my one and only chance to question Paddy Maloney and maybe, just maybe, get to the bottom of the Adonis Club Massacre.

"Dorothy, get a cab and go home. I have to follow that man."

As I started to hurry away, she grabbed my coattail and yanked me back.

"Screw that. If you have to follow him, I'm going with you."

It was a choice between letting her come along or knocking her down and the latter would have attracted some attention. I shushed her, put my arm around her shoulders like we were sweethearts, and we started off after Paddy. Fortunately, we didn't have to go far. Paddy strode quickly down Mulberry, across Canal, through the remaining few blocks of Italian residents that then still held on south of Canal, and into the burgeoning narrow streets of Chinatown. While much smaller, New York's Chinatown in 1928 would be familiar to anyone who knew the neighborhood today. Vendors and shoppers screamed at each other in Chinese, standing over displays piled high with fish and chickens and unidentifiable meats, as well as herbs and vegetables. The streets were improbably narrow and impossibly crowded, making it easy to trail our conspicuous Irish target without being spotted. We almost lost him though, when he suddenly took a hard right down an even narrower alley which was in stark contrast to the busy thoroughfare we were on, being nearly deserted.

I backed Dorothy against the wall of the building at the mouth of the alley and we watched Paddy walk away from us. As I expected, he darted a furtive look back and forth, then hustled up a stoop and into a building on the downtown side of the alley. I waited, waving at Mrs. Parker to be quiet, and was rewarded by the sight of a light on the fourth floor coming on.

"Dorothy, I have to talk to that guy," I said earnestly. "You don't want to be there."

"Don't tell me what I want or don't want, Jimmy O'Neal." Dorothy's black eyes flashed angrily. "This was supposed to be my night, for me to help Sacco and Vanzetti. If I have to tell everybody I got nothing, at least I want a little excitement. Is this about the Adonis Club killings?"

That stood me up straight.

"How'd you know that?"

"It was your big story and you dropped it like a hot brick. I figure it's been eating at you all this time that you never cracked it. Who's the lamster? Let me guess: Paddy Maloney."

My mouth dropped open. Cracked it? The lamster? Where did Dorothy Parker, Girl Detective come from?

"Don't stand there looking like a fish," Dorothy said. "Woollcott and I make a hobby of murders, you know that. We followed your stories on the Adonis Club. Friend Paddy went to the bathroom at a very strategic moment, just before the shooting started. You noticed that and so did we."

Dorothy straightened my tie and patted my shoulders.

"Come on, Jimmy. Let's go solve those murders."

What could I do? Dorothy Parker was beyond most men and way beyond me. I told her to follow my lead and we went down the alley and into the apartment building where Paddy Maloney was hiding out.

Building security then wasn't the way it is now. We met no lock as we went into the entryway, tramped as quietly as we could up four flights of stairs, and reached the door of what I figured must be Paddy's apartment. I knew he'd have a gun and he'd looked nervous talking to Charlie Lucano, though most people did. It didn't seem prudent just to knock. I was considering options when Dorothy astonished me again, by rapping on the door and bursting into a sing-song stream of Chinese-sounding gibberish. At least it was gibberish to me, and no doubt to Paddy. He called repeatedly through the door that she should beat it, but Dorothy's recitation just grew louder and more insistent.

Finally, able to stand it no more, Paddy opened the door a crack to throw her out, giving me the moment I was waiting for. I kicked against the door as hard as I could and followed it with my shoulder, knocking Paddy backward and opening the door sufficiently that Dorothy and I could tumble in.

Paddy was stripped down to his pants and undershirt, but of more interest at the moment was the fact that he held in his right fist a cocked revolver. I slammed my hand down on it and sent it flying across the floor. We rolled around on each other for a bit, then Dorothy once again came through by picking up the revolver, putting it in Paddy's face, and ordering him to freeze. He responded wonderfully.

"You speak Chinese?" I demanded when I caught my breath.

"Hell, no, that was just nonsense," Dorothy said, holding the gun with a two-handed grip, pointing it at Paddy's skinny chest. "I once played a coolie girl in a school play."

"You are certainly full of surprises."

"Who are you people?" Paddy demanded.

"Excellent question, Paddy."

I stood, shut the door and took the revolver from Dorothy.

"I think you'll be pleasantly surprised. Get up from there, let's move into the living room, and we'll talk."

Dorothy flashed a smile at him and helped him to his feet. A bottle of some sort of homemade hooch was on the table so I took a pull and handed it to Paddy, who took two.

"My name is James Cornelius O'Neal. We only met once, but I'm betting you know who I am."

Paddy looked morose and jumpy at the same time, like the trapped rat that he was.

"You're the reporter."

"That's right, Paddy, the crime reporter for the *Journal*. You may not be much of a reader, but I expect you read my stories on the Adonis Club Massacre, didn't you?"

Paddy glanced over at Dorothy. "Who's the skirt?"

"The skirt," I said quickly, "is a very well-known and talented lady whom you should forget you ever met. I want you to focus on me right now."

"I'm not telling you nothing."

I took another swig of the whiskey, which was vile, but in Prohibition one made do.

"I don't want you to tell me anything, Paddy. I don't need you to tell me anything."

Dorothy narrowed her eyes at me, but I ignored her.

"Let me tell you some things that I know, things that are obvious. The Adonis Club was a set-up. The Italians paid you to lead Lonergan and his friends into the club that night. You knew Frankie Yale would be there with his boys. They knew you'd lead Lonergan in there. You went to the men's room just before the shooting started so you'd survive. You were paid off by the wops and you went underground and now here you are, living with chinks and begging for scraps from Charlie Lucano. How'm I doing so far?"

"Fuck you."

I considered Mr. Maloney. Superficially, he was a typical Irish bhoy from Brooklyn: nasty, balding, skinny, consumptive, face shaped like a potato. Somewhere, though, buried deep in those dark eyes, I saw a spark suggestive of an active intelligence. Paddy was studying us and thinking about his chances. Just like I hoped.

"You are in a tough spot, Paddy. Your Irish buddies must have been getting suspicious or you'd still be with them, so they're looking to kill you. Your eyetie buddies think you're a rat and if they get tired of you, they'll kill you dead and feel like they were scraping shit off their shoes. What did they promise you, Paddy? Let me guess: the scissors-grinding concession at the Festival of San Gennaro?"

I handed back the bottle and he took a long drink.

"They told me it was big," he said. "Told me I'd be their guy to run the Irish longshoremen on the docks. Said a dago couldn't do that. They said it'd be a hundred grand a year minimum for me."

I nodded.

"Get anything up front?"

"Five grand. They said it was peanuts next to what was coming."

I nodded. What a chump. Always get it up front.

"So you're not running the Irish longshoremen?"

Paddy smiled ruefully.

"That was such shit, I tell ye. Yale is running the whole dock now, whether the Irish like it or not. What can they do? Like you said, here I am, begging for scraps from those dago bastards. It's just a question

142

whether my old friends find me or the wops get tired of me and take me out. Fuck." He pronounced it "Fook."

We sat silently a moment, contemplating the sad fate of Paddy Maloney. Dorothy glanced over at me, wondering where this was going. I wondered, too.

"One little thing I'm curious about."

I didn't look at Paddy, just let the words lie there a moment.

"I thought Frankie Yale ran the docks, but you were just talking with Charlie Lucano. He's Masseria's man. How big is this?"

I didn't mention seeing Yale and Lucano and Capone and Anastasia and Altieri, all cozy at Yale's beach cottage the morning after the massacre, but that was the memory that had gnawed at me for more than two years.

"What's big to you, Mr. Reporter?" Paddy was getting drunk now, which took a lot. "A million a year? Five million a year? That's nothing, boyo. Word is there's a deal to be made with a new heroin source, a big one, and that'll mean more money than this town has ever seen, it will. Bootlegging's good right now but it won't last because liquor will be legal again soon. Heroin will last forever. It's a whole new world."

Dorothy broke her silence.

"It sounds to me like you need to disappear, Mr. Maloney."

"Fuckin' right I need to disappear, darlin'. Got any ideas?"

Dorothy smiled, the smile I had seen a thousand times in the Rose Room at the Algonquin, just before she skewered someone with her acid tongue.

"I have a friend, Mr. Maloney. A friend who likes murder. And he could use a roommate."

So it was. I sprang for the taxi and we took Paddy to Alexander Woollcott's new apartment on the third floor of a luxury building at the very end of 52nd Street, overlooking the East River. Woollcott was understandably reluctant until we explained Paddy's story and then he was on the case with the enthusiasm of an effete bloodhound sniffing a bloody kidney.

With my star witness safely stashed in Woollcott's spare bedroom and Dorothy placed in a cab and sent home, I paused for a moment to watch the dawn come up over the East River. What in bloody hell to do next?

16

An Honest Cop

Cornelius

My cousin Mikey looked like he was trying to pass a kidney stone. Actually, he was just trying to process what I'd told him, that I had stashed a witness who could crack the Adonis Club Massacre and pin the murders on the unholy confederation of Frankie Yale, Al Capone, and Charlie Lucano, all looking to solidify control over the Red Hook docks to allow the smuggling of massive quantities of heroin from a mysterious new source. This was heady stuff for a mere patrolman, even one as well-connected and politically astute as Mikey Toolan.

It was a quiet Saturday afternoon in Red Hook. We were sitting in Mikey's parlor, drinking beer, his family sent away so we could have a private conversation. Mikey sat in a sleeveless undershirt. He sipped his beer slowly as he considered the ramifications of what I told him.

According to Paddy Maloney, heroin was about to flow into the city at unprecedented levels and the Italians wanted to make sure the White Hand was never going to challenge them for control of it. Thus, Lucano and Anastasia approached him about leading Peg Leg Lonergan into the trap at the Adonis Club, bribing him for his cooperation. Maloney said that Frankie Yale was in charge of the deal and Capone was just a handy gun who happened to be in town and owed Yale a return favor for the O'Banion hit. Maloney knew that Lucano normally worked for Joe the Boss, but he didn't think Masseria was involved in the plan, or at least he never heard his name associated with it.

"Mikey, listen to me," I said, leaning forward on his sofa for emphasis. "This is very, very, very big. If you get credit for solving the massacre and putting away Frankie Yale, you can write your own ticket."

He laughed ruefully.

"Ticket to the morgue, you mean."

"That's the problem," I acknowledged. "Half the cops and judges in town take money from men like Yale and Masseria. That's why I need you. You must know who the honest cops are. That's what we need. We're family, Mikey."

Of course, I hadn't visited the Toolans' home more than twice in nine years despite numerous invitations, but still, family is family.

Mikey put his face in his hands.

"You still don't understand what you're dealing with, Jimmy. When you say half the cops and judges are crooked, that's an understatement. Just about all of them are on the take to somebody, most of the time to a lot of people. It's hard for a cop to stay honest in this town. It's like the old saying: an honest cop is someone who once you bribe him, he stays bribed."

"You telling me you can't help me, Mikey?"

There was a very long pause. Mikey's big brow was furrowed and his lips were smacking in and out. He was obviously thinking hard. Finally, when I was thinking he might never come out of his trance, he spoke.

"All right, Jimmy, but for something this big, we have to go to the top. The very top."

"Coolidge?"

"No, not Coolidge, you dummy. The mayor."

I spat a mouthful of beer back into my glass.

"Are you nuts? Jimmy Walker is supposed to be the crookedest mayor this town's ever seen! Word is he's on the payroll of everybody from Arnold Rothstein to the parish card clubs."

Mikey raised his hand to soothe me.

"Don't believe all you hear. This is big. Sure, Walker takes graft, just like everybody, but a guy in his position can't turn a blind eye to something this big. Anyway, I never heard that Walker is tied to Masseria or any of the Italians. Arnold Rothstein, sure. He's close to Rothstein. Is Rothstein involved in this?"

"I don't think so."

"There you go, then. Walker's the only guy with enough clout to deal with this and it'd be great politics for him. Plus, I know him a little. He owes me for some favors I did him. If I'm going to tell anybody about this and try to help you, it's got to be the mayor."

I stood up, disgusted.

"Then forget it, Mikey. I can't risk it, Walker's too dirty. I'll figure out something else."

I headed for the door, Mikey following.

"You're making a mistake, kid. Walker's your best chance. If you don't trust him, you better forget this whole thing."

"I should trust Jimmy Walker? After all Runyon's told me about him? Not a chance."

Mikey's voice followed me as I walked down his stoop.

"God be with you, Jimmy," he said.

That evening, I went to the Algonquin to forget my troubles by watching the game at the Thanatopsis Literary and Inside Straight Club. Every Saturday night, FPA presided over a poker game in a suite at the Algonquin, attended by many of the Round Table regulars. Runyon sneered at the practice, saying the Algonquin writers wanted to play at poker so they could pretend they were real newspapermen. Of course, Runyon despised the Round Table folks. I was actually lunching at the Round Table rarely by this time as the competition to be witty was annoying. Still, I saw no harm in showing up for the poker game occasionally.

I walked in and was met with the usual clouds of tobacco smoke and high-spirited chatter of the gamblers seated around the poker table in the middle of the room. I stopped cold when I recognized the player directly across the table from me, seated between Harold Ross and that fat eunuch Woollcott, grinning and puffing a cigar and raking in chips. Paddy Maloney! The shiftless Irish hoodlum, my precious witness who was supposed to be hiding for his life in Woollcott's apartment, sat there laughing and joking and twitting George Kaufman on losing the last hand. Once word got out that Maloney was talking to me, which now it clearly would, he was a dead man and I probably was, too.

Obviously, one person was responsible for this.

"Woollcott!" My voice snapped across the smoky room and stilled the chatter. "I need to talk to you out in the hall, please."

Woollcott was unperturbed. He sucked daintily at his damn cigarette holder and gave me a mildly pained expression.

"Mr. O'Neal, why so rude? Oh, are you concerned about Paddy? No worries, we're all friends here. I wouldn't introduce Paddy to anyone who wasn't already a friend. After all, the mob is after him." Woollcott actually giggled. "Isn't that exciting, everyone?"

"Mr. Woollcott's been taking grand care of me," Maloney chipped in. "We went to the theatre and last weekend we had a party for his friends out at his country place. Oh, it was grand."

Maloney was plainly drunk as a bishop and it made him expansive.

"Sure, we had the grandest time," he continued. "Mr. Kaufman was there, and Mr. Ross here, and some lovely ladies and we played the grandest games."

"Paddy was especially good at the game of Murder," Kaufman chipped in.

"Oi, you're the wise one, you are," said Paddy, his brogue filling the room. "You should hear the things this man says. He could be a writer, he could."

"I doubt it," snarled FPA. "Let's play cards."

It was hopeless. However furious I was, however much I wanted to put my fist in Alex Woollcott's fat face, there was no keeping the Maloney secret now. I'd agonized over telling Mikey, but felt it was necessary. Now, Woollcott's unquenchable thirst to be the smartest, most admired wit in the room led him to parade Maloney before his Algonquin friends repeatedly, like a new pet poodle, doubtlessly telling them all that Paddy Maloney was a critical witness in the Adonis Club case and Woollcott was going to crack it wide open. Why did I ever trust that buffoon? Why did Dorothy? Now that this many people knew the story, it was bound to get to the mob and they were bound to react with deadly force, against Maloney and me and maybe Woollcott, too.

I stayed at that game until I could get Maloney out and take him to my apartment, with him whining and complaining about being separated from his friend Alex. I figured I had maybe two days at the outside before Yale and his minions tumbled to what I had planned and came after us. Two days to find an honest cop in New York City.

17

Mr. Rothstein Reveals His Nature

Cornelius

As it turned out, two days were too many. It was on the very day after the Thanatopsis game that all hell broke loose.

I barely slept that night, stewing over where to stash Maloney while I searched like Diogenes for an honest cop in New York City. Maloney's piggish snores echoing through the apartment didn't help my repose. He wasn't a happy Irishman when I roughly shook him awake shortly after dawn.

"Oi, what you pushing me for?" he snarled.

"I'm trying to keep you alive, you goon. Throw some water on your face and let's go."

"No breakfast, are ye sayin'?"

"Charlie Lucano will have you for breakfast, and me too, if we don't get you somewhere safer than this. Move!"

Lacking any better ideas, I had decided to take Maloney to my cousin Mikey's place in Brooklyn and beg him to hide the crook away in his cellar for a few days. I didn't know if Mikey would do it, but I thought his wife might take pity on me and make him agree. Maloney completed his toilet, which consisted of a considerable amount of peeing and burping, and I hustled him out the door and down to the street. I stood on the sidewalk in front of the little grocery store next to my apartment building and waved for a cab.

It was neatly done. As I stood waving my hand, a covered truck with panels advertising a fruit company slammed to a stop right in front of me. A machine-gun barrel immediately poked out of the passenger side window, covering both Maloney and me. The doors at the rear of the truck swung open and four hoods swarmed out, encircled us, and pulled and pushed the two of us to the back of the truck, up and into the rear compartment, clambering in after us and slamming the truck doors behind them. There were benches along the sides of the compartment where we sat, the hoodlums covering us with handguns and not saying a word. We didn't speak, either. There didn't seem to be much to say. The truck started rattling along, bouncing on underslung springs so that it was all I could do to keep seated on the bench and not bite off the tip of my tongue. Paddy was in bad shape, hands trembling, teeth chattering, but even he found no words as he looked at the impassive and brutal faces of the mobsters guarding us.

There were no windows in the compartment and the truck made enough turns that I lost all track of where we might be going. I recall it as being about twenty minutes gone by, but it could have been more or less, when the truck pulled to a stop and I heard muffled shouts giving orders. There was the sound of an overhead door slowly opening, then the truck moved forward and stopped again, then the sound of the door closing. At this point, one of the hoodlums threw open the back doors of the truck, revealing that we were in some sort of small garage or storage building with just enough room for the truck and the few men inside. They grabbed our arms and led us up a few steps, through a door, and then up more steps in a dirty narrow stairway typical of the slums. We went up three, maybe four flights. At each floor, there was an industrial-sized door closed tight, bearing a hand-lettered sign that read "The workers here do not speak English; do not attempt to talk to them." On the top floor, our escorts slid open such a door and pushed us inside.

A peculiar stench had been growing worse as we ascended the stairs and it hit us with an oppressive blast once the door slid open. Inside, in the dim light, I could see the cause. We were in some sort of bizarre butchery. Chinese men in filthy white garments smeared with blood and grease were hurriedly, silently doing their work at and around a series of wooden tables that filled the large loft-like space. The entire floor was just this one cavernous room. Around the circumference of the space, skinned carcasses hung from open rafters. I noted what I believed were pigs, goats, sheep, and some sort of monkey, and there were a number of animals I didn't recognize and didn't want to think about. Well-muscled young Chinese men and boys would cut down a carcass, let it fall across their backs and carry it over to one of the tables, where an older Chinese wielding a bloody cleaver would quickly and efficiently hack it to pieces. Bone would be roughly separated from the meat, at least for the most part, and then the butcher would slide the meat onto a pan which a boy would carry to one of three meat grinders at the far wall, to be dumped into the chute and ground to chopstick-sized pieces.

That was the basic work flow that I took in at a glance. On a second look, my eyes fixed on three white men over near the grinders, one seated and the others standing and flanking him. I was disheartened to see that the two men were Legs Diamond and Albert Anastasia, but the sight of the man seated in the middle gave me a moment of foolish hope. It was Arnold Rothstein.

To that moment, I still harbored the common delusion about Rothstein. He was a gambler and a bootlegger and he was no doubt crooked in some ways, but he was not in the same league with men like Joe Masseria or Frankie Yale. Rothstein hung out at Lindy's, and went to shows and ball games, and knew all kinds of politicians and society types, and was friends with Damon Runyon. He was fun, like Polly Adler or Fanny Brice's husband Nicky Arnstein, the sort of shady character who livened up parties and made the Broadway scene so stimulating. Even though bootlegging was a rough trade, requiring Rothstein to associate with hard boys like Diamond, Rothstein himself couldn't be all that bad a fellow or he wouldn't be so prominent and all those politicians and judges wouldn't take his money or drink his illegal booze. This gave me some hope that Rothstein's presence in the room, when I had never associated him with the Adonis Club Massacre or Frankie Yale or Charlie Lucano, might be some sort of good omen.

I was very wrong, of course. This was the day I began to learn the truth about Arnold Rothstein. He knew how to act the harmless rogue, but he was as vicious and brutal as any of them. In fact, it was Arnold Rothstein, with his brilliance, imagination, business sense, and sheer sociopathic malice, who created the organized crime template that his successors Lucano, Meyer Lansky, and others would follow. He was about to show me just how violent he could be.

Rothstein was sitting on a little wooden chair, primly as always, munching on an apple. It would have been laughable in that setting, but nobody was in the mood to laugh. I thought Rothstein was someone I could reason with, so I spoke up.

"A.R., what's this all about?"

He raised his hand to silence me. He gestured at the fruit in his hand.

"This is a particularly good apple," he said. "They are hard to find at this time of year. Please let me finish it."

My mouth dropped in astonishment, but he kept chewing away. After three more bites, the apple was down to the core. He removed a handkerchief from his side pocket, carefully folded the core in it, and placed it back in his pocket. He swallowed, covered a small belch with his hand, and looked blandly at us.

"Now," he said. "Mr. Diamond, please kill Mr. Maloney."

Paddy barely had time to raise his hands and say "Wait." Diamond smiled, pulled a gun from beneath his coat and shot Paddy four times in the chest and abdomen. Paddy buckled at the knees and collapsed to the floor like a suit falling off a hanger. Diamond gestured and two of the hoodlums who had delivered us raised Maloney's body off the floor and dragged it away. I was relieved that they didn't throw him in the grinders with the goats and monkeys. Poor Paddy never got the breaks in life.

By this time, my teeth were chattering like Paddy's had been. So much for the thought that Rothstein would help the situation. As always in a tight spot, I wondered what Riley would do. I started looking around for a chance to run, but felt hoodlum arms grabbing mine and holding me in place.

"Mr. Anastasia," Rothstein said. "Please."

I stiffened, expecting Anastasia to pull his piece and do me in. Instead, Anastasia simply walked over to me, his gorilla face staring grimly. Suddenly, he planted one enormous fist in my gut, then the other. The men holding me let go, while I bent and dry-heaved. Anastasia calmly put on a pair of brass knuckles. He fired a left into my kidney, which straightened me up and allowed him to hit me in the ribcage with a right. When I fell, the men lifted and held me so the beating could go on. I'd been beaten before, notably in a German prison shortly after World War I, and I would be beaten again, but this was a bad one. Anastasia was a bull-strong longshoreman and he knew how to hurt a man. When he was done, I lay in a heap at Rothstein's feet. I was a mess, but I was alive.

The Chinese workers hardly glanced up, either when Paddy was shot or while I was beaten. They simply kept on chopping up carcasses and feeding them to the grinders. Admirable work ethic, I suppose.

"Prop him up," Rothstein said.

Another wooden chair appeared and I was hoisted up and plopped onto it, jolting my aching ribs such that I nearly passed out. Rothstein hitched his pants up on his knees and looked intently at me.

"Don't try to talk right now, Mr. O'Neal. I am sure you are in a great deal of pain. Unlike some of my associates, I do not enjoy violence for its own sake. However, at times, violence is a necessary tactic in the businesses in which I am engaged. In this case, I felt that the dramatic dispatch of Mr. Maloney and your own rough treatment by Mr. Anastasia were required to ensure that you understand how serious is your situation."

The room was swimming before me. Each time I breathed, a demon seemed to be striking a hammer on my injured ribs.

"What are you talking about?" I croaked.

"Shh, please don't talk. You will only embarrass yourself if you pretend to be even more ignorant than you are."

Rothstein took a deep breath.

"Like you, I am an ambitious man, but my ambitions are far greater than yours," he said. "I see crime as a business potentially greater in scope than oil, steel, or any of the various industries that have so enriched the propertied class in this country. Crime, after all, is simply profiting from human weakness, and what commodity is more abundantly, inexhaustibly available than human weakness? I mean to be the Rockefeller of crime, Mr. O'Neal. And for a number of sound business reasons, the product of the future is clearly going to be narcotics."

I remembered Paddy Maloney telling me of the great amounts of money that would be made from heroin and opium smuggled through the Red Hook docks and saying that control of that traffic was behind the Adonis Club killings. But Rothstein? I'd seen Yale, Lucano, Anastasia, Capone, and Willie Altieri at Yale's place after the massacre. What did Rothstein have to do with these Italian hooligans?

"So, eliminating Mr. Yale's competition for control of the docks was an important business objective and the Adonis Club incident achieved that. The Irish White Hand has been in total disarray since then and Italian control is complete. As you by now have realized, I work closely with many of those Italian gentlemen, the best and most forward-thinking of them like Mr. Anastasia and Mr. Lucano and, at least at one time, Mr. Yale. I watched your investigation of the Adonis Club affair, doubting you could get to the bottom of it, but alert to the potential danger. Then you made that rather silly attempt to purloin my notebooks. Yes, I knew all along that was you, since I foolishly allowed you to accompany Damon and myself to see the art in my office and you got to see where I kept my notebooks. I took steps, then, to get you under my control. A few days ago, when I heard that you found Mr. Maloney and intended to use his testimony to expose the purpose behind the Adonis Club killings, I knew that it was time to exercise that control."

Rothstein stood and looked down at me.

"You see, the reality is that I own you, Mr. O'Neal. Here is why. First, you will recall that whole business with J.P. Morgan. You will probably not be surprised to hear that the desk of the Pope's Usurer was in fact actually stolen from its owner by associates of mine. The bill of sale was forged. A Vantine's ship brought the desk into this country. Vantine's workmen in my employ installed within it a hidden compartment, and within that compartment is a certain quantity of heroin, straight from my supplier in China."

In my wounded condition, I was struggling to follow. I was beginning to sense that a web was ensnaring me.

"I arranged for you to broker the transaction with Mr. Morgan to gain control over you and because, incidentally, it amused me to use an anti-Semite like Morgan for my purposes. Think about it. If I drop the word to one of my friendly police officials, Mr. Morgan's own home can be raided and not only will the police find the stolen desk of the Pope's Usurer, they will find heroin in a secret compartment within." Rothstein flashed one of his imitation smiles. "Very amusing. I am enough of a realist to recognize that a man like J.P. Morgan will never suffer more than embarrassment over this. He will fume and deny and say he was misled by the criminal behind it all, whom he will identify as none other than James Cornelius O'Neal, whose endorsement"— he flashed the check from his breast pocket—" will be found on this canceled check from Mr. Morgan, paying for the stolen desk. You will say all kinds of things implicating one Mr. Arnold Rothstein, but Mr. Morgan will never have heard of me and my friends in the court system will have little trouble classifying yours as the ravings of a vicious criminal and putting you away for many, many years."

My mind raced through the events surrounding the Morgan transaction. By God, he was right. I was cooked.

"I see you recognize the seriousness of your situation now," Rothstein said. "There is one more thing for you to know. I have to be absolutely sure of your loyalty, because I need to entrust you with a very important assignment that will ensure that I will be at the head of the heroin trade in this country for the foreseeable future. I thought long and hard, deciding that while it was regrettable, I needed to arrange one more act of violence in order to be sure I had your absolute fealty."

Rothstein nodded at the henchmen behind me, who placed firm hands on my arms. I was neither in physical nor mental condition to resist.

"The key to a man is his father," Rothstein said.

I stiffened in the henchmen's hands.

"Long ago, I made inquiries with friends in Kansas City about your family situation. I learned of your son, Walter Hal, and your parents, Jack and Rose, and your friendship with the Riley family."

I was seething at this point, but what could I do?

"I sent a man to your family when I learned you had found Mr. Maloney. I just heard from him. He has done the violence I ordered. You will need to go to Independence and I understand that. When you return, I will inform you of what I require."

A name and a face came to me. Hal. I'd seen so little of my son, by my own choice. Even the image of his face in my mind was fuzzy. Suddenly, the thought that these barbarians might have harmed that little boy seemed to me the worst atrocity I could imagine, one I could not bear.

Rothstein spoke to me for several more minutes, telling me exactly what his minions had done in Independence and lecturing me on how helpless I was to do anything but obey his commands. Then he nodded to the henchmen. I was hustled out, back down the stairs, back in the truck, back to my apartment.

When I got there, a telegram was waiting. I already knew what it would say.

Part Three

The Death
of
Arnold Rothstein

18

A Break from Reading

Jim

When I finished the chapter of the Cornelius notebook that was set in the Chinese butchery, I joined Riley on the patio in back of his house. He sat looking out on the desert. I drew up a chair next to him.

"I need a break," I said.

"How far are you?"

"Paddy Maloney just got killed. Rothstein says he has Cornelius in his power."

Riley nodded.

"Well, he did. Cornelius was in bad trouble. Bad enough that it even reached us in Independence."

I looked at the cigarette pack on the table in front of Riley and was thankful I never smoked. It was bad enough for me that I tried to keep up with Riley's drinking: trying to smoke with him while I worked on the notebooks would have killed me.

"This has been a little strange," I said. "The first book, you and Cornelius were together all the time, or almost. Now I've read from 1919 to 1928 and it seems like you were never in the same town."

"Pretty much true," Riley said. "Cornelius loved New York and never wanted to leave it. Not even for his son."

"I can't imagine how Grandpa Jimmy could have abandoned his son like that," I said. "Dad never really talked about it, not with me."

"Not with anyone, I expect. Hal wouldn't have talked about that sort of thing, not about his feelings or anything that might make his family look bad. Learned that from me, maybe."

"What were you doing all those years that Grandpa Jimmy was enjoying Broadway?"

Riley took a deep breath, closed his eyes, and started talking.

19

Death Comes to Independence

Riley

While Cornelius was in New York, I was farming. It was exciting as it sounds. Real life has lots of parts that ain't so exciting.

Oh, farming's good for some folks, it just never was for me. Don't know how I stuck at it long as I did. There was one little adventure in the early twenties, where Churchill gave me a job to do that I might talk about some other time. Mostly, I farmed, I went back to boxing at Skelly's, and I drank more than I should. Not much to tell. I grew a mustache some time back then — I accomplished that much.

Ma was a wonder. Strong a woman as ever was. One time, I saw her lift up a fallen log ten feet long and throw it out of her way like it was a toothpick. She could plow a field with a mule, bake apple pies, choose what crops to plant each year, and sew baby outfits for Fern and Hal, sometimes all in one day. But Ma had rigid ideas about menfolk and womenfolk. She stepped in when she had to, when I was off at war, but now that I was back, there was a man in the house again and she didn't think it was fitting for her to run things. She made that plain to me on my first night home. I was in charge of the farm.

Our family had eighty acres out east of town, about ten miles from our homestead on the edge of Independence. Doesn't seem like much now, but in those days it was enough to sustain a family if you knew what you were doing. Trouble was I didn't. Pa had tried to teach me when he was alive, but I never listened and he wasn't the sort of father who'd make me. As a kid, I'd run off to Kansas City to box at Skelly's and then I ran off to Mexico and eventually to the war. Farming was just tedious labor and I never got the knack for it. Ma would have been better off staying in charge or letting Jesus the migrant run the farm than giving it over to me. She did what she did and I had to make the best of it.

We raised Fern and Hal, of course. Cute little kids: Hal such a little soldier, Fern so like Marta. They were inseparable, more than brother and sister, and I guess they're still like that. Marta did most of the raising, to be honest. I kept reminding Marta how she told me she wanted to find a job, something to do outside the house, but she never could settle on anything. Kind of like me, that way. Maybe she was scared to try new things. I know I was. It's funny to me how Cornelius keeps making me out as brave all the time. I never felt brave, it was just that some things bothered me and some things, like fighting, didn't.

One thing I came to like was going with Jack O'Neal down to the colored neighborhood at Twelfth and Vine to listen to the jazz. You have to credit the Pendergast machine that ran Kansas City, it made Twelfth and Vine possible. The liquor flowed, Prohibition and all. The clubs lined the streets: the Subway, the Blue Room, the Boulevard Lounge, the Hi Hat, on and on. A few more years and those streets would jump to the music of Count Basie, Lester Young, Charlie Parker, and more. Jack and I would sit at the clubs and listen to bands like the one called Beenie, Bailey, and Dude, or BB&D. It was called that after the nicknames of the main players, but everybody called them Big, Black, and Dirty, because that's what they were. Wow, that music. Deep and rhythmic, like sex in your head.

I got to know Tom Pendergast over the years, since he was a boxing fan and took to betting on me when I fought at Skelly's. Once, one of his toadies told me to take a dive and I decked the guy. After that, Boss Tom let me alone and just made money gambling on me. He told me to come to him if I ever wanted any favors, which made me wonder if I was part of the Pendergast machine. I won most of my bouts, fighting middleweight.

Anyway, time went by. Cornelius only came to visit us once, which was a disappointment. I think it was 1923. He hardly had a word to say to his son. He took the train out, stayed a week, and the whole time he looked like he couldn't wait to leave. He didn't bond with Hal at all, didn't even tell his parents he'd been married and divorced. I only found out about that much later. It made me sad. I had no idea what Cornelius was up to in New York, except he worked for a newspaper. We didn't really enter into his story at all until 1928, right around the time Arnold Rothstein had him beat up in that Chinese butcher place, like the notebook said.

Around then, Jack O'Neal and I were down at the Blue Room, listening to Big, Black, and Dirty. It was soon going to be planting time, so I wanted one last night out. The band was really hot and tight that night, so we stayed a lot later than usual. Jack didn't drink much, but I had a lot of bourbon, which I've always held pretty well. Still, I let Jack drive us back to Independence.

Rose was already in bed when we let ourselves into the O'Neals' bookstore and went upstairs to the living quarters on the second floor. Jack was in mid-harangue about the 1928 election, whether the country had gotten broadminded enough that Al Smith could get the Democratic nomination, being he was a Catholic. Smith also favored getting rid of Prohibition, which suggested to me he had some sense. Mr. O'Neal being a Marxist, he didn't have much use for any of the candidates who might actually win, but he was rooting for Smith anyway.

"You got to understand, Walter, this country won't always be run by old Protestant white men," he said from his favorite position, squatting on the floor like an Indian with a coffee cup in one hand and a cigarette in the other. "First there'll be a Catholic president, then Jewish, then colored. Even a woman."

I nodded, deciding I shouldn't ask if there was any whiskey in the house. I never paid a lot of attention to Jack O'Neal's speechifying, but it was soothing to me. Like listening to Cornelius.

That's when the bad things started. There was a smash of shattering glass from downstairs. This wasn't one of those maybe-it's-something-maybe-it-isn't night noises where you wonder if you should get out of bed to check. Somebody had definitely broken a window downstairs, with no attempt to muffle the noise. Then we heard the front door of the shop open.

"Call the police," I told Jack.

165

I started for the stairs. Jack told me not to go down there, but I paid no attention. Figured it was probably a high school kid looking for spare change—real crime didn't happen in Independence. For a fleeting second, though, I did wish I had my gun.

I eased my way down the stairs. Only illumination was from a little night-light the O'Neals kept in the shop. When my foot made a noise on the step, there was a scurry down below like cockroaches when the light goes on. There were at least two of them, maybe three, but I wasn't sure.

"Get out of here now," I told them firmly, though the bourbon was probably slurring my words a bit. "Police have been called. You don't want to be here."

A book hit the floor somewhere to my right, from one of the back shelves of the store. When I'd taken three slow steps toward the noise, another book hit the floor behind me, from a shelf near the front. I turned and walked toward that noise.

Turns out there were three of them. An arm wielding a blackjack popped out from the shelves as I passed and rapped me on top of the head. I doubled over but didn't lose my footing. I pivoted and sank a right into the man's gut, then his two buddies were on top of me, beating me over the head and shoulders with their saps. Knocking a man unconscious isn't as easy as it looks in the movies, but four or five head-shots with a leaded blackjack surely make a man woozy, especially one with some bourbon on board. They quickly had me flat on the floor, seeing double and wanting to throw up. Two of the men headed upstairs while the third held a gun on me. He didn't need it. I was too punchy even to get on my feet, much less to save anybody. To this day, I still think about whether the result of that night might have been different if I hadn't been drunk to start with.

I don't want to dwell on what happened next. Didn't seem long before the two men came back down the stairs. The one who acted like the leader came over to me. He was a little blond guy with a face like a mean rat. He kicked me hard in the side.

"Have a nice evening," he said.

Then the three of them took off.

I was still wobbly, but I forced myself to rise and head upstairs fast as I could. When I reached the living room, I saw Jack O'Neal lying dead on the floor, his arms spread wide like he was Christ. Rose, in her

166

nightgown, was bent over him, sobbing. Two knives stuck out from Jack's front: one from his belly, one from his heart. My best friend's father, the children's grandfather, this kind man who liked jazz was dead now. I stood immobile, not able to take it in yet. We called the police and when they were done with us, I took Rose home and told the family. We spent the night sobbing.

The next day, I marched into Tom Pendergast's office in Kansas City. One of his bullies tried to stop me, but I pushed by him.

"You know what happened last night," I said. "Those killers, they weren't young kids, they were professionals. Nobody gets killed in Independence by men like that where you don't approve it."

Tom Pendergast was a big, beefy, bald man, the very picture of a big city political boss. He chewed his cigar and glared at me.

"Close the door," he said.

When I did, Pendergast rose from his desk and walked very close to me, right in my face.

"I'm sorry about what happened, Riley. I don't know why it happened, but somehow, that friend of yours, the O'Neal kid, he got in dutch with some very bad people out in New York. These aren't your normal crooks, Riley. These men don't stop, they kill anyone in their way, they kill their families, sometimes they kill for no fucking reason at all. They're rich, and they're powerful, and they get what they want. You stay out of this and you stay away from your friend in New York. He's a dead man."

Pendergast walked back to his desk.

"Now, get the hell out of my office."

20

Cornelius Goes Home

Cornelius

Rothstein's cold, precise words at the Chinese butchery were resounding in my head as I looked at the telegram I found at my apartment, a telegram which said my father was dead. Rothstein had told me the Kansas City mob was watching my mother and my son, in case further orders had to be given.

"I own you now," he had said to me. "You may think you can harm me, kill me, have me arrested, but you can't. I own this city and all the police and courts that it has. I proved that to you when Jimmy Walker told me about you and Maloney. Yes, your cousin the copper told the mayor about that and he did it to help Walker, not you. He knew this was too hot not to tell his protector about and Walker knew to come to me. I ordered the death of your father to show you that I could and would. The threat to your family and the threat of ruin and imprisonment bind you to me more firmly than a simple threat of violence to you, personally, ever could. I own you now."

He had said even if I succeeded in doing him harm, killing him, his minions would kill the rest of my family and produce the Vantine's evidence against me, regardless. He had said I had no choice but to do his bidding and, if I satisfied him, he would forgive my obligations.

He had said something else, just before Anastasia pushed me out the door of the Chinese slaughterhouse.

"Mr. O'Neal, I do want you to know that I understand familial obligations. Family is very important. You will need to go to the funeral and I will allow it. Be back here by the middle of next week. I will have instructions for you."

Then I was out in the street.

I've wondered, from time to time, why a man like Rothstein would follow his chilling description of the horrors he was prepared to visit on me with a pious reference to familial obligations. I think Rothstein's childhood in a strong, cultured Jewish family still ate at him, despite everything. Not that I gave a damn: his family should have flushed that bastard down the nearest sewer when they had the chance.

I took the first train to Kansas City and was met at the station by Ma Riley, by herself. She looked as grim as I've seen her, maybe grimmer than after her husband was killed in a tornado. A different kind of tornado had come to Independence.

"Where's my mother?" I asked immediately.

"At our place. She's staying with us now so we can look after her. Walter wants all of us to stay close to home until we can figure out what is happening." Ma's gaze softened a bit and she pulled me into an embrace. "I'm sorry about your father, Cornelius. He was as good a man as I've ever known."

I held her close. I loved Ma deeply and almost began sobbing. Ma Riley was a strong, solid woman. Her big hands were chafed and callused from constant work, both a woman's work and a man's work. Riley drew his force from her, like Antaeus from the Earth. I knew that my mother and I needed both Riley and Ma if we were to get through this.

"Come on, Cornelius," she finally said. "Let's get you to our place. You need to see Rose and Hal and you need some food in you, I expect."

We bundled into the Rileys' car and Ma, an excellent driver despite her prejudice against women handling automobiles, put us on the road to Independence.

It was dark when we pulled into the driveway at the Riley home, the place where I spent as much time as a teenager as I did at our apartment above the bookstore on Maple Street that my parents owned. Riley stood on the porch, Ma's shotgun cradled in his arms, his pistol from the war at his hip. I could have told him not to bother. Nothing would happen as long as I remained Rothstein's slave.

"You have a mustache!"

That was the first thing I said to my best friend after not seeing him for years.

"You still talk like a fool sometimes, Cornelius," Riley said.

He looked grim under the mustache he was to wear the rest of his life. It was thin but not too thin, like Clark Gable was later to grow.

"Get in the house," he said. "We don't know who killed your pa and we don't know if it's safe for the rest of us, so get inside and we'll talk there."

Ma berated him for speaking so rudely to me, but I noticed that Ma then complied with the admonition to get inside quickly. As soon as I dropped my bag at the door and stepped into the living room, my mother flew from the sofa and wrapped me in her arms, sobbing. Over her shoulder, I saw Marta, the children, and Riley's sisters Ann and Hazel. Marta was standing near the sofa looking sympathetic, plainly having been comforting my mother before I arrived.

Fern and Hal were standing in the middle of the room. They'd been tiny when last I'd seen them on a visit home, but they were genuine people now: both almost ten years old, if my calculations were correct. Fern, a pigtailed little girl in a homespun dress, was looking at the carpet. Hal looked right at me, serious and, in my imagination at least, disapproving. My mother broke our embrace and said the worst thing possible.

"Hal, come hug your father."

The boy and I looked at each other. For a moment, I thought he might refuse, but without changing expression, he stepped across the room and gave me the briefest of hugs, then walked back to his place. Neither of us said a word. Well, I couldn't blame him.

Marta took Fern's hand and led her over to me. Rather than a hug, Marta reached out her hand and gave mine a brief shake. She said she was sorry about my father. She told Fern that I was Cornelius, Hal's father, which Fern took in silently. All in all, a quiet homecoming.

The rest had finished their dinners, but Ma made me a plate. Hazel told me she'd married and lived in Kansas City. Ann remained a spinster in Springfield. I asked after the missing Riley sisters. Bessie had apparently been expelled from Harvard and was last heard of in Indiana, where she had founded a small church. Gussie had married and lived in Florida. Fayette married a lawyer in Illinois. This news shared, the room again fell silent.

I draped my arm around my mother's shoulders as we sat together on the sofa. I was haunted by the knowledge that it had been my actions in New York that caused my father's death. Very little was said by anyone. The evening drew to an early close, the funeral scheduled for the next morning. My mother weakly rose and headed for bed, facing a tough day. Marta accompanied her. I asked Riley to take a walk with me. He looked uncertain, but Ma immediately said she would keep her eyes open while we walked—she had to wash dishes anyway. She picked up the shotgun as we left. Riley and I strolled down Blue Road, as we had so many times in our youth. He lit a cigarette and handed me his flask, which I accepted gratefully.

"We've known each other too long to let something fester inside without talking about it," Riley said.

"The hell does that mean?" I asked. "You hardly say anything ever, good or bad. You're the most silent person I ever met."

Riley took a deep breath.

"You know I'm sorry for what happened to your father. He was a fine man, almost like a father to me, too."

"I know."

Now it was Riley's turn to take a pull from his flask.

"You need to be with your boy, Cornelius. It's not right."

Criticisms hurt the most when they're true. We walked in silence a few steps.

"You think I don't know it, Riley? I know what my father thought, I know what you and my mother and everybody thinks, but I didn't ask for that boy, Riley. You should see New York. It's nothing like here. New York is action, Riley, twenty-four hours a day, every day. Action. I'd be bored to tears and frustrated here and what good would I be to anybody then? Hal's a lot better off with Ma and Marta and my parents... with my mother. I just couldn't take care of him in New York. I can't imagine it."

Riley nodded. I knew him well enough to know that the farm in Independence was no life for him, either.

"Well, anyway," Riley said, "stay around here until we figure out why your father was killed and whether the family's in any danger."

"Riley," I said, "nothing's going to happen to any of you. Not now, anyway."

Riley stopped for a moment and looked at me curiously.

"Tom Pendergast said this was about you. What's going on?"

I emptied my bag. I told of my Adonis Club stories and dead Paddy Maloney and being shanghaied off the street by mob hoodlums. Mostly, I told him all about Arnold Rothstein, who now owned me. Riley never shows his thoughts, but I have to say I think I astonished him.

"You're telling me the greasers who killed your dad were working for this New York gambler?"

"Right."

"And they did it just to show you they could?"

"Basically. The men who killed my father were working for Rothstein. This is all about Rothstein wanting to dominate the narcotics business in this country."

Riley's eyes hardened. Normally that was a bad sign for someone who crossed him, but what could he do this time? The enemy we faced was just too powerful for us.

"I guess we've both been idiots, Cornelius. You went poking the wrong hornet's nest and I've been drinking myself to death out here. Now your father's dead and our families are at risk. This'll take some thinking."

It would take more than thinking. If thinking were enough, we'd be fine since I'd been thinking about nothing else since leaving Rothstein and Anastasia. We walked in silence for at least ten, fifteen minutes. Suddenly Riley stopped.

"He did all this to get a lever on you. We need a bigger lever on him."

"Meaning what?"

"What does this Rothstein care about? I mean really care about, in his soul?"

"We can debate whether that little shit has a soul," I replied, "but I'd say power, money, gambling, maybe his wife but probably not."

Riley drew deeply on his cigarette.

"We need a real threat, something we could use to take away all

173

that if he doesn't let us alone. A lever bigger than what he's got on you. So, what is there?"

The answer should have been obvious to me, but I struggled.

"I don't know. He said even if we killed him, his men would still hurt Hal and put me in jail. Rob him? That wouldn't... Wait a minute." How could I not have seen it right away? "The ledgers!"

"What?" Riley asked.

I grabbed him by the shoulders.

"Rothstein keeps detailed notebooks recording every shady deal he's ever done! I tried to steal them once already, just for the newspaper story. If we get our hands on those ledgers, we've got him!"

"Ledgers? You mean like accounting books?"

"Yeah, ledgers!" I said impatiently. "Little notebooks filled with handwritten incriminating notations! I always thought those ledgers would blow New York sky-high if I could ever get them. That's the lever on Rothstein."

"Where does he keep them?"

That took my wind a bit.

"I don't know. He carries the latest one around with him and he used to keep the old ones in his office, but he moved them when I almost got hold of them. I don't know where they are now."

Riley tossed away his cigarette.

"Well, we'll have to find them. You sure nothing's going to happen around here unless you don't do what Rothstein tells you?"

"Think about it. The whole idea was to get control of me. Why would he do anything more as long as he thinks he's got it?"

Riley nodded, as if this made good sense.

"Then day after tomorrow we're both going to New York. I think I need to get to know this Rothstein fellow."

I looked in Riley's eyes as he spoke. Even though Rothstein held all the cards, right at that moment, I'd have bet on Riley.

21

Bad Times

Marta

April 18, 1928

Oh, diary, bad times again. I haven't written since the tragedy. Poor Mr. O'Neal! And poor Rose, and Hal, and all of us! He was such a wonderful man, so warm and kind, so caring a grandfather for both our children even though it was Hal to whom he was related. I don't understand the world. Such cruelty. I knew from my own experience how cruel it can be and I hoped at least this violence was all in our past. But no.

Cornelius came home tonight. It has been years since I saw him, yet he seemed unchanged. I'm sure he thought me much changed, older and getting fat. I do not understand Cornelius, any more than I understand the world. He was so brave in Mexico, almost as brave as my Walter. He can be funny, he seems to care for all of us, yet he stays in New York, deserting his fine son. Yes, diary, deserting, that is the word. I love Hal as my own, we all do, but he should be with his father. Though I think it might kill my Fern if he ever left. They are so close, always together, always taking care of each other. They never even argue, which is amazing for a boy and girl their age. We joke that they will marry, but they seem too close for that, too much like brother and sister.

I prattle on. I fear I want to talk about everything except the most important thing, Mr. O'Neal's death and whether it means danger to the rest of us. Walter walks the house grimly and believes more violence may come. It is time for planting, yet Walter will not go to the fields as he won't leave us alone. When I think of our beautiful children being in danger, I go wild! Yet at least the men who killed Jack are not crazy, not like that monster who killed my brother Miguel. Why would such men harm children?

I hear my Walter coming back from his walk with Cornelius. I will close for now. Writing does help me. Perhaps next, a poem?

April 21, 1928

I missed another day, but I have reason, my diary. My Walter is gone, off to New York with Cornelius! I don't know what we will do.

Walter said nothing when he came back from his walk, just grunts, even though I tried to draw him out about what will happen next and what he had discussed with Cornelius. Then, yesterday morning was the funeral. Some of us went in the wagon while Walter drove Rose and Cornelius in the automobile.

We were in the little country church out by the east eighty, where we have sat so many Sunday mornings. We had talked about whether the funeral should be in a church, since Mr. O'Neal did not believe in God, but Rose had insisted.

"For once, Jack O'Neal will hedge his bets," she said.

The pastor spoke, things he could have said at anyone's funeral. Then Cornelius rose to speak. I did not take notes, but I remember some of the things that Cornelius said:

> Some will remember Jack O'Neal as an atheist and a communist. If you asked him, he would have told you he was both of these things. What they meant to him and how he reached those destinations after a very long thought journey would be different than what you might imagine. I hope, as we stand surrounded by ideologies and philosophies and factions, that ultimately Jack O'Neal will be measured by much more sensitive instruments. He was a kind, caring, loving, and instinctively generous man. Measured by this standard,

there is nothing to which I would sooner aspire and nothing which I would have a more difficult task to become.

This is why I have such trouble deciding how I feel about Cornelius. He seems so shallow and full of himself, then he can speak words such as these.

The service ended. The ladies of the church hosted a short reception in the church basement, then we returned to the Riley homestead. If we thought we would have a rest from thinking of our problems, we were misinformed. Walter called us all into the parlor, sending the children out in the yard to play.

"There's good news, but I'll have to go to New York with Cornelius for a little while," Walter said. "Cornelius will explain."

Cornelius told us that Mr. O'Neal wasn't killed by the local criminals, but by some criminal in New York whom Cornelius has been writing about in the newspaper. He said this criminal had Mr. O'Neal killed to stop Cornelius from writing and the rest of us are safe as long as he doesn't write. But he and Riley need to see that this criminal is put in jail for what he did. He said they can't rely on the police, because the criminal has bribed the police and the judges.

"All of them?" Ma asked scornfully. "All the police in New York City have been bribed by this one gangster?"

"Ma, it's like Kansas City," Walter said. "You know that Tom Pendergast runs the show there. This fellow is hooked into the same kind of machine that the Pendergasts have."

My heart ached when he said that.

"Walter, you can't be against men like that," I implored him.

Walter shrugged off my worries and we hardly got any more information out of the two of them. Even tonight, when we were alone, I couldn't talk Walter out of doing whatever it is they plan to do in New York. They leave in the morning. They wouldn't even tell the children themselves, they left that to me. Fern cried so much. I could have told her she is entering a world where the men leave it to the women to clean up after them. It is always so.

22

Deep Waters

Cornelius

"Have you ever heard of a man named Alfred Loewenstein?" Rothstein was looking at me with his usual cold intensity. It was all I could do to keep from throttling the son of a bitch, but this would have been contrary to the plan Riley and I had worked out back in Independence. In any event, it would probably have resulted in Legs Diamond shooting me dead. I merely responded that I had never heard of Mr. Loewenstein.

"Perhaps that is not surprising since he lives in London, but I might have thought you'd have heard his name. He is reputed to be the second-richest man in the world."

"Who's first? You?"

Rothstein smiled humorlessly at my little joke.

"Hardly. I believe Mr. Rockefeller holds that distinction. However, that is not relevant. What is relevant is that I have an appointment to meet Mr. Lowenstein in three days and you will be there as well."

Rothstein didn't wait long to summon me after my return to New York. Riley, who'd insisted on traveling from Independence separately from me to avoid being observed if Rothstein was having me watched, had yet to reach town when a messenger brought over a note from A.R., commanding me to go to his office at the Park Central suite. He'd characteristically wasted no time on pleasantries, immediately asking me about this Loewenstein fellow.

"Mr. O'Neal, I am now going to reveal to you some important and highly confidential information," Rothstein said. "I do this because of the hold that I have over you. Not only do I have evidence linking you directly to the narcotics traffic in this city, evidence which I assure you would be sufficient to get you a lengthy sentence from the New York courts where, as you know, I wield significant influence, I also have shown you how far my reach extends. You lost a father, but I left you a mother. The one parent could be taken as easily as the other, and your son as well. You are now in position to do me a considerable service and I believe I have succeeded in ensuring you will do so. Do you agree?"

Bile rising in my throat, I said I would do whatever he asked.

"Well, then," Rothstein said, unwrapping what appeared to be a cough lozenge and placing it on his tongue, "let me tell you that I have been studying Mr. Loewenstein from afar for a long time. He is an interesting man. No one seems to know how he acquired his wealth. By the time he came to anyone's notice, he had many investments all over Europe and North America and other places as well. His horses are his passion. He owns the best riding stable in England and likes to make a big show at races. He owns his own airplane, travels extensively, and is well-known to be a hard man to deal with."

"Hard? Meaning what?"

Rothstein waved his hand dismissively.

"Meaning ruthless, untrustworthy, deceitful, unpredictable. As likely to make millionaires of his partners as to cheat them savagely. An enigma, in other words, and not a man to approach lightly."

"So why are you approaching him?"

"As I said, I've made a study of Mr. Loewenstein. He came to my attention when I learned of a source of opium and heroin production out of Turkey. It is a very large source. Product is shipped from Constantinople to Marseille and from there throughout all of Europe. As far as I've been able to tell, however, this source has not been making deliveries to the United States, where the potential market in my opinion is far larger than in Europe."

"And you would like to remedy that situation."

"Indeed I would. You see, Mr. O'Neal, Prohibition will soon be repealed, but it seems to me we are still very much on the ground floor of the narcotics opportunity. Heroin has only been against the law for five years. Up to this point, much of the supply for businessmen like me has been unreliable and small scale: rogue physicians, that sort of thing. I've used the Vantine's shipments to bring in a small but profitable flow from the Orient, but I'm having a very hard time keeping up with the demand. There seems to be no end of people who are anxious to sample our wares and who quickly become so addicted to our product that they are willing to steal to get the money to pay for it. It really is an excellent business, a model of inelastic demand. I suppose I shouldn't criticize, since I have been accused of being addicted to gambling myself."

It occurred to me that Rothstein was being unusually chatty. He appeared to read my thoughts.

"You must wonder why I am telling you all this. It is partly because I need you to do something for me and partly because you are in my power and I feel free to say whatever I wish to you. But time is passing and I must move along."

"You think this Loewenstein is behind the Turkish supply source?"

"I know he is. It took me two years and a lot of money, but I was able to trace the ultimate organizer behind the traffic to the mysterious Mr. Loewenstein. I sent the Diamond brothers to France and Turkey, where they greased palms and threatened witnesses until they'd followed the line all the way to the top. We tried repeatedly to communicate with Loewenstein and, finally, his assistant who runs the Turkish farms convinced him to meet with me to discuss a distributorship arrangement in the United States. This assistant, a German, believes we would be the best-positioned partner for them here, which we are. Unfortunately, I have learned that I have a rival. And that is where you come in, as they say in the theatre. You know Mr. Frankie Yale."

I nodded.

"I thought Mr. Yale was my associate in this endeavor and would ensure free use of the Red Hook docks for the Turkish shipments. I suggested his elimination of Mr. Lonergan at the Adonis Club for that very reason: yes, that is how long this move has been in the planning stage. But Mr. Yale has proven to have ambitions beyond his station. Loewenstein's assistant, the German who is promoting our cause, recently let me know that Yale has been in direct contact with

Loewenstein about becoming his U.S. agent, cutting me out completely. It is not clear to me where Mr. Masseria stands on all of this, assuming he is even aware of it, but it is possible that Masseria is behind this latest betrayal by Yale. I believe, however, that I have that flank protected and it is simply a matter of convincing Alfred Loewenstein that his interests lie with me and not a Coney Island saloonkeeper. To do that, I need to discredit Yale, to make him seem too unreliable and dangerous to be an appropriate business partner. You are ideally suited to accomplish just this."

"What are you talking about?"

"You are the reporter who has repeatedly published on the Adonis Club Massacre. You will come to my meeting with Mr. Loewenstein and you will inform him that you are about to conclude your series with a devastating article revealing Mr. Yale as the mastermind who planned the murders at the Adonis Club. You will report that your evidence is so strong that Mr. Yale will be behind bars or electrocuted in the near future, rendering him most unsuitable as a business partner. You will convince Mr. Loewenstein that, if he wishes to tap into the lucrative New York market, his only viable partner is his fellow Jew, myself. Do you understand?"

On first hearing, it didn't sound as bad as I expected Mr. Rothstein's favors to be.

"How much do I tell him?"

"You can tell him what has been in your articles to date and about finding Paddy Maloney as your witness, omitting that Mr. Maloney is now dead."

That would be a safe lie to tell. As far as Frankie Yale or anyone else knew, Paddy Maloney had vanished and could well still be alive. There was never any news of Paddy's body being found anywhere. Perhaps he'd gone into the grinders after all.

"Make no mention of Al Capone, implicate Yale only," Rothstein continued. "Mr. Capone and I continue to have an arrangement and Mr. Capone is rather upset with Mr. Yale for plotting against me. You see that these are deep waters, but your role, Mr. O'Neal, should be quite simple."

I nodded and picked up my hat. I wanted to get back to my apartment, hoping Riley was there by now. I needed him.

23

The Big Bankroll
Meets a Bigger Bankroll

Cornelius

Riley had indeed arrived. I found him sitting stolidly on the floor of the hallway in front of the door to my apartment. It was time for business, so we didn't even exchange greetings. I just opened the door and we went inside. I led him to the kitchen table, we sat down, and I recounted the entire conversation I'd just had with Rothstein. Riley, as usual, hardly said a word.

He finally spoke when I had finished.

"Least we know what he wants from you. One of the things, anyway."

"That's exactly it, one of the things," I said. "This won't stop. Not until he's squeezed the last usefulness out of owning the crime reporter for the *Journal*. Then I'm dead."

"Well, you're not dead yet. Stay as close as you can to Rothstein. Pretend you're starting to like being a criminal and do whatever he tells you, 'less if he asks you to kill somebody or something, but he won't. He's got plenty of better qualified people to do that. Find out where his notebooks are. Then maybe we've got something."

"How about my job? I'm supposed to come up with a crime

story every day, six days a week! I can't be running errands for Arnold Rothstein."

Riley looked at me impatiently.

"If you don't, your son or your ma is killed and you go to prison. You'd better work it out."

He had a point, so I changed the subject.

"What are you going to be doing? You came all the way to New York. Where are you going to start?"

He shrugged.

"I've been thinking I might go to Brooklyn, eyeball this Frankie Yale. A lot of this mess seems to be tied up with the Brooklyn docks. I want to look at the boss over there."

"Be careful with Yale, Riley. He's a killer."

Riley put his hand on my shoulder.

"Cornelius, so far it seems like everybody you know in this town is a killer."

We were to meet Loewenstein at his suite in a hotel on 42nd Street. A little before the scheduled time of the meeting, I joined Rothstein in his office at the Park Central. He was wearing his most elegant and conservative suit, an understated blue serge with a club necktie instead of his usual sporty bow.

"It's very important that he sees me as a businessman, a safe partner to go into an enterprise with," Rothstein said. "The whole object today is to convince him that Yale is a vulgar, murderous thug, likely to be in prison before he can even start taking heroin deliveries. That's your job. Then it's my job to show him I can run the Red Hook docks without Yale."

"Can you?"

Rothstein gave that little grimace that he thought was a smile.

"Don't you know me better than to ask? Mr. Yale would be surprised to know the connections I've made. It's time to go."

If the desk clerk at Loewenstein's hotel wondered why the most notorious gambler and fixer in New York was meeting with a fabulously wealthy businessman, he didn't show it. He simply called Loewenstein's room and waved us up once he got the all-clear.

The suite was sumptuous, matching its occupant's bankroll. We were shown in by someone who appeared to be a personal secretary, but he quickly made himself scarce. The suite's living room was about three times the size of my apartment, with thick and tasteful rugs, dark wood furnishings, and a bar and dining table big enough to have hosted the Versailles peace talks. Rothstein sat down primly on the leather sofa, briefcase clutched in his lap. He nodded to me to sit down as well and, to my amusement, quickly put his finger to his lips to warn me that we might be overheard. So we sat, for nearly an hour, without a word spoken. I doubted that Loewenstein was sleeping or conducting important business in his bedroom. I suspected he just wanted Rothstein to wait, so there would be no question who was boss.

My guess was confirmed when the man burst into the living room, for he was ostentatiously perusing a sheaf of papers that he held in his hands, not looking up from them, plainly seeking to convey the impression that whatever was in those papers was far more important than anything the mere Arnold Rothstein could have on his mind. Rothstein was far smarter than he needed to be to get this message, but he showed no sign of annoyance. He snapped to his feet the instant Loewenstein entered the room and stood respectfully waiting for his host to look up. I did the same, though I did not rise with A.R.'s alacrity.

I looked over the great man from London. Europe's leading financier and horse fancier looked the part of a wealthy self-made man. I later learned he was about fifty, though he looked a tad older. He was of medium height, burly build, with a handsome and strongly-featured face: prominent nose, wide mouth, deep dimples, deep-set and piercing eyes. He was dressed to go out, wearing a dark pinstriped suit and expensive shoes polished to gleaming brilliance. When he finally looked up from his papers and spoke, he betrayed the slightest of German accents, something of a surprise in a man who had lived so much of his life in England. His voice was loud and his gestures authoritative. He was not a man to cross.

"I have ten minutes," he barked. "I am meeting with a board of directors and must be on time. Then I fly to Montreal."

He sat across from Rothstein, still holding his papers. We sat and Rothstein began his pitch, all smiles.

"We are both businessmen and we understand the importance of a busy schedule," he began, drawing from Loewenstein a subtle crinkling of impressive eyebrows. "You are aware of the general nature of the business proposition I am here to discuss. In my turn, I am aware that I have a rival who seeks to do business with you in my stead. It is not clear to me that you know all of the implications of dealing with this man and for this reason, I've brought here Mr. James Cornelius O'Neal, the reporter for the *New York Journal* who has done a series of pieces on Mr. Frankie Yale, in particular his unfortunate involvement with a very violent incident in Brooklyn three years ago."

Loewenstein sniffed.

"I am familiar with the articles. You sent them to me and I read them. I always read what comes to me by way of business." The large head rotated my way. "Mr. O'Neal, are you somehow affiliated with Mr. Rothstein? Is that why you are here on his behalf?"

Rothstein tried to answer for me.

"Mr. O'Neal is a reporter…"

"I know who he is," Loewenstein snapped. "I am interested in his motivations."

I decided what the hell.

"Same as yours, just on a different scale, Mr. Loewenstein. Rothstein's paying me $5,000 to tell you what I know about Frankie Yale and the Adonis Club. Reporters don't make a lot of money."

Actually, Rothstein was paying me nothing, but I thought this would be a good response.

Loewenstein's lip curled.

"That is a lot of money to you? Enough for you to lie about Mr. Yale to promote Mr. Rothstein?"

"Oh, no, sir. A lie would have cost him ten."

I won't say that Loewenstein laughed, but he gave out a loud bark that sounded like "Ha!"

"I like you," he said. "You are honest with me. Go ahead, Mr. O'Neal, earn your fee. Tell me about this Frank Yale."

Rothstein had rehearsed me repeatedly in my part, which was hardly necessary since most of it was true or close enough. I talked about my investigation of the Adonis Club Massacre. I told him that I recently located a critical witness, omitting the fact that Paddy Maloney had become somewhat less critical by becoming dead. I told him this witness would swear that the Adonis Club Massacre was a put-up job by Frankie Yale to murder Peg Leg Lonergan, all for the purpose of assuming total control of the Brooklyn docks as part of a long-term plan to expand smuggling operations, especially narcotics. I assured him that when my witness went public, Mr. Yale would go to Sing Sing or some similar place of accommodation to rot or fry as his luck provided.

"In sum, Mr. Loewenstein, Frankie Yale would be a very bad bet as a long-term business partner. He's showy, violent, and devious, but more to the point, he's about to be convicted of murder after a very public trial." I put on my hat, ready to go. "And that's what's Mr. Rothstein paid me $5,000 to tell you. The truth."

Loewenstein raised his hand to detain me.

"And what of Mr. Rothstein himself? What sort of long-term business partner would he make?"

I considered my answer while Rothstein stewed, his knuckles white on the handle of his briefcase.

"Mr. Rothstein is a very different individual," I said. "He's never been linked publicly to anything violent. He's known as a gambler, but every banker on Wall Street is a gambler and no one holds that against him. He has tremendous influence with everyone in government and law enforcement in the city, which must be handy in all kinds of ways. So I'd say Mr. Rothstein would be a good investment for a man like you."

All true, though I'd have said it even if it wasn't.

For all his brains, Rothstein could have a tin ear. While he should have stayed silent, he piped up.

"I'm very flattered by Mr. O'Neal's remarks," he said, "and I encourage you to check them out by asking around town, Mr. Loewenstein. I have always tried to be a sound businessman who takes care of his partners. I learned this from my father, a well-regarded man in the Jewish community here. A credit to our mutual heritage."

Rothstein all but simpered, which was the wrong tone to take.

Loewenstein had been warming up, but Rothstein's playing of the brother Hebrew card seemed to upset him. He frowned and stood to dismiss me. He did offer his hand to me.

"Mr. Rothstein and I have perhaps three more minutes of business, if you will excuse us, Mr. O'Neal. I enjoyed meeting you and I hope we meet again."

I tipped my hat and walked out. I waited around in the lobby, curious if Loewenstein indeed kept Rothstein to three more minutes.

It appeared so, for suddenly the Big Bankroll was striding toward me, looking agitated indeed.

"That prick. That fucking prick."

"Whoa, A.R., simmer down."

"He wouldn't even listen to me. Just said he had no intention of associating with a man like me and what he did or didn't do with Yale was none of my damn business."

"He didn't appear to like you harping on your Jewishness."

"Can you imagine that? Objecting to a respectful reference to our mutual Jewish heritage. Fucking kike."

"Look, I did the best I could. I did everything you asked."

"Not now, I have to think. If that prick is going to Montreal, I'm going to Montreal. I'm going to make him see reason. I'm clearly the best man for him to take on as his partner and that's what's going to happen. I'll talk to you later."

He strode out of the hotel, looking for a cab.

Rothstein went to Montreal all right, but it did him no good. He came back in a few days and said Loewenstein wouldn't even talk to him. If anything, Rothstein was more coldly furious than he had been in the hotel lobby. He told me he wanted me to go to London and take one more crack at convincing Loewenstein to see reason, since the man seemed to take to me. The fact that this would take at least two weeks and that I had a job didn't matter to him, so it couldn't matter to me. Worse, he gave me a traveling companion from my nightmares: Albert Anastasia.

I didn't know why Rothstein thought that a gorilla like Anastasia and I could make headway with Lowenstein when the Big Bankroll couldn't. Even so, I still would have put my money on Rothstein, since my experience with him was that he always got what he wanted. I didn't know it then, but A.R.'s luck was finally beginning to change.

24

The Pointing Nun

Riley

I went off to find Frankie Yale while Cornelius and Rothstein met some rich man at a hotel. I don't know why, but I guess I had to do *something*. Maybe I thought if Yale was in competition with Rothstein for the drug connection, he might help us somehow. Maybe, if we could start a full-scale war between them, it might help. Anyway, I went to Coney Island.

Cornelius insisted I ride the electric railway, as I called the subway back then. I'd never done such a thing and it worried me. Following directions from Cornelius, I made my way down some dirty stairs with people pushing past me—some things haven't changed that much since 1928. When I got to the bottom, I saw the machines that Cornelius warned me about. There was one where you could put in a dime or a quarter and get the right number of nickels back from it. I'd never seen a change machine before. Then you put your nickel in a slot and you pushed yourself against this barred wheel that turned and let one person in per nickel. I'd never seen a turnstile before either, so I had to watch a few people go in before I risked trying it myself.

Years later, they raised the fare to a dime and changed out all the turnstiles to accommodate the different coin. Then, when they raised the fare to fifteen cents, they came out with little slugs called tokens that went in the slots. The man in the street objected that, with the tokens, they could easily raise the fares however often they wished, but who cares what the man in the street says? As Cornelius used to say, if he were worth listening to, he wouldn't be in the street.

I made it through the barred wheel and followed the signs like Cornelius told me. It wasn't hard to find the right train. The weather was getting warm and the amusement parks were open, so if you just got on a train full of folks heading for a beach, you'd get to Coney Island. The train crossed under the river and made what seemed like a lot of stops. By the time we got to the station with a big sign saying "Coney Island," the car was full to busting with families who had that cranky look that people get when they're going out to have a good time.

I used the train ride to decide on a plan. I would approach Frankie Yale to warn him that Arnold Rothstein was out to get him. I'd say I was working for Rothstein, found out the plan, and wanted to warn him because I hated Rothstein and would prefer to work for Yale. If he didn't believe me, I'd tell him I knew about the competition for Loewenstein's drugs, which he'd figure I had to learn from Rothstein. I preferred not to do that, because he might just decide to kill me because of what I knew. I figured I'd deal with that if it came up.

Coney Island featured a row of privately-owned amusement parks along the boardwalk: Luna Park, Steeplechase Park, Dreamland. While the crowds lined up to get into them for the Coney dogs and the thrill rides, I made off down Surf Avenue like Cornelius told me and found Yale's new favorite restaurant, Ciccone's. It was a cheery enough little place, with pictures from Italy on the walls. There were only a few patrons, which suited me. I took a seat at the bar and ordered a soda. The bartender was a thick-set Italian guy, friendly until he poured my drink and I asked him when Frankie was coming in.

"What Frankie?" he asked. "We got a million Frankies. Half the Italian guys in Brooklyn are named Frankie."

"This one's the main Frankie," I said. "You know who I'm talking about."

I thought he'd get cagey on me, but he didn't. He thought about it and decided, for whatever reason, to give me a straight answer.

"I suppose you mean Mr. Yale," he allowed. "Mr. Yale is a good customer of ours, but not today. Today, he's over at St. Rosalie's for the ground-breaking ceremony."

"The what?"

"The ground-breaking ceremony for the new parish school. Mr. Yale was one of the big donors. He's a very charitable guy. You won't hear a bad word said about Mr. Yale anywhere in Brooklyn, buddy."

"You won't hear it from me, either. I just want to talk with the man."

I paid for my soda, drank it, and started to walk out.

"Hey, mister, wait a minute." He waved me back and spoke in a lower voice. "Don't think I'm stupid. I don't know you from Adam and I don't know why you want Frankie Yale. He's a great man and I'm proud to call him a friend as well as a customer. I told you where he is because everybody in Brooklyn knows he's at the ground-breaking. It was in the papers. But if it turns out he didn't want to see you, it's better you don't mention my name."

"I don't know your name," I said.

I headed for St Rosalie's. It turned out that was a nickname, for the old lady on the street who gave me directions told me the formal name of the church was St. Rosalia. It was the main parish for the Italian Catholics in the neighborhood. I walked up to the place just as the ground-breaking ceremony was starting. It was the usual program for such events. A small set of bleachers had been set up between the construction site and the church, a solid, substantial building with a bell tower and the usual Catholic saints and crosses for decoration. They apparently planned to build the school next to the church, for the lot there had been razed and was roped off for the occasion. No seating was provided other than the bleachers, but a large crowd had still gathered to watch the ceremony.

On the bleachers sat a line of maybe a dozen dignitaries, the usual pack of well-fed and self-important aldermen, wealthy parishioners, and Knights of Columbus who speak at such events, with a priest standing at the dais acting as master of ceremonies. He was just beginning to introduce the quality behind him, but I knew without being told which one was Yale from the description given me by Cornelius.

"Big, big dago-looking guy," Cornelius had said. "Slicked-down hair, dark skin, round face, Cupid lips. Massive arms, massive chest, and little legs. Looks like a longshoreman in fancy dress. Always in expensive clothes, with lots of jewelry including a wide belt set with diamonds. I am not kidding."

That was Yale, all right, in the front row, second from the end on the left.

I was worried the speeches would go on forever, but the priest didn't give anybody the chance. He said a few nice things about each of the dignitaries, generally to the effect that their contributions would assure them a free pass from St. Peter, and then it was on to the shoveling.

A small knot of reporters and photographers were in attendance and a lot of flashbulbs went off as Yale took his turn with the shovel and moved some dirt around. When the last shovel was turned, the crowd applauded and slowly headed over to the church for the refreshments the priest had promised. I was able to sidle through the throng until I was next to Yale.

"Mr. Yale, I need a word with you," I said.

It seemed that Frankie really could be a generous man, for he smiled broadly at me even though I'm sure he sensed I was leading up to putting a touch on him.

"Sure, my friend. Come and share some food with me inside the church. The ladies here are all wonderful cooks and I want to get started on the spread they put out."

He put his arm around my shoulder and started walking me toward the door of the church. He towered over me and pulled me close. I knew he was checking me out and he felt the revolver in my right jacket pocket, just as I felt the gun he carried in his waistband under his coat.

Folks made way for us, or I should say for Yale, and we made our way quickly through the crowd, up the steps into the church, then down an interior stair into the basement where a massive spread of food was laid out. There was a long line, but the people smiled and gestured for us to move ahead of them. Yale accepted this as his due. These were mostly working-class Italians, laborers, and housewives, with the occasional professional person. All were dressed in their best and seemed happy about everything: the new school, the nice weather, the food, and the chance to show their respects to their *padrone*, Frankie Yale. An outsider might have wondered if he could be as bad a guy as Cornelius said, but by this time I had a fair amount of experience with the world. I knew the same person could be very good and very bad, that if any of these sweet parishioners crossed Frankie Yale where it mattered, he'd kill them without mercy. They knew it too and they respected him for it.

Yale greeted everyone by name and kissed the old ladies on the cheek, but he kept moving swiftly toward the food. His eyes bulged at the sight of the dishes on the long table, which I have to admit was an impressive spread. All kinds of noodle dishes I didn't know the name of, but they smelled awfully good. Salami, sausages, cheeses, fruits, all sorts of cakes. Yale greedily scooped more and more food onto first one plate, then another. As he did, he kept advising me to try this or that.

"I'm not much of an eater," I said.

He looked at me like I had said I wasn't much of a breather.

"*Marone*," he said in mock surprise. "You want to be a big man, not have to ask for favors. You want some meat on your bones."

He finally had his plates full to overflowing and a woman behind the table put a small glass of red wine in his fingers. He nodded me over to a quiet corner and we sat at a tray table that had been provided for the occasion. He shook hands with a couple more folks and waved the rest away.

"Now, what can I do for you, Mr. Doesn't Eat When It's Offered? You know, where the people here come from, that is considered rude."

"I apologize," I said, "but you'll want to hear this. I work for Mr. Arnold Rothstein."

That brought Yale's head up out of his plate. He looked hard at me.

"Arnie? Arnie's a loner, not many men work for him. I've never seen you before."

"I've never seen you, either. In fact…"

I stopped short. Over Yale's shoulder, I saw a man appear in the main entrance to the basement hall we were in. He was looking around the crowd and I knew right away he was looking for Yale. It was the skinny, blond, tough little gunsel with the rat face, the one who kicked me in the side the night Jack O'Neal was killed. That night, he'd seen my face, so if he saw me now, he'd know I wasn't an Arnold Rothstein flunky. That would blow my whole plan for starting a war between Yale and Rothstein, eliminating any chance of taking these mobsters by surprise.

Another second and the gunsel's eyes would light on Frankie Yale and he'd come over to us. Without another word, I shoved away from the table, pulled my jacket up around my face, and headed for the back door, then up a flight of stairs leading back behind the main altar of the church. I heard Yale bellow "Hey!" behind me and figured he and his blond henchman would be up the stairs and on me in a moment. I got to the main sanctuary, which seemed to be empty of people. On the side wall, there was a door to the outside, but instead of leaving by it, I flung it open and then crouched down behind a pew. I figured my pursuers would think I left by the door and I could escape while they were diverted.

Sure enough, the two gangsters appeared in the sanctuary, spotted the open door, and headed for it. Right then, I saw a nun I hadn't noticed before. A kindly-looking woman in a traditional black habit, she was kneeling on the rail in the row in which I crouched, hands folded on the pew in front of her in prayer. Rather than communicating with her maker, though, she had her head turned and she was looking straight at me. I clasped my hands in front of me in supplication and silently mouthed to her what she had to know was a plea for asylum.

She didn't hesitate.

"Frankie!" she brayed, pointing right at me. "He's over here!"

I was on my feet and running in a crouch before she finished her sentence. I pulled my jacket over my face to keep the gunsel from recognizing me.

"Not here," I heard Frankie yell, "this is my church!"

I suppose that meant he stopped his man from shooting me. The pews must have blocked their way, for I made it down the aisle and out the front door and I was gone. I scurried down a half-dozen alleys before I was satisfied they weren't after me.

Ever since, I've never really trusted nuns.

25

The End of Frankie Yale

Riley

Cornelius was already back when I got to the apartment. His day had been a bust and so had mine, but now we knew one new thing.

He opened a bottle of bootleg whiskey and we both took a glass.

"You're saying this guy with Yale who chased you was in the bunch who killed my father?"

"Same guy. Skinny, mean-looking, big nose. Never seen an Italian with blond hair like him."

Cornelius nodded.

"I know the guy. Willie Altieri. He's Yale's favorite assassin. They call him Two Knives."

I leaned forward.

"What did you say?"

"Two Knives. You know, it's one of those gangster nicknames. Dumb one."

I emptied my glass.

"Well, he's the one killed your father, all right."

I explained about finding Mr. O'Neal with one knife in his heart and one in his belly. I hadn't told him about those details before, to spare his feelings. Cornelius sat still for a long minute.

"If he killed my father, Altieri must be working for Rothstein, maybe without Yale knowing," he finally said. "Rothstein told me that he had the docks covered if Yale goes down. Maybe Altieri and Anastasia are his men in Brooklyn, set to take over when Yale's gone. Jesus, Two Knives Altieri."

Cornelius was again silent.

"Riley?" he finally said. "We get the chance, I want us to kill that bastard."

I told him I'd keep it in mind.

More than a month went by after Rothstein had struck out with Loewenstein and I'd made a fool of myself at St. Rosalie's with Frankie Yale. Rothstein sent Cornelius and this Anastasia hood over to England to take another crack at negotiating a deal. I was left to pace the apartment, trying to come up with another idea. I kept out of sight as much as possible, so nobody would notice that there was a man staying at the apartment with Cornelius. Marta wrote me almost every day and I wrote her back some, though it may have increased the risk that somebody would figure out I was there. It was nice getting Marta's letters and it made me miss her, but there wasn't much to say back. I can never think of what to say in letters, anyway.

Finally, I couldn't just sit around the apartment any more. The best idea I could come up with was still to start a war between Yale and Rothstein in the hope that Rothstein would lose or get killed and the whole Cornelius business would be forgotten. Since I could hardly approach Yale about helping him after the embarrassing powder I took at St. Rosalie's, I decided to convince Yale that Arnold Rothstein wanted to kill him and hired me to do it. I figured I'd take him somewhere and tell him Rothstein hired me to eliminate him as a rival for Loewenstein's business. I'd wing him in the shoulder or leg or somewhere, then leave him and hope he'd take out Rothstein next.

Sticking my revolver in my jacket pocket, I headed for Brooklyn. I swung by Ciccone's but Yale wasn't there, so I took a taxi over to a building that, according to Cornelius, contained Yale's office. Sure enough, there was a brown Lincoln coupe parked on the street in front, matching the car Cornelius had told me that Yale drove. I didn't see anybody watching over the car. I guess the boss of Brooklyn always got the best parking spot and didn't need a guard for his car.

Didn't need to lock his car either, for when I sidled by, I noticed the doors weren't locked. On an impulse, I pulled open the door and squeezed into the back. Though it was a coupe, it was a pretty large car and I found room to lie down. My thought was to surprise him once he started the car. I figured he probably wouldn't have more than one person with him and might be alone.

Once I got myself settled, with my revolver in my hand, the idea started losing its appeal to me. What if he didn't show up for the whole afternoon? What if he saw me right away and never got in the car? What if somebody walking by saw me? The ways this could go bad were multiplying in my head. I was about to reach for the door handle and slide out of there when Frankie Yale threw open the driver's door and plopped down behind the wheel.

He seemed wrought up and he didn't notice me. I could see the folds on the back of his neck, sweating and red as he started up the Lincoln. He revved the engine, threw it into drive, and pulled away with a screech of the tires that threw me backward in a way that might have caught his notice if he hadn't been preoccupied about something. At least he was alone.

Yale tore down the street at what was definitely an unsafe speed. I didn't know how far we were going or what might happen next, so I decided I'd better act quickly. I stuck the muzzle of my revolver at the back of Yale's head.

"Slow down, Frankie," I said softly. "You don't want to kill yourself."

Yale inhaled sharply, but was otherwise silent. A man like him, a gun to his head wasn't that big a surprise. He'd be thinking about his next move. He only slowed a bit.

"We're taking a ride, Frankie," I said, trying to sound like these hoods sounded. "Just keep on going nice and easy and I'll tell you where to go."

I suddenly realized this was a problem. This car idea had come up so fast, I hadn't thought where I was going to take him and I wasn't all that familiar with New York. Where would be a good spot to take a mobster and shoot him in the leg?

Yale glanced back at me.

"Hey, I've seen you. You were that guy at St. Rosalie's."

"Shut up."

I knew he'd recognize me, but that was all right since I'd told him then I worked for Arnold Rothstein. That's what I needed him to believe. Of course, my plan wouldn't work if Altieri had recognized me at the church, but I didn't think he had.

"What the hell are you doing? Didn't you say you work for Rothstein?"

"I do work for Rothstein. Keep your eyes on the road, Frankie. I don't want to spill your brains all over your nice new Lincoln."

I have to say, Yale didn't seem frightened a bit.

"Hey, are you behind that call I got about my wife? Did you fake that? That was a shitty thing to do!"

He pounded the wheel.

"I don't know what you're talking about. Keep your eyes on the road."

"You're a dead man, you know that? Call me and tell me my wife's in the hospital just to get me in my car. Where do you think you're taking me, anyway?"

I had to come up with something. Where would be a quiet and secluded place?

"Central Park," I blurted.

That actually got Yale laughing.

"Central Park? You want to go to Central Park? I'll tell you where we're going, you asshole. We're going right to the Brooklyn Police Department and talk to my friends there. We'll see what happens to you and your little popgun."

And he gunned the Lincoln so we were flying.

I was again thrown backward for a moment, but I recovered and stuck my gun barrel back against his head, harder this time.

"I swear, Yale, you slow down and head to Central Park or—"

BOOM. The rear window exploded, sending glass all over me and the back of Yale's head. I heard a couple more cracks, pistol shots. I looked back and saw that a black sedan was right behind us, with a gunman leaning out the passenger window and getting a bead on us with his pistol again.

Our car careened right and then left as Yale struggled to keep control. He floored it now, with the sedan right on our tail.

"Who are those guys?"

"I don't know," I shouted, burrowing as deep as I could into the floor in the back. "They're not with me."

"What the fuck is going on today?"

More shots came. Yale flung the car back-and-forth to avoid them. One clipped the side mirror. I snatched another look and saw that the sedan was pulling alongside us. There were four men inside, in overcoats and fedoras. I saw a shotgun barrel come out the back window as they came next to us.

BOOM.

A shotgun blast through the side window caused an explosion of blood from Yale's head and neck. He slumped onto the wheel and the speeding Lincoln spun in an arc across the sidewalk and crashed head-on into the stone steps of a brownstone. I put my arms over my head as a spray of bullets poured into the car to make sure Yale was dead, which he definitely was. Dead as they come.

I heard the sedan peel off. I put my gun back in my pocket and pushed my way out of the car. Onlookers were gathering, but I kept my head down and hurried off. No one tried to stop me. My plan to involve Yale in a gang war flopped again. Turns out he was already in one.

26

Marta's Lament

Marta

June 29, 1928:

I don't know what to do, diary. It's been almost two months that Walter's been gone. I write and I write and hardly a word do I get in return. It is hard on the children, for they don't understand. Especially poor Fern.

Today, we were in the kitchen, fixing dinner for the men in the fields. With Walter gone, Ma is again working with them, but she comes back to help put dinner together. To make sure I do it right, I mean. Fern and I were filling the baskets with bread when Fern asked me when her daddy was coming home.

"I'm not sure, my darling," I replied, trying to be honest with her. "Soon, I hope. He will come as soon as he is through helping your Uncle Cornelius with some problems that he has."

Fern worked this answer over in her smart little nine-year-old mind.

"What problems does Uncle Cornelius have?"

"I'm not sure, darling, but it is something your daddy has to help him with. He will come back as soon as he can."

I hoped that was true, but sometimes I cannot help but wonder. Walter is such a restless man. I know he loves me and I know there is no other woman, but could he be realizing the life here is too quiet, too safe for him? He is such a strange man, so quiet and gentle, yet he can be so harsh. He said he has to see that men in New York don't hurt the rest of our family like they hurt and killed poor Mr. O'Neal. But how can that be? If he and Cornelius know who killed Mr. O'Neal, why can't the police help?

And what of me, diary? I am restless, too. I am so busy with the children and helping Ma with the farm, yet I feel there should be more to life. I have said many times I should find work, something outside the house to be taken up with, but I see nothing that makes me really want to do it. Every time I try, the bad thoughts come and I don't dare take on anything new. Now I don't even have Mr. O'Neal to talk with about the books I read. Without him, I truly believe I could go mad. Fern and Hal are wonderful, but I need to talk with someone about the world outside this place. Is that wrong of me? Perhaps I am like Sister Carrie in the book by Mister Dreiser, always wanting more and never happy with what I have. When Walter is overcome with such a feeling, he goes off to New York. What can a woman do?

Walter's absence cannot be a good thing for Hal, especially since his own father has been absent his whole life. Hal must think it is life's way, that men go off while women stay at home and do the real work in life. Perhaps he is right.

27

A Rich Man Takes a Dive

Cornelius

No *Ile-de-France* suite for us. Anastasia and I were put in adjoining cabins on a cramped passenger schooner bound for Plymouth. From there, we planned to take a train into London to seek an audience with Alfred Loewenstein. Fortunately, Anastasia was no more inclined to be sociable with me than I with him. He suffered from seasickness and stayed in his room most of the time. Occasionally, I tried to draw him out to see if he knew more than I did about how we were supposed to persuade Loewenstein to do something he plainly didn't want to do, but it was like trying to charm Dracula. The whole time you were talking with him, you sensed he just wanted to chew off your throat and drink your blood. He was a man born in a state of rage and his only natural language was violence. Decades later, when I heard he'd been shot down in the barber shop of the Park Central, I only hoped they remembered to cut off his head and stuff it with garlic.

We arrived in London and checked into the cheap hotel where Rothstein had reserved us rooms. My instructions were to ring up Loewenstein's office and request an interview, so I did. I left a message and was told I would be called back. I wasn't. I called again and again and again, and it was the same routine. After the fourth try, I told Anastasia that we might as well go home.

"No dice. We're staying here until Uncle Arnold says we go home. You ain't got it so bad. See the town."

I had to admit, he was right. It was my first time in London and I liked what I saw. Big but horizontal, not like vertical New York. I liked the people, liked the sights, liked the beer. I especially liked walking around Speakers' Corner in Hyde Park to listen to the orators. But I was still there as a lackey for Arnold Rothstein and that knowledge soured everything, plus I had a job to get back to. I had a back-up doing the crime stories I was supposed to be writing, but Mr. Hearst wouldn't allow that to go on indefinitely. As the days passed, I grew increasingly sick of getting the runaround from Loewenstein's staff. I even showed up unannounced at his London office and was shown off the premises by the security goons. Anastasia was amused by it all. Then he disappeared for three or four days, but I didn't know if his secret business related to Loewenstein or to something else entirely.

It was a Monday morning when Anastasia dropped his bombshell. He knocked on the door of my room and delivered the news as soon as I opened up, without even saying hello.

"Frankie Yale got whacked," he said. "That should make your job easier."

And he turned on his heel and left.

This must be it, I realized. The Rothstein plan. He was behind Yale's murder, I thought, and indeed I later learned he had hired Al Capone's men to do the job, promising Capone a cut of the coming profits from the Loewenstein connection. This is why Rothstein and Anastasia didn't care that Loewenstein wasn't returning my calls. They wanted me on scene and ready to swoop in to talk with Loewenstein as soon as Yale was eliminated, since now Loewenstein would have no one but A.R. to hook up with. Yet, it seemed funny to me. Rothstein had made a big deal about Loewenstein liking his partners to be respectable, but murdering a rival like Yale wasn't particularly respectable. It seemed that Rothstein was getting desperate.

I searched through the British papers for a description of Yale's murder, but found nothing. I was hoping that Willie Altieri went down with his boss. I also wondered what Riley was doing. I tried calling Loewenstein's office again to see if Yale's killing had changed my reception. No soap. This time, the man who answered the phone threatened to call the constables if I didn't stop bothering him. That's what he called cops, "the constables."

I didn't see Anastasia again until the next evening, when he stopped by as abruptly as before and told me to be ready on short notice: we would be seeing Loewenstein the next day, the Fourth of July. By this time, I'd given up asking for explanations. I simply asked what time we'd be leaving and he told me to be ready to go any time after noon.

"I want to hear some sweet talk tomorrow," he said menacingly. "Rothstein sent you here to get a deal done. He don't want excuses."

Something about the look behind Anastasia's eyes drove me to the pub that night, for whiskey instead of beer.

It was mid-afternoon on Wednesday the fourth when Anastasia pounded on my door to bring me to Loewenstein. I had celebrated the American holiday by rubbing the bell man's nose in 1776, but my heart wasn't in it. I was too busy wondering what Albert Anastasia would do to me if I couldn't persuade the arrogant multi-millionaire to tie the knot with the Big Bankroll.

When we got in a taxi, Anastasia surprised me.

"Croydon Airport," he growled to the driver.

I hadn't been told to pack anything and Anastasia wasn't carrying a bag. I wondered if I was just supposed to tackle Loewenstein as he was boarding a plane. In fact, that's almost what happened.

Long since closed, Croydon was the main London airport back in the early days of commercial flight. There was a beautiful neoclassical terminal and an air of high-class adventure associated with the place, given it was only a year since the Lindbergh flight and there was still some feeling of derring-do surrounding air travel. I expect that appealed to an aggressive and demonstrative man like Loewenstein, who maintained a small state-of-the-art Fokker monoplane at Croydon for his personal use.

Anastasia bustled me out of the cab and led me to the main entrance to the terminal, where we were greeted by a handsome young man in the leather jacket and jodhpurs of a pilot. He and Anastasia nodded at each other, clearly having met before. Anastasia made no effort to introduce me, so the man stuck out his hand.

"How do you do?" he said with a smooth English accent. "I'm Donald Drew."

"Jimmy O'Neal," I said.

Here I was, with a murderous longshoreman from Brooklyn and a dashing young bloke who looked like he had stepped out of a Noel Coward drawing-room comedy. The social situation was new to me.

"Yes, well, you'll be wanting to get on the plane," Drew said. "Mr. Loewenstein is expected shortly."

Donald Drew walked us through the terminal, past a sign that read "Private Aeroplanes" and through a glass door onto the tarmac. He waved familiarly at attendants as we passed. No one stopped or questioned us. We came to a line of planes, with various workers idly standing about and smoking, which struck me as a poor idea around aircraft fuel. This early in the days of commercial aviation, these private planes must have been owned by men both rich and forward-thinking. I had no idea so many private planes existed.

Drew led us to a plane in about the middle of the line. I am no aviation expert and this one looked no different to me than the others, though Drew patted it admiringly.

"She's a beauty, isn't she? Flies like a dream."

"Just keep the fucker up in the air," Anastasia said.

I suspected that, like me, Anastasia had never flown and was a bit nervous about the idea.

The plane had one wing stretching out both ways atop the main cabin, with a large propeller at the nose. A series of letters were emblazoned on the sides, but I didn't know what they signified. It didn't look all that fancy to me for such a rich man's toy. It was the biggest of the private planes on view, though.

I only saw one door and it was toward the back of the plane on the side facing us. When Drew knocked, a man opened it from inside and started lowering a flight of steps so we could enter.

"Bob Little," said Drew. "Our mechanic."

Anastasia looked at him sourly.

"What do we need a mechanic for?"

Drew smiled.

"You should hope that we don't, but if we do, we'll need him very badly."

Anastasia didn't think this was funny.

We all climbed on board, Drew last so he could pull up the steps behind us and shut the door. To my surprise, once we'd stepped through the only outside door to the plane, we were immediately in a small chamber that contained a toilet and washbasin.

Drew saw my expression and laughed.

"The big man designed this plane himself. Not sure why he wanted the loo to be the first thing you see when you come aboard, but there's no accounting for taste."

Drew gestured for us to pass through a door to our left, which brought us into the main cabin. The cockpit was plainly visible to us, as only a transparent partition separated it from the passenger area. There were bench seats along each side wall and a large throne-like chair in the front, facing backward, where the great man would no doubt sit. I've never seen another airplane quite like it but, as Drew pointed out, there is no accounting for taste, especially that of the world's second-richest man.

It was obvious that Anastasia had been communicating with Drew and Little, having bought them off. Maybe this was the only way to get a moment with Loewenstein, but the cabin of his plane seemed a crazy place to try to negotiate a narcotics deal. No doubt Loewenstein would have some sort of entourage. How were we to have any privacy in a private plane? Go to the privy together? Then it occurred to me that a beast like Albert Anastasia might simply kill all the witnesses who weren't safely bribed. Difficult thing to explain once we landed, it seemed to me.

The fact that I was entirely in the dark about what the plan was, what I was expected to say, and what I could offer Loewenstein as inducement to join up with Rothstein nearly caused me to leave my seat and bolt from the plane. I'd given up trying to pump my companion for information or instructions. Anastasia sat next to me, eyes closed, looking like he'd chosen this moment for a nap. Drew was in the cockpit, doing whatever pilots do before a flight. Little had disappeared. I could do nothing but wipe my sweating palms on my knees and await developments.

It was a fine, warm mid-summer evening. As the sun dropped near the English horizon, I heard a car pull up very near the plane. I leaned forward to look out the opposite window just as a chauffeur opened the door of a long elegant limousine and Alfred Loewenstein stepped out. The rich man was dressed too warmly for the weather: he sported a heavy fur-collared coat, with a derby hat perched on his head. Behind his vehicle was a less imposing auto from which two men and two women disembarked. As Loewenstein stepped onto the gangway leading into the plane, Anastasia sidled over next to the entry to the main cabin.

Good God, I thought, *he's going to chloroform the man. Or strangle him.*

I was close. The moment Loewenstein flung open the cabin door, Anastasia's big hand closed on his wrist and pulled him roughly inside. Loewenstein stumbled and dropped his cane, but he kept his feet. Drew had opened the door to the cockpit partition to welcome his employer and his mouth dropped when he saw the rough treatment.

Drew's shock was nothing to the amazement and indignation on the face of Alfred Loewenstein. No coward, Loewenstein raised his fists to attack the interloper, but Anastasia's gun barrel in his face stopped him cold.

"Sit down and shut your trap," Anastasia hissed at him. "We're going for an airplane ride."

Loewenstein snapped his head to his nearest employee.

"Drew, what is the meaning of this?"

Drew shrugged helplessly while Anastasia grasped Loewenstein by the shoulder and pushed him down onto a seat opposite from where we'd been sitting.

"I said sit down and I mean it. This guy's gonna talk to you and you're gonna listen to what he has to say. You give him a hard time and I'll slap you around." Anastasia turned back to the cabin door, where Loewenstein's entourage was standing dumbfounded. "Get in here, all of you. Let's get this plane moving."

Here, I thought, everything would fall apart. These new arrivals would join with Loewenstein in an assault on Anastasia and it wasn't clear to me that he could overcome all of them. I certainly wasn't going to help him, though my position was an awkward one. To my amazement, the two men and two women who accompanied Loewenstein simply put their heads down and moved silently to their seats. Little, behind them, closed the exterior door and moved to his seat in the front next to Drew. Loewenstein's mouth dropped open as he realized this monstrous invasion was no surprise to his loyal retinue. They were in on it.

The fact is, those days that I'd wandered London while Anastasia went missing, he'd been bribing and intimidating the employees whom he'd learned were flying to Brussels with Loewenstein. Drew, Loewenstein's pilot, was the first he'd approached. Drew had easily persuaded Little to join the plot and he'd told Anastasia the critical link was Arthur Hodgson, Loewenstein's secretary and chief assistant, a lean, pale fellow who just now was sitting quietly in the far end of the plane, glaring hatred at his employer and smiling grimly. The others—Lowenstein's valet and two female typists—succumbed to the combination of Rothstein's money and Anastasia's intimidating ferocity. As Anastasia would explain to me on the return voyage home, "They hated the bastard's guts. I gave them the choice between making a bunch of money by fucking him over or getting dead. They saw my point of view."

Anastasia signaled Drew to get back in his place and get the flight started. In a few minutes, we heard Drew speaking over the radio to the control tower and Loewenstein began shouting for help in the hope the tower would hear. Anastasia leaned over with his pistol and slapped Loewenstein across the head with it, removing any doubt as to whether he was prepared to do violence to the great man. This bought a period of sustained horrified silence from the occupants of the cabin, except for Hodgson, who rather seemed to want Anastasia to take another whack. The engines revved, the wheels turned, we lumbered down the runway, and we were off to God-knew-where to accomplish God-knew-what.

Once we'd leveled off, Anastasia told me to start talking. Loewenstein was glaring at me as he held his palm against the spot where Anastasia had clipped him. He did not appear to be a receptive audience.

"Look," I said, "it's too bad we had to start like this." God, it sounded ridiculous. "You wouldn't see me any other way. You know that Frankie Yale is dead?"

Loewenstein said nothing.

"Well, he is. He was killed three days ago, in New York. That's all I know. I don't know who killed him."

Loewenstein gave a grim smile at that, but still said nothing.

"I'm here for Arnold Rothstein. I'm authorized to say the proposal he made to you in New York is still good. Mr. Rothstein sincerely wants to be your business partner. Respectfully, Mr. Loewenstein, Mr. Rothstein could have lowered his offer once Mr. Yale passed, since there aren't really any qualified competitors now. But he respects you as a businessman and knows that your connection and your product are excellent opportunities, so he keeps his offer where it is, as a sign of good faith."

This brought another smile from Loewenstein and it was not a friendly one.

"'Sign of good faith,'" he repeated. "I hate that phrase. It means nothing, but confidence men use it when they are trying to cheat a fool."

"You are no fool, Mr. Loewenstein," I said quickly. "Neither is Arnold Rothstein and he's not a confidence man either. He has connections in New York's government and the police that are second to none. He conducts the highest-class bootlegging operation on the east coast. He's constantly in the public eye as a gambler, but he's never been convicted of anything, never even been arrested since he was a kid. Do you have something against him, Mr. Loewenstein? He's such an obvious choice, yet..."

"Stop!" Loewenstein pounded his fist on his knee, and the cold fury in his voice made even Albert Anastasia straighten up in his seat. "I will never associate myself with Arnold Rothstein. He is a gangster! I would never have associated with Frankie Yale, either. I made it clear to both of them. I am a respected businessman and I do not associate with such people."

Anastasia and I were both staring at him with our mouths open.

"Don't take this wrong, Mr. Loewenstein," I finally stammered, "but don't you sell, um, heroin?"

Loewenstein drew his knees together primly.

"I export agricultural products of various sorts, including processed opium poppy. I do not control the processing operations, though I hold a significant equity position in them. These are just one of many operations for which I am responsible. I am not a hoodlum, regardless of what Mr. Rothstein might think."

The human race amazes me.

Anastasia felt the same way.

"So who the fuck you gonna get to run your dope for you? Henry Ford?"

Loewenstein curled his lip, treating Anastasia to a sneer that anyone who knew Albert's reputation in Brooklyn would have regarded as suicidal.

"Whom I choose to associate with is none of your concern, nor your employer's. When we arrive in Brussels, I intend to have the lot of you arrested for kidnapping. And that is all I am going to say."

He clamped his mouth shut with an air of finality. I started to remonstrate, but Anastasia held up his hand and waved at me to forget about it. This surprised me, since I figured he'd want me to keep trying, but maybe Anastasia had more sense than I thought. Loewenstein was clearly not going to budge, as ludicrous as were his pretensions to clean hands, and I had no authority to sweeten the deal. I didn't even know what the deal was, so I was happy to sit back and keep silent for the rest of the flight, figuring I'd done my duty for Rothstein and Anastasia wouldn't tell him any different. I decided not to worry about Loewenstein's threat of arrest in Brussels, for Rothstein would have planned for this contingency. I had a feeling we were not going to Brussels.

We were not. Loewenstein became suspicious as the plane crested the French coast and immediately started to descend.

"Drew! What are you doing!" he demanded, pounding on the partition that led to the cockpit.

Drew didn't react, but Anastasia did. He drew his gun from his waistband and held it on Loewenstein. Words were unnecessary: the rich man immediately put his hands in his lap and shut his mouth. He was having a bad night.

I became nervous myself, for I looked out the window behind me and saw no lights below, just a strip of beach backed by a range of hills, with an old tower of some sort at water's edge. The tower was a single column of stone, apparently the remnant of some medieval structure. It was maybe twelve stories high and at the top was a parapet surrounded by a crenellated stone battlement. The whole structure looked like a rook from a giant's chess game. To this day, I don't know where we were, other than somewhere on the coast of France or Belgium, probably near Calais.

I didn't see how we could possibly land on this dark beach,

but I needn't have worried for Drew proved himself an adept hand at piloting. He landed that Fokker gently on the sand and brought it to as easy a stop as if we were on the tarmac at Orly. I thought Anastasia might at least have tipped him a thumb's up for the flying exhibition, but he was all business. He immediately stood and waved Loewenstein to rise and exit the plane ahead of him. As they walked toward the door, Anastasia turned to the assembled passengers.

"All of you keep still. We'll be back. Don't talk, don't do nothing. Just wait for us." Then he noticed that I was still seated. "Come on, O'Neal. You come with us."

I didn't think I wanted to see whatever was going to happen.

"Look, I've done my bit. I'll just stay here."

"Your bit is done when I say it's done," he snarled, his hand on Loewenstein's shoulder to hold him still. "Follow me or you know what'll happen. Rothstein's waiting for my report on you."

I knew he was right. Whatever I was about to witness, I'd have to deal with it.

We scrambled off the plane and stood on the sand. At last Loewenstein's icy composure was cracking, as it should have been. Instead of a civilized airport in Brussels, he was stranded on a dark, deserted beach with a murderous ape holding a gun on him. If I were Loewenstein, I'd have been offering Rothstein all the poppy in Turkey, with a ride on one of my racehorses thrown in, but Loewenstein was a tough bird and kept his counsel.

Anastasia gave him a shove to start him walking toward the tower, which was the only destination in sight unless Loewenstein was simply to be shot where he stood. We came to an opening in the wall at the bottom of the tower, leading to a winding set of stairs that no doubt climbed to the parapet at the top. I wasn't eager to take the twelve-story walk and was sure Loewenstein didn't relish the idea either, but we didn't have the gun. At Anastasia's direction we started up, me in the lead and Anastasia bringing up the rear, lighting our way with a flashlight he'd pulled from his coat pocket.

Our shadows loomed in front of us as we trudged upward. I noticed footmarks in the dust on the steps, suggesting someone had passed this way not long before. When we finally neared the top, I was winded, but not so much that I wasn't startled to see light coming from the parapet at the top. Someone was there.

I paused a moment, but Anastasia urged me upward. When my head cleared the opening to the parapet, I saw a man holding a flashlight, leaning against the battlement with his feet crossed and arms folded, seemingly quite relaxed. He was a barrel-chested fellow of middling height, with neatly-slicked dark hair surmounting a sour-looking face. He wore a pea jacket and dark trousers, giving him a slightly nautical look. As the three of us all mounted to the parapet, he spoke with a sharp, nasal voice.

"*Guten Abend, Herr Loewenstein.*"

I recognized a Berliner accent, similar to those which surrounded me in that city during the Spartacist Revolution. I speak excellent German because my dad drilled me in it as a child, so I could read Goethe and Schiller in their original tongue. I wondered if I might be here as a translator.

Loewenstein started when he saw the man and gazed at him with loathing and surprise. He unleashed a torrent of German at him.

"You! Richter! Are you in league with these hoodlums? Have you lost your senses, man? How could you betray me?"

That brought Herr Richter across the parapet and into Loewenstein's face.

"Now you will know. For thirteen years you treated me like a slave. I built the poppy farms, I negotiated with the Turks, I opened the shipment routes to Europe. You just sat in London and played with your racehorses."

"How dare you?" Loewenstein snapped, drawing himself to full height.

Not, apparently, the right response. Richter spat in his face. Anastasia stuffed his gun in his waistband and wrapped his meaty longshoreman arms around Loewenstein.

"Enough of this shit."

Anastasia was a strong guy. Loewenstein was no lightweight, but Anastasia pulled him off the floor and over to the wall. Richter picked up his feet, called him a pig-dog, and presto, they tipped him over and off into space.

I don't remember a scream, just some guttural grunts as the world's second-richest man fell to his death on the beach below. Whoever had been number three just got promoted. I couldn't help stepping to the wall and looking down at Loewenstein's broken body, face down in the surf. I didn't regard the delusional heroin dealer as a great loss to the world, but I was concerned about my own position in the matter. Was I about to follow Loewenstein's deep dive? Even if not, I was now a witness to first-degree murder, linking me more irrevocably than ever to Rothstein and his mobsters. Little wonder I nearly threw up on the corpse below. How could I ever get out of this?

At least I wasn't meant for the Big Jump. Anastasia, who seemed no more concerned than if it had been a peach pit that he threw over the side, turned to me.

"Now's when you earn your trip to Europe, newspaperman." He pointed to Richter. "This guy don't speak no English. Tell him the deal is set just like we planned. We'll take care of the people on the plane and he needs to get his men to move the stiff."

I relayed this in German to Richter, omitting some of the gangster slang. He smiled.

"Your friend may rest assured we will do our part. You see below, we are already starting." He pointed downward, where a fishing dinghy had appeared and was being rowed steadily toward the corpse. "That arrogant bastard will be floating in the Channel before your plane is in the air."

I translated for Anastasia, who saw the fishing boat and nodded. Richter held up his palm.

"There is one more thing. The money you've given me so far was just for my help with arrangements here. Now I require a down payment, a non-refundable down payment, before my shipments will start for Red Hook."

Anastasia's eyes narrowed at my translation, but he told me to ask how much.

"Five million American dollars, to be delivered to me in Marseille. Then and only then will Mr. Rothstein be our distributor. It is a small thing in comparison to the amounts involved."

I didn't think Anastasia would think it a small thing and I was right. As soon as the number was out of my mouth, Anastasia snarled like a dog and grabbed Richter by the lapels. I knew Rothstein wouldn't be happy with either of us if Richter went off on the flying trapeze, so I took Anastasia by the arm.

"Don't do it, Rothstein wouldn't like it. This guy is the key to the connection. Let A.R. decide if he wants to pay or not."

That made sense and Anastasia knew it. Reluctantly, he released Richter. I told Richter we'd get Rothstein's answer and the party broke up. Sure enough, by the time we got down those damn stairs, the dinghy was barely visible out in the Channel and the corpse was gone. The tide had even washed away the imprint of the rich man's body, as though he'd never been there. As far as the world has been concerned, he never was.

I didn't anticipate it at the time, but we created a mystery that bedeviled the world's press and law enforcement agencies for years: the mystery of the Man Who Fell from the Sky. Anastasia bribed and scared the passengers and crew of the plane sufficiently that they adhered to the story he had impressed into their brains, that Loewenstein got up during the flight to Brussels to go to the bathroom and he never came back. That's what they said when Drew landed the plane briefly on another beach, Saint-Pol, where they told authorities their passenger simply vanished from the plane. That's what they told the police when they returned to London and what they said when asked about the subject for the rest of their lives. The implication was that Loewenstein had mistakenly opened the plane's exit door rather than the door to the cabin after he had done his business and had stepped into open space. Sure enough, his body was found in the Channel about two weeks after the flight and it looked like he'd had a bad fall. The man must have stepped out the wrong door, a sad accident.

The problem, people soon realized, was that it couldn't have happened. Tests showed that one man couldn't have forced the exit door open in mid-flight against the air pressure that would have existed. In any event, the opening of the door would have shaken the whole plane in a way that the passengers could not fail to note. Yet they all insisted that Loewenstein simply went to the bathroom and never came out, with no one noticing any problem until they thought to look for him, at which time the exit door was found to be shut and in perfectly normal condition.

Rothstein was called the Brain for a reason. In typical fashion, he had lined up the disgruntled Mr. Richter, Loewenstein's operations manager in Marseille, as his fallback if he couldn't convince Loewenstein to be his partner. He chose the most intimidating assassin available to him to buy the cooperation of Donald Drew and the other people who were set to travel in the plane and to terrify them into sticking to the script once the deed was done. Knowing there was no hope of changing Loewenstein's mind, he sent me along, not to persuade a man who refused to be persuaded, but to translate between Anastasia and Richter and incidentally to be an eyewitness to Loewenstein's murder, making me even more effectively his slave.

It was Rothstein who came up with the idea of throwing Loewenstein from the tower and planting his body in the water, to suggest he fell from the plane. He knew the death of such a wealthy man would inevitably draw heavy police attention if it were done by an ordinary murder, but a dive from the plane in mid-Channel wouldn't even be clearly in any particular force's jurisdiction. A.R. was not a very jolly man, as you've probably gathered by now, but he actually chortled as he read the press coverage of the Man Who Fell from the Sky. He figured a body falling from twelve stories and being found out at sea would look on autopsy close enough to a body that fell from an airplane that no one would notice the difference. No one did. Numerous commentators obsessed over the mystery and a number of ingenious theories were posited, but none was remotely close to the truth.

The theorists failed by embracing complexity. They came up with fancy explanations when they should have simply accepted the inevitable consequence of the fact that the exit door could not possibly have opened in mid-flight.

It didn't.

28

Rothstein Feels the Pinch

Cornelius

"*Five million dollars?*"

Rothstein shouted the words, looking surprised, angry, and sick all at the same time. He was far more upset than I expected, given that he was such a high roller. Apparently five million was a lot of dollars, no matter who you're asking.

Anastasia and I had wasted no time shipping back to New York. We'd both kept in communication by telegraph with Rothstein on and off, but we weren't going to get into detail about drugs and murder over the wires. Anastasia had slipped off as soon as we reached New York, so I made my report to the boss by myself. This was the first he'd heard the figure that Richter was demanding.

We were in Rothstein's suite at the Park Central. The story of our adventures with Loewenstein amused Rothstein. I remember him smiling as I said the cops were going nuts trying to figure out how Loewenstein fell out of the plane. But the smile vanished when I mentioned the amount Richter demanded as the price of admission to the biggest heroin-smuggling operation then in existence.

"This was never part of the deal. This crook is holding me up."

I shrugged.

"So what? If this deal is worth that much to you, just pay him. You've already killed I don't know how many people for it."

Rothstein stared daggers at me. He bit his lip, looking worried. Abruptly, he pushed himself to his feet and paced to the window, gazing down on Seventh Avenue.

"It's a bad time, that's all," he said finally. "I'm a little short."

That brought up my eyebrows.

"You? The Big Bankroll? You don't get short, you make everybody else short."

He was rubbing his fingers on the window sill, as if to rub away his situation. I didn't think I'd ever seen Rothstein nervous before.

"Listen, Cornelius. That's what Damon calls you, isn't it? Cornelius?"

I nodded.

"This can't get around town. I can't let people know I'm short. It'd be bad for my reputation. Times are tough right now. Just temporary."

"I know you got hit at Aqueduct a couple of times this summer, but that's nothing new. Nobody wins at the horses, not when they bet as often as you or Runyon."

Rothstein shook his head.

"It wasn't just a couple of times. It's been every time I go, I lose a bundle. Memorial Day was the worst, but I just can't get even. That's not the worst of it, though. It's the real estate. I got taken by a bunch of politicians on a stadium deal in Detroit. That housing development out on Long Island, it's sucking the money right out of my pockets. The casino deal is still costing me. And investments in Saratoga and everything else I touch is going down the toilet. But the Long Island thing is the worst."

"The bootlegging must make money. I haven't noticed anybody's stopped drinking."

"Too many partners. I pay the suppliers, I pay the distributors like Owney Madden and that *gonif* Dutch Schultz, I pay a cut to Masseria, and at the end of the day there's not enough margin to float my losses at the ponies, much less real estate." The troubled little bastard let out a long sigh. "You can't imagine the expenses I've got, Cornelius."

"Vantine's?"

Rothstein's fist hit the desk.

"That's been my biggest disappointment. What I get for relying on Chinamen. Narcotics should be the surest bet in the world, the way people get hooked on that stuff, but you have to have a steady supply if you want to make money and I never know if the product's going to show up or not. It's just not business-like, Cornelius. That's why I'm so anxious to make a deal with an established business run by white men, so I can keep the supply flowing."

Rothstein was nowhere near the first crook in America and he was not even the first organized crook, but it was Rothstein who taught all the other crooks to talk like they went to business school. Most of them, it must be said, didn't do it as well as Arnold.

I wasn't sure what I was supposed to say to all this, but I was intrigued to see the always unflappable Rothstein becoming indisputably flapped. He must indeed have been feeling the old pinch to look so stressed and to blab so much to a mere civilian, even one he had over his barrel. Of course, maybe since Loewenstein's murder, he didn't so much think of me as a civilian anymore. Maybe he was right, maybe I was joining the underworld, bit by bit. That was a disturbing thought.

Rothstein seemed to have a thought just then, too. He narrowed his eyes and looked at me, then he gave that creepy imitation of a smile and sat back down at his desk.

"We're going to have to work together on this, Cornelius. Believe me, I know how to make it worth your while. I always take care of my partners."

I expect there might be some tombstones in Brooklyn inscribed "Here because A.R. always takes care of his partners."

"I need some time to get this money together," he continued. "That means you have to talk to this Richter, get him to wait awhile. You speak German, you can charm him, let him know I'm good for it, that I just need time. It's a cinch. He can ask anybody on Broadway, they know I'm the Big Bankroll. Speaking of which…"

Rothstein pulled his wad from his side pocket. He peeled the first two hundreds off the roll and froze. He jammed the dough back in his pocket, but I had caught a glimpse of George Washington peeking at me from the next bill down. Of all people, the great Rothstein was flashing an East Side bankroll! Now I knew he was in trouble.

He handed me the two C-notes and tried to smile.

"That's just a token. You buy me time to make this deal and

you'll see a lot more. Let's say one hundred thousand smackers once the dope money is flowing. Even better, Cornelius, the day the first shipment lands at Red Hook, I'll tear up all the papers that link you to the Pope's Usurer sale. You'll be free to be a straight citizen again, if you want. Or you can keep working for me and make more money than you ever dreamed about. Sound good?"

No, actually, A.R., it does not sound good. It sounds like you need me to work with Richter because I speak German and you have a handle on me. It sounds like you're promising me a hundred large and my freedom from you because you have no intention of giving me either one. Meaning the day you close this deal, I'm dead.

"Sounds terrific," I said.

I shook his outstretched hand. Rothstein wasn't the only one who needed time.

When I came out of the Park Central, it was lunchtime. I walked over to Lindy's in part to eat some chopped liver, but mostly to find Runyon. He was sure to have the dope on Rothstein's financial woes. Whether he'd tell me was another question.

It was a hot July day and I was sweating when I pushed open the door at Lindy's and scanned the room. Runyon was at his usual table, the same one where I first bearded him all those years ago. It could have been the same moment in time: Runyon sat there reading a paper, smoking a cigarette, drinking coffee over the remains of some egg dish he'd had for lunch, looking just as he did in 1919. Runyon never changed. He still watched New York through his rimless glasses, saw much, wrote well, said little.

He didn't look up as I sat at his table and waved for a waiter. He finished the story he was reading. When done, he raised his eyes and looked at me, mutely inviting me to say something or not, as I chose.

I chose.

"What's up with Rothstein these days? Have you heard anything about him being down on his luck?"

Runyon frowned.

"And the reason you're asking is what?"

Morrie, one of the oldest waiters at Lindy's, took my sandwich order and Damon lit another cigarette. When Morrie had buzzed off, barking at the busboy, I shrugged.

"I'm the crime reporter and Arnold Rothstein is our biggest criminal," I said. "I try to keep up."

"Are you writing about Rothstein? It's good to see you writing about something, you're taking too much time off lately. But writing about Rothstein would not be a healthy undertaking."

"Relax. Deep background. That's your specialty, isn't it? What's going on?"

Runyon glanced around for eavesdroppers. Apparently satisfied, he leaned across the table and spoke even more softly than usual.

"The Brain's been acting peculiar lately. You know he's always so cool, placid, like he's clammy. This summer, he's different, barks at people, all high-strung. He dropped a hundred and thirty grand at Aqueduct on Memorial Day and now he's betting the horses almost every day, more and more. Betting wild and always covering with markers, no cash up front. I watch him at his table here and he doesn't push across with the shekels anymore when he gets a sad story from a citizen. Word is that he's losing a bundle on real estate deals, too, but I wouldn't know about that." Runyon smiled and waved his cigarette, dropping ashes on the table. "It happens. Nobody wins at the track. But this is Arnold Rothstein we're talking about."

"Meaning what?"

"Meaning he's not like other guys." Runyon paused for a moment, marshaling his words. "A.R. is involved in nearly every dirty deal in this dirty town, yet he sits here in Lindy's every day where anybody can find him. The mayor, the governor, the big Broadway stars, they all shake his hand with smiles on their faces. He's a cold and bad man, but he's got a heart. Did you know, even though his father disowned him long ago, he visits his mother every month? A couple of years ago, he even gave his father's synagogue an anonymous gift of a Torah cabinet, with a replica for his old man thrown in? He's an unusual man, the Brain. He's not all bad and he's thought up more ways to make money than anybody on Wall Street ever heard of. He'll be back."

That was what I worried about. He'd be back. He'd pay the German his money and then, I was dead certain, James Cornelius O'Neal would go into the Gowanus Canal and never come out. I couldn't let that deal be made until we found the ledgers and had leverage on Rothstein.

Until then, I had to keep him broke so he couldn't conclude the deal and he'd still need me. How in the name of all that's unholy was I going to do that? Who could sink Arnold Rothstein?

That was the moment when Fate sat down at the table and called for a new deal. As I looked around the restaurant, the door to Lindy's opened and in walked a tall, rail-thin road gambler in a fancy fedora, sharp linen suit, and newly shined shoes. In walked the unbeatable proposition man who always bet to the sky.

I waved my hand to him.

"Hello, Titanic," I said.

29

Marta Gets Fed Up

Marta

August 4, 1928:

I've come to a decision.

I've written and written to Walter, pages and pages, and he writes hardly at all. Then today I was excited, for another letter came from him. What did it say? I will put every word in my diary:

> *Darling:*
> *I miss you. And little Fern and everybody.*
> *Nothing to say here. Still trying to help Cornelius.*
> *Take care. Love, Your Walter*

I can't bear any more. I don't care if he is a silent man, if this is all he can write after he has been away for three months, I fear I am losing him. I told Ma today, I am going to New York. I will come back to help during harvest time and I hope to bring Walter back with me. Ma and Rose can look after the children. I won't tell Walter I'm coming, I will just go. I'm taking the train tomorrow.

I will not let my Walter drift away from me. Not without a fight.

30

Recruiting Titanic

Cornelius

Being a guy who was out and about along Broadway more than somewhat, as Damon Runyon would say, I saw Titanic Thomas occasionally and heard lots of stories about him. I heard that he'd collected the scalps of half the financiers on Wall Street in a string of high-stakes poker games. He'd gone to the Polo Grounds and made a pile on crazy side bets, like how far he could throw a peanut—he'd planted lead shot inside the peanut shell to help, of course. He sank all the golfers he played, after hustling them into making the biggest bet he figured they could pay. His only losses were at Aqueduct since, like Rothstein and Runyon, he couldn't beat the ponies and he couldn't stay away from them.

Most interesting to me, I heard about Titanic's relationship with Arnold Rothstein. Back in the spring, shortly after he got into town, Titanic was standing in Times Square with Rothstein and Runyon. He bet them that if you read license plates as poker hands, the next New Jersey plate they saw would beat the next New York plate. The New Jersey plate won with three threes, because the driver of the car was waiting to drive by until Titanic took off his hat. Runyon was a born sap when it came to gambling, but Rothstein should have known that Titanic would always know the odds and then improve them.

After losing small amounts on a couple more of Titanic's propositions, Rothstein swore off, saying he'd never bet against Titanic again. Indeed, after Titanic had been in Manhattan less than six months, much of the greater New York area swore off him as well. This was the great problem of the road gambler: once word on him got around a town, his action dried up. Then he would have no choice but to leave for another place, another population of suckers. And Titanic was starting to run out of towns. He knew he'd have to leave New York soon, but first he was determined to accomplish one of his main goals in the Big Apple. He wanted to bust Arnold Rothstein, the greatest gambler in the biggest city in the country.

I explained all this to Riley the day I saw Titanic at Lindy's.

"Titanic Thomas is to gambling what Babe Ruth is to home runs," I said. "If he could play Rothstein at anything, Rothstein wouldn't be able to put up the money for the heroin deal for months. But he can't help us if Rothstein won't play him."

We were sitting at my kitchen table. Riley was eating a baloney sandwich. He looked thoughtful.

"You can't talk him into playing with this Thomas fellow? Seems like Rothstein's getting to like you."

I shivered.

"That little shark doesn't like anything but money. He's figured out that Titanic sinks everybody, even him, and he won't touch him."

Riley closed his eyes and thought for a moment.

"He won't bet against him," he said, "but what if he bets with him?"

"Meaning?"

Riley rose and poured himself a shot of whiskey.

"You remember how I played a lot of poker in the army? One time, this guy was winning all the pots, making bets no one should make and cashing in more often than not. Another one of the players who had a little more experience than I did figured that this guy was playing partners with his buddy and they were signaling each other how to bet and what their hands held. I never knew you could do that, but it's a big advantage. 'Less you get caught, of course."

"What happened to the cheaters?"

"Oh, we beat the hell out of them. I expect a man who did that to Rothstein'd get shot."

I nodded.

"He would. Titanic's killed four men on the road. It's a rough profession. Where are you going with this?"

Riley sat back down at the table and looked hard at me.

"Say Rothstein thought he and Titanic were partners. Say a game was set up by someone Rothstein trusted, with patsies ready to bet high. Seems like Rothstein might view that as a chance to get his deal money all in one sitting, if he thinks this Titanic was helping him instead of betting against him. If Thomas is as good as you say he is, I'd think he could figure a way to turn the tables and bust Rothstein instead of being his partner."

It sounded crazy to me, but I didn't know enough about gambling to evaluate it.

"Well, I can't think of anything better. Let's see what Titanic says."

We tracked Titanic down at the Union League Club, where he was playing cribbage with a member who hadn't yet gotten the word about him. We arrived just as Titanic, who had lost a number of rounds, was raising the stakes.

"Bill, you got to give me a chance to get even," Titanic was pleading in his Arkansas drawl as we crossed the ornate game room and approached their card table.

Titanic's opponent was a fleshy captain of industry, bald on top with red hair on the sides, and he was obviously pleased with his winnings to that point.

"Now, Alvin," he said, "maybe you should take it easy. You're a beginner at this game. It's not as easy as it looks."

"Consarn it, Bill, don't come all superior with me. I may be an Arkansas country boy, but I'm entitled to a game if I want one. Tell you what, I'm a fool but I feel my luck's turning. I'll bet you ten thousand dollars on one hand. You win, we call it a day and you can go back to your office with all my money. What do you say?"

Bill was plainly tempted.

"I don't know, Alvin, that's a lot of money."

"Come on, show me some respect, give me a chance to get ahead.

Not much of a chance at that, you've taken every hand so far. They told me you have a little gamble in you, were they wrong?"

Of course, Bill made the bet. Riley and I took seats against the wall and waited. I had no idea how it was possible to cheat at cribbage, but I figured Titanic knew. He bet on everything.

Sure enough, one hand later, Bill was scrawling out a check and storming past us. Titanic carefully folded the check and put it in his pocket, then walked out and signaled us to follow him. He'd seen me looking at him, but didn't want me to disturb his pigeon.

We took a table at a nearby sandwich place and laid out Riley's idea. When we finished, Titanic stared into space and didn't speak for several minutes. He was calculating odds.

Finally, he spoke.

"It's got to be poker. Rothstein thinks he's better at poker than he really is, so that's our edge. And I need a partner."

To my amazement, Riley said, "I could do it. I've played some poker."

Under other circumstances, Titanic would instantly have played Riley as a mark. Here, though, there was serious money to be made, so he looked scornfully at Riley.

"Rothstein's a pro and I need a pro. I'll get Nate Raymond. I played partners with him back in Chicago, taught him the system I worked out with Nick the Greek. Nate'll do it." Titanic looked at me. "You sure you can set up the game?"

"Better. I can get to a guy Rothstein trusts and he'll set up the game. This guy is so stupid, Rothstein will take him at face value."

I had already decided to use Hump McManus, as he had set up other games for Rothstein and he was as dumb as I said.

"What do you expect for a cut?" Titanic asked.

I'd anticipated this question.

"We don't want a cut. We have reasons of our own to want Rothstein cleaned out. You do that, you keep all the money and split it with this Nate Raymond however you want. Just don't ask why we want to take down Rothstein. It's not your business."

Now there was only a short pause before Titanic stuck out his hand.

"You get me the game," he said as I shook it, "and I'll pick him clean."

Such was my faith in Titanic's mythic powers that I felt Rothstein was already as good as busted. Riley caught my enthusiasm and we were in the best of moods when we headed back to my apartment. All of that changed when we saw who was waiting for us there, standing at the door like a mother who had finally caught up with her errant boys.

It was Marta.

31

Riley's Breakfast

Jim

I met Riley for breakfast in the kitchen. The night before, I had gotten to the point in my reading where Riley and Cornelius came upon Marta in the hall outside Cornelius' apartment.

"Must have been quite a shock," I said to Riley.

"What?" he asked.

He took a puff on the unfiltered Camel that, along with a few cups of black coffee, served him as breakfast.

"Coming upon Marta in the hall outside Cornelius' apartment when you didn't know she was coming. Or did you know?"

I poured a bowl of Grape Nuts for myself, though I knew they were stale.

"No, I didn't know. Couldn't blame her though. I ran off without telling her much and here I'd been gone three months. No wonder she got fed up. That as far as you've read?"

"I looked at the next chapter, but it skips ahead to the poker game when Grandmother was already gone. So I thought I'd stop reading until I asked you what happened with her."

Riley nodded.

"Well, that's good. Because I think what your grandmother did during the rest of the story might surprise you. I know she surprised me."

32

The Lady of the Hacienda

Riley

Being the daughter of a Mexican don, Marta knew how to be haughty and dignified when she wanted. That's how she was when Cornelius and I got back to the apartment. She didn't blow up at me about how long I'd been gone or for hardly writing her or anything like that. She was ice-cold when I leaned in to kiss her hello, though. Once we went inside and got settled in the living room, with Cornelius perched only halfway onto his chair like he was ready to bolt at the first sign of Marta getting emotional, she folded her hands in her lap and spoke like the lady of the hacienda.

"I am glad you are both here, because what I have to say is for both of you. Walter, you have to come home. The children miss you. Your daughter misses you. Your mother needs help on the farm. This isn't fair to any of us. I don't know what you've been doing here with Cornelius and you don't have to tell me. You just have to come home."

My head was sinking lower and lower as she spoke. I felt like a damn dog. I'd been trying to help my friend, but did he need me as much as my family back home? You know how you tell yourself something but you know it isn't really the whole truth, because the whole truth hurts so much worse and says something so bad about you that you can hardly bear it? That was me then. I knew that helping

Cornelius and getting some sort of payback for Jack O'Neal was part of why I left home, but not all. The fact was, home was boring to me and I'd been enjoying New York and Cornelius and having some action again, like during the war or afterward in Berlin. What's the matter with me?

Even so, I had to shake my head.

"Sweetheart, I know I've done wrong. I should've told you more about what's happening, I just didn't want to scare you, is all."

I reached for her hand and this time she didn't shy away.

"Scare me? Mr. O'Neal killed, you gone for months? How could I be more scared, my husband? Nothing is worse than not knowing. We have had trouble before, Walter. You should have known that I can survive trouble."

God, the look on her face when she said that. I glanced over at Cornelius, who nodded.

"We'll tell you everything," I said.

So we did. We told her all we knew about Rothstein and Runyon, the Adonis Club, Paddy Maloney, Vantine's, Two Knives Altieri and why Jack O'Neal was killed, the murders of Yale and Loewenstein, Rothstein's need for money and our need to keep him from getting it, the hunt for the ledgers to get Cornelius and the family in Independence out from under, everything. We even told her about Titanic Thomas and how I had to stay until the poker game where we'd fleece Rothstein. We must have talked for an hour, but she sat still, taking it in.

When she finally spoke, she was all business.

"It sounds like the whole key is to get these notebooks Mr. Rothstein keeps, to have some power over this gangster and force him to leave us alone."

"That's the idea," I said. "Don't know if it'll work, but it's all we can think of except killing the man."

"We're not doing that," Cornelius interjected. "Even if we survived it and no one came after us later, which we'd never know, the Pope's Usurer evidence could still come up. Somehow we have to get Rothstein to give it back to us and the only way I can think to get any leverage over him is to be holding his ledgers."

"Tell me everything you know about Arnold Rothstein," Marta

said to Cornelius. "About the sort of man he is, what is important to him, who is close to him, his family, everything. It may give us an idea."

That took quite a while, too, since Cornelius knew a lot about Arnold Rothstein. We went out to supper with Cornelius still talking. From that day on, Marta was a full partner with us in trying to get out of the mess we were in. In the end, it was Marta who saved us. She saved everything.

33

Coney Island

Marta

August 18, 1928:

Such a strange day, my diary. It started so gay and wonderful, even with all the troubles pressing on us. Then I embarrassed myself, and then something even worse. I will try to tell you everything as honestly as I can.

While Cornelius was at work, Walter and I spent hours and hours in his apartment or walking the streets, trying to imagine where a man like Rothstein would keep his precious ledgers. Once, I suggested that I should follow Rothstein to see if that gave me a clue, but Walter wouldn't hear of it. I told him they wouldn't suspect a woman, but Walter said yes, they would, and he couldn't bear the thought of the danger I would be in. He can be sweet.

Cornelius finally heard back from the gambler Thomas, who said his friend Mr. Raymond was agreeable and the game could be arranged. Cornelius was sure he could persuade a man named George McManus to set it up. This man's nickname is "Hump," which sounds very amusing. Anyway, he is working on a location and getting Mr. Rothstein and other gamblers to agree to play. I hope this plan of Walter's works. It sounds very risky to me. If this man Rothstein is as smart as everyone says, won't he know he is being cheated?

I've been here a week and I know I have to go home. Women cannot ignore their responsibilities as men do. My little Fern misses me and Hal does too. When I told the boys I would take the train home and would keep thinking about Rothstein and the ledgers, neither of them exactly tried to talk me out of it, but Cornelius was very nice.

"Marta, you can't go back without enjoying New York at least a little. This is the greatest city in the world. You and Riley need to relax and take in the sights. I know where you should go: Coney Island!"

I couldn't help being excited. The whole world knew of Coney Island, the greatest amusement park ever constructed. It was said to be a magic place where people of all sorts came in droves to witness amazing sights, bathe in the ocean and ride the brand-new and exciting roller coasters that were so famous. I'm sure my expression showed my eagerness, as Walter immediately promised to take me there the next day.

"Wish I could go with you, but I've got an interview set up and I have to work tomorrow," Cornelius said. "You'll have a ball. Listen, there are these two pinheads in the freak show, Pipo and Zipo. If you see them, rub their heads. It's supposed to bring good luck and Lord knows we need some."

Diary, the day started out so beautifully. Walter and I left early and found the train station where we could catch a subway to Coney Island. We had no bathing costumes, but we dressed casually and for a fun outing. I wore a white blouse and my black jodhpurs that I used to wear riding my horses back in Mexico. Walter was surprised! I thought perhaps I was being too daring by wearing pants instead of a skirt, but when I saw the bathing costumes the girls at the beach were wearing, I realized I needn't have worried. So much skin above the knee was showing, it was almost like the girls were in their underwear!

It was my first ride on a New York subway. You go down long stairs into darkness, put a nickel in a machine, push through what they call a "turnstile," and wait in the crowd for the next train. The car became so jammed with people dressed for Coney Island that I wondered how on Earth we were going to get all the way through Brooklyn without the train just exploding on the tracks. We were so crowded together we could hardly move and everyone was hot and sweating, but there was still such excitement and happiness that no one minded. We were going to Coney Island! The people certainly looked like they needed a break in the sun. These were working-class people: fathers in patched clothes, mothers carrying baskets of food, and laughing children finding ways to pester each other even in the massive crowd. They were smiling, holding hands, and singing. It was wonderful.

I didn't think the train could get any more crowded, but at each stop more people poured on and somehow we found room for them. It seemed like no one ever got off, for everyone was going to the same place. Finally, we reached the Stillwell Avenue Station and were carried by the force of the crowd out to Surf Avenue and the storefronts and facades that marked the start of the amusement areas.

"Look, Walter," I said as I pointed, "there is Nathan's, where Cornelius said to get Coney dogs."

He'd told us the red hots at Nathan's were only a nickel and were just as good as the ones at Feltman's, where they were a dime.

"You want a Coney dog?" Walter asked me.

I smiled.

"Not now, Walter, later. Now is for the beach. I've never seen the ocean and now is the time."

My excitement dimmed when we walked onto the boardwalk and looked down onto the beach. It was only mid-morning, but already so many bathers were there that the strip of sand between boardwalk and sea was as crowded as the subway train. Men, women, and children, all in bathing dress, stood straight up, crammed one against the other, as there was no room to lie down. There were people frolicking in the water, looking like they were enjoying themselves, but there seemed no way to get there without horse soldiers to force a way through.

I had to laugh, because Walter was looking at me so pitifully, fearing I would insist on putting my feet in the ocean.

"Don't worry, my Walter," I said. "I have my whole life to wade in oceans. Let's go on a ride."

And we certainly did. We went on a ride called the Whip that would start and stop so suddenly we'd be tossed helplessly against each other. We went on a Ferris wheel so tall it made the little ones I'd seen at carnivals back in Kansas City seem like toys. We went on roller coasters called the Thunderbolt and the Tornado that shot up and down the track at speeds that took your breath away. Walter didn't want to dare going on those, but I insisted and thought they were wonderful. Walter looked very grim and a little green when we were done.

Oh, just walking down the boardwalk was special. We saw men playing a game with three cups and a ball where the player would try to keep his eye on the one cup that held the ball as the "pitch man" (that's what they call them) shuffled the cups around and around, crying "By gosh and by golly, let's follow Miss Polly!" We saw a holy man from India walking an elephant and scantily-dressed Egyptian women doing what the pitch man called a coochie dance and a show where you could talk with "a beautiful Mexican girl who murdered her father and mother." I don't know about her parents, but she definitely was not Mexican. We walked by a "kissing marathon," where couples would keep their lips locked together for hours or even days to win the prize for being the last person standing. It was all crazy and colorful and delightful.

And then I spoiled it. Just as we were about to leave the park and head back to the subway station, I was startled to hear a pitch man's holler from behind me.

"You, miss! Yes, you! The lady in the lovely boots and riding pants! Come over here. I must ask you something."

Walter and I smiled and shrugged at each other. He took my arm as we walked over to the pitch man. I hadn't even noticed him or what he was pitching before he called me over. He was a very tall, very thin man with a long and droopy mustache. His height was accentuated by a stovepipe hat that he wore, yellow with red polka dots, while his suit was red with yellow polka dots. He sported a wooden cane with a curved handle that he waved in the air as he spoke. He stood on a platform in front of some kind of show or exhibit, but I wasn't paying much attention.

"Young lady," he said in a deep and sonorous tone, bending over to stare into my eyes. "Do you have the courage? Do you have the strength? Are you prepared for the horrifying mysteries of"—and here he waved his cane at the structure behind him—"the Bandit's Cave?"

My heart stopped.

I now focused on the attraction behind the man and saw with horror that it was a pavilion painted with devils, evil djinnies, ghosts, flames, and people screaming with terror. The largest painted figure, right over the entrance, was a demonic-looking fiend in Arab costume, a sword in each hand, a hellish expression glaring out from under a sheik's headdress.

Walter understood immediately why I went pale and swayed on

my feet as I took in this childish sideshow attraction. The Bandit's Cave. It brought me back to the unimaginable time, the time I don't think about, cannot think about, in the cave in Mexico where the Spaniard's men abused me, over and over, did things to me that I cannot think of but never can forget. The Spaniard gave me to them to be raped while he tortured and murdered my little brother Miguel. All of this came rushing back to my mind when I saw The Bandit's Cave. I almost fell to the ground, maybe would have fallen had not Walter gripped me by both arms.

"Let's go, Marta," he murmured, drawing me away.

But I resisted.

The pitch man saw my terror.

"Look," he shouted, pointing at me with his cane, "this beautiful young woman faints at the mere thought of the frights that await in the Bandit's Cave. The fiendish tortures of the Orient, here at Coney Island, only 10 cents a visit."

"Marta, come home with me. Now."

"No, my Walter," I finally said. I took his hand and squeezed it tightly. "I need to face this, *querido*. Those men who hurt me have too great a hold on me. I cannot let them defeat me."

The horrid old pitch man, all yellow teeth and greasy mustache under his ridiculous hat, leaned down toward me.

"That's the stuff, young lady, you go right in and face those bandits and I'm sure your young fellow here will be happy to protect you."

"Don't say one more word to her, snaggletooth," Walter snarled.

Even so, he nodded to me and we walked to the ticket booth, where Walter handed over two dimes and we climbed onto the platform where the old man stood. He didn't seem the least bothered by Walter's ferocity, but simply turned his attention back to hustling the crowd once he saw that he had our money.

The entrance to the Bandit's Cave was a dark open doorway underneath the fearsome Arab with the swords. Inside we saw only blackness, a sharp contrast to the sunny brightness that illuminated most of Coney Island. The exhibit must not have been a popular one, for no one else was entering. Hesitant as little children, we stepped into the dark and realized that our way was almost immediately blocked by a black wall. The hallway made a sharp turn to our left. The darkness was nearly absolute as we shuffled along, holding hands. We gradually became aware of quiet strains of Oriental music, melodic yet somehow threatening, like a snake charmer might play. Sounds of mechanical things and muffled booms came from somewhere unseen, ahead of us.

As we walked, we passed writing on the walls in glowing phosphorus paint, which told of a boy named Aladdin searching for treasure in a bandit's cave, but instead finding the devil himself. Drawings of Aladdin on the walls made me think of my poor brother.

"Your pulse is running like crazy," Walter said, looking concerned. "We should get out of here."

I shook my head. I was determined to be strong, even though I was perspiring and my heart was racing. I wanted to show that I could be as brave as Walter. It was so hard though, as everything in this dreadful place reminded me of the cave in my nightmares. I was even imagining the tall pitch man was the Spaniard himself.

We turned another corner and were on a platform that was a little brighter than the corridor. We could see, dimly, stuffed figures filling the chamber, requiring those entering to feel their way through, shifting right and left among them. They were mock-ups of frightening fiends: demons, ghouls, ax-wielding murderers. I nearly broke down when one of the figures, an actor who had been standing frozen, suddenly jumped at us and swung his ax in the air near us. Walter didn't move a muscle when the actor swung the ax, other than to support me.

"For God's sake, Marta, let's go," he said.

I shook my head, determined to conquer my fear. When we passed into the next chamber, invisible threads hanging in the entrance slipped across our faces like spider webs. Gas pipes ran along the floor on each side of the room, shooting flames along their length from tiny openings. All along the walls, demons writhing in hellfire were painted and illuminated with ghastly light. At the far end of the chamber was a round entry that led into a rotating cylinder, one which revolved in a continuous circle such that we would have to run quickly through or be knocked down by the motion. Above the entry to this cylinder were painted the famous words from Dante: "Abandon All Hope Ye Who Enter Here."

We slowly approached, watching to take in the speed of the spinning cylinder. I stepped on something soft and suddenly a wooden scimitar, suspended from the ceiling above the entry by a cable, swung down and swished across the opening, back and forth, adding one more obstacle to be timed in order to get through. At the same moment, a tall actor dressed as the devil himself stepped from a hidden side passage and flung his arms upward, making wings of his red cape.

That was more than I could take. I screamed with terror, for in that moment the devil was the Spaniard and the Spaniard was the devil. Walter put his arm behind my knees, lifted me up, and carried me back the way we had come, past the painted devils, through the stuffed figures and out into the daylight.

The pitch man pointed his cane at me and shouted, "Behold, the terror the Bandit's Cave creates."

I think Walter would have struck him if he hadn't been preoccupied with me. Walter carried me to a nearby bench and we sat. I sobbed deeply, with Walter wrapping his arm around my shoulders and patting me.

"There, there," he said.

For normal, healthy adults, the Bandit's Cave would have been very silly, but I am not normal or healthy. I never have been since the Spaniard set his men upon me and it is pointless for me to pretend this is not so. I felt, at that moment, there was nothing I could do. I would forever be damaged, forever prey to nightmares, forever unsure when terror might overwhelm me. I wondered if this was a life worth continuing, if I could be a good mother to Fern with so much fear inside of me.

Then something very strange happened. I was trying to get control of myself. Passersby looked at me with sympathy, probably wondering what had so frightened this crazy woman. Suddenly, just as I had finally stopped weeping and was calming a bit, I became aware of a man. He stood perhaps ten feet from us, staring with an expression of intense hatred. How could this man hate us, when we did not even know him?

He was a thin man with blond hair, a prominent nose, and eyes that squinted malevolently. His hands were in the pockets of his jacket. Something about him made me very uncomfortable. Walter sensed this and looked over. To my astonishment, he immediately stood between me and the blond man.

The man smiled coldly.

"Well, well. Welcome to Coney Island, Mr. Riley. Looks like your lady had a fright."

Without a word, Walter pulled me to my feet and led me away. The blond man watched us go, still smiling, hands still in his pockets.

"Who was that?" I kept asking Walter as we hurried toward the subway. "How did he know you? Who was he?"

Finally, Walter answered.

"That was the man who killed Jack O'Neal."

August 21, 1928:

Well, diary, I am on the train home. I did not want to go like this. When I went to New York, I planned to insist that Walter come home with me. That plan failed when I knew I had to get back and Walter showed no sign of being ready to come along. Then Coney Island happened. Now I just feel I am a weak woman who will never control her life, who will always have things done to her instead of doing them herself.

Why is it like this? Could it be otherwise? Walter went through tortures in the Spaniard's cave, too, yet he is still strong. Are men truly stronger than women about such things? Many times they do not seem strong. Or does Walter drink and smoke and fight and run from his home, all to control his memories? I do not know. It is confusing to me.

I want to be home.

34

"I Like to Drink and Smoke"

Jim

"You didn't go with her?" I asked incredulously.

As a grandchild, with the blithe ignorance of younger generations, I always assumed the long marriage of Riley and Marta was a happy one. Yet Marta's diary was making Riley out to be one of the worst husbands she could have had, about as bad as Cornelius was as a father. You want so much to love your family, but you cannot help judging and taking sides.

We were sitting in the study, as usual, each with our glass of bourbon, Riley smoking. I didn't work too hard to hide my disapproval of how Marta was treated. From the vantage point of the 1990s when Riley and I were talking, I could see that she required counseling and careful medical treatment to address her post-traumatic symptoms. Logically, I knew this wouldn't have been so obvious back in the 1920s and medical care then might well have consisted of electrical shock or lobotomies that would only have worsened things and might have killed her. But Riley was easy to blame, so I did.

Riley never ran from anything and he didn't run from my tone.

"I should have," he acknowledged. "She was in bad shape, worse shape maybe than I realized. But we had the big poker game with Rothstein coming up and I figured I had to be around for that in case something went wrong… oh hell, I don't know. I just wasn't ready to go back to the farm and the kids and to sitting around all winter not doing much and then working in the fields all summer. I just couldn't do that life much longer. So I stayed in New York and I'm a bad man. You'll have to live with it."

I poured myself another drink.

"You think she was right?"

"About what?"

"You drink and smoke so much because you were traumatized in the Spaniard's cave?"

"Hell, no," Riley snorted. "I like to drink and smoke. Let's not get off the subject."

35

The Game

Cornelius

Marta came to New York because she was sick of waiting for Riley to go back to Independence. She stuck around for a while, but eventually went back home without her husband. Riley stayed with me. I could always depend on Riley when I had trouble. He was my best friend.

All in all, it took a few weeks to get the game lined up. I didn't want to pitch the idea to A.R. myself, since it would backfire on him in a big way and I didn't want to get the blame. Instead I mentioned casually to Hump McManus, who regularly set up games for Rothstein, how I thought it would be a fine thing if Rothstein and Titanic Thomas would ever hook up and play partners, because who could ever beat the two best gamblers in the world? Predictable as always, big Hump checked with Thomas and found he was willing, and then it was easy to sell Rothstein. After all, Titanic was both the world's best poker player and the world's best cheat. To play as his partner and split his winnings was a sure bet, and Rothstein needed sure bets then as much as he ever did in his life.

Meanwhile, Thomas put in a call to Nate Raymond and he didn't have to ask twice. Raymond would have *walked* from California to get the chance to fleece Arnold Rothstein with Titanic Thomas as his partner. As it happened, Titanic told us, Raymond had just married some third-rate Hollywood actress, so he made the trip to New York into a honeymoon.

The game was set for Saturday night, September eighth, at the apartment of Jimmy Meehan. Meehan was a young gambler and hanger-on who rented out his apartment by the hour for games like this. The other players were all professional gamblers and high rollers, but not in the same league as Rothstein or Titanic Thomas. At the last minute, I wangled an invitation from A.R., not to gamble but just to watch. I didn't want to miss the show.

Around noon on the day of the game, Riley and I met Titanic in the lobby of the Waldorf, where Raymond and his bride were staying. We wanted to size him up and Titanic needed to go over their signals for the game. The idea was that Titanic would start out playing partners with Rothstein as promised, then find an excuse to cancel that deal and secretly start partnering with Raymond. The desk clerk told us to go on up to room 802.

I never liked the Waldorf. It tries to be both fancy and big, but they don't go together. We waited too long for the elevator and finally Titanic was rapping on the door of Raymond's room. A cute, tiny little lady in a negligée opened up. She had Clara Bow lips, a flapper's hairstyle, and a figure that made Nate Raymond a lucky man.

Titanic tipped his chapeau.

"How do, ma'am. We're here to see Nate."

"Good luck with that," the lady said, turning to allow us to enter.

We heard a low moan. Walking in, we found a man sprawled on the bed looking very pale and very sick indeed. Titanic instantly abandoned his cornpone chivalry.

"What's the matter with him?"

Before his bride could answer, Nate gave his own form of response by clutching his belly, leaning over the side of the bed, and upchucking into a wastebasket.

"Tell me about it," the lady said. "This is supposed to be my honeymoon and all I'm doing in New York is watching this guy puke into a bucket." She kicked the bed, drawing a sharp moan from her hubby. "Come on, Nate, I want to go shopping."

Nate flapped a hand to silence her. Titanic bent over and grasped him by the hair to look in his eyes.

"What the matter with you?" he repeated. "We have a game tonight."

"Can't do it, Ti," Raymond gasped. "Sick."

He fell back onto the bed, lips smeared with vomit that he didn't bother to wipe off.

"Dumb lunk took me to some chink place downtown and ordered this weird fish," said Nate's bride. "I didn't eat any of it, didn't smell right to me, but my dumb husband chowed it right down, didn't you, dummy? Jesus, I've never seen anybody so sick. I've had to empty that wastebasket six times."

The number seemed to outrage her, as she started pounding her fists on Raymond's chest.

"*It's my honeymoon!*" she shouted.

"Jiminy," said Titanic.

He jerked his head toward the door and we went out in the hall, giving the lovebirds privacy.

"Well, that tears it," Titanic said. "Game'll have to be straight. Maybe I'll partner with Rothstein for real and make some dough that way."

"That's no good," I insisted. "We need to bust Rothstein, not make money for him. He's bound to hit some bets soon or get some money from his rackets. We need to do this game tonight."

"I got an idea," Riley said. "I'll substitute for him."

Even I thought this was crazy. Titanic instantly shook his head.

"No chance, you're an amateur."

"I'm better than you think," Riley said. "We got until tonight for you to teach me the signals, then it's just following your lead. This Raymond is from California, not known around New York, right?"

Titanic nodded.

"So I'll be him. We're about the same size, both have dark complexions, both have black hair. I'll be him, we'll fleece Rothstein, you keep all the money, and you won't have to split it with anybody. And for the rest of your life, you'll be the man who sank Arnold Rothstein."

That last argument was appealing to Titanic, who weakened. At my suggestion, we went back in the room and grilled the ailing Raymond on whether he'd ever met any of the game's participants. He hadn't.

"All right," Titanic finally said. "We'll go back to O'Neal's place and see how you do. But I'm not going into this game unless you convince me you can handle it. I don't care what they do to you, but I would personally prefer not to get myself shot."

On that cheery note, we went back to my apartment to practice. We sat at my kitchen table for hours, Titanic dealing hands and issuing instructions in a stern, staccato tone that was as different as possible from the cornpone drawl he affected when trolling for a victim.

"The game will be five-card stud, no limit," he told us.

He dealt eight dummy hands on the table in front of him. Titanic glanced over the hands for a moment, but did not turn over the hole cards. He made his selection and shoved a hand over to Riley, who flipped over his hole card. He had a seven and a nine, both hearts. Best visible card on the table was a ten of clubs, fourth hand along the row. Titanic tapped it.

"This is Rothstein." he said. He tapped the hand just to the left of it. "This is me." He tapped the first card in the row. "This is the dealer." He tapped a hand to the left of the dealer. "This man checks. Next man bets a hundred. Rothstein raises him a hundred. I call, so do the next three. What do you do?"

"Call."

Titanic showed neither approval nor disapproval. He kept dealing the cards, stating the bets, folding players as seemed right. When the fourth cards were dealt, only Riley, Thomas, and the putative Rothstein were left. Riley had no face cards, but his hearts were holding up: he only needed one more to fill the flush. Rothstein had a pair of tens showing. Thomas had a pair of sixes showing. Two sixes and a ten had already been dealt to other players.

"How much is in the pot?" Titanic suddenly asked Riley.

I had no idea, since no real money was used and I certainly didn't carry all those bets in my head.

Riley didn't hesitate.

"Forty-two hundred."

Titanic pointed to the Rothstein hand.

"He bets two grand. I fold. It's two to you, to see if you get the flush. What do you do?

"I fold."

Thomas leaned over the table toward Riley, signaling the next would be the important question.

"Why?"

"It's two grand to me, with the chance of winning a little over six grand. That's about thirty-four percent. There are twenty-four cards left in the deck. After you take away my four hearts and the three I see on the table, that's six hearts left, and some of them may be in the hole for the other guys. So I've got less than a twenty percent chance of getting my heart, compared to pot odds of thirty-four. In the long run, it's a bad bet."

I never liked it when writers talked about somebody "goggling," as I didn't believe people actually did that. But that was what I did on hearing Riley speak his lessons like a mathematics professor. I goggled.

"Riley, where did you learn all that?" I asked in amazement. "You could barely do your sums back in school."

"Never saw much use in it, then," he replied.

Titanic nodded.

"I was just the same."

He pulled in the cards and shuffled. I asked to see if Riley would have made his flush, but they ignored me.

"If you're wondering, I know these cards are marked," Riley said to Titanic as he dealt.

"How?"

"Because you're not looking at the hole cards to bet."

"That's not a good reason. You need to learn to spot the marks themselves. But we're not using marked cards tonight, so you don't have to worry about that. Lots of other ways you can get us shot, we don't have to mark any cards."

We sat for about an hour, with Titanic dealing mock hands and testing Riley's betting judgment. Then he started on the signals.

"I'll only signal you when the cards tell me to. I'll signal when I'm about to signal, then I'll signal what you bet. We'll have signals that mean do it, signals that mean don't do it."

"What's 'it'?"

"You'll know when it happens. I'm only giving you signals to tell me if you've got the nuts or you don't got the nuts, so you don't have so much to remember. We'll have master signals that change all the other signals around, just in case. You still want to do this?"

He did. We spent three more hours rehearsing signals, until Titanic was reasonably satisfied that Riley had them straight. I didn't envy him. The signals were kid's stuff—scratching a nose to mean a high card, tugging an ear to mean fold, that sort of thing—but there were a lot of them and they had to be inconspicuous so they wouldn't be spotted. Worse, the master signal meant a sign would then say the opposite of what it said before. I couldn't keep it straight for two minutes, but Riley was as cool as ever. It must be said: Riley is a surprising man.

At last, Titanic was satisfied. He slapped his palm on the table. "Gentlemen," he said, "let's play some poker."

It was an unusual Saturday evening, for Runyon was not at Lindy's. I was glad. I would have been expected to converse with him and I was too wrought up. As it was, I could nod silently to the wise guys and flappers of my acquaintance, while sitting alone at my corner table and eating brisket, potato pancakes, and my own liver at the thought of Riley trying to remember all those signals. Riley was at my apartment with strict instructions not to show up at the game until Titanic had several hours to partner with Rothstein and study the other players.

Titanic sat with Rothstein at the great man's table. Unusual partners, soon to be sworn enemies if the game went as planned. I wondered if Rothstein intended to betray Titanic as Titanic planned to betray him. It would have been fitting, perhaps, but I doubted it. To play partners with Titanic Thomas was a sure enough moneymaker without the need for embellishment. I could tell from across the room that Rothstein was being his typical cold, milk-drinking self, while Titanic was playing the Arkansas jokester.

At eight o'clock, Max at the register pointed the telephone mouthpiece in A.R.'s direction. It was McManus: the game was on. Rothstein jerked his head at me as he and Titanic left the restaurant and I tagged behind. I couldn't miss this, whatever was going to happen.

Jimmy Meehan, our host, was a tall, thin Irish boy. When we arrived, he was still arranging the liquor bottles and snacks to his liking on a table by the window in the living room. A large rectangular table with seating for nine dominated the center of the room. A sofa and a pair of easy chairs had been pushed back against the walls to make space for the gambling. All the invited players except Riley (or excuse me, Nate Raymond) were present. They greeted Rothstein with that air of false friendliness that A.R. often provoked. Rothstein was regarded in that apartment with much respect and some fear, but no affection. As for Titanic, they looked at him warily, eager to take him on, but knowing he was the best cheat in their cheating world.

I was introduced to the short and stocky Boston brothers, whose name was actually Solomon but everyone called them by their hometown. There was a slick-looking Jew named Joe Bernstein, another one named Abe Silverman, and Red Bove with the red pompadour. Hump McManus was pouring himself a large scotch when we came in. Most of these players were pros and didn't booze much while they gambled: Rothstein and Titanic, of course, didn't drink liquor at all. Hump made up for them and drank heavily the whole game, though I can't say it made him any more boorish and dumb than he was to begin with. Some people have a gift.

There was little small talk. These men knew why they were there and in moments they were seating themselves at the table and shuffling cards. The room was already heavy with tobacco smoke. I'd been told to expect a marathon lasting into late Sunday or even Monday and I tried not to think of the state of the room when we finished.

"Aren't we missing someone?" Rothstein asked as he seated himself directly across from Titanic.

"That California guy, the one they call Nigger Nate," McManus responded. "Fuck him, we're not gonna wait."

"Why they call him Nigger Nate?" one of the boys asked.

"I don't know. Ask Thomas, he's the one who knows him."

Titanic smiled and shrugged.

"Some people say it's on account of his dark skin, some say he likes dark meat for his women. Take your pick."

"Maybe it's because he's too dumb to show up on time, like a nigger," McManus hooted.

No one else smiled. No one ever smiled when McManus made jokes, because his jokes were stupid.

"Come on," said one of the Boston brothers. "Let's play cards."

As the game organizer, Hump got the first deal.

"Gentlemen, the game is five-card stud, no limit."

They were off. I took my seat on the sofa against the wall, where I was to remain for a very long and mostly tedious time. I tried to follow the play and note each gambler's style and mannerisms, as I knew that poker players were supposed to do. My trouble is that I have always found gambling to be one of the most tedious ways to pass time that mankind has invented. I spent the decade of the twenties surrounded by men like Rothstein and Runyon who lived to gamble. That was also the decade when gambling in the stock market seized the soul of my country, especially my city, but for the life of me, I never felt anything from gambling except boredom and, if it was my money, fear. Thus, it was usually not my money.

I can't say that I rose from that sofa any more knowledgeable about whether Joe Bernstein blinked when he had a good hand or whether Red Bove sweated when he bluffed. Although I knew that Rothstein and Titanic were playing partners, I had no idea what signals they used. They both sat nearly motionless for hours, dead-eyed and monotone, so I couldn't catch any of their signs even though I knew they were making them. They both were doing well, of course, and by midnight each was a few thousand up.

I must have dozed, for I suddenly heard Riley's voice and I hadn't heard him come in.

"Sorry I'm late, boys," he was saying. "Not too sorry, though. I was shooting craps and I'm up eight grand. I think this is my night."

"Your night?" Rothstein said. "Let's see how they gamble in California. I'll high card you for your eight grand, right now."

Eyebrows raised around the table. This could more than offset all Rothstein's winnings so far. Titanic pulled his ear, the "do it" signal. Riley nodded, picked up a deck, and cut a nine. Rothstein cut a six.

"That's how we gamble in California," Riley said.

Titanic called for a break and, while the rest of us ate sandwiches, he and Rothstein strolled out in the hall. I knew this was when Titanic would tell Rothstein their partnering was off and I figured, accurately, that he'd use the wild high card bet as his excuse. Meanwhile, McManus was asking Riley why people called him Nigger Nate.

"They don't," Riley said. "Not to my face."

I was pleased to see that Riley's stone face worked as well at intimidating Hump McManus as it had worked on the playground in Independence, Missouri.

The game resumed with no abort signal from Titanic, so apparently the split with Rothstein went smoothly. As the hours passed, A.R. became increasingly strange. He showed far more emotion than

254

was his custom even on the street, much less in a poker game. He bet high and aggressively, losing often—to everyone. He started making crazy side bets, like ten thousand he had a higher hole card than McManus or five thousand his hand would beat Bove's hand, whoever took the pot. He was sweating, his hands shook a little, and he gulped at his milk like he was sucking it from a teat. I never saw Rothstein anything like this before and I figured the strain of not having his big bankroll was getting to him. He bet like a rich man, but he sweated like a sucker. And that's the one thing Arnold Rothstein never was, a sucker.

Not only did I know that Titanic and Riley were signaling each other, I knew what the signals were, but I still rarely caught them. I hoped to God that Riley was better at it than I was. He must have been, as the chips kept piling up in front of him. Titanic won, too, but he saw to it that "Nate Raymond" was the big winner. Every half hour or so, while raking in a pot, Riley would say, "That's how we gamble in California," just to tweak Rothstein and get him to bet higher. It's amazing how you better the odds in a long poker game by playing partners, giving signals just when the occasion calls for them. Everyone at this table, except maybe McManus, knew how to calculate the odds so skewing them just slightly, by giving two of the players more information than anybody else had, meant a shift in the odds that brought big money when the game went on long enough.

This game did go on. Sunday morning became afternoon, then evening. Breaks were short and Rothstein complained even about those, since he couldn't win back his money with everyone eating sandwiches. Finally, breaks were abandoned and they ate while they gambled. The smoke hung over the table so thickly I wasn't sure Riley could still see the signals, but he kept winning. In fact, everybody was winning except for Rothstein and McManus, but Riley won most of all. Rothstein grew increasingly angry that he was always being stuck with the deadliest hand in poker, the one that is second-best at the table.

"Did an Irishman like you get gefilte fish for the sandwiches, Meehan?" Rothstein said at one point. "Something is smelling very fishy in here."

Later, after losing again to Riley, he said, "I begin to get the idea of how you gamble in California, Mr. Raymond. More skill than luck."

Riley just smiled at him.

"If you're making an accusation, Mr. Rothstein, just go ahead and make it. But be prepared to back it up."

There was a long pause while most of the players stared intently at the tabletop. Finally, Rothstein muttered "Deal" and play resumed.

By midnight Sunday, Rothstein was down half a million dollars, more than half of it to "Nate Raymond." He'd been handing out markers, not cash. This was a major loss even for the Big Bankroll, but I knew just how small that bankroll had become. It would be months before Rothstein could make his payment to the German, giving me time to find his ledgers or figure some other way to get out from under.

Ice man Arnold Rothstein was hot, sweaty, and desperate. On losing what proved to be the last hand, he pounded the table and rose to his feet.

"That's it, Raymond. I'll cut cards with you one more time and it'll be for forty thousand dollars. You have the stomach for it?"

I saw Titanic touch his nose, the "don't do it" sign. But Riley didn't hesitate. He picked up a deck and held it out to Rothstein, who promptly cut a deuce.

"My night, not yours," Riley said as he cut a jack.

Rothstein was now a wreck, no longer the King of Broadway, instead an embarrassing loser.

"You're a pack of crooks," he snarled.

He marched out. Titanic broke the silence that Rothstein left behind.

"All we've got are markers," he said. "What's this joker trying to pull?"

McManus waved him off.

"He's good for it. He's the Big Bankroll."

I knew better, and so did Titanic, but it was Hump's job to make sure Rothstein paid up, cheating or no cheating. Even I figured he'd do it. Rothstein hated to lose and could be a slow pay, but in the long run, nobody could welsh who wanted to show his mug on Broadway again. That's the way it was.

Before long, Riley and I were out on the sidewalk with Titanic Thomas. I thought we'd be celebrating, but Titanic's voice was hard as stone.

"What were you doing, cutting cards for forty large with my money?" he hissed into Riley's face. "I should kill you for that."

Titanic opened his coat and put his hand on the pistol in his belt.

"Maybe I will," he said.

Riley looked at him, calm as in church.

"Go ahead. Pull it."

I stepped between them and put my hand on Titanic's shoulder.

"Before you pull that thing, Ti, let me tell you something about my friend. I've heard you brag about how you killed four men during your years on the road. Well, I won't talk about the first man I saw Riley kill, back when he was eighteen. And I won't talk about the dozen or so German soldiers I saw him kill at Cantigny, in the war. I just want to tell you about the time I saw Riley put down five armed men with five bullets in about, oh, fifteen seconds. That was after being tortured by two Indians he also killed, with a knife. My friend is an interesting fellow. And you know, I've never heard him brag about any of it."

Titanic seemed to weigh what I was telling him.

"All right, as you were," I said, stepping out of the way. "I'm just telling you, Ti, I don't like your end of this."

Titanic was silent a moment. Then a grin cracked his face and the cornpone was back.

"Shoot, you boys are too serious," he drawled. "We had us a good night! Let's go get some soda pop."

So we did.

36

Marta Makes a Plan

Marta

October 20, 1928:

At last, harvest is over and Ma won't be so stretched with all she has to do at the farm. Fern and Hal are settled in at school and it almost seems peaceful here. If only Walter would come back.

Once again, I feel I have to go to New York to fetch him. This time, I won't leave without him. Walter must decide if he means to be a husband to me and a father to Fern or not. I have wondered which would be the best for us.

There is something else, diary. Every day since I came back to Independence, I have gone over in my mind what happened when we went to Coney Island. It was a silly carnival ride, one that should scare only young children, yet I made such a fool of myself. The darkness, the creatures jumping out at me, the presence of devils and a cave, it brought out my worst memories all at once and I was overwhelmed. Will I never be free of the past? Never be safe from the dreams and from the terror that chokes me, which can be brought on by even innocent provocations? How can I be a good mother to Fern or accomplish anything good in this life if I never know when what happened in that cave will come back to me? There was a time when I felt safe with Walter, but Walter is gone. Even when he is here, he is gone.

I have an idea, though, my diary. I so want to prove to Walter that I am not just a useless woman, a drag on him, that I can succeed at things even he finds difficult. Walter and Cornelius think their problems might be solved if they find the ledgers kept by this bad man, Rothstein. I thought and thought and thought about everything Cornelius told me about that man and I think I have an idea. If those ledgers are so precious to him, I think I can guess where he might be keeping them. I won't tell the boys. When I get to New York, I will find a way to check on my idea by myself, so I am not embarrassed if I am wrong. If I am right, perhaps Walter will see that I can be a true partner to him, and he will come back with me to Independence and we can get on with our lives.

Why is it not easy to be happy?

37

Rothstein the Welshman

Cornelius

We were on Corregidor in '42, just before the Philippines fell. Riley and I were supposed to make sure Douglas MacArthur got out of there alive, which he did, but no thanks to us. The general that our pal from Independence Harry Truman liked to call "that showboating cocksucker" made it all the way to Mindanao and lived to fight again, while Riley and I fell out of his boat and had to swim to what was, at that moment, the most dangerous hellhole on earth. But that's another story, for another notebook.

I mention it because the tension that dominated Corregidor reminded me of nothing so much as New York in the fall of 1928, as Broadway waited to see if Rothstein would pay his gambling debt. Just as the soldiers and sailors and even the coolies in the hot Philippine swelter were unusually silent, glancing repeatedly north as though Hirohito's minions would appear on the horizon any moment, so denizens of the speakeasies and the automats spoke softly, shook their heads often, and averted their eyes when Rothstein entered Lindy's or the Park Central. A.R., normally the most cold-blooded and predictable of men, was acting strangely. Wise guys who barely knew him could see he was tense, jumpy, and irritable. For the King of Broadway to be acting this way, while welshing on his bets, unsettled all Times Square and put the scent of regime change in the air. Even my Algonquin friends Benchley and Harpo heard of the situation and talked about it in my presence, though they had no idea I was involved.

As the official organizer of the game, Hump McManus was responsible for making sure all markers were paid. Titanic and the Boston brothers pestered Hump for weeks and even people with no stake in the proceeds would ask Hump what was going on and why Rothstein wasn't paying up. As for Rothstein, everyone who knew him well enough, from Runyon to Nicky Arnstein to Polly Adler, told him he had to pay.

"It doesn't matter if they cheated," I heard Runyon tell him. "You know you have to pay up. You gave your marker. If you welsh, you're dead in this town. That's how it is, even for you."

Rothstein just waved his hand, as though brushing off a fly.

"They can wait," he insisted. "I got a big parlay on the election and when that hits, everybody gets well. Meanwhile, let them sweat a little. Teach them to pull that crooked stuff on me. It was Thomas and that California buddy of his behind it. I still need to design their comeuppance and I will."

At least Riley was off the hook. Nate Raymond and his bride slid out of town with Nate clutching Titanic's marker for a cut of the winnings once Rothstein paid up. We heard no suggestion that the man who cut cards with Arnold Rothstein for forty thousand dollars was anyone other than Nate Raymond and that's how the history books spell it out. Even later, when the real Nate returned to New York, nobody noticed the switch. Either his passing resemblance to Riley was good enough to get by or the folks at the poker game decided it was better not to raise too many questions about that particular event.

September became October, then November was approaching. I tried to stay in close touch with Rothstein, fearful that he was stockpiling cash for the narcotics deal while ignoring his gambling debts. As far as I could tell, his luck had turned against him and stayed turned. He kept gambling and losing, spreading markers like confetti though none as large as his markers from the big game with Titanic. The real estate he owned in Long Island was a sinkhole for dollars. He insisted that I call Richter on the newly available transatlantic radio phone to ask for more time and see if I could talk him down from his five-million-dollar demand. Richter was polite, but he wouldn't reduce the down payment and he said he was considering other offers.

"I would like to work with your principal, Cornelius," Richter said to me in his guttural German. "His reputation is excellent, much better than the Italians who are my next option. But I cannot wait much longer. There is too much money to be made."

"Just wait," I said. "Election day here is November 6. My principal has so many bets down that he will have the money in your hand right after."

I didn't even know how much Rothstein stood to win or who he'd bet on, so I had no idea if what I was saying was true. I hoped it wasn't, since I was more certain than ever that once Rothstein didn't need me to deal with Richter, I was looking at a short swim in the Gowanus Canal with an anchor around my neck.

The situation couldn't go on forever. Riley and I figured we'd have to bring things to a head by election day, but we didn't know how. The only idea we ever had was to get the ledgers and blackmail Rothstein with them, but we still had no idea where they were. We started to tiptoe around the idea of killing Rothstein, just murdering the bastard outright and making an end of it. Problem was, we didn't know if that would be the end or if some henchman of Rothstein's would take revenge, not just on us but on our families, who were still being watched. Besides, as good at killing as my friend had proven to be, cold-blooded murder in a civilized city was a big step further than we had ever taken. It took some thought.

Then, just to make matters more complicated, Marta showed up again! This time she sent a wire and Riley was waiting for her at Grand Central. I can't say I was a very gracious host when he brought her into my apartment that night.

"I'll be honest, Marta, I wish you hadn't come," I told her as she removed her hat and Riley took her bag into my bedroom. "We're getting close to working this out and you'll only be a distraction."

She looked at me coldly, very much the haughty Mexican aristocrat.

"You have monopolized my husband for too long, Cornelius. He needs to be home, to be a husband to me, to be a father to his child. And to your child, too."

Well, she had me there. She had changed the subject in a way that left me no conceivable response. Women can be so unfair.

Riley came into the living room at that moment and Marta gestured for us to sit.

"Cornelius says you are getting close to solving your problem. I want to hear about it."

"It's not so much that we're close to solving it," Riley said as we seated ourselves. "We just have to. Rothstein claims he's going to win a bunch of money next Tuesday on the elections, so he might make enough to cut the deal with Richter and he won't need Cornelius any more. We've got to finish this thing."

Marta nodded.

"All right. Tell me your plan."

We were embarrassed. The silence made it clear that we had no clue what to do next, despite months of thinking.

"Well, I have an idea," this remarkable woman said. "I've been going over everything you told me about Mr. Rothstein. Walter, the election day is next Tuesday, correct?"

"You know it is."

"And Cornelius, Sunday is the day gamblers are supposed to pay their debts, what you call wash day?"

"That's right, but so what?" I responded. "We've had almost two months of wash days since the poker game and Rothstein hasn't paid up yet."

"We don't want him to pay, we want him to leave us alone. So here is what I think we should do."

And by gosh, she had a plan.

38

The Key to Every Man

Marta

November 3, 1928:

I am determined to write in my diary, even though I am in New York and I am so distracted with what is happening with Walter and Cornelius. I really do believe I am being helpful to them in ways they did not expect. We will see how it works out.

When I arrived in New York, it soon became apparent that the boys had no idea how to get back the evidence against Cornelius and convince Mr. Rothstein to leave us alone. All the time I was back in Independence, I went over and over what Cornelius had told me about Rothstein. I kept coming back to his childhood: raised an Orthodox Jew, in a family dominated by a patriarch with the amazing name of Abe the Just, a man respected above others in his community for his righteousness and his wisdom. How could a boy raised by such a man, and with a brother who became a rabbi, turn to gambling and bootlegging and all the evil things that Arnold Rothstein does? And what would happen to such a man inside?

"The key to Mr. Rothstein is his father," I told Walter and Cornelius that first night when I arrived.

I could tell that Cornelius was skeptical.

"How do you know that?"

"Because the key to every man is his father. Mr. Rothstein himself told you that."

Perhaps it was cruel of me to say this, as he knew I was thinking of how he'd abandoned Hal and how his actions had led to his own father's death. But it is true and Cornelius had really not earned excessive sensitivity for his feelings.

"I know very little about the Jewish faith or Jewish traditions," I went on, "but being the son of such a respected and devout man, then turning out to be so evil that your father disowns you, has to have a major effect. I even talked to the rabbi at a temple in Kansas City and he confirmed what a powerful combination of love and hatred would result in Arnold Rothstein."

Cornelius scoffed.

"Rothstein loves money. That's it."

"No, Cornelius. That is never all there is to someone. Our parents, our childhoods rule us, whether we know it or not. The rabbi told me that for Rothstein's father to announce his son is dead to him, that would resonate in his very soul. The strongest grip we can get on Arnold Rothstein will be through Abraham Rothstein."

Walter reached across the sofa and took my hand.

"What's your idea, Marta?"

I told them. At least I told them one of my ideas, the one that played on the love for his father that must be buried deep within Arnold Rothstein. The other idea, the one that depended on an equally strong hatred he must have for his father, I kept to myself. I wanted to see that idea through without their help, if I could.

The idea that I shared with them was to present Rothstein with false "evidence" that his father was having an affair with a woman from outside the Jewish faith. I would play the paramour. I would find a way to sidle up to Abraham Rothstein and get as close to him as I could, while Cornelius secretly took photos. Cornelius suggested the added idea of stealing some article of Abraham Rothstein's clothing and putting perfume on it. Walter would confront Rothstein with this evidence and threaten to ruin his father's good name unless Rothstein turned over to us the evidence linking Cornelius to the desk of the Pope's Usurer. Cornelius would promise to leave New York City and never reveal what he knew about Rothstein and the drug trade or the killing of Alfred Loewenstein. Walter would also agree, as Nate

Raymond, to tear up the markers that Rothstein gave him at the poker game. Titanic Thomas might not like that, but what did that matter?

I could tell the boys were not impressed by my plan. Cornelius was openly mean about it and even Walter looked doubtful. In the end, though, they agreed they had no plan at all, so we would try it. We needed to hurry with election day so soon.

To his credit, Cornelius handled the arrangements very well, despite not believing in the plan. He learned where Abraham Rothstein lived and we waited outside until he came out. As he walked down the street, I quickly circled the block so I could be waiting for him. When he came even with me to pass, I pretended to swoon and fell right into his arms! My, what an impressive man he is. Tall, handsome despite his years, with a thin face and the nose of a hawk. He wore a broad-brimmed black hat and carried a walking stick. He was so shocked by my faint that he almost dropped me onto the sidewalk. Cornelius was hiding across the street and was able to get pictures of us together, which he had a friend at his newspaper develop. I pretended to be not right in the head and I gave the elderly Mr. Rothstein a kiss on the cheek for saving me. This disturbed him to no end, but gave Cornelius an excellent photograph! Cornelius also found out that Abraham Rothstein frequented a Turkish bath and he was able to steal the man's necktie from the changing room while he bathed. All in all, we were quite the efficient conspirators.

Tomorrow is Sunday, which the gamblers call "wash day" because it is when they are to pay their debts from the week. I have noticed it is the fashion here to give funny nicknames to terrible things. Anyway, election day is this coming Tuesday, November sixth, so we need to act now. Tomorrow, my Walter will find a way to get Arnold Rothstein alone, and he will present the "evidence" and we will see. Even if this idea fails, I have hopes for my other plan.

39

A Secret Compartment

Marta

November 19, 1928:

It is over and we are home.

I feel I must finish here the story of what happened in New York, even though no one but me will ever read what is written here. I do not know if I will continue writing after that. There is so much in life that is harsh or sad. Does it need to be recorded?

But I must now describe what happened on the day Arnold Rothstein was shot. It was a Sunday. The boys left me in the middle of the afternoon, off to show Mr. Rothstein the photograph of his father and me, and to threaten to blacken the father's name if he did not let Cornelius alone. They thought I would stay alone in the apartment, but that was not my plan. I had a second way to get power over Mr. Rothstein, if my theory was correct. I thought I knew where Mr. Rothstein's famous ledgers might be hidden.

I meant it when I told Cornelius the key to all men is their fathers. This would be especially so with a man like Arnold Rothstein, an evil man whose father was said to be admired by everyone for his piety and goodness. He would, deep inside, love his father, so the plan to threaten him with the photograph might work. But he would also feel hatred for his father, I thought, a father who was not proud of his son and disowned him in a very hurtful way. Through August and September, I had wondered if somehow his hatred for his father might be useful to us.

Then, I remembered two things that Cornelius told me about Arnold Rothstein. First, he told me that Rothstein must at least have feelings for his mother, because he visited her every month and spent most of a day there, while his father stayed away from their home on those days so he wouldn't see the son he had disavowed.

Then, Cornelius told me that Arnold Rothstein must still have feelings for his father, too. Mr. Rothstein had donated a valuable old Hebrew cabinet to the Rothsteins' family synagogue as a place to keep the Torah scrolls. At the same time, he'd donated a replica of the cabinet to Abraham Rothstein himself. Both gifts were anonymous.

I remember I was mopping the kitchen floor when I got the idea. Cornelius described the ledgers as being thin, small notebooks that fit in the inside pocket of a man's suit jacket. Mr. Rothstein engaged in many transactions and made many notes in his ledgers. It sounded, then, like these notebooks might have space for one month's worth of entries. And Mr. Rothstein visited his mother once a month. Surely he could find a few moments to place a completed ledger into a hiding place in the house where he was raised and where his father still lives! There would be spiteful satisfaction in knowing that the records of his evil deeds were kept safe, not only in his hated father's home, but in a cabinet that symbolized the Jewish faith that the father adored and the son had abandoned. Hiding contraband in a piece of furniture that was also a work of art was not unknown to Rothstein, who did the same thing with the heroin he placed in the desk for J.P. Morgan. Cornelius said Rothstein made the anonymous gifts about two years ago, which was about the time that Cornelius tried to rob Rothstein's desk and caused him to find a new hiding place for the notebooks.

I knew it was little more than a wild guess, but it seemed right to me and I knew I must attempt to look in that cabinet. I did not tell Walter or Cornelius, because they never would have let me put myself in that sort of danger. Besides, I have to admit, I wanted to do this myself so I could show them the ledgers in triumph if I was right, but would never need to tell them anything if I was wrong. This was petty of me, but it so aggravates me that Walter pines for adventures and finds excuses to run off with Cornelius to have them. I wanted to show that I could be adventurous, too.

Here is what I did. Because I had already been there to carry out our blackmail plan, I knew where Abraham Rothstein lived, in a nice neighborhood in what they call Manhattan's Upper East Side. From the research done by Cornelius, I had a good idea of his schedule, which was very regular. Every Sunday afternoon, he took long walks in Central Park, leaving his wife Esther at their home. After the boys left on that Sunday afternoon when they planned to blackmail Arnold Rothstein, I quickly made my way to the Upper East Side and took a position across the street from Abraham Rothstein's home, a very handsome building. Luck was on my side, for I didn't wait very long before I saw Abraham Rothstein, walking with a stick and wearing a black overcoat and the same large-brimmed black hat as on our first meeting, stride down the stairs of his building and toward the park. I was careful to stay hidden, of course, and I waited five minutes after the man disappeared from view before I crossed the street and knocked on his door. I was wearing my most conservative black dress and had a shawl over my head, for I was hoping to pass for an Orthodox Jew. I also carried a very large handbag which I bought on the street. I hoped it would soon contain as many of Arnold Rothstein's notebooks as it would hold.

I expected a servant to answer, but the door was opened by a dignified matron who could only have been Esther Rothstein, mother of the biggest criminal in New York. A heavy woman, short, she wore a simple dark housedress that was no fancier than what I wore. Practical shoes with flat heels, no jewelry at all, gray hair pulled back from a pale, kindly face. She greeted me with an inquiring smile. I did not smile back, but looked anxious and worried.

"Mrs. Rothstein?"

I was careful to keep any trace of an accent out of my speech, which I could do if I concentrated, having lived in Missouri for more than ten years.

"Yes. What can I do for you, my dear?"

She seemed used to strangers coming to seek help from Abe the Just.

"I am very sorry to trouble you, ma'am. Is your husband at home?"

"He is out for a walk. You just missed him."

"Oh. Well, may I wait for him? I'm sorry, I know this seems strange."

Mrs. Rothstein's smile only broadened.

"Not at all, dear. Many people come to talk with my husband and for all sorts of reasons. Come in, come in."

The first step accomplished, I walked into the Rothstein home and she shut the door behind me. The house was what I expected. I stepped into an immaculately clean foyer with much hardwood and simple, sturdy furnishings. The feel was perhaps more masculine than feminine. It seemed a house for serious, quiet, and studious people.

"Let me take your things and then we can have a cup of tea in the parlor while we wait…"

Not the parlor. The cabinet wouldn't be in a parlor. I interrupted her with a sob and put my hands over my face. She put an arm around my shoulders.

"What is it, dear?"

"I'm sorry, but I'm in so much trouble… I came all the way from Kansas City and…"

I broke down again.

"It can't be as bad as that. What is your name, dear?"

"Hannah Rosenbloom."

I had picked something that I hoped sounded Jewish.

"Oh, my. From the Kansas City Rosenblooms?"

"Yes," I said. "Distantly."

She seemed a little puzzled by "distantly" and I couldn't blame her. I said it because I feared she might start quizzing me about mutual acquaintances, but she didn't.

"Well, you just step into the parlor and we'll wait for Abraham. He always wants to help members of the community."

"Do you think—I know this sounds foolish—do you think I could wait in Mr. Rothstein's library? I've heard so much about what a scholar he is, I think I would find that soothing. I'm sure he has so many books."

Mrs. Rothstein nodded, somewhat regretfully.

"Oh, yes, there are many books. We have no space left for them and Abraham keeps buying more. All right, it's over here, dear."

She led me to the right, into a long and narrow room just off the foyer. She hadn't exaggerated. All the walls were lined with shelves up to the ceiling and all the shelves were packed solid with books. Big, weighty volumes that looked to be used, not simply placed conspicuously as a decoration. There was a leather easy chair with a lamp for reading, a desk for study, and, glory be, a beautiful ornate cabinet, standing on four curved oaken legs. This was truly a piece that would be a standout in any museum. The dark wood sides, the doors, even the legs were intricately carved with both figures and letters. The letters, I was sure, were Hebrew. The figures seemed Biblical: I recognized men carrying the Ark of the Covenant and Moses with the Burning Bush.

"Oh, my goodness!" I exclaimed. "What a beautiful piece!"

"Yes, it is nice. My husband was given it when he was president of the synagogue. Do you know, the donor was anonymous so we couldn't even thank him."

"You don't say? Remarkable."

I had moved near the easy chair and suddenly I let my knees buckle and dropped into it. Mrs. Rothstein rushed to me.

"What's the matter?"

"I'm sorry," I managed to say. "It's just been so long since I've eaten…"

Plainly, Mrs. Rothstein couldn't allow a hungry guest in her home. She wrung her hands, called me a poor thing, and hurried out to the kitchen to get me some sustenance. I hoped it would be something complicated, as I had work to do before she came back.

I hurried to the cabinet and looked it over carefully. It was essentially a wardrobe standing on four legs. The doors were open, revealing three shelves containing tall leather-bound books. These were obviously special. They were expensively bound, with gold lettering in Hebrew, and they were unlike the other books in the room because they did not seem worn at all, as though they were too precious to be touched. I wondered if they could be hollowed out and contain the notebooks, but that seemed far-fetched. If I was right and the notebooks were in this cabinet, there had to be a secret compartment, as in J.P. Morgan's desk.

"Dear," I heard from behind me.

Mrs. Rothstein was back! I whipped around to face her.

"My, you do like our cabinet, don't you? You were staring at it so."

"It's the most beautiful thing I've ever seen, I think. Our people in Kansas City have nothing like this."

"Oh, you might be surprised," she said. "Get a look inside Ethel Waterman's house some time, you'll see some things. I just came to say, I'm heating up some chicken soup. I know it's a cliché, but I really do think it's the best when you need some comfort. Is that all right?"

"Wonderful."

Just make it slowly, I wanted to add. She smiled, nodded, and headed back to the kitchen.

I didn't have much time left. I knocked gently on all the sides, top and bottom of the cabinet. I wasn't sure what I was listening for and I didn't hear it. It did seem to my eye like there was more room than there should have been between the floor on the inside of the cabinet and the outside bottom. If the notebooks were in the cabinet, that must be where they were. But how to open it?

Growing more tense, I scanned the various scenes depicted along the outside walls. Many were familiar from the stories the priest told when I was young. There was Moses, there the Ark, there Daniel in the lion's den, there Abraham... the name stopped me. On one side of the cabinet, toward the bottom, was a carving of an old bearded patriarch holding a child on an altar. The patriarch's eyes were lifted to Heaven, but in his hand was a vicious-looking knife, poised to strike at the child. Plainly, this was Abraham about to follow God's order to sacrifice his own son. The father Abraham, cruelly willing to murder his boy. It seemed to me that Arnold Rothstein might be taken with this carving.

I knelt beside it and traced it with my fingers. Was there something strange about the knife in the father's hand? It seemed to stand out from the background more than would be expected. I put my fingers against it and pushed with all my strength.

Yes! A drawer of surprising depth dropped down from under the floor of the cabinet, caught by an ingenious hinge mechanism. Inside was the treasure I sought: it looked like perhaps fifty small notebooks, shaped to fit in a man's breast pocket. I picked up my bag and started scooping notebooks into it as quickly as I could.

I was about to shovel the last few notebooks into the handbag when, suddenly, the library door opened. This time, instead of Mrs. Rothstein with chicken soup, it was Abraham Rothstein himself!

He stood in the door frame and drew himself to his full height, an expression of astonishment on his face. He looked like Jeremiah.

"You!" he exclaimed, recognizing me as the woman who bumped into him on the street. "What are you doing? What is this?"

His eyes had taken in the precious religious artifact, the cabinet, now with the undreamt-of secret compartment open to view and plainly being looted by a villainous woman.

He strode across the room and grabbed my arm roughly. He was distraught and angry.

"You invade my home, grab at my things? What are you putting in that bag?"

Esther Rothstein was now in the room, looking concerned and mystified.

"Don't hurt her, Abraham. She's only a girl."

"Mr. Rothstein," I said as calmly and firmly as I could as he was shaking me. "I will explain if you let me go. It's about your son, Arnold."

The name stopped him and he threw aside my arm.

"Of course it is about my son. All that is evil is from my son."

I pointed to the cabinet.

"You see there was a secret drawer here. Your son was the anonymous donor who gave you this. Every month, when he would visit Mrs. Rothstein, he would place one of these notebooks in the secret compartment."

Rothstein glared at his wife.

"Mrs. Rothstein didn't know, of course. This was all your son's plan."

The father stumbled to his chair and sat, shaken to his soul.

"But for what? What are these notebooks?"

I handed him one at random.

"They are the records of his evil deeds, Mr. Rothstein. Your son sits at Lindy's and keeps the records of his gambling and bootlegging and whatever else he is up to in these little notebooks. As he finishes one, he places it into this drawer and he starts another."

Esther now sat at the chair by the desk, looking ill. Her husband thumbed through the notebook I'd given him, then placed his face in his hands, miserably.

"Why would he do such a thing?" he asked in a pleading tone.

I considered my answer.

"I think to him it is a sort of joke."

Rothstein's head snapped up to look at me. He heaved the notebook violently across the room.

"Yes, that is my son. That would be his joke. Who are you? You can't be with the police."

"Mr. Rothstein, I think if I have these notebooks, I can bring your son to justice. It is time for that."

Mrs. Rothstein began to sob. Mr. Rothstein looked over at her, but did not approach her. He waved at my bag.

"Take them. Take them and go."

I didn't wait. I snatched up the bag, even picking up the notebook Mr. Rothstein had thrown, and I bolted from the room. I felt so badly for this couple, but what could I do? I had my own family to protect.

I must admit, when I reached the sidewalk and breathed in the chilly November air, I felt exalted. I had done it! Cornelius hoped for years to get his hands on Arnold Rothstein's ledgers and now I had them safely in my grasp, ready for the boys to use to pressure Rothstein into letting Cornelius alone. Then Walter and I could go home to Fern and to Hal and we would never be involved with bad men again. I was picturing how Cornelius would look when I showed him the notebooks.

Right at that moment, a man stepped from behind a stoop, directly in front of me. It was the blond, greasy man who Walter said had killed Jack O'Neal. He punched me, very hard, in the stomach. He grabbed my arms and bundled me into a parked car, throwing me into the front passenger seat. From his back pockets, he pulled a pair of handcuffs and he cuffed me to the armrest on the door.

"Don't worry, missy," he sneered. "This will be fun. We're going to Coney Island."

He got behind the wheel. I had just the sense to notice that he threw my bag with the notebooks into the back seat. Then we sped away.

40

Big Night on Broadway

Cornelius

Marta's plan was crazy. She insisted that Rothstein would be irrational about his father, so if we cooked up phony evidence showing his father was having an affair, he'd be so worked up he'd give us whatever we asked. It made no sense to me, but I couldn't come up with a better idea and Riley was for it, so there we were.

It's actually pretty easy to create fake evidence, on a superficial level. Marta waylaid old Abe on the sidewalk with a pretended faint, with me taking pictures from the bushes. I heisted one of Abe's ties from his Turkish bath and we sprinkled it with some perfume. Weak stuff, but Marta insisted that A.R. would cough up the evidence against me without thinking too hard, especially if Riley tore up the markers to Raymond and if Riley kept a gun to Rothstein's head until it was over.

The toughest part for me was that Marta insisted I'd have to promise to leave New York. This was devastating, but I saw her point. As long as Arnold Rothstein ruled Broadway, this would not be the place for me, so I went along with Marta's plan. I figured I'd talk to Hearst about a job in Los Angeles. I heard they had crime there.

We decided to spring the trap on Sunday night. We knew Rothstein would be at Lindy's and Hump McManus had taken a room at the Park Central to get away from his wife for the weekend and party. Lots of Broadway types used the Park Central that way. Riley, as Nate Raymond, would beard McManus in his hotel room and get him to ask Rothstein over to discuss the gambling debt. I'd be stationed at Lindy's and call ahead if anyone else left with him. Once all three of them were in the room, Riley would pull his gun on the other two, then pitch the trade of the evidence against me for the evidence against Rothstein. Whatever happened, Riley wouldn't let him out of sight until we had our deal. Not alive, anyway.

I know, it sounds crazy and it was. Maybe you have better ideas, but we didn't.

So, there I was, sitting with Runyon at a table in Lindy's, just another wash day. The usual Broadway crowd was present. Runyon was a loser that week, as always, and was in a grouchy mood. I listened to him grumble as I kept my eye on Rothstein, sitting alone at his table by the cash register. He was acting per usual, but I noticed that the wise guys weren't coming to him for loans or favors. Word on the street was that the Big Bankroll was welshing in a very serious way, so nobody wanted to be too close lest a creditor start expressing offense with a submachine gun.

I saw Max, the counter man, pick up the telephone. He listened, then called Rothstein to the phone. I thought this was McManus, making our planned call inviting Rothstein to the Park Central to meet Riley. But after just a few seconds of conversation, Rothstein calmly walked back to his table and sat down. Almost another hour went by.

In the noise of the restaurant, I barely heard the telephone the next time it rang. As before, Max answered, listened, and beckoned to Rothstein, who rose and held the phone to his ear before shrugging, nodding, and hanging up. I expected that this time, the voice on the telephone belonged to Hump McManus. Rothstein walked over to the door, pulled a handgun from under his coat, and handed it to Jimmy Meehan, who was sitting there. This was obviously for safekeeping, as I knew that Riley would have told McManus to specify there should be no guns at the meeting.

Rothstein went out into Times Square. I asked Max for the phone and, with some irritation, he handed it to me. I called the Park Central, asked for Hump's room, and Riley answered.

"He's on his way," I said softly. "Alone."

Riley hung up. My work was done, now it was up to Riley.

After a half-hour or so had passed, bad news in the form of Charlie Lucano and Albert Anastasia walked through the door into Lindy's. News doesn't come much worse than that. They looked at Rothstein's empty table, then scanned the room and focused on yours truly. They strode to the table where Runyon and I sat, with a purposefulness that weakened my knees, even sitting down.

We didn't know that night that Charlie Lucano was soon to become forever known as Lucky Luciano, soon to enter legend as the rare man who survived a one-way ride. Nor did we know that he was a few years away from murdering his mentor Joe Masseria and taking not just Masseria's lead role in New York crime, but the top job in a new commission that would rule organized crime across the country. Still, that chill autumn night at Lindy's, we knew that Lucano had an air about him. Anastasia was a thug, with no mystery. Lucano radiated cold, murderous intelligence and was plainly a leader of men. Very evil men.

"Hello, Mr. Runyon. How ya doin'?" he said suavely to Runyon, his eyes never leaving my face.

"Good to see you, Charlie," said Runyon. "What brings you up here? It's a long way from Little Italy."

Lucano turned to glare at Runyon.

"Why shouldn't I come up here? You saying Italians aren't welcome in a Jew joint like this?"

Runyon was the least perturbable of men, but even he swallowed hard at the change of mood. Fortunately, Lucano grinned.

"Just fooling with you, Damon," he said. "You boys don't mind if we join you, I'm sure."

They pulled up chairs at our table. There was noticeable silence around us, for Lucano and Anastasia were known, even this far uptown.

"Well, ain't this nice?" Lucano said, unbuttoning his suit jacket. "O'Neal, I hear you and Albert are old shipmates. Old flying mates, too."

Anastasia shifted his weight uncomfortably.

"Don't run off at the mouth, Charlie," he said, looking over at Runyon.

"Oh, don't worry about Damon," Lucano said, smiling. "Everybody knows Damon Runyon is a square guy. He hears everything, he sees everything, he knows everything, but he don't say nothing and he don't write nothing. Nothing important, that is. Ain't that right, Damon?"

It was more right than Runyon liked.

"You boys keep talking," he said, rising to his feet. "I'm taking a walk."

And he did, leaving me with the two charmers. Lucano wasted no more time on pleasantries.

"We came to give Arnold a message," he said. "He's out of time. There's a whole lot of money in that Turkish deal that we're not collecting. He keeps telling us he'll get the down payment from his election bets, but he needs to understand. That's his last chance. If he don't come up with the down payment then, somebody else makes the deal and not him."

I was confused.

"Why doesn't Masseria front the money if you want the deal done?"

They both stayed mum, looking down at the table, and it dawned on me.

"Masseria doesn't know, does he? You're cutting your boss out of the picture. Rothstein is looking to you two for muscle, but you don't have that much dough."

Lucano smiled.

"Let's just say I like Arnold. He helps me pick out my suits."

"But Masseria's bound to find out, when you start bringing in the heroin. What happens then?"

This time, even Anastasia smiled.

"Oh, the future," Lucano said. "Who can foresee the future? It is a mystery indeed."

I wondered if they intended Joe the Boss to have much of a future.

That's when the world turned upside-down, on Broadway at least. A young kid, couldn't have been more than sixteen, flung open the door and shouted with a clear, pure voice that echoed across the restaurant and stopped all the conversations cold.

"Arnold Rothstein's dead!"

Lindy's was silent for perhaps three long seconds, then the room exploded. Gamblers and their ladies ran to the kid, demanding explanations. A waiter dropped a tray. Titanic Thomas slapped his forehead in disgust, thinking of his worthless markers. I joined a throng that was pouring into Times Square, looking to find out what had happened. Just as I stepped onto Seventh Avenue, Riley came running up to me. He was panting and wild-eyed.

"We've gotta get to Coney Island," he exclaimed. "Altieri has Marta!"

"What the fuck?" a deep voice said from behind me.

It was Anastasia. He and Lucano had followed me out the door and were close enough to hear Riley's statement. Riley grabbed my arm.

"Let's go!"

He ran right in front of a cab to wave it down and we barged in. Looking out the back window as we drove away, I saw Lucano and Anastasia hail a cab as well and follow us. Riley pulled out a gun and put it to the cabbie's head.

"We need to get to Coney Island fast as this cab can go," he hissed in the driver's ear. "Floor it. You stop or even slow down and I'll kill you."

So, while throngs of cops and citizens hurried in the direction of the Park Central to see the corpse of the King of Broadway, Riley and I were barreling through New York, setting the world speed record for travel from Times Square to Coney Island, with Lucky Luciano and Albert Anastasia on our heels. It was an interesting night.

41

In the Beach Cottage

Marta

November 19, 1928 (continued):

Handcuffed to the armrest as I was, I could do nothing to escape. The blond man said nothing, he just drove, the streets quiet on a Sunday afternoon. He was smiling, really a sort of leer. His teeth were more yellow than his hair. His long thin fingers gripped the wheel tightly. He said nothing, he didn't even look at me.

Once again, I was shivering with panic. I remembered the cave, being tied, what the men did to me. I remembered my Walter shooting them, every one. I could only think that this man, this gangster, would be like the bandits and I would again be raped, perhaps by many men. This time, I thought, I would not survive. I did not think I would want to survive.

We crossed a bridge and drove into what I thought was Brooklyn. As we kept going across town, I wondered if he was really taking me to Coney Island. Why there?

I recognized Surf Avenue and the sausage stand that said Nathan's. We pulled into an alley and stopped near the side door of a little house, like a beach cottage. It fronted right on the Coney Island boardwalk. The area was deserted: there was no reason to come to Coney Island in

November. Perhaps that in itself was a reason for a man such as the one who had me now.

The man left the car and went in the side door of the cottage. In moments, he returned with a funny-looking little fellow, small and round and dark, wearing a sweatshirt with a turtleneck like a bully in the movies. The blond man opened the door, released my handcuffs, and led me into the cottage, telling the funny-looking man to take my bag from the back seat.

The side door led to a small shabby kitchen, just an icebox, stove, a table, and some chairs, into one of which I was roughly deposited.

"Now, sweetie, let's see what you got in here," the blond man said as he opened my bag. His jaw dropped. "Holy Christ. Are these what I think they are?" Then, remembering the man in the sweatshirt who stood near the door, he said to him, "Get in the living room. Make yourself scarce. I can handle her."

The man looked irritated and curious. He sneaked a look at my bag, but he obeyed. Without even hearing him speak, I judged him for a weak-willed man, no match for the icy blond assassin who was now left alone with me.

He picked up a notebook and scanned through it.

"Holy Christ," he said again. "Where'd you get these? From Rothstein's parents? Holy Christ."

He didn't wait for me to answer and I didn't. He took out his gun and held it on me.

"I've gotta make a call, right there in the hallway. Don't go anywhere, sister. I'm right through this door."

He stepped into the hall and I heard him ask an operator for Lindy's, then when someone at Lindy's came on the line:

"Get me Rothstein. ... A.R., this is Altieri. You will not guess what I'm looking at right now. I am looking at one of your little notebooks you're always writing in. That's right, from May of 1927. First goddam name I come to is Jimmy Walker, you giving him ten grand. You got a interesting life, A.R. ... I picked up Riley's girl off the street coming out of your parents' house. She had them. ... I followed her to your parents. ... I was watching O'Neal's apartment, that's how. ... Yeah, that's right. Your parents keep them for you? ... She's right here at the cottage. I got a gun on her right now. ... Well, how long you gonna take to get here? ... Shit, that long? ... Yeah, I know, you got business, you always got business. Get here as soon as you can. I need my beauty sleep. You want I should get the story from her before you get here? … No, I guess there's no hurry. … Okay, just don't keep me waiting all night."

I heard the slam of an earpiece onto the phone and the blond man, Altieri, returned.

"We're gonna wait for a while, sister. The Bankroll has wash day business that's gonna keep him until late. Then we'll see what's what. Meanwhile, I'll figure where to keep you."

He gestured for me to walk down the narrow hallway into the living room, where the henchman sat cleaning a gun. Altieri put me in a chair and cuffed me to the armrest.

"Make yourself comfortable. It's gonna be a long night for you and it ain't gonna be over when A.R. gets here. It's just gonna be starting."

"Fuck's going on?" the henchman asked.

"Don't worry about it. Rothstein wants to talk to the girl. He's not gonna get here till late, so we just have to wait."

The henchman seemed to take this in, slowly. Then his big calf eyes moved over to me and looked me up and down.

"She's a good-looking skirt," he said. "How 'bout we take her upstairs and, you know… pass the time?"

My heart stopped. Suddenly I was back in the cave, the Spaniard telling his men that I was for them. Altieri looked me over and seemed to consider the idea.

"Better not," he said. "Rothstein might have something different in mind. Hell, stay up though, Sonny. Maybe A.R. will give you the leftovers."

Hours passed, I don't know how many. It grew dark outside. Altieri sat on a sofa across the room from me, reading the notebooks and laughing. The one called Sonny finished cleaning his gun and fell asleep in his chair. My mind was racing. Of course, I was thinking what would happen when Arnold Rothstein arrived or if Walter would keep him from coming and what would happen then? Most of all, I was thinking that somehow Altieri knew Walter's name and that I was his woman. Altieri had seen Walter in Independence and seen him with me at Coney Island. Did Rothstein now know it was Walter in the poker game, not Nate Raymond?

I stayed awake, hoping for some sort of chance, even handcuffed as I was, but while Sonny slept on, Altieri never seemed to close his eyes at all. He took a salami from the kitchen and sat eating hunks that he carved off with a knife he took from a scabbard at his belt. I saw that he wore two of them. He caught me looking at them and winked at me. He threw pieces of salami to me, like he was feeding a dog.

It may have been close to midnight. I don't know. I may even have been dozing, for the sudden sound of gunshots shocked me and caused me to bolt up, though restrained by the handcuffs. The henchman and Altieri pulled out guns and dropped to the floor, but no shots came into the room. The shots were coming from in front of the cottage, but seemed to be fired in a different direction.

More shots came. Altieri crawled on his belly to me, released my handcuffs from the chair, and cuffed me to his wrist. He was careful to keep my body between him and the front windows.

"They may have surrounded us," he said to the henchman.

"Who are they?"

"Fuck if I know. Somebody who either wants the bag or the girl. You hold the front, I'll hold the back."

Picking up the bag and yet again hauling at my arm, Altieri dragged me down the hallway. Instead of "holding the back," he immediately took me out the side door and down the alley.

"We're getting out of here, sister. I know just where to hole up."

And he dragged me, running, toward Luna Park.

286

42

Bullets on the Boardwalk

Cornelius

We were speeding toward Coney Island, with Lucano and Anastasia right behind us. I looked over at Riley, still holding his pistol to the cabbie's temple.

"What the hell happened back there?"

"Not here," he snapped.

I knew he was right. If the cabbie heard that his passengers were involved in the murder of Arnold Rothstein, he'd probably faint and crack us up right there.

As it turned out, Rothstein wasn't dead, not yet. It took the bastard the rest of the night and much of the next two days to die. As we drove onto the Brooklyn Bridge and headed across the East River, word of Rothstein's demise or near-demise was flying all over New York. Jimmy Walker heard it while dining with the beauteous Betty Compton and immediately sped to Times Square to figure out what the hell. Runyon, I am told, actually ran to the Park Central, something impossible to imagine. Judges, cops, and aldermen said Hail Marys. Everyone in the city knew that Rothstein kept detailed records of his dirty deeds and everyone in the city was wondering what would happen to those records and whether their names were in them. Unbeknownst to us as we barreled across the bridge, those records were in fact in the possession of none other than Riley's ever-loving Marta. Unfortunately, Marta was in the possession of Two Knives Altieri.

Riley and I sat in tight-lipped silence as we careened through Brooklyn and, at my direction, skidded to a stop on Surf Avenue, across from Nathan's. I made to get out of the car.

"Not yet!" Riley said.

He flung open his door and, quick as light, moved around the other side of it, so it was between him and Lucano's car, just pulling to a stop maybe forty feet behind us. Riley squeezed off three rounds into their car's grillwork.

"Now!" he shouted.

I jumped from the car and the two of us tore down Surf Avenue and jerked to the right, into the first alley we saw. The cabbie stayed on the floor of the front seat. He didn't get his fare, but I doubt he complained about that.

For myself, I didn't think that our pursuers were intending to kill us. Why should they? More likely, they wanted to see what was going to happen when we got to Altieri, since Lucano would have figured his crew had an interest in all things crooked in Brooklyn and with Rothstein dead, who knew what would happen next? It didn't seem a good idea to stop and discuss it with them, though.

We were running toward the ocean, down the alley that leads to the Wonder Wheel. I could see it in the distance, the big red wheel fronted by its sign flapping and creaking in the darkness and the cold November wind. We stopped at a corner where the boardwalk passed across the alley. I could hear running feet behind us, but I couldn't see them.

"Yale's place is over there," I said, pointing. "Only place with lights on. That's where they'll be."

Riley scanned the ground quickly. Looming over each side of this stretch of the boardwalk were cheap carny stands, unlit, with painted faces leering from the plywood, hawking tattoos, ice cream, fortune tellers. There were no guards and no fences, as there was nothing to steal and no people around, except in the cottage that had the lights on.

We only had the one gun between us. Riley handed it to me, along with a box of ammunition.

"Take up position there behind that ticket booth. Start firing and hold off those guys and whoever comes out of the cottage. I'm going in the back."

There was no time to argue. Riley pulled a knife out of his sock, jumped, grabbed hold of the roof of a small Coney dog stand, and hoisted himself onto the top. He started running toward the cottage, bent over, jumping from stand to stand just as Lucano and Anastasia rounded the corner at the alley and appeared on the boardwalk. I let off two shots above their heads, not trying to hit them, and watched them dive back for cover. I hoped to God I wouldn't have to kill Charlie Lucano or Albert Anastasia since I knew Joe Masseria would never rest until he'd gotten his revenge. On the other hand, I hoped to God they wouldn't kill me, too.

I got into the ticket booth and ducked down. As a shield against gunfire, it was ridiculously flimsy. My teeth were chattering and my hands shaking, but I still managed to replace the cartridges I'd fired so I had a full load. I knew I might not have time once the men in the cottage came out to see what was happening.

One of them did. He put his head out the door, at the top of the stoop. He was a heavy guy, wearing a turtleneck sweater. His arm appeared through the crack in the door and he pointed a gun at me. I knew the bullet would go through the plywood that was my only shield and I had no option but to hope the door to the cottage was no sturdier. I planted three, maybe four shots into that door, where the man's torso had to be. The door swung open and the man behind it dropped, face forward, his corpse wedging itself in the opening. I hoped he wasn't Joe Masseria's cousin or some damn thing.

I thought I heard glass breaking from up above and figured Riley was busting through a window on the second floor of the cottage. With just a knife, he had his work cut out for him. Anastasia stuck his head around the corner and I got off another shot in his direction. Then, seeing no one at the windows of the cottage and knowing I had to get inside to help Riley, I sprinted to the front door, hurdled the corpse, and dove prone to the floor, gun extended with both my hands. Nobody home.

"Riley?" I shouted.

"I'm here," he answered. "Upstairs is clear."

I figured that meant downstairs was my job. Moving slowly, gun forward, I edged toward an entry into a hallway. I heard Riley come down the stairs. I pushed open the first door and saw an empty bedroom. I was moving to the second when Riley shouted.

"There!"

He was looking out a front window of the living room. A man and a woman were just disappearing in the distance, around the corner on the boardwalk. Altieri and Marta.

"There must be a side door," Riley said.

He barged into the kitchen at the end of the hall, me following. Sure enough, a side door. Forgetting caution, Riley hit the alley through the side door and I was on his heels, watching for trouble and hoping this wasn't Marta's last night on earth.

43

Charlie's Suit

Cornelius

A s I went through the cottage door into the alley, a scene like from a movie greeted me. I saw Riley, knife in hand, reach the end of the alley and turn sharply to his right, running down the boardwalk.

I took a deep breath to start after him and two men appeared at the end of the alley, pointing guns at Riley. Anastasia knelt on the boardwalk to steady his shot, Lucano right behind him. They were perfectly framed in the mouth of the alley, easy targets in the bright moonlight, but I still hoped to avoid killing these particular men.

I knelt and assumed firing position with my barrel fixed on the small space between them.

"Freeze! Both of you! Drop your guns on the ground or I swear to God I'll blow you to hell!"

One tries to be emphatic in such situations.

I saw both of them eyeing me sideways, figuring the odds. The odds broke my way this time, for they opened their hands and their guns dropped to the boardwalk.

"Kick 'em away… Now belly down, hands behind your heads."

These were experienced men. They calmly lay prone, fingers interlocked on their necks, waiting for the next instruction, as though they had done all this before. I knew they were looking for any chance I might give them.

I picked up their guns and shoved them in my waistband. Now what? I heard two shots from the direction of Luna Park and knew I had to get over there. Here I had three guns and Riley none. But if I just left Dracula and Frankenstein free on the boardwalk, next thing I knew they'd have the whole Brooklyn mafia joining in the fun. A pretty problem, solved by a glance around. There, just inside the alley, was the most beautiful big garbage bin I'd ever seen, complete with a lid. A glance inside told me the bin was empty, waiting for the start of the next season.

"Albert," I said, "get to your feet slowly and keep your hands above your head. Walk over here. Charlie, stay flat or I'll plug both of you…"

I pointed to the bin and told Anastasia to get in.

"No fuckin' way, *fanook*," he said.

Lucano intervened.

"Albert! Do what he says. I want to go home tonight, you understand me?"

Lucano's word was apparently already law, for Anastasia gave me one last glare and hoisted himself into the dumpster. Lucano followed without needing to be told, though when he looked into the bin where Anastasia already lay, I heard him sigh, "My suit."

"It's a very nice suit, Charlie," I said as I slammed the lid down.

I dragged the corpse of the dead man in the doorway to the dumpster and hoisted him onto the top to weigh it down and delay the gangsters' escape.

More gunshots in the distance. I ran to Luna Park.

44

The Bandit's Cave

Marta

November 19, 1928 (continued):

A thought flashed into my mind as the gangster dragged me down the boardwalk: he was taking me to the Bandit's Cave. I knew it with certainty. My terror would make me easy to manage and he was a man who would enjoy that terror. As we ran, I expected to find in myself the same overwhelming panic, the same unconquerable hysteria that so vexed me before, but it wasn't there. In fact, I became calmer and for the first time since I was taken, I felt able to think clearly. I knew that Walter was somewhere behind us, that he would remember the Bandit's Cave, and that he would find us there however well we were hidden. If this Altieri could defeat my Walter, I would be much surprised.

But we weren't yet at the Cave. We passed into Luna Park, which was as unsecured as the rest of off-season Coney Island. The deserted, ghostly attractions were familiar to me as we passed them: Midget City, the Love Nest, Trip to the Moon. They looked so different. Without all the lights, they were sad and sinister. He was taking me to the Bandit's Cave, all right. Suddenly, when we were about level with the ride called the Red Mill, Altieri stopped and cocked his head. Over my own panting, I could hear running footsteps approaching from behind. I was sure it was Walter. Altieri foolishly fired two shots into the night in that direction, perhaps thinking of them as warning shots for he could see no one. The footsteps paused. After one more shot, Altieri pulled me forward and urged me toward the great facade of the Bandit's Cave, whose painted figures had so terrified me. Now, they only looked cheap and foolish. I had a real devil to worry about.

A gate barred the entrance to the Cave, so Altieri simply used his knife to slash a new door in the canvas wall beside it. He pushed me inside, into the darkness. Altieri took another wild shot through the slash, maybe this time seeing someone. Then the hammer of his gun fell on an empty chamber. He cursed. He felt his side pockets and cursed again.

"The one night I'm not carrying ammo," he said.

He looked at me, pulled one of his knives from its scabbard and held it to my throat.

"Don't get your hopes up. You ain't getting rescued tonight. That's your boy out there—I saw him duck when I took my last shot. I'll make sure you get to kiss his cold dead face before I give you to Rothstein."

Still handcuffed together, we moved forward into the darkness. I'd been through at least part of the Cave before and I doubted Altieri had. I only hoped this would be an advantage.

45

Two Knives

Cornelius

I crossed 12th Street cautiously, not wanting to get shot. There was no more gunfire coming from Luna Park. It was eerie seeing the place, for at night I was used to the park with its famed quarter-million bulbs illuminated bright as the sun, but now there was only moonlight and an occasional glow from a lamppost. Through the arched doorway to Luna Park, I trotted briskly but quietly in the direction of the shooting, expecting any moment to feel a bullet through my ribs. I'd never been shot, despite the Kaiser's best efforts in the war, and I didn't want to spoil my record.

I reached the main courtyard of the park, past the Coal Mine, past the Love Nest and the Pit ("More Laughs to the Minute Than Any Broadway Play Ever Produced" read the sign), past the Red Mill. Then my eyes fell on the next attraction to my right, the Bandit's Cave. This was the place, I thought, where Marta had panicked and Altieri saw her and Riley. That drew me to step closer and look more carefully at the attraction and I saw two slashes in the canvas that made openings, one by the main entrance, one far along the wall to my left. Instantly I knew, without thinking about it, that one of the slashes was made by Altieri to hide inside with Marta, the other by Riley going after them. Did the silence since the last shot mean that Altieri had gotten him?

There was no alternative but to push forward. I thought I could hear feet shuffling off to my left, but I couldn't see a damn thing. *Jesus, did everybody else blunder their way through this blackness?* Fuck that. If I was chasing after a hoodlum with a gun, I wanted to see where I was going. Quietly as I could, I felt along the front wall, hoping against hope to find a light switch. I heard cursing from the darkness and thought it was Altieri. I was running my hands up and down the canvas, from the floor to as high as I could reach. I came to what felt like a post and, sure enough, there was a switch on it! Startling light, not real bright but still light, revealed a small empty chamber oriented perpendicular to the front wall through which I'd entered. The walls were canvas hanging on two-by-four posts. An opening in the left wall led to more blackness.

I stepped through and felt around to my right, thinking perhaps there were light switches in each room at roughly the same location. Heavy breathing was now not far ahead. Just as I was about to flip the switch, I heard a sharp thwack and a grunt, then a loud thud and a curse. I threw the switch and saw a tableau that could have been part of the show, except it was deadly real.

I was at one end of a room painted up to look like a childish vision of Hell. Two gas pipes ran along the floor, one on each side. At the other end of the room, there was a round entry filled by one of those large rotating pipes they put in carnival funhouses to make you run through. The pipe was rocking back and forth, but just on its own momentum, it wasn't under power. Above the entry was lettering: "Abandon All Hope Ye Who Enter Here."

I hoped not, for Marta was lying sprawled in the cylinder, handcuffed to Altieri who lay half on her and half off. His arm was raised, knife in hand, poised to slash down onto her throat. I couldn't get off a shot with the two of them so wrapped up together.

I didn't need to. Suddenly, through the damn swinging pipe, I saw Riley standing on the opposite side. Quick as the light had filled the room, Riley reached his hand behind his head and flung his knife at Altieri's back, just as he'd learned from Jesus back at the farm. The blade flew straight, piercing between Altieri's shoulder blades. He fell forward and dropped his knife.

But one stab wound doesn't usually kill a man, certainly not instantly. Altieri reached for the knife he'd dropped, fumbling for it.

Marta reached out, grabbing for it with her left hand. I was trying in vain to get a shot I could take. Riley sprinted forward, into the tunnel but, as soon as he did, the cylinder shifted and he fell on his belly.

And then, what do you know? The jerk of the cylinder jarred Altieri just a bit. Marta grabbed his knife and slammed it, hard, into the killer's throat. Riley half-ran, half-crawled to Marta's side, but it was over. Altieri dropped on his face, still gurgling and bubbling down in his throat. He was dying. Riley felt Altieri's pockets and found the handcuff key. He released Marta and pulled her to his arms.

"Marta, darling, *te amo*, I love you," he said, etc., etc., kissing her all over. "Are you all right? Are you hurt?"

Marta, remarkable woman that she is, actually gave a little smile.

"No, *mi esposo*, I am not hurt. I'm just glad I am left-handed."

Altieri gave up one last gurgle, then the ghost. Riley looked down at his corpse.

"I guess he was right after all," Riley said. "Two knives is better."

46

Polly Adler's Peace Conference

Cornelius

Some might think we were now sitting pretty. We'd survived one of Broadway's most hectic nights, which is more than Arnold Rothstein and Willie Altieri could say. We had possession of what every wise guy in the city was looking for and afraid someone else would find: the business records of the Big Bankroll. I sat in my hotel room and read every page. Incredible stuff, stuff that would blow the top off City Hall, Albany, Wall Street, and just about every other New York institution, legal and not. Throughout the twenties, Arnold Rothstein seemed to have his hand in every crooked deed of the decade, usually as financier or fixer, but often enough as mastermind and direct participant.

There was the prominent New York Supreme Court judge who was blackmailed into throwing out a case against one of Rothstein's cronies lest his predilection for little boys be revealed. The loan to the newly-elected governor, Franklin Roosevelt, when he was a very young man and had a gambling debt. Rothstein's fixing races in Saratoga. The Broadway star who'd begun her career at Polly Adler's. A detailed accounting of monthly payments to cops, prosecutors, judges, aldermen, just about everyone in the city who could do Rothstein some good. And, of course, there was yours truly, seller of heroin to J.P. Morgan and accessory to the murder of Alfred Loewenstein.

Why, I wondered, would Rothstein even think of keeping such records? I knew his memory and he would never forget a transaction, he didn't need to write it down. At a minimum, he could have put the entries in some sort of code. Yet there they were, in plain English and neatly transcribed, easily read and understood by anyone who might get hold of them. They may not have been admissible in court, but the roadmap they would give to an aggressive prosecutor could put half the politicians and all the mobsters in New York in jail, if there were any judges left to preside at their trials. At the time, I couldn't fathom the psychology of a brilliant criminal who would be so cocksure and so deluded as to make careful records that could lead to his own undoing. Of course, as I write this, I am an old man in the nineteen-eighties and we've all learned a lot more about this phenomenon from Richard Nixon.

Anyway, we were not sitting pretty. In fact, we were sitting pretty ugly. Lucano and Anastasia were no doubt looking to kill us, if nothing else for the damage to Charlie's suit. If Jimmy Walker or the wrong kind of police found out we had Rothstein's journals, we were equally dead: no single individual featured more prominently and often in the notebooks than Beau James, New York's elegant mayor. I could try to get the *Journal* or somebody else to publish all this stuff, but after all that happened, I couldn't see the mob ever regarding retribution as moot. While I could destroy the references to me in the notebooks, I didn't know what other evidence might be out there with my name on it. I shivered when I thought of that, given that everyone and his brother and his late maiden aunt were rooting everywhere in the city, looking for Rothstein's notebooks as they sat in Marta's handbag on the sofa in the hotel room where we were hiding out.

We three also sat in that room, analyzing our position, considering and rejecting options to slide out from under. Riley explained what happened when Rothstein was mortally shot. As I might have expected, it was all the fault of that numbskull Hump McManus. At first, Riley told us, all went as planned. He braced McManus in his hotel, room 349 at the Park Central. McManus was flirting in there with the hotel maid, but shooed her out when Riley arrived. As far as Hump knew, Riley was still Nate Raymond, aggrieved gambler.

Riley told Hump that for reasons of his own, he needed Rothstein to pay his debt now, immediately, yesterday would be better. Hump said Rothstein kept claiming he'd get well in two days, from his bets on Herbert Hoover for president and Roosevelt for governor. Riley said well then, Nate Raymond was by God going to be the first creditor paid out of those winnings. He demanded a sit-down with Rothstein, right there in Hump's hotel room. He told Hump to make it clear there were to be no guns and he opened his coat to show he was unarmed. Fortunately, Hump was so stupid he didn't even frisk Riley, whose pistol was jammed in the back waistband of his pants, beneath his coat.

Hump made the call to Lindy's, which I witnessed from the Rothstein end. Rothstein left his gun with Jimmy Meehan and went to the Park Central, all so far as planned. After Hump made his call, Riley pulled his gun and held it on Hump while taking my call from Lindy's. Rothstein arrived and Riley covered him as well. But before Riley could go into his pitch about Rothstein's father and the photograph with Marta and the like, the Bankroll topped him.

"This is your move, is it? McManus, haven't you figured out who this is? He's not Nate Raymond, his name is Walter Riley and he's a friend of O'Neal's."

"I don't know how he found out, but he did," Riley told me. "I guess when Altieri recognized me that time at the Bandit's Cave in Coney Island, he told Rothstein who I was and that I was in New York. When and how he figured it was me in the poker game, I don't know. Maybe he saw a picture of Nate Raymond or something. Anyway, there it was."

Riley kept his gun on Rothstein, still planning to work the father angle. Then Rothstein pulled another bunny from his hat.

"You might want to put that gun away, Mr. Riley. When I was at Lindy's, I got a call from your friend Willie Altieri. He's got your wife. He followed her from O'Neal's apartment and grabbed her. She's stashed in Coney Island, waiting for me to show up. Hate to think what might happen to her if I don't get there. Want to call Willie, see if I'm giving you the straight dope?"

Or something like that. Anyway, at that point Riley was focused on Rothstein, he told me, and Hump decided to be a hero. He jumped Riley, wrestling for the gun. It went off, shooting Rothstein in the privates, so Riley bolted for Lindy's, where he fetched me to help find Marta.

"Wait a minute," I said when he'd finished the story. "The paper

301

said they found the gun that shot Rothstein on the street outside the hotel, like it had been thrown from Hump's room."

"Yeah, that's McManus again," Riley said. "Turns out, he had a gun in the desk and before he ran out, he threw it out the window. Didn't want to have a gun found in his room after the shooting, I guess. Dumb guy. But the gun on the street wasn't the one that shot Arnold Rothstein." He held up the weapon that I had returned to him after Coney Island. "This one did."

So that's the genuine story of who shot Arnold Rothstein and why. Rothstein died at Polyclinic Hospital. I'll say this for A.R., he didn't blab anything to the police about who shot him. I don't think it was any gangster code that stopped him from squealing: Rothstein didn't have any code and I know for a fact he squealed on Legs Diamond and others when it suited him. I think Rothstein believed he'd live and wanted to kill us himself. Well, screw him.

While Rothstein was now dead, we still had to figure out a way to make peace with the remaining gangsters and come out of this alive and not on the run. Our only hole card was Rothstein's notebooks, the hottest commodity in town, and we had them. How could we make use of them?

Then it came to me. I needed to involve someone. A man who made a career of never getting involved in anything.

Riley, Marta, and I showed up early for the meeting at Polly Adler's place. Sex being a good business for the procurers, Polly had come up in the world. She now ran her shop out of an impressive townhouse on the Upper East Side. She didn't hesitate a bit about hosting the meeting I had in mind. Her place was often used as a neutral site for conflict resolution purposes and Lord knows we had a conflict to resolve. When I told Polly who would be attending the meeting, she grinned all over.

"Why, Jimmy O'Neal, I'd have been so insulted if you asked anyone else to host this meeting! With that guest list, it's going to be quite a party."

I knew we would need babysitters for security, to be sure the party didn't turn violent. Off-duty cops would be the best choice. I wasn't going to ask my cousin Mikey or any of the Toolans after Mikey had blabbed my secrets to his sugar daddy Mayor Walker. Maybe he didn't know that would get my father killed, but he sure knew he was betraying me. Instead, I called on the policeman I knew next best, Rory McGunnigle, the detective who had let me into the Adonis Club murder scene back in 1925. I thought he'd need some convincing, given the people we were dealing with, but he seemed amused at the prospect and he enlisted a couple of his cop friends. McGunnigle was well enough known that I figured our guests would recognize him as a cop, even in plainclothes.

Polly extended the invitations to the guests, telling them they would receive information as to the whereabouts of Arnold Rothstein's notebooks, which made them lathered up to come. The first two to arrive were Lucano and Anastasia. When they rang the bell, I slipped into the library with Riley, Marta, and my little surprise. I could hear Polly's charming voice.

"Charlie! And you must be Mr. Anastasia. Wonderful to see you, come on in, please."

There was a few moments' pause while McGunnigle and his buddies frisked the gangsters, per my instructions. They must have been satisfied, for I heard Lucano and Anastasia pass into the living room and Lucano asked Polly where the notebooks were.

"Be patient, boys," Polly responded. "There's one other guest coming, then all shall be made clear."

Polly then launched into gracious chat about the theatre, the weather, and many other extraneous topics while her listeners waited silently, no doubt glowering.

The last arrival was nearly twenty minutes late, but he came. I joined Polly at the door to welcome him, since we could now get the meeting started. Riley and Marta came along, Marta carrying her big flowered bag. When the door opened, Polly and I both laughed, for the newcomer's face was entirely wrapped in a woolen muffler that concealed his features.

"Oh, Mister Mayor, take off that silly muffler and come on in. I don't know why you bother. No one's going to see you here."

Jimmy Walker took off the muffler and revealed his handsome features.

"Well, Polly, I just didn't want people to think I have to pay for sex," he smiled.

"You don't have to pay for it, but that's just because I never charge you. Right this way, Jimmy."

Walker looked at me as we stepped into the living room.

"Two Jimmies here, I see. I heard you were on the lam, Mr. O'Neal."

"Why would I be on the lam when I have such charming friends?" I said, gesturing toward Lucano and Anastasia.

Walker froze. He no longer looked so debonair.

"Don't worry, Mr. Mayor, these gentlemen are interested in the same things you are, the things that half of New York is looking for. We're all going to sit peacefully and discuss it. First, just to show good faith, you and I and my friends are going to be frisked, just like these gentlemen were when they got here. Polly can frisk Marta. Detective?"

McGunnigle grinned while frisking the mayor, which I thought was gutsy. Then I had Polly and the cops head upstairs to stay out of the way and I gestured for everyone to sit down. Riley and Marta weren't sure about my plan, but I was confident it would work and I was starting to feel exhilarated, like a long ordeal would soon end. Lucano looked unpleasantly at Marta.

"You bring a broad into this?"

"She's our partner," I answered.

Marta smiled at me for that, but it was the simple truth. We wouldn't have the notebooks without her.

"Now, as you know, my friends and I got ourselves crossways with Arnold Rothstein. Maybe it was my fault, maybe I was too pushy about the Adonis Club thing. Anyway, that's in the past and so is A.R. What all of us need to be concerned about now is the future."

"I ain't concerned about the future," Lucano snarled. "My future is just fine. You're the ones who should worry about the future."

Walker held up his hand.

"Charlie, let's hear him out."

I rose and paced the room as I talked, warming up, feeling the flow.

"Sure, we're worried about our futures, Charlie. You haven't forgotten our little altercation in Brooklyn and you're not a good enemy to have."

"Ruined my fucking suit," he said.

"But everybody should worry about the future, Charlie. Why is everybody running all over New York looking for Arnold Rothstein's records? We all saw him, night after night at Lindy's, scribbling everything he did into those little notebooks he kept in his breast pocket. I bet you wonder if your names are in them, don't you? And you, Mr. Mayor, I expect your name is in there a lot. Wouldn't all of you like to know those notebooks are safe, never to see the light of day, guarded by a man everybody on Broadway can trust?"

"What are you talking about?" Lucano asked.

"Fuckin' guy," Anastasia grumbled.

"So where are the notebooks?" Walker asked straight out.

I paused, for effect. Then I said, "Right there."

I pointed at Marta's bag, resting on her lap. She opened the bag and showed the notebooks to the room. Walker strode over to her, grabbed a notebook, and paged through it. He nodded to the others.

Charlie asked the obvious question.

"What's to stop us from grabbing that bag and walking out of here right now. Those cops you got upstairs?"

"Them," I said. "And him."

Riley reached under the cushions on the sofa where he and Marta were seated. He drew out his pistol.

"Polly didn't know about the gun," I said. "We were all frisked, but that didn't stop us from coming early and finding a way for my friend to plant his piece in the sofa."

"Jesus," Walker said. "There can't be any shooting here. I'm the mayor, for God's sake."

"Exactly," I said. "I'm sure you're all busy men, so let's get to the point. All we want is our lives back. My friends want to go back to Missouri, I want to be able to walk into Lindy's without somebody shooting me. Here's the proposition. These notebooks get stashed with a third party. He's instructed to keep them hidden away and never to release them or any of the information from them, unless he gets wind that my friends or I or any of our families are harmed by any of you. Then the notebooks get sent to the newspapers and the federal prosecutors and God help us all. Oh, and as part of the deal, I quit being a crime reporter and move to some other beat. Too much grief in this line of work anyway. If you don't take this deal, we release the notebooks to the newspapers and run like hell. That's it."

I'd modified our prior plan so that I'd stop being a crime reporter, but I could stay in New York. Rothstein was dead now and anyway, I couldn't leave Broadway.

Again, Charlie asked the obvious question.

"And who is this 'third party' we're supposed to rely on to keep his mouth shut when he's sittin' on the hottest thing in town?"

"Somebody you all trust to keep his mouth shut already."

"Trust?" Walker was amused. "This is New York. You're talking trust to two gangsters and a politician? Tell me another."

"I think you'll be satisfied," I said.

I walked over and opened the door to the library.

"Will you join us, please?" I asked.

Damon Runyon walked into the living room. Eyebrows rose, jaws dropped.

"Runyon? You'll do this?"

Runyon gave Lucano his thin smile.

"Sure, Charlie. If you all agree you want it, I'll do it."

Lucano, Anastasia, and Walker looked at each other for a moment. Riley told me later that he never believed they'd buy this idea, but Riley wasn't a citizen of Broadway. Everybody on Broadway knew Runyon and everybody knew Runyon was a right guy who didn't flap his lips about nothing. That's how Runyon got to be Runyon.

"Oh, hell," Charlie said. "If Runyon's got the notebooks, I'm satisfied. I got more important things to worry about than chasin' some two-bit reporter."

Anastasia and Walker nodded their agreement. We were done. And I was done, done with mobsters, madams, murderers, the whole scene. Life was going to be different, but at least I still had a life and my friends and our families had lives.

Runyon picked up the bag with the notebooks and the guests headed for the door. As they were leaving, I heard Lucano talking with Walker.

"Hey, Mayor, you always look good. Who does your suits?"

47

Marta's Prayers

Marta

November 19, 1928 (conclusion):

And so, diary, I have more memories I will have to live with. My husband killed Arnold Rothstein. I killed that terrible Altieri man, the man who killed Jack O'Neal. Afterward, I almost made a joke about it, telling Walter I was glad I was left-handed.

That was not me, not my real self. I said it because I thought it was something Cornelius would say, wanting to get him and my Walter to admire me. I think they did. Cornelius treats me differently now, with more respect, I think. Because I killed? Men are so strange.

There is nothing good or heroic about killing. I pray my Fern and my Hal (yes, I call him mine) never are in any trouble where such things happen. I can still feel how the muscles in my arm tensed up when I was pushing in the knife. At night in the dark, I still see his eyes bulge, hear him sputter as he died. I thought of myself, my whole identity as a victim of violence, and I am a victim of this violence as well, even though I was not the one who died. Walter, with everything he has seen and done, seems to sleep so soundly next to me. Ma has lost a husband, yet she goes on as before. Is it only I who feels too deeply about these things?

I don't know if I will write in this diary again. As much as I try to be strong, all is so dark. Tonight, I will say the prayers that I always say. I pray that Walter finds the peace to stay by my side, not to wander, not to seek the excitement he seems to need, but to find his satisfaction in his family, in the farm. I pray for Fern and Hal and Ma and Rose, yes, and Cornelius. And for me, I pray to rest.

48

So Who Did It?

Jim

I was tired, having stayed up late into the night to finish Marta's journal entries and Cornelius' notebook. I joined Riley for breakfast in the dining room, poured my coffee, and told him I was finished.

"What did you think?"

"Pretty much what I thought of the first one. Crazy stuff, hard to believe any of it. My grandfather killed Arnold Rothstein? Not something I ever thought I'd hear myself say."

Riley pushed back from the table.

"Well, you don't have to worry about it, because I didn't."

"Didn't worry about it?"

"No. I didn't kill Arnold Rothstein."

He said it as calmly as if he were asking me to pass the sugar.

"You didn't? You're saying Cornelius lied about that?"

"No, Cornelius tells the truth in these notebooks, much as anybody can. He thought I killed Rothstein because I told him I did and I told your grandmother I did. Only one who knew I didn't was Hump McManus and, so far as I know, he never told anybody either. Hump seemed to enjoy people thinking he did it, made him a big man, I guess."

Riley lit a cigarette.

"Well, you can't leave me hanging," I said. "Are you going to tell me who did it?"

"If you want."

49

The Son of My Sorrow

Riley

Everything in that hotel room happened just like I told Cornelius, until the moment Rothstein said that Altieri had Marta. McManus didn't jump me. What happened was, there was suddenly a pounding on the hotel room door. A man's voice out there said something in a foreign language. Rothstein looked like a rattlesnake had bitten him.

"Papa?" he asked in wonderment.

McManus was standing near the door and he opened it, like a fool. A tall, very distinguished-looking old man walked in, looked at Rothstein, and raised his hand to point a gun right at Rothstein's heart.

"No!" I shouted.

I dove for the man. As we fell, he squeezed the trigger and the bullet hit Rothstein in the groin. He sank unconscious to the floor, looking dead. The man, Rothstein's father, immediately dropped the gun and lay still, his job done. McManus grabbed the gun and threw it out the window, then he took off running.

"Shoot me or do as you will," the old man said to me.

I was tempted, since I'd wanted to get more information from Rothstein about Marta. But I'd heard that Rothstein's father was a decent man and he plainly had very good reason to be ashamed of his son. Anyway, I didn't really think, I just took Mr. Rothstein by the arm and got him out of there before anyone came in response to the gunshot.

We went down a stairwell. Out on the street, Abraham Rothstein looked at me.

"What now?" he said.

"Why'd you do it, Mr. Rothstein?"

"That was my son, my *ben-oni*, the son of my sorrow. He was dead to me, though the shame never left. But today, today I found out he was not content with shaming me by his life. He desecrated a work of my people, a beautiful work with a holy purpose in my faith, and he kept the records of his wickedness there, in my home, my wife's home." He closed his eyes, seeking to master himself. "It was too much."

I took him by his shoulders.

"Go home, Mr. Rothstein. No one will ever hear from me what happened tonight. Go home and live your life."

And I ran to find Cornelius and go to Coney Island for Marta.

50

An Old Testament Kind of Way

Jim

"That's it? Arnold Rothstein was killed by his father? Abe the Just?"

Riley nodded.

"That nickname about summed him up, I'd say. In an Old Testament kind of way."

He was standing at the window of the living room, looking out at the desert.

"Cornelius told me that one of Rothstein's last visitors at the hospital before he died was his father. Abraham Rothstein sat and held his son's hand for hours."

"He did?" I asked. "After firing the bullet that killed him?"

"I guess relationships can be complicated."

Riley lit another cigarette.

"But how did he know where to find Rothstein?"

"Not sure. Maybe Jimmy Meehan told him, maybe somebody at the Park Central tipped him off. I never heard."

Riley walked out of the room. When he came back, he had with him the next Cornelius notebook.

"This one is about the Depression," he said. "I was a bum."

He tossed the notebook on the table in front of me.

51

Wrapping Up

Cornelius

My life changed, all right. Oh, I don't mean my job, that proved surprisingly easy. I told Hearst I was done as a crime reporter and hinted that my safety depended on getting a different beat. With Runyon's encouragement, Hearst moved me to the City Hall political desk, figuring that way I could keep reporting on criminals. That's how I got into political reporting, which took up most of my career after that.

No, when I said my life changed, I was talking about Hal. I got to thinking about what Marta said. The key to every man is his father. I'd been pretty much of a disaster as a father, but maybe I could try to make up for it.

At Christmas time, I went to Missouri and announced my intention. I guess I'd say the response was mixed. The adults in the family (by now I thought of the Rileys and the O'Neals as one family) were sad at the thought of Hal moving away, since I wasn't about to live anywhere but New York, but they were glad I finally decided to live up to my responsibilities. It was the children who were devastated, I'm afraid. Couldn't blame them, of course. They'd been inseparable all their lives and they hardly knew me at all. I doubt if Fern stopped crying for months after we left. Hal was a good soldier, just like he's been all his life, but he wasn't happy. Still, I figured he'd get over it. Who wouldn't love New York City?

As for Rothstein's murder, it quickly moved from being the talk of the town to being the joke of the decade. Most everybody assumed Hump McManus did it, but despite a great show of activity, the cops really did almost nothing to investigate the crime. They didn't even dust the gun found on the street for fingerprints. Finally, after almost a year, the pressure to do something overwhelmed the politicians in Tammany Hall and Hump was arrested for the murder. The trial was a thing of beauty. Titanic, the real Nate Raymond, and all the other players in the card game at Jimmy Meehan's testified. I watched them on the stand and they came up with such a confused pile of non-statements that you wondered if these guys had all been at the same game. The papers, incidentally, got Titanic's name wrong and called him Titanic *Thompson*—Titanic must have liked it because he used the name Thompson ever after. Just like it was reporters getting his name wrong that turned Charlie Lucano into Lucky Luciano and Dean O'Banion into Dion O'Banion. Sometimes I'm embarrassed for my profession.

Hump sat at the defense table with a dumb grin on his face for the whole trial and you knew the fix was in. He was acquitted and, most importantly from our point of view, my name and Riley's never came up. I don't know who the bozo was who first said "truth will out," but he wasn't from New York City.

You probably know what happened afterward to the main players in the drama. My one-time date Anne Morrow married Charles Lindbergh, the most famous man in the world, and later became a distinguished author. The Algonquin crowd kept first-nighting and drinking and cracking wise. Dorothy Parker, maybe the most talented of the group, stayed a friend of mine, meaning I had to watch her spiral downward over the years. Poor Dorothy, I don't think she ever figured out what she was so unhappy about.

Lucky Luciano arranged for the murder of Masseria and then of Masseria's chief rival, putting Charlie at the top of the gangster heap, where he stayed until a prosecutor named Dewey had him deported to Italy. Tom Dewey was a bit of a prick, but he was honest. The second distinction was a lot less common in New York than the first.

Anastasia did well, for such a murderous thug. He succeeded

Frankie Yale as boss of the docks at Red Hook. Lucano also put him, along with another charmer called Lepke, in charge of Murder, Incorporated, the syndicate's official enforcement bureau. Anastasia didn't meet his own end until the fifties, when he was rubbed out after getting the most famous haircut in history, in the barbershop of the same Park Central Hotel where Arnold Rothstein was shot. Humanity did not weep.

Jimmy Walker eventually went to jail for corruption, but not because of Rothstein's notebooks. And Runyon? He became a famous author of Broadway tales, sanitized for public consumption and amusement. Rothstein appears in Runyon's world as the Brain and Nathan Detroit, Titanic as Sky Masterson, and even Frank Costello, a mobster who replaced Rothstein as the city's chief fixer, was given the Runyon moniker Dave the Dude, who gets all weepy-eyed about the fate of an old lady called Apple Annie. Now, Runyon knew very well that Costello was a hard-hearted bastard who wouldn't get sentimental about an old lady if his grandmother got the clap, but Damon couldn't write a story about a guy like that. It wouldn't be Runyonesque.

Runyon died of cancer on the tenth of December, 1946. I hadn't seen him for years: we lost touch after the Rothstein business. I sat at his funeral with emotions that were, I will say, mixed. I've never been able really to forgive Runyon for writing cute stories about killers and whores and drug peddlers, never shared in the admiration for how he would be the guy who saw everything, knew everything, but wrote nothing truthful about it. On the other hand, Damon Runyon was a great friend to me. He was a terrific writer, with a gift for language and dialect very few have had. With his snap-brim fedora, his ever-present cigarette, and that glint in his eyes behind wireless spectacles, he was the essence of New York in the twenties, a bright world I loved intensely and miss every day of my life.

A day or two after Runyon's funeral, I saw his widow and second wife Patrice sitting alone at the bar in the Algonquin and I sat down next to her. I'd never met her, but I was curious about something. I introduced myself and said I was sorry for her loss.

"Yeah, my loss," she said, thoughtfully stirring the ice in her Old Fashioned. "Funny, I didn't see Damon for two years before he croaked. He wanted me to visit him and I didn't. I got a nice boyfriend now, things are good."

She knocked back the last of the Old Fashioned and I ordered another for her without waiting for her signal to do it.

"But you know," she continued, "it is a loss. Runyon was Runyon. There was nobody like him."

The bartender brought our drinks.

"I gotta ask, Patrice, you ever hear anything about Arnold Rothstein's notebooks?"

She laughed.

"Oh, those. Yeah, Damon told me about them. That was you?"

"That was me. You ever see them?"

"What, the notebooks? Oh, hell, no. Damon told me he burned those things as soon as he got them home. You don't think Damon Runyon would hold onto anything as hot as those notebooks were, do you?"

No, I thought. I suppose not.

It must have been January, two months after Arnold Rothstein died. I'd just settled Hal into my apartment and was starting up my new job as a political reporter. I stopped at Lindy's. All the Marx Brothers were sitting in there, even the one who wasn't in the act but still had a funny nickname. I went over to talk to Harpo.

The brothers, as usual, were carping and cracking wise with each other. They were feeling pretty frisky. George S. Kaufman had taken Benchley's advice from that long-ago Algonquin lunch and started writing for them. Their second show with Kaufman, *Animal Crackers*, was packing them in at the 44th Street Theater. Chico looked over at Groucho, who was intently reading the stock exchange results in the paper.

"Look at this guy," my old buddy from Polly Adler's said. "And he says *I'm* a gambler."

Groucho looked very different without his greasepaint mustache. He folded up the newspaper and looked scornfully at his brothers.

"You don't get it, do you? Everybody else is getting rich in the stock market and you mugs throw away your money on dames and gambling. Get with the times! It's 1929!"

Author's Note

Three of the wisecracks attributed to members of the Algonquin Round Table in this novel are not the author's creations, but were allegedly spoken by the three wits to whom they are attributed in the text. These are the jokes about leading a horticulture, slipping into a dry martini, and the Yale Prom.

The author also thanks Ken Liebman for his advice on poker.

THE RILEY SERIES
James Anderson O'Neal
riley.threeoceanpress.com

" Riley was my grandfather on my mother's side.
He was born on May 6, 1898.
He died on October 18, 1993.
Every day in between, he was a tough son of a bitch. "

Riley produces a box of memoirs written by the late Cornelius. The memoirs, spiced with Riley's salty comments, recount wild adventures the two friends supposedly engaged in. The old men claim that, in their younger days, they battled Lucky Luciano and Chairman Mao, spied for Winston Churchill, traded barbs with Dorothy Parker, marched with Martin Luther King, enraged J. Edgar Hoover and Roy Cohn…

Who can believe these guys?

Believe them or not, you'll have a great time following Riley and Cornelius as they roam through history from Pershing's expedition against Pancho Villa to the fall of the Berlin Wall, around the world and across the 20th Century.

Previously in the Riley series:

RILEY AND THE GREAT WAR

Riley and Cornelius ramble from revolution to war and back to revolution. In Missouri and Mexico, Paris and Munich, they match wits with historic icons like George Patton, Pancho Villa, Rosa Luxemburg, and Winston Churchill, as well as a sadistic master spy. Even if they make it through the Punitive Expedition, World War I, and the Spartacist Revolution, they'll still have to face a dachshund and a tiger.

threeoceanpress.com